Interfictions

an anthology of
interstitial writing

Edited by Delia Sherman
and Theodora Goss

Interstitial Arts Foundation
Boston, MA

Interstitial Arts Foundation
P.O. Box 35862
Boston, MA 02135
www.interstitialarts.org
info@interstitialarts.org

Distributed to the trade by Small Beer Press through Consortium.
Printed on Recycled Paper in Canada by Transcontinental Printing. Text set in ITC Esprit.
Library of Congress Cataloging-in-Publication Data available on request.

ISBN-13: 978-1-931520-24-9

First edition: 1 2 3 4 5 6 7 8 9 0

Table of Contents

For Terri Windling, artist,
inspiration, and fellow
IAF founder.—DS

For Kelly Link, who inspires so
many of us to make our stories
stranger and more real.—TG

Introduction

Heinz Insu Fenkl

I. An Introduction

I worked on my first book for twenty-three years, from the time I was twelve to the time I turned thirty-five. I am not an especially slow writer; this was writing that had deep meaning for me, writing that was at the beginning of a life-long series of interlinked works. In 1996, this book, *Memories of My Ghost Brother*, was published as a novel.

But *Memories of My Ghost Brother* is not a novel. It is the story of my childhood in Korea, drawn from life but told in such a way that there is a clear aesthetic consciousness behind it.

The decision to call it a novel—and not a memoir—was made by the publisher's marketing department, not by me.

I had told my editor that given the current state of literary theory, I was comfortable calling my work either thing—a novel (because of its literary style, its use of tropes, its collaging of time and character) or a memoir (because nearly everything in it is true, in the factual sense, within the realm of flexibility for that form). I had just come out of a PhD program in Cultural Anthropology, having spent the last several years heavily engaged with the theory of ethnographic writing. *Memories of My Ghost Brother* was what I had written in response to, and in implicit criticism of, both ethnographic and theoretical works I had been reading. It was what I was compelled to finish instead of my dissertation monograph.

Nearly a decade after its initial publication, there is now another publisher that would like to repackage *Memories of My Ghost Brother* as a memoir.

I have directly experienced the power of binary oppositions in the world of publishing. As an academic with a background in a wide range of theoretical approaches, including semiotics and structuralism, it is no surprise to me; but as a first-time "novelist," this experience was both disillusioning and educational. It gave me that proverbial eye-opening look behind the scenes, and as I began to work later with small presses, I learned things that helped me become a more realistic academic. For me as the writer of an autobiographical narrative that pushed the envelope in both directions, the problem of categories was: memoir or novel (fact or fiction)? I approached it head-on by labeling my work "autoethnography."

In an essay I called "an autoethonographic recursion," I looked at my own writing as if I were an anthropologist looking at a text, and this exercise helped me put to rest a tangle of theoretical and writerly problems. I had been familiar with various theoretical approaches to texts, which examine their "liminality" or "hybridity," often applying terms with the prefixes "inter" or "trans" ("intertextuality" and "transnationality," for example), but these approaches all rely on an implicit notion of dichotomy combined with the idea of moving from one state to another or combining (intersecting) one thing with another.

In the world of publishing, this way of thinking presents itself as a series of either/or decisions: Fact or Fiction, Fantasy or Science Fiction, Genre or Mainstream, Mystery or History? I present these categorical problems as dilemmas of a sort, but in many cases the possibilities are not initially limited only to two; and yet, when a particular work is hard to classify, its final label is then often compared to or contrasted with a series of other possibilities, one at a time.

The result may be that an either/or decision (which implicitly negates neither/nor) produces a thing that then follows an and/or logic—and then transcends it, perhaps by ignoring it altogether.

II. The Interstices

An interstice is not an intersection. (That is why a concept like hybridity, by itself, is not adequate to the idea of the Interstitial.) The word "interstice" comes from the Latin roots "inter" (between) and "sistere" (to stand). Literally, it means to "stand between" or "stand in the middle." It generally refers to a space between things: a chink in a fence, a gap in the clouds, a DMZ between nations at war, the potentially infinite space between two musical notes, a form of writing that defies genre classification.

An interstitial thing falls between categories, and so one might think of "interstitial" as coterminous with "liminal" (from the Latin "limen," meaning threshold, or "limes," referring to boundary—the word "limit" comes from the same root). Liminality is a concept made prominent (in Anthropology) by Victor Turner, who used it to refer to that strange "betwixt and between" state initiates go through in rites of passage. Liminality is a suspended state, but there is an underlying idea that it is also transitional.

In the field of Cultural Studies, the figure most identified with the idea of liminality is Homi K. Bhabha, who deals with various boundaries and borders, concepts directly relevant to the issue of *Interfictions.* In his introduction to *The Location of Culture*, he writes: "It is in the emergence of the interstices—the overlap and displacement of domains of difference—that the intersubjective and collective experiences of nationness, community interest, or cultural value are negotiated." Bhabha is writing about nations, cultures, and marginalized peoples, but what he says is just as applicable to the world of literature. In place of "nationness" we can think "genre" (or, more widely, "marketing category") and the parallels are quite clear. Imagine the "domains of difference" being the vaguely-articulated features that distinguish the category "Fantasy" from "Mainstream Fiction" and the ideas of "community interest" and "cultural value" become apparent. And this is not an inappropriate application of Bhabha's ideas—we are still dealing with domains of discourse and the relationship among centralized power, the margins, and minority groups. In the realm of discourse, the dynamics are remarkably parallel.

In the world of genre literature, there are few venues that seek "to authorize cultural hybridities" (as Bhabha puts it) except perhaps some recent e-zines and web resources. *Science Fiction Eye* comes to mind as a forum for genre discourse, but its circulation was small, and one could argue that even with its elite readership and contributorship, its general impact was minimal. And yet we are clearly in one of those moments of historical transformation.

III. In the Interstitial DMZ

There is a major difference between liminality and interstitiality. Unlike the liminal, the Interstitial is not implicitly transitory—that is to say, it is not on its way toward becoming something else. The liminal state in a rite of passage precedes the final phase, which is reintegration, but an interstitial work does not require reintegration—it already has its own being in a willfully transgressive or noncategorical way. Interstitial works maintain a consciousness of the boundaries they have crossed or disengaged with; they present a clear awareness of the kinds of subtexts which might be their closest classifiable counterparts.

The problem with an interstitial work is in its relationship with the audience—both its initial audience (which we may construe, for economy's sake, as the publisher) and its eventual audience, the readers. The relationship between reader and text, as we all know, is integral because each separate reader of the same text creates a unique work in his or her mind. Our general agreements about the plot or theme of a work are essentially the same as our agreements about the "real" world, which is actually determined by cultural consensus. Interstitial works have a special relationship with the reader because they have a higher degree of indeterminacy (or one could say a greater range of potentialities) than a typical work.

For example, if an interstitial novel is determined to be Fantasy by its publisher, a reader, having the parameters of initial engagement with the text predetermined, might experience it as a Fantasy novel exhibiting odd dissonances or interesting novelties in relation to that genre.

Barry Hughart's *Bridge of Birds* is a novel that did well in its genre classification, winning the World Fantasy Award in 1985. Fantasy readers found the work uniquely vivid and full of a sharp and lively humor. The backdrop, a "China that never was," proved the novel feature, and all of the representations of that mythic China (a collage of different historical periods and literary sensibilities) were what made the book unique in the genre. But read outside the genre by a reader unfamiliar with the built-in expectations of Fantasy, say, a reader of Mystery novels, *Bridge of*

Birds presents an updated twist on an old tradition started by the Dutch diplomat Robert Van Gulik, with the Judge Dee series, set in T'ang Dynasty China. Yet another category of reader—say, one with background in Asian Studies—might appreciate Hughart's mixing of history and fiction, something Van Gulik's could not do as brilliantly after the initial Judge Dee novel (which happened to be a translation of an eighteenth-century Chinese novel set against a T'ang Dynasty backdrop).

Bridge of Birds spawned two sequels, but then Hughart quietly disappeared from the Fantasy radar, having worn out the quality that made his mythic China a novelty in that genre. Hughart's is a case of initial success as a result of forceful classification into a genre, but the eventual outcome is negative.

One might say that what I've described is merely the sad reality of the publishing business. But Hughart's case shows the problems of initial perception and the eventual effects of forceful classification based on a publisher's (mis)perception of a text. Playing devil's advocate, one might argue that Hughart had his chance with readers, that he simply represents a cases of a text that lost its potential readership to other texts more competitive in the marketplace. But both readers and publishers know the importance of initial reviews, packaging, and classification. What if *Bridge of Birds* were to be re-released into a different classification, with careful attention to sending the book to appropriate reviewers? Would it suddenly find large numbers of new readers who had not appreciated it in its first release?

Hughart's situation exemplifies how things are complicated in the DMZ of the Interstitial. Interstitial works are self-negating. That is, if they become successful to the degree that they engender imitations or tributes to themselves, or if they spark a movement which results in like-minded works, then they are no longer truly interstitial, having spawned their own genre, subgenre, or even form. The DMZ they initially inhabit becomes its own nation, so to speak.

What I am trying to illustrate is the oddly ironic quality of interstitial art. Once it manifests itself, regardless of the conditions of its creation, the interstitial work has the potential to create a retroactive historical trajectory. Further, if this historical trajectory is prominent enough, the work that sparked its discovery (or creation) then may become a representative—though not necessarily the first—work in a newly-identified genre or subgenre whose parameters the work has helped illuminate.

An example might be the form of the Revisionary Fairytale, which has become a clear subgenre by now. Although its current form is best represented by the works collected in the six volumes edited by Terri Windling and Ellen Datlow as well as books like Emma Donoghue's *Kissing the Witch*, there are numerous recent works that make use of the same trope, some by established writers like Robert Coover, who enjoy a highbrow credibility for their Postmodern writing. Once this subgenre exists and is identifiable by various consistent characteristics, it is possible to begin tracing the history of the form. We might begin with a work with strong elements of Revisionary Fairytale like the film that made Reese Witherspoon famous—*Freeway* (1996)—and then look for other works that perform similar transformations on the Little Red Riding Hood story and arrive at Angela Carter's collection, *The Bloody Chamber* (1979). Carter is recognized now as one of the originators of the contemporary Revisionist Fairytale, but while doing some random reading, one might run across an even earlier text, Djuna Barnes' perplexing novel, *Nightwood* (1937), which uses tropes very similar to Carter's, and may, in fact, be a formative influence on her work. But by this time we will have noticed the Red Riding Hood motif in perfume commercials, music videos (by Tori Amos and Sarah Evans), and other recent films (Pieter van Hees's short, *Black XXX-Mas*: a.k.a. *Little Red in the Hood*).

IV. Illuminating the Interstitial

What the Interstitial does, actually, is transform the reader's experience of reading. Formerly invisible historical trajectories become visible to the reader. The interstitial work, in combination with the reader's particular perception of it, manifests itself in that particular way because the reader's "reality" has changed. We have figures of speech for this kind of transformation at a profound level—"I have seen the light," for example—but the transformation caused by the Interstitial is far more subtle. Perhaps instead of something as extreme as "The scales have fallen from my eyes," one might characterize this change as "A scale has fallen from my eye." In any case, the reader has learned to see in a different light, and that change causes a reinterpretation of the reader's experience of the past—in general—though perhaps this begins with a re-examination and reinterpretation of other texts the reader has experienced.

An interstitial work provides a wider range of possibilities for the reader's engagement and transformation. It is more faceted than a typical literary work, though it also operates under its own internal logic. At Readercon, on a panel discussing Metafantasy, I used the term "bilocation" (borrowed from the practice of Remote Viewing) to describe the reader's state of mind when reading works like John Crowley's *Little, Big*, which are Fantasy but also aware of the fact that they are Fantasy and make the reader aware of that awareness. Readers can lose themselves in the world of the novel, but simultaneously maintain an awareness of the act of reading. This "bilocation" (more precisely, a "multilocality") of the reader's awareness produces a form of engagement characteristic of metafiction and altered states of consciousness. Many readers find this state of mind so uncomfortable that they reject works of this nature (often rationalizing their rejection by focusing on some perceived flaw). Interstitial works also induce a sort of multilocality in the reader's consciousness, but at a different threshold of perception. The reader may not be aware of this phenomenon, and therefore stays with the work, achieving the effect of multilocality over repeated engagements over time. This multilocality then extends to the reader's perception and memory of other works. (And once again, this is not to suggest that interstitial works cannot be metafictions.)

Once one engages with the underlying logic of the Revisionary Fairytale, for example, one can see its structural qualities in other works in various orders of magnitude. What Carter and Barnes do with the story of Little Red Riding Hood is to take an extant structure and then transform its elements or its structural dynamics, thereby creating a work with clear knowledge of its subtext but with a distinctly different rhetoric. This is what the Romans did with Greek myths when they renamed the Greek gods and goddesses and appropriated them into their own religious practices. This is also what the Romans did by attaching their mythic history *The Aenead* to the Greek epic *The Iliad*. This is what the writers of the Gospels did when they took the story of Jesus and worked it into a classic Hero tale that parallels the stories of Krishna, Mithras, Apollonius, Buddha, and even Julius Caesar.

But before such historical trajectories become apparent, the works that reveal them are interstitial—sometimes only for a short while, yet sometimes for several centuries—and by being unclassifiable, they present readers with a uniquely new literary consciousness.

In transforming the perceptions of the reader, interstitial works make the reader (or listener, or viewer) more perceptive and more attentive; in doing so, they make the reader's world larger, more interesting, more meaningful, and perhaps even more comprehensible. The reader, who has been seeing black-and-white, suddenly begins not only to see color, but to learn how to see other colors.

What We Know About the Lost Families of —— House

Christopher Barzak

But is the house truly haunted?

Of course the house is haunted. If a door is closed on the first floor, another on the second floor will squeal open out of contrariness. If wine is spilled on the living room carpet and scrubbed at furiously and quickly so that a stain does not set, another stain, possibly darker, will appear somewhere else in the house. A favorite room in which malevolence quietly happens is the bathroom. Many speculate as to why this room draws so much attention. One might think that in a bathroom things would be more carefree, in a room where the most private of acts are committed, that any damned inhabitants could let down their hair or allow a tired sigh to pass through their doomed lips.

Perhaps this is exactly what they are doing in the bathroom, and we have misunderstood them. They turn on the shower and write names in the steam gathered on the mirror (never their own names, of course). They tip perfume bottles over, squeeze the last of the toothpaste out of its tube, they leave curls of red hair in the sink. And no one who lives in the house—no one living, that is—has red hair, or even auburn. What's worse is when they leave the toilet seat up. They'll flush the toilet over and over, entranced by the sound of the water being sucked out. This is what these restless inhabitants are endlessly committing: private acts.

The latest victims

Always there has been a family subject to the house's torture. For sixty-five years it was the Addlesons. Before that it was owned by the Oliver family. No one in town can remember who lived in the house before the Olivers, not even our oldest residents. We have stories, of course, recountings of the family who built —— House, but their name has been lost to history. If anyone is curious, of course there is the library with town records ready to be opened. No one has opened those records in over fifty years, though. Oral history, gossip, is best for this sort of situation.

Rose Addleson believed the house was trying to communicate something. She told her husband women know houses better than men, and this is one thing Rose said that we agree with. There is, after all, what is called "Women's Intuition." What exactly the house was saying eluded Rose, though, as it eludes the rest of us. Where Rose wanted to figure out its motivations, the rest of us would rather have seen it burn to cinders.

"All these years?" Jonas told her. It was not Rose Addleson who grew up in the house after all, who experienced the years of closeness to these events, these fits that her husband had suffered since childhood. "If it's trying to communicate," he said, "it has a sad idea of conversation."

Rose and Jonas have no children. Well, to be precise, no living children. Once there had been a beautiful little girl, with cheeks that blushed a red to match her mother's, but she did not take to this world. She died when she was only a year old. On a cold winter's night she stopped breathing, when the house was frosted with ice. It wasn't until the next morning that they found her, already off and soaring to the afterlife. "A hole in her heart," the doctor said, pinching his forefinger and thumb together. "A tiny hole." They had never known it was there.

After their first few months of marriage, Rose and Jonas had become a bit reclusive. Out of shame? Out of guilt? Fear? Delusion? No one is able to supply a satisfactory reason for their self-imposed isolation. After all, we don't live in that house. If walls could talk, though, and some believe the walls of —— House do talk, perhaps we'd understand that Jonas and Rose Addleson have good reason not to go out or talk to neighbors. Why, even Rose's mother Mary Kay Billings didn't hear from her daughter but when she called on the phone herself, or showed up on the front porch of —— House, which was something she rarely did. "That house gives me the creeps," she told us. "All those stories,

I believe them. Why Rose ever wanted to marry into that family is beyond me."

Mary Kay has told us this in her own home, in her own kitchen. She sat on a chair by the telephone, and we sat across the table from her. She said, "Just you see," and dialed her daughter's number. A few rings later and they were talking. "Yes, well, I understand, Rose. Yes, you're busy, of course. Well, I wanted to ask how you and Jonas are getting along. Good. Mm-hmm. Good. All right, then. I'll talk to you later. Bye now."

She put the phone down on the cradle and smirked. "As predicted," she told us. "Rose has no time to talk. 'The house, Mother, I'm so busy. Can you call back later?' Of course I'll call back later, but it'll be the same conversation, let me tell you. I know my daughter, and Rose can't be pried away from that house."

We all feel a bit sad for Mary Kay Billings. She did not gain a son through marriage, but lost a daughter. This is not the way it's supposed to happen. Marriage should bring people together. We all believe this to be true.

Rose heard a voice calling

She has heard voices since she was a little girl. Rose Addleson, formerly Rose Billings, was always a dear girl in our hearts, but touched with something otherworldly. If her mother doesn't understand her daughter's gravitation to —— House, the rest of us see it all too clear. Our Rose was the first child to speak in tongues at church. Once, Jesus spoke through her. The voice that came through her mouth never named itself, but it did sound an awful lot like Jesus. It was definitely a male voice, and he kept saying how much he loved us and how we needed to love each other better. It was Jesus all over, and from our own sweet Rose.

We do not understand why, at the age of twelve, she stopped attending services.

But Rose also heard voices other than the Lord's. Several of us have overheard her speaking to nothing, or nothing any of us could see. She's hung her head, chin tucked into breastbone, at the grocery store, near the ketchup and mustard and pickles, murmuring, "Yes. Of course. Yes, I understand. Please don't be angry."

Rose heard the voices in —— House, too. This is why she married Jonas: The house called for her to come to it.

It was winter when it happened. Rose was eighteen then, just half a year out of high school. She worked in Hettie's Flower Shop. She could arrange flowers better than anyone in town. We all always requested Rose to make our bouquets instead of Hettie, but Hettie never minded. She owned the place, after all.

On her way home from work one evening, Rose's car stalled a half mile from —— House. She walked there to get out of the cold, and to call her mother. At the front door she rapped the lion-headed knocker three times. Then the door opened and wind rushed past her like a sigh. She smelled dust and medicine and old people. Something musty and sweet and earthy. Jonas stood in front of her, a frown on his sad young face. He was already an orphan at the age of thirty. "Yes?" he asked in a tone of voice that implied that he couldn't possibly be interested in any reason why our Rose was appearing before him. "Can I help you?"

Rose was about to ask if she could use his phone when she heard a voice calling from inside. "Rose," it whispered. Its voice rustled like leaves in a breeze. "Please help us," the house pleaded. And then she thought she heard it say, "Need, need, need." Or perhaps it had said something altogether different. The walls swelled behind Jonas's shoulder, inhaling, exhaling, and the sound of a heartbeat suddenly could be heard.

"Are you all right?" Jonas asked, cocking his head to the side. "Rose Billings, right? I haven't seen you since you were a little girl."

"Yes," said Rose, but she didn't know if she was saying yes to his question or to the house's question. She shook her head, winced, then looked up at Jonas again. Light cocooned his body, silvery and stringy as webs.

"Come in," he offered, moving aside for her to enter, and Rose went in, looking around for the source of the voice as she cautiously moved forward.

Mary Kay Billings didn't hear from her daughter for three days after that. That night she called the police and spoke to Sheriff

Dawson. He'd found Rose's car stuck in the snow. They called all over town, to Hettie's Flower Shop, to the pharmacy, because Rose was supposed to pick up cold medicine for Mary Kay. Eventually Rose called Mary Kay and said, "I'm okay. I'm not coming home. Pack my things and send them to me."

"Where are you?" Mary Kay demanded.

"Have someone bring my things to —— House," Rose said.

"—— House?!" shouted Mary Kay Billings.

"I'm a married woman now, Mother," Rose explained, and that was the beginning of the end of her.

Jonas in his cups

He had many of them. Cups, that is. Most of them filled with tea and whiskey. Jonas Addleson had been a drinker since the age of eight, as if he were the son of a famous movie star. They are all a sad lot, the children of movie stars and rich folk. Too often they grow up unhappy, unaccustomed to living in a world in which money and fame fade as fast as they are heaped upon them.

Jonas Addleson was not famous beyond our town, but his family left him wealthy. His father's father had made money during the Second World War in buttons. He had a button factory over in Pittsburgh, Pennsylvania. It's long gone by now, of course. They made all sorts of buttons, the women who worked in the factory while the men were in Europe. Throughout —— House you will still find a great many buttons. In the attic, on the pantry shelves, in the old playroom for the children, littered in out-of-the-way places: under beds, in the basement, among the ashes in the fireplace (unburned, as if fire cannot touch them).

This is not to say Rose Addleson was a bad housekeeper. In fact, Rose Addleson should have got an award for keeping house. She rarely found time for anything but cleaning and keeping. It was the house that did this eternal parlor trick. No matter how many buttons Rose removed, they returned in a matter of weeks.

When Rose first arrived at —— House, Jonas showed her into the living room, then disappeared into the kitchen to make tea. The living room was filled with Victorian furniture with carved armrests, covered in glossy chintz. A large mirror hung on the wall over the fireplace, framed in gold leaf. The fire in the fireplace crackled, filling the room with warmth. On the mantel over the fire, what appeared to be coins sat in neat stacks, row upon row of them. Rose went to them immediately, wondering what they were. They were the first buttons she'd find. When Jonas returned, carrying a silver tray with the tea service on it, he said, "Good, get warm. It's awfully cold outside."

He handed Rose a cup of tea and she sipped it. It was whiskey-laced and her skin began to flush, but she thanked him for his hospitality and sipped at the tea until the room felt a little more like home.

"The least I can do," he said, shrugging. Then remembering what she'd come for, he said, "The phone. One second. I'll bring it to you."

He turned the corner, but as soon as he was gone, the house had her ear again. "Another soul gone to ruin," it sighed with the weight of worry behind it. "Unless you do something."

"But what can I do?" said Rose. "It's nothing to do with me. Is it?"

The house shivered. The stacks of buttons on the mantel toppled, the piles scattering, a few falling into the fire below. "You have what every home needs," said the house.

"I'm no one," said Rose. "Really."

"I wouldn't say that," Jonas said in the frame of the doorway. He had a portable phone in his hand, held out for her to take. "I mean, we're all someone. A son or daughter, a wife or husband, a parent. Maybe you're right, though," he said a moment later. "Maybe we're all no one in the end."

"What do you mean?" asked Rose. She put the teacup down to take the phone.

"I'm thinking of my family. All gone now. So I guess by my own definition that makes me nothing."

Rose batted her eyelashes instead of replying. Then she put the phone down on the mantel next to the toppled towers of buttons. She sat down in one of the chintz armchairs and said, "Tell me more."

The first lost family

Before the Addlesons, the Oliver family lived in —— House. Before the Olivers lived in —— House, the family that built the house lived there. But the name of that family has been lost to the dark of history. What we know about that family is that they were from the moors of Yorkshire. That they had come with money to build the house. That the house was one of the first built in this part of Ohio. That our town hadn't even been a town at that point. We shall call them the Blanks, as we do in town, for the sake of easiness in conversation.

The Blanks lived in —— House for ten years before it took them. One by one the Blanks died or disappeared, which is the same thing as dying if you think about it, for as long as no one you love can see or hear you, you might as well be a ghost.

The Blanks consisted of Mr. Blank, Mrs. Blank, and their two children, twin boys with ruddy cheeks and dark eyes. The photos we have of them are black and white, but you can tell from the pictures that their eyes are dark and that their cheeks are ruddy by the serious looks on their faces. No smiles, no hint of happiness. They stand outside the front porch of —— House, all together, the parents behind the boys, their arms straight at their sides, wearing dark suits.

The father, we know, was a farmer. The land he farmed has changed hands over the years, but it was once the Blank family apple orchard. Full of pinkish-white blossoms in the spring, full of shiny fat globes of fruit in autumn. It was a sight, let us tell you. It was a beautiful sight.

The first to disappear was one of the boys. Let's call him Ephraim. He was the ruddier of the two, and often on his own, even though his parents taught him not to wander. One afternoon he and his brother went into the orchard to pick apples, but in the evening, when the sun began to set, only Ephraim's brother returned to —— House, tears streaming down his face.

"What's the matter?" asked Mrs. Blank. "Where's your brother?"

But the boy (William, we'll call him) could only shake his

head. Finally he was able to choke out this one sentence:

"The orchard took him."

Then he burst into tears again.

This, of course, sparked a heated debate around town. We who live here have always been a spirited group of people, ready to speculate about anything that might affect us. The general consensus arrived at was that the boy had been taken. Someone must have stolen him, like the fairies did in the old country. A stranger passing through, who perhaps saw the perfect round ruddy globes of Ephraim's cheeks and mistook them for apples. It is a dark thought, this possible narrative. But dark thoughts move through this world whether we like it or not.

Mr. Blank died soon after his son's disappearance. He died, as they say, of a broken heart. Mrs. Blank found him in the kitchen, slumped over in his chair, his head on the table. She thought he was crying again, as he often did after his son's vanishing. But when she stroked his hair and then his cheek, she found him cold, his heart stopped up with sorrow.

They buried Mr. Blank in the orchard, beneath the tree where William last saw Ephraim. And only two years later Mrs. Blank woke one night to find that she was alone in —— House. She searched every room twice, but could not find her last remaining family member, her young William.

It was the middle of winter, in the middle of the night, and when Mrs. Blank stepped outside onto the front porch, she found a set of footprints in the snow that gathered on the steps. She followed them down and out the front gate, around back of the house and through the orchard, where they came to a stop at her husband's grave, at the tree where William last saw Ephraim. Mrs. Blank called out for William, but she only got her own voice back. That and the screech of an owl crossing the face of the moon above her.

Suddenly a rumbling came from inside —— House. Mrs. Blank looked at the dark backside of the house, at its gingerbread eaves and its square roof, at its dark windows tinseled with starlight, and shuddered at the thought of going back in without anyone waiting for her, without her son beside her. The house rumbled again, though, louder this time, and she went without further hesitation. Some women marry a house, and this bond neither man nor God can break.

William's body was never found, poor child. Like his brother, he vanished into nothing.

But we say the orchard took him.

Everything you need

It took Rose and Jonas Addleson less than a year to make their doomed daughter. Full of passion for one another, they made love as often as possible, trying to bring her into this world, trying to make life worth living. This was perhaps not what Rose felt she needed, but Jonas wanted children, and what Jonas wanted, Rose wanted too. That's the thing about marriage. Suddenly you want together. You no longer live in desire alone.

What Rose wanted was for Jonas to be happy. She would marry him within a day of meeting him on the front porch of —— House during that fateful blizzard, knowing this was to be her home. The house had told her. And soon it had become apparent that Jonas didn't want her to leave either. When she went to call her mother, he had interrupted to say, "Would you like more tea?" When she had moved toward the front door, he'd stood up and said, "Would you like to lie down and rest?"

They shared more whiskey-laced tea, and before the night was over Rose found herself sitting next to Jonas on the sofa, holding his hand while he told her his family's story. How his grandfather had owned the button factory during the war, how his father had killed himself twenty years ago by placing a gun in his mouth and pulling the trigger. How his mother had worked her fingers to the bone taking care of everything: the house, Jonas, his father's bloody mess in the bathroom. "I found him," Jonas said. "I was ten. On the mirror in the bathroom. There was blood all over it. He was lying in a pool of blood on the floor. Mama scrubbed and scrubbed, but it wouldn't come out. Not until she asked the house to help her."

He paused, gulping the story down again. Rose watched the

way the column of his throat moved as he swallowed. She wanted to kiss him right there, where the Adam's apple wriggled under the skin. Instead she asked, "What did the house do?"

He looked at her, his eyes full of fear. "She told me to leave the bathroom. So I left, closing the door behind me. I waited outside with my ear against the door, but I couldn't hear anything. After a few minutes passed, I knocked. Then a few more minutes passed. I was going to knock again, but before my knuckles hit, the door swung open, and there was Mama, wringing her hands in a damp rag. There was no blood on her, not even a speck. And when I looked behind her, the carpet was as clean as ever, as if no dead body had bled to death on it."

"The house loves you," Rose said.

Jonas looked at her curiously. "What do you mean?"

"It loves you. Can't you feel it? It's trying to tell you something."

"If it's trying to communicate," said Jonas, "it has a sad idea of conversation."

She held those words close as soon as he said them, she pressed them to her chest like a bouquet. This was why she had been brought there, she realized. In this instant she knew she would translate for him. She would bring back all that he had lost. She'd be his mother, she'd be his father, she'd be his wife, she'd have his children. A family, she thought. With a family, he'd never be alone.

She leaned into him, still holding his hand, and kissed him. Without moving back again, she looked up through her eyelashes and said, "I have everything you need."

A child bride

The story of the Oliver family is a sad one. No, let us revise that statement: It is not sad, it is disturbing. We don't like to talk about it around town anymore. We are all glad that —— House took the Olivers, for they were a bad lot, given to drinking and gambling, as well as other unwholesome activities.

The Olivers moved into —— House just past the turn of the

century, after Mrs. Blank died. Our grandparents found Mrs. Blank several weeks after her passing, due to the smell that began to spread down Buckeye Street. It was one of the only times they'd gone into —— House, and we remember it to this day: the hardwood floors, the chintz furniture, the stone mantel over the fireplace, the stairs that creaked as you stepped up into the long hallway of the second floor, the second floor itself, the lower half of the hall paneled with dark polished wood. And the bathroom, of course, where all of the trouble eventually focused its energy. It was a fine house, really, with wide windows to let light in, though even with all of that light the house held too many shadows. Our grandparents did not linger. They took Mrs. Blank's body to the county coroner's office in Warren and left the doctor to his business.

Less than a year later, Mr. and Mrs. Oliver came to —— House with their three children: two boys, one nearly a man, one still muddling through adolescence, and a girl about to bloom. At first our grandparents didn't think badly of the Olivers. It takes a certain amount of time for a family to reveal its secrets. So for the first few years, they welcomed the Olivers as if they had always lived among us. The Olivers began attending the Methodist church on Fisher-Corinth Road. They sent the younger boy and girl to school with our children. The oldest boy worked as a field hand for local farmers. His work was good, according to Miles Willard, who paid the boy to clear fields those first few years, before all of the madness started to happen again.

How to tell about that madness? We suppose we might as well start with Mrs. Oliver's murder. Two of our children found her body in Sugar Creek. They had been going to catch crayfish, but found Mrs. Oliver's body tangled in the roots of a tree that grew out of the bank instead. She had been severely beaten: her face covered in yellow-brown bruises, her skull cracked on the crown. Dark fingerprints lingered on her throat, so we knew she had been strangled. We still do not forgive her murderer for leaving her for us to find. People should take care of their own dirty work.

Since they had a murder on their hands, our grandparents called on the sheriff to deal with the matter. They marched him right up to —— House expecting trouble. But what they found was the front door open and, inside, Mr. Oliver's body spread out on the dining room table, a butcher knife sticking straight up out of his throat. The sheriff asked several of our grandfathers to back him up as he explored the rest of the house. And so they did, each carrying a rifle as they descended into the basement, then up to the second floor, finding nothing suspicious. It was when the ceiling creaked above them that they knew someone was in the attic.

They tried opening the attic door, but it had been locked from the inside. So they busted it down, only to be met with a blast from the rifle of Mr. and Mrs. Oliver's middle child. The sheriff took the shot in his shoulder. He fell backwards, but our grandfathers caught him. Several of them returned fire at the boy. He left a smear of blood on the wall as he collapsed against it.

They found the oldest boy and the girl bound and gagged in the attic. They were wild with fear. Their brother had killed their parents and was going to kill them, too, they said. This was all over a fight the boy had had with his parents about a debt he'd run up over in Meadville, playing poker with older men who knew how to outwit him. He wanted his parents to pay his debt, but they wouldn't. They insisted he work to pay for his debts and his drinking, just as their oldest son did. After he killed his parents, he wasn't sure what to do with his siblings, so he tied them up, and there they still were, alive and none the worse for wear, and we thought perhaps we had salvaged something from that house's evil.

The oldest Oliver boy and his sister stayed on at —— House. They had nowhere to go, no people. Just each other. The boy kept working as a field hand, the girl continued her schooling. But soon her attendance dropped off, and then she stopped coming altogether. She started working to help with the keeping of the house and the paying of her brother's debts. She took in wash if people gave it to her. She mended stockings. She raised chickens, selling eggs at the general store to make extra money. Anything she could get her hands on she turned into cash.

At first she seemed awfully hard-working and a good girl, but we soon discovered not only was she working to pay off her brother's debts, but to prepare for the child growing inside her. When her stomach began to round out the fronts of her dresses, we knew what was going on up at —— House. This was something our grandparents could not abide, so they stopped giving the girl work. They stopped buying her eggs, and the farmers released her brother from his duties. In no time at all, the brother and the child bride packed up their things and left. Without the aid of our grandparents, they could not live among us. This is the way all of the families that lived in —— House should have been dealt with all these years maybe. Without mercy. But Lord knows we are a merciful lot.

Word came several months after the siblings left that they had been seen in Cleveland, living together, posing as a married couple.

The baby's room

Here it is, in the same condition as when the baby was living. The crib with the mobile of brass stars still spinning in space above it, the rocking chair near the eastern window, where sunlight falls in the morning, the walls painted to look like the apple orchard in summer, the ceiling sky blue, as if the baby girl had lived outdoors forever, never inside the confines of —— House.

We know the room is still like this because Mary Kay Billings has seen it. Twice since the baby died she has gone to visit her daughter, and both times the baby's room was as it was during her last visit. Two years after the child's death it begins to seem a bit odd, really. She suggested changing it into a sewing room maybe, but Rose shook her head. "No, Mother," she said. "That's not allowed to happen."

Mary Kay Billings has no patience with her daughter. We all understand this. If our daughters had married into a family that lived in —— House without our permission, we'd have no patience either. Poor Mary Kay is one of the pillars of our community. She is one of our trustees, she sings in the church choir. At the elementary school, she volunteers her time three days a week, three hours each of those days, to aid in the tutoring of our children. Mary Kay

Billings has raised her daughter, has lived through the death of her husband, God rest his soul (for he would roll in his grave to know what happened to his child), and yet Mary Kay still gives to others for the good of her community. This is the way a town works, not how Rose would have it. We all think Rose is a bit selfish, really, leaving her mother to struggle alone, leaving Hettie without any warning (we liked her flower arrangements better than Hettie's and better than the replacement girl's, so it's even more selfish of her to have done this). Leaving the community altogether, to go live in that place.

We must mention that not all of us think she is selfish, but only has the appearance of selfishness. Some of us (the minority) believe Rose is noble. A bit too noble, but noble nonetheless. Who else but a self-sacrificing person would take on —— House and its curse? We say a crazy person, but some of us say Rose is doing us a favor. If it weren't Rose, who would the house have brought to its front door when it needed another soul to torment?

But the baby's room is a bit too much really. We asked Mary Kay Billings what the rest of the house was like and she said, "Buttons! Buttons everywhere, I tell you! I said to Rose, 'Rose! What's the matter with you? Why are all these buttons lying about?' and she says to me, 'Mother, I can't keep up with them. I try, but they keep coming.' And in the baby's room, too, I noticed. Right in the crib! I said to Rose, 'Rose! In the crib even?' and she says to me, can you believe this, she says to *me*, her own mother, 'Mother, I think it's best if you go.'"

"And Jonas?" we asked, leaning in closer. Mary Kay narrowed her eyes and sucked her teeth. "Drunk," she told us. "Drunk as usual."

Life during wartime

In the nineteen-forties, most of our men had been taken overseas to fight against the devil, and our women stayed behind, keeping things about town running smoothly. All over America, women came out of their houses and went into men's workplaces. We still argue about who was made for what sort of work, but in the end we know it's all a made-up sort of decision. Nothing fell apart, nothing broke while the men were off fighting. In fact, things maybe went a bit smoother (this of course being an opinion of a certain sector of our population and must be qualified). In any case, the factories were full of women, and in Pittsburgh, just across the state border, James Addleson, the grandfather of our own Jonas, had his ladies making buttons for the uniforms of soldiers.

The Addlesons had bought —— House several years before the war had broken out, but we rarely saw them. They were a Pennsylvania family and only spent part of their summers with us. Occasionally we'd see them in autumn for the apple festival. The Addlesons had money, and —— House was one of their luxuries. They had passed through our town during their travels and Mrs. Addleson had seen the house and wanted it immediately. James Addleson didn't argue with her. Why on earth she would want to buy a house in the country, no matter how stately and beautiful, was beyond him. But he had gotten used to giving the woman what she wanted. It was easier. And it soothed any guilt he might have felt for other, less attractive activities in which he participated. Especially later, after the war started.

Now Mrs. Addleson was a beautiful woman. She had a smooth complexion, high cheekbones, and a smile that knocked men over like a high wind had hit them. She wore fire engine red lipstick, which we must say is a bit racy but something to look at. Occasionally she'd come to town without Mr. Addleson. She'd bring their children, a girl in her teens and the little boy who would later grow up to be Jonas Addleson's father. During the war, we started seeing her and the kids more often. We'd find her shopping in the grocery store, or coming to church on Sundays, sitting in the last pew as if she didn't want to intrude on our services. Eventually we got used to her being around, and some of the women even got to be something like friends with her.

Mr. Addleson often stayed in Pittsburgh to look after his factory. We felt bad for the Addlesons. Even though James Addleson didn't go to war since he had a business to manage, his family suffered like anyone's. Whenever we asked Mrs. Addleson how her husband faired, she'd say, "Buttons! Buttons everywhere!" and throw her hands in the air. She was a strange lady, now that we think about it. Never had a straight answer for anyone.

For a while we thought perhaps —— House had settled into a restful sleep, or that even the spirit that inhabited the place had moved on to better climates. We hoped, we prayed, and during the war, it seemed our prayers had been answered. Finally a family lived in —— House without murdering one another or disappearing altogether. We thought perhaps we'd been foolish all those years to think the house haunted. We shook our heads, laughing a little, thinking ourselves to be exactly what everyone who makes their homes in cities considers us: backwoods, superstitious, ignorant.

But then our peaceful period of welcome embarrassment broke. Like a cloud that's been gathering a storm, holding inside the rain and lightning and thunder until it bursts forth, flooding the lives of those who live below it, so —— House released its evil upon our town once more.

This time, though, we realized its hand reached further than we had previously thought possible. This time we knew something was wrong when detectives from Pittsburgh began to appear on our doorsteps, asking questions about the Addlesons. How long had they been living in our town? How often did we see them? Did they go to church? Did they send their children to school with our children? What were they like? What did we know about their doings? In the end, we realized we knew little about the Addlesons. As we have said already, it takes time for families to reveal their secrets.

They found the first body in the basement, the second in the attic, the third buried in the orchard, and the fourth stuffed in a defunct well on the property. All women. All girls from Pittsburgh, the detectives told us. All pregnant with James Addleson's babies.

We were disgusted. Oh, but we were disgusted. Never had the house erupted with such evil before. Never! We thought the Oliver family massacre and the decline of its surviving children to be the worst, the worst possible manipulation the house could imagine. And here we were faced with something even more despicable.

While Mrs. Addleson raised her children in the quiet of our country town, James Addleson had been manipulating his women workers into sleeping with him. At first we assumed the women were a bad sort, and possibly their lust had gotten them into this trouble (as any of the great sins will surely do) but then we heard the news that seven other girls in the button factory had come forward. He had threatened to take their jobs away from them, they said, if they wouldn't give him what he wanted. They had been lucky, they said. They hadn't gotten pregnant. "It could have been us," one of the girls said in an anonymous interview. "It could have been any one of us."

It took the police a week to find the bodies of all four girls. The one in the well was the hardest to locate. We all prayed for their poor families back in Pittsburgh, for their poor husbands at war, off fighting that devil while another devil pursued their wives at home.

We had a notion to burn down —— House then, and were going to do that. We were gathering, the old and the young and the women left behind by their husbands. We were gathering to destroy the place when word came that Mrs. Addleson would not be leaving. She was going to stay and raise her children here among us. Her husband's factory would be closing; he'd be going to prison. She needed a place for her children. The children, we thought, oh what sacrifices we make for our children! This we understood all too well.

So we left the house alone, and her in it. And even after her daughter grew up to be a fine, respectable woman, graduating from our very own high school, and went off to college to marry a doctor, even after Mrs. Addleson died and left her son, the heir of James Addleson, alone in —— House, we allowed him to live there without any interference as well.

He was smart enough not to court our daughters. He went to college like his sister and came back a married man, his wife already expecting. This was in the nineteen-seventies, mind you, and such things happened among our children, it seemed, without them thinking much about it. We said nothing. We scolded ourselves and told ourselves it was not our business, and to stop caring.

But if it is not the business of one's community, whose business is it?

If we'd have intervened, if we'd have tried to get the Addlesons some other living arrangement, perhaps poor Jonas would not have walked into the bathroom at the age of ten to find his father's dead body, the blood spilling out of his shattered skull.

Why did the son of James Addleson kill himself? You are probably wondering. The answer is simple. It was those girls his daddy murdered. We have seen and heard them ourselves on occasion, wandering through the orchards, climbing out of the well, beating on the windows of the cellar and attic. We have seen and heard them, and continued on our way, ignoring them.

James Addleson's son was not so lucky. He lived with them. He heard them day and night, talking about his father's evil. In the end, they convinced him to join them.

A visit

But not our own sweet Rose! How could this have happened? We often wondered where we went wrong. Through all the years of that house's torments, never did our own children go near it. We taught them well, or so we thought. But that house would get what it wanted. Our own sweet Rose. How we have fretted these past three years she has been gone from us. How we pray for her and for Mary Kay Billings nightly. And how Mary Kay suffers. How she holds herself together, never mentioning her daughter unless we ask after her. Never wanting to burden us. And how we all have our crosses. Which is why we did what we have done.

We had let the Addleson family linger under the spell of the house's evil, and because of that Jonas's father took his own life, and Jonas himself became the wreck he is today. We thought we were doing best by them, leaving them to their own choices, trying not to interfere with the lives of others. But we saw how wrong we were when —— House took our Rose, when it took our Rose's little girl. And then, recently, when Mary Kay Billings mentioned to one of us that Rose had been asking after her cousin, Marla Jean Simmons. "Could you send her on up here, Mother? I'm sort of lonesome. And I could use some help around the house."

It was then we decided to take action. Not one more of our children would we let that house ravage.

We approached Mary Kay Billings with our plans, and tears, buckets full of them, were shed that day. Poor Mary Kay, always trying to be the tough woman, the one who will not be disturbed, yet when we came to her and said, "We shall make that house a visit," she burst, she broke like a dam.

"Thank you," she told us. "Oh thank you, I can't do it alone any longer. Maybe with all of us there she'll let us talk some sense into her."

So we selected representatives. Mr. Adams, the town lawyer. He inspired fear in his opposition, so we chose him hoping the house would fear his authority. Mrs. Baker, the principal of our elementary school, who Rose once respected as a child. Pastor Merritt, since a man of God in cases such as this is necessary. Tom Morrissey, the undertaker, who has dealt with death long enough not to fear it. And Shell Richards, one of our school bus drivers, because she is simply a force to be reckoned with, and we all of us stay out of her way, especially when she's been drinking.

Together, led by Mary Kay Billings, we trudged up the road to —— House on a cool spring evening when the buds were on the trees, the sap rising. At the gate, we hesitated for only a moment to look at each other and confirm our convictions by nodding. Then Mary Kay swung the gate open and up the path we went.

As soon as our feet touched those porch steps, though, we felt the life of whatever lived there coursing beneath us. We shuddered, but continued. Since it was not a social visit, we didn't bother knocking, just opened the door and went straight on in. "Rose!" we called loudly. "Rose!" And soon enough, she appeared on the landing above us, looking down at us with a peculiar glare, icy and distant.

"What are you all doing here?" she asked. Her voice sounded far away, as if she were speaking through her body, as if her body were this *thing* that came between her and the rest of the world.

Her hand rested on the newel post of the landing, massaging it as she waited.

"We've come to help you, darling," Mary Kay said. We all thought it best that she spoke first.

"I don't need any help now," said Rose. "What help would I be needing, Mother? Why didn't you send Marla Jean like I asked?"

We immediately saw Mary Kay's resolve fading, so Mr. Adams spoke up. "Dear," he said. "Come down to us. We're taking you out of this place. We're taking you home this very instant."

Rose cocked her head to the side, though, and slowly shook it. "I don't think so," she told us. "I'm a grown woman. I can make my own decisions. And my home is here, thank you very much."

"Where's your husband?" asked Mrs. Baker. But Rose didn't answer. She only looked at Mrs. Baker suspiciously, as if a trap were being set.

"We're going to help him, too, dear," said Pastor Merritt. "But we need to get you both to safety. We must ask God to help us now."

"God?" said Rose, and we shivered. We'd never heard a word so full of goodness said in such a way that it sent chills up and down our spines. "God?" she said again, then started down the stairs toward us. "I haven't heard Him in a long time," said Rose. We nodded. We remembered. She hadn't come to church since she was twelve.

"He is always listening," said Pastor Merritt. "All you have to do is ask for His help, and He will provide."

"I don't talk," said Rose. "I'm the one who listens."

We didn't nod this time. We weren't sure what to make of what she was saying.

"Enough of this," said Shell Richards suddenly, and we all, even Rose, looked at her, puzzled by her outburst. "Enough dillydallying," said Shell. She stepped right up to Rose, grabbed her arm and said, "You're coming with us, little girl."

Mary Kay ran up the stairs to gather a few things for her daughter while Rose fought to free herself from Shell's grip. "Stop struggling," Shell warned, but Rose struggled. She slipped, and as she fell buttons poured out of her sweater pockets, scattering across the floor.

Then a scream spilled down the staircase and we knew Mary Kay Billings was in trouble. We abandoned Rose on the floor and rushed up the stairs, one after the other, the steps creaking beneath us, until we came to the baby's room with the mural of the orchard painted on the walls and the sky on the ceiling. Mary Kay stood in the center of the room, near the crib, staring apparently at nothing. We followed her stare, and in the mural we saw the Blank boy, Ephraim, sitting in an apple tree, looking out at us. You could tell it was him by the dark eyes and the ruddy cheeks.

We took Mary Kay Billings by the arm and led her back down the stairs then, only to find that Rose had disappeared on us. "Who saw her last?" we asked each other, but no one had stayed with her. We had all gone running to Mary Kay when she called.

We searched the house from top to bottom, shouting for either of them to come to us. "Rose!" we called. "Jonas!" But all we found were buttons, and all we heard were the screams of dead mothers, and all we smelled was the house's evil circling us like a dark cloud.

We were too late. Our chance had come and we had failed her. The house had taken her and Jonas before we could free them, and so we left, defeated, not bothering to close the door behind us. Let the wind have it, we thought, let the rain flood it, let it all fall down in ruin. For that was the last family that —— House would take, we decided at that very moment. Never again would we allow anyone to go near it.

If walls could talk

And they do talk, if you know how to listen. If you know how to pay attention to the way a roof sighs, or a window slides open with relief, or a step creaks its complaints out. If you know how to hear what those walls are saying, you will hear unbearable stories, stories you would never imagine possible, stories we would rather turn away from. But we cannot turn away, for they will only follow us. They will find us, one by one, alone and frightened, and tear us apart if we try to stop our ears up.

The Blank family is still with us. The Olivers too. And those poor dead girls from Pittsburgh still linger, howling through the night as we try to sleep. And Jonas's father, the gun cracking his life open like a pocket watch, to let all of the time spill out of him. And now Jonas, too. Wherever he is, we hope he's restful. And Rose. Poor Rose. We don't hear from Rose, though. She never talked to us. She only listened.

~

"What We Know About the Lost Families of —— House" was written after I'd left my rural hometown in Ohio and had lived in a variety of suburbs, cities and beach towns only to come home years later and find the same voice of that town speaking in its same rhythms about the factories and the farms and the fields and the families that worked them. Hearing that voice again made me understand I had crossed many boundaries in my life. I was the only child in my family to graduate from college, the only one to leave the town my parents themselves had been born and raised in to live in other places, to learn another language even, when I eventually moved to Japan where I lived and worked for two years. That town's voice was a touchstone to the family that made me, but also revealed how I'd crossed out of that rural working class family into a world where I was able to be an academic, a writer, a world traveler, and many other things as well. That voice, the collective "we" of the story that knows so much about its citizens and yet so little of their inner lives, reminded me that I was both of that place I was born to, but not of it now as well, that I stood on a border between the many places that have shaped me ever since. The town in "What We Know About the Lost Families of — House" was the first place to mark my passage through this world, and no matter where I live and who I become I will always stand on its threshold, with one foot in those fields and farms and the other in the whole wide world beyond.

Christopher Barzak

Post Hoc

Leslie What

Her boyfriend dumped her two months ago, and so far Stella hasn't been able to trick him into answering his phone. Caller ID. She should sue the guy who invented it. Because they really need to talk. At least, she does. Christopher's already said what he has to say; he's made that clear. Their last time together, they fought over who should have remembered the rubber. "This is why it should have been you," Christopher explained. He wasn't sure he wanted a baby. Neither was she, but now she's gonna have one.

Stella calls and leaves another message Christopher won't answer. If he only heard her voice, his heart would soften with compassion. If he saw her now, he'd see her changed body, her tall frame slightly stooped on account of the cramps the doctor said were normal, her nipples darkened to the color of freckles, the flattering swell of her breasts. He'd take pity on what she has become. She stares into her phone and wills him to answer. It's not much of a contest. His will doesn't give a damn.

She tries yet another foolproof tactic and speed dials Pizza Schmizza to order a pizza, *their* pizza, heavy on the sliced red onions, black olives, and anchovies. She knows she shouldn't charge things over her cell phone, because criminals could steal personal information, but a case of credit card fraud might be an improvement to this feeling that nobody is listening. She adds a five-dollar tip to motivate the delivery guy, in case there's any problem at the drop-off.

She imagines Christopher's look of confusion when he opens the door and inhales the irresistible aromas of sweet tomatoes and mozzarella toasted to a golden transparency. Naturally, he'll think of her, and hesitate before accepting the box. He'll lock the doors, slide home the bolts, and lower the blinds before sitting on the couch to contemplate the wisdom of eating a pizza of unknown origin. He'll resist flipping open the box until the aromatic premonition of salt and tang and sweet makes his stomach growl. It will only be a matter of time before he succumbs. She pictures him opening his mouth, tongue darting out to lick up sauce that's fled the tyranny of cheese. He'll chew, and think of her. She'll seize the moment, call him again; this time he'll pick up. They'll work things out. They'll marry. Hilo for the honeymoon. Snorkeling and hiking. Her last chance wearing a bikini without stretch marks. They'll have to hurry, or it could be a second trimester wedding. Higher chance of stretch marks. The dress will cost more, too. Extra fabric. She'll bear their son, and the boy will look just like his father. Christopher Junior. Thick, dark lashes that old ladies will notice and gush, "Why is it that only the boys have long lashes?" A child of such intelligence and kindness he will bridge the widening gap between her and her family, who think she's made too many poor choices in her young life and are practicing a modified form of Tough Love.

Only one problem with her fantasy: the very act of visualizing the pizza produces nausea and she spends the rest of the night curled around the toilet, bent over in a bathroom interpretation of the Swan Lake ballet, the chance for a perfect moment ruined by hormonal imbalances. She's so sick to her stomach she can't calm her nerves with a cigarette, just as well. The doctor warned her smoking was bad for the baby.

She needs another plan. Enough with the candygrams and e-cards, even an off-duty process server hired to deliver her proclamation of love. She's running out of options and there's only one thing left: mail herself to him. It's all done online now. Takes five minutes and ta-da! Insuring herself for the fifty dollars costs a buck thirty-five. The price doubles for each additional fifty. Since she's broke, there's no sense fretting about true value when the minimum is enough to ensure special handling. She arranges for her postman to pick up. Good thing she's doing this now, as the rates go up in another week. Some things never change, but postage isn't one of them.

She prints Christopher's name, address, and postage onto a label, and recycles the shiny backing, a bit prematurely, as now she must wrestle with the sticky label and think about where to stick it. She checks the mirror to see if applying the label to her chest or forehead is more dignified, dignity being hard to come by when you're mailing yourself to your boyfriend. Ex-boyfriend. At least, according to him.

Forehead it is.

Stella waits on the porch and at noon, her carrier—Joe—arrives, and hands her a catalogue from the community college she attended for one semester. Also a past due notice from the medical lab. Three rabbits, all dead, but she had to be sure. Joe notices the address label on her head and takes two seconds to understand what she's up to. His nod is sympathetic, patient. He says, "Gotta put you in back until I'm done for the day."

"You do what you have to," Stella says, disappointed Joe has made it so obvious she's not the first to resort to desperate measure.

The postal van idles at the curb. "While you're at it," she says, "would you mind taking my outgoing mail?" There's a postcard she's been meaning to send and a trial subscription to *Working Mom*.

"Be happy to," says Joe. He hoists her down the driveway and opens the swinging doors at the back of his van.

She squats inside a nest of media mail lining a white plastic tub, one of many white tubs with slots cut out in the sides for easy lifting. Some of the tubs are small and filled with a toss of Number 10 envelopes and some are large enough to hold microwave ovens. On the side of each tub is a modernist silkscreen USPS blue eagle, a reminder there is order in chaos.

Joe takes his seat in front, on the right side, and putt-putts up the street. "Feel free to read magazines," Joe says. "Just don't tear out recipe cards, or I'll get complaints." He pauses at the next mailbox, picks up a bundle of mail, and gently taps it home. He drives on. On the floor by his foot sits a copy of *Post Office* by Charles Bukowski.

She pretends she's on her honeymoon, that she and Christopher are walking over warm beach sand, the fine, dry kind that doesn't stick to your skin or get trapped in your butt crack. She breathes into her sleeve to escape the mushroomy odor of newspapers, exhaust, and detergent samples. She is smelling for two, and it stinks.

Joe finishes his route by five. He parks in the post office alley and transfers his white tubs onto a conveyor belt. He stamps Stella's cheek, *Hand Cancel* with red ink. "Oops," he says, and wets his thumb, rubs small circles across her skin. "Didn't mean to smudge."

"It's okay," she says, a little embarrassed by the personal attention.

"Got it," he says, and stops rubbing. "Have a good night."

"I will," she answers before disappearing behind a rubber flap that separates the natural world from the post office. The echo of footsteps tapping concrete punctuates the buzz of sorting machines that spit out stacks according to zip code. The conveyer belt transports her through the cryptic and industrious night world of the post office. There are no windows and no doors. It's a lot like being on one of those theme park rides, where you're told to keep your hands and arms inside the boat. Stella expects to hear the "It's a Small World" song cycle endlessly until it's a meme she can't get out of her head without deprogramming. She can't find a comfortable position, and in order to lie down in her box she must twist her body like a Möbius strip or her forearms and calves jut out from the sides. The night passes slowly and she considers giving up and going home, but she's too lonely to want to be alone. She watches the clock, counts the seconds. The shift supervisor takes note of her insomnia. "Let's see what we can do," he says. He unlocks a cabinet, removes a thick roll of plastic, tears off lengths of bubble wrap and cushions her white tub with doubled-over sheets. "Double bubble," he says.

Memories of that sickly sweet pink chewing gum scent make her want to throw up. Her eyes are so dry the lids won't close without great effort. She's almost too tired to sleep. Her mind is still sorting facts, just not into neat stacks, and it's obvious that her life lacks the zip codes to make everything fall into place.

The night shift supervisor says, "I have an idea," and covers her tub with another just like it, building a cabin, of sorts, more of a box. The opaque plastic lets in the light, provides privacy and space to sit up. Her cabin is cozy enough, though you're never as comfortable as in your own bed. She dozes, wakes, dozes. In the morning she's processed alongside the rest of the local mail. They date stamp her elbow and cancel her lips. She bonks her forehead against the scanner, but as long as the address is still readable, she's told she's good to go. She's transferred to a crate containing other mail requiring special handling. There's a taxidermy skunk with no return address, a ripe pork sausage—casing ready to burst—with a note that says, "Thinking of you," an oil-stained cardboard box labeled "Blubber from Alaska." It's as if they are in this together, a frightening thought.

Joe strolls past, wearing a short-sleeved permanent-press shirt that matches his blue pants. How is it that every man looks good in a uniform unless it's postal? When she met Christopher, he was wearing his Swiss minimalist lifeguard togs: red Speedos, a white whistle on a red cord, a red foam rescue tube with RESCUE printed in large white letters. She'd fallen hard after that first taste of CPR. He'd saved her life, only to ruin it later.

Anonymity is difficult in a small town, impossible on a postal route. Since Christopher lives close, along with all they've shared, they share the same carrier.

"How you doing?" Joe asks. He's a poet, but he never says anything worth remembering.

Her boobs feel lumpy and heavy, like someone filled them with buckshot during the twenty-five minutes she managed to sleep. "Not so great," she says.

"Sorry to hear it." Joe transfers the white tubs to his van, leaving hers for last. "You okay with this?" he says, with a nod to the skunk.

She shrugs. "It doesn't smell," she says. "But thanks."

Her boyfriend's house is near the end of the route. Stella, in her present state especially, won't fit inside the mailbox, so Joe carries her to the door and rings the bell. He gives it a few tries before setting her on the concrete slab porch. "What are we gonna do now?" he asks, but she knows a rhetorical question when she hears it, and sure enough, he takes out form PS 3605-R from his pocket and starts filling out the blanks. The paper is yellow. He copies the zip code and checks a box informing the occupant a parcel awaits pickup.

"Can't you just leave me?"

"Sorry. Someone has to sign to show they've accepted you."

She doesn't protest. She knows about rules, about rigidity. Her mother was a civil servant. Her father, a career soldier. "There's no democracy in bureaucracy," he told her. When you work for the government, there's nothing to do but bide your time until retirement. So back she goes, back to her padded crate and night workers who couldn't be kinder. They feed her Vanilla Wafers and saltines and let her use the employee bathroom. She feels special, like the post office cat. She waits to be claimed. And waits. Joe brings her a science fiction book called *The Postman* by David Brin, but she's not much of a reader, and sets the book on the counter while she uses the bathroom. By the time she remembers, it's disappeared. She becomes friendly with a sorter named Michelle, whose asthma is exacerbated by the glues used to seal envelopes. Twice, she's sent Stella to the lockers for her inhaler, and Stella has stood by, doting, until the rasp of Michelle's wheezing fades and her breathing comes easier. Stella learns the wisdom of having a friend who is in worse shape than she is.

Michelle has two kids and works night shift while her husband sleeps. She goes home in time to get the children ready for school. Four hours of sleep and then there's after-school activities and cooking. "Not much of a life," she says. "But it takes two incomes."

After a week, Joe brings disturbing news. "You can't stay," he says. "You need to go home."

"He's coming," Stella says. "Just another few days." She looks at her watch, which makes no sense, not that anything about her life makes sense. She just expects it to.

"Sorry," Joe says. "Regulations." He flips through a manual and points to a page, but when she sees the heading *Mail Recovery*, formerly called the Dead Letter Office, Joe says, it makes her sad, and she only pretends to read the words in question, and nod her head. In the morning, he transfers her to his van and when he gets to that place on the route, delivers her to her house, where she's supposed to sign for herself so he can leave her on the porch.

Only she won't do it.

Joe fills out another form, this one chartreuse and marked PS 941-X. "We just had in-service on this," Joe says. "New form." They return to the post office to file a report about unaccepted mail. Joe boils water and makes her instant soup. His voice is gentle. "Stay as long as you need," he says. "You're on my route. Around here, that means something."

"Thank you," answers Stella. When her calf seizes up and she has to stretch, she's allowed to walk around unsupervised in the storage room, a space that, like the center of the earth, has seen neither fresh air, nor natural light.

"Look where you step," says an old man sitting next to a shopping cart on a green canvas cot. The shopping cart is filled with lumpy black plastic bags and crushed soda cans. Oil-stained buckets from Kentucky Fried Chicken form a makeshift parapet around his encampment. He smells like sour milk and stale tobacco. A dried maple leaf curls through his hair.

"Do you live here?" she asks.

He shrugs. "Yeah. It's not so bad. I worked here forty years," he says in a gentle Southern accent. "Service before that."

She does the math and it adds up to Vietnam. Sure enough, he's wearing a black tee shirt under his flak jacket with an evil-eyed golden eagle and gold letters that proclaim, "Remember the POWs."

"What's your name?" she asks.

"Bartleby," he says. "Like Melville's scrivener. But you can call me Bart."

"Like the Simpsons," she says, being unfamiliar with either Melville or scrivening. She introduces herself.

"Like Stella Kowalski," he says. "I once lived on Desire."

"No," she says. "Not like anyone." This isn't true. She just doesn't know who she was named for. Maybe if she did, she'd understand better how she'd ended up living in a post office. She sees misshapen figures like shadow puppets fluttering across the back wall. "Do they live here, too?" she asks.

The old man shushes her. "It's best not to mention it. Don't ask, don't tell," he says, "or they'll make you fill out a squatter's form." He chuckles at his joke and lies back down, leaving up one hand to guard his cart. "First thing you do," he says, "you get yourself a cart. Unless you can convince one of the blue shirts to give you a locker."

"I'd prefer a locker," Stella says.

"I'm kidding. Sorry, little post office humor. I'll ask one of the boys to bring back a cart next time he makes groceries."

Stella wanders out, finds the break room. She'd like a cigarette, but the machine is out of everything except Snickers and Wintermint gum. Her stomach roils. She sits with her head between her legs for fifteen minutes until she's able to stand, then go out and find somebody to talk to. She sees why Bart might like it here.

"Would you like to help sort the outgoing mail?" asks the night supervisor. "Makes the time go faster when you've got something to do." He finds her a blue uniform she can grow into.

She works an hour or so before seeing her boyfriend's name whisk by, and she pockets that envelope, and though shamed by her felonious act, her shame is not so strong it prevents her from doing this again. And again. In less than a week, she's a serious serial mail thief who lines her tub with Christopher's correspondence. She steals utility payments, his Texaco charge, and his entry to Publisher's Clearinghouse. She lets him pay his telephone bill.

She sleeps from four in the morning until noon, and sometimes manages to sneak in a short afternoon nap, but her slumber is frequently interrupted by vivid dreams that leave her exhausted. Today, for instance, she's dreamt she was a sand crab coming up for air just as an animated Swiss Army Knife—with blades for limbs—dashed away. She's dreamt Bart asked Joe to deliver a postal money order, but Joe said it was against regulations to reveal her zip code. She's dreamt she was about to add her name to Christopher's mailbox, but couldn't find a Sharpie. This last was a waking dream, and her eyelids flutter into consciousness just as Bart asks her something she doesn't quite get. "Could you repeat that?" she must say, and he shuffles away, muttering, "Sorry to interrupt."

She feels bad for him, but also wary. Two days ago, Bart got mad and kicked a man hard enough the man flew out of his shoes. The man was one of the shadow people she's been warned to stay away from. These are very bad people, people who've been caught opening Christmas cards to steal money meant for children. As punishment, they must walk the floors in darkness, pulling heavy bags filled with mail. The bags are locked with heavy metal locks that clank against the chains. The shadow people moan and groan from the weight. It's very creepy. On the night Bart kicked the man hard enough for him to fly out of his shoes, Michelle, Stella's friend in mail sorting, broke up the fight with a cardboard mailing tube, reinforced with quarters from the stamp machine, and told Bart he'd be asked to leave if it happened again.

"It's the veterans who go postal," Michelle had said. "This one's got a temper you need to watch out for."

So Stella lets him go, feeling bad to have hurt his feelings by being half-asleep. He was married once, but his wife took the children and left him. She knows Bart's had a hard life, and knowing this helps her keep things in perspective, because as bad as things are, they could always be worse. At the back of her mind she holds the hope she'll suffer a miscarriage, fit back in her own clothes, but that seems more and more unlikely once she graduates from the first trimester. She's made a decision by making no decision, not for the first time. Maybe it's her training in a military family, where people tell you what to do.

The night supervisor organizes a pool and swiftly collects over a thousand dollars, half of which goes to her. "I'm betting on February 31," he says with a wink.

Joe saves out some crafts magazines that can't be forwarded because the subscribers have moved.

Stella learns to knit a scarf with postal twine she finds in the storage room. They don't use it anymore—the fibers get snared in the machines. She knits potholders and a bath mat. Linda, on the cleaning crew, brings her a few skeins of yarn and Stella starts on a yellow and white striped baby blanket. Soon, everyone's bringing in their leftover yarn. She knits compulsively. Wrap. Cast. Purl. She appreciates the smooth touch of the needles, how they clack and tap, the soft bump of the knots beneath her fingers. Knitting produces a tactile bliss that's almost as satisfying as smoking.

The night shift supervisor shows her how to develop a business plan for a mail order business. She figures out the sales points for personalized lap warmers. Postage is a break point, but fortunately, the lap warmers can go First Class in a Tyvek envelope. A casual observer might believe things are looking up for her. It's Bart who discovers Stella one night, sitting in the center of a maze of sorting boxes. She's writing postcards to Christopher and has accumulated a hefty stack. "Having a wonderful time," she's printed on the reverse of a Disneyworld train station. "Wish you were here."

"For when the baby comes," she explains. "So he knows I'm still thinking about him. In case I don't have time to write him then."

Bart nods. "You can't forget a person just because they forget you," he says, and shows her to a box of letters written to his son in Seattle. "There might come a point," he says, "where you stop writing them and stop mailing them. It happened to me."

She doesn't want to argue. Just because their paths have intersected in the mailroom doesn't mean she must abandon hers and follow his.

Bart pulls out a rolled up book from his jeans. It's *The Postman*. "I hope you don't mind me borrowing this," he says. His fingers curl around the spine. He isn't so much returning it as coveting it.

"Was it any good?" she asked.

His expression is animated. "Great," he says. "Maybe sometime I can read it again."

"Why don't you keep it?" she says. The hand clutching the book is already halfway to his pocket.

"Thanks," he says. "Much appreciated."

The old man was a medic. "You need vitamins," he says, and the next day, Joe brings forth a discount vitamin catalog in the bulk mail pile.

One of the women on the day shift brings in old maternity clothes, and the night shift supervisor finds a mattress that fits a clean white tub and is a perfect crib.

One night, when Stella is sorting mail, the machine mangles an envelope, creasing it into an origami heart with hard corners. It's addressed by hand, from a Kara G. on Portland Street to a Danny L. on Emerald Ave. Whatever message was inside is absent now. This happens sometimes, when people don't seal the flaps. She's supposed to go to the night supervisor, who will stamp it with the auxiliary marking that says, "We're sorry that your article was damaged during processing," but the futility of this correspondence intrigues her, and she keeps the envelope to add to her collection of Christopher memorabilia. She thinks about what might have been in the letter. A copy of expenses from an automobile accident? A complaint about services rendered; maybe Danny was the overzealous gardener who butchered the azaleas. Maybe it was love. Would Kara try again, or give up when there was no answer?

The missing letter haunts her. The next night, curious, she cautiously opens a few promising letters and reads. A child has written a note, thanking his grandmother for a bicycle. Marie is sending a picture of her dream family room to a contractor before getting a bid. James is writing Martha to ask for a recommendation to grad school. At first, she's careful when replacing the contents, and gluing the envelopes shut. By the end of the week she no longer cares. When there's something she wants to keep, she either pulls out the letter and sends the envelope on to the supervisor, or hides the entire thing. This kind of thing is difficult to trace.

Bart catches her, and though she worries that he'll turn her in, instead, he volunteers himself as the baby's godfather. "That would be great," Stella says. "Really, great." She's no longer afraid of him.

The old man gives her a hug. His clothes are dirtier and more beat up than when she first met him, but the odor doesn't bother her nearly so much. She decides to knit him some hand warmers.

She likes the name Christopher for a boy and Christine for a girl. She reads about correspondence schools and mail order degrees. She's comfortable living here; this will be a good place for a child to grow up. Her last trimester, her ankles swell and she's tired all the time. "Why don't you cut back," says the night shift supervisor. "Get a little more rest."

Being pregnant is practically a full-time job, utterly exhausting. She reduces her shift to two hours a night and is in bed in time to catch the last few jokes on Letterman. One night Michelle bakes her a tray of homemade cinnamon rolls that Bart promises to guard, to prevent sneaky nighttime raids upon her buns. Michelle's asthma has improved since Stella ordered a bottle of essential oils made from Thyme, Eucalyptus, Sage, and Lemon. Stella also ordered Lavender oil for Bart, though she hasn't had the nerve to suggest he use it sparingly to mask the other smells.

Bart tucks her in and pats down her hair with a fatherly hand. "Sweet dreams," he says. She falls asleep. They say you don't pick your family and sometimes that's true. But sometimes, you get lucky and your family picks you.

I became interstitial when my sister was born three years after my birth, transforming me from little sister to middle. In case you didn't know, middle children wrote the book on interstitial relationships, a tragicomic memoir. On one page, there you are, siding with big sister to form an unbeatable pair, relentless in tormenting your younger sibling. Turn the page, and big sister sides with little, forming an equally daunting pair who torment you. You're the in-between girl. One foot crosses into future mysteries and big sister's new high heels; the other foot plays dress-up with the baby, whose idea of *grown-up* is to imitate your mother. The lines have been drawn, and they are blurred. Did I mention I also have astigmatism?

Like many readers, I learned of the interstitiality of the Post Office from Eudora Welty. Like many writers, the PO is my conduit between artistic endeavors and audience. It's a surreal place, where intimate conversations stack atop bulk mailings, and where civil servants work beyond what can reasonably be asked, all in service of keeping the world interconnected. Thanks to my mailman, Joe.

Leslie What

The Shoe in SHOES' Window

Anna Tambour

The shop says SHOES because that is what it sells, just as the bakery next door says BREAD. When milk jumps out of a cow's eyes, it would make sense to call a shoes-shop 'Liliana's' or 'Mode', but that, incredibly, is what is done in those places where chaos reigns.

Truly, where chaos reigns, even at night, nonsense and evasion shine where people look for straightforwardness, but where they look for inspiration, something beyond the realm of daily existence, they are then shown only things, and who can feed his soul with that? For a tired man or mother, a few moments of my treatment is like taking off socks and shoes and dipping your feet into a cool stream on a hot and stinking day. I restore the mind and nourish the soul—myself and my colleagues, I should say: window dressers to the People.

I dress the windows of SHOES, as well as the shops FOOD, STATIONERY, CLOTHING, and TOYS. This year I won the Hero of Culture Award for SHOES, but my most consistent triumphs, I think, have been in TOYS.

For years my days have been filled with the dual necessaries of life: creativity and undisturbed peace. That is a state unachievable to the workers in the shops, disturbed as they are from shop opening to shop closing, by constant interruption. It is impossible to do a proper inventory! But I am glad to say: that is not my problem.

I have cordial relations with them all—or *had*.

Today SHOES was in an uproar, and I was dragged into the middle of this unpleasantness.

A man came in last week, who wanted a shoe in the window.

Not only did he want a shoe in the window, but someone told him (was it the young girl from the provinces, or sour old Luka?) when I would be coming back to work on the window: this afternoon.

He appeared at my elbow after I had unlocked its shop-side door and just as I raised my leg to climb up. He wanted a certain shoe in the window, he said, and he said this with such audacity that I banged my knee turning toward him.

He has one leg.

I was so startled that he spoke to me, that I acted stupidly. 'H'm,' I said, as if this *h'm* meant *yes*. I climbed up into the window and locked myself in, but he had disturbed my creativity so much that my hands shook.

He waited for about five minutes while I sat on the floor of the windowcase. He pounded on the door, but I was safe inside. Then he ran outside and attacked me from the pavement, using his eyes and one finger. But he could do little from the pavement unless he wanted to become a display himself. He left the ranks of the window gazers—a curious old woman and a girl whose eyes were only for the window.

I thought that I had taken care of him, so I felt it was safe to climb down.

I was met by the whole SHOES unit, who had called an urgent meeting. Though I am technically not part of their unit, I had no choice but to attend, the window being the source of unrest.

Everyone was in the most vile of moods, the air thick with the bad breath of people who need to eat and haven't since their mid-day soup at the canteen.

I argued: I cannot have my materials stolen. What would the window look like then?

Then I asked the meeting if anyone had tried to interest the man in the shoes in the shop. No one had thought of that, but why would they have anyway, several argued. They could not sell the man one shoe, and he—'*sensibly,*' he had emphasised, didn't want to pay for what he didn't need. When he added '*patriotism*' to that argument, no one knew what to do with him.

The meeting discussed needs, and I had to defend myself against accusations that I hadn't discussed materialism with *him*. 'That would have rusted his face,' Kishov said, his head bent as he shook dandruff from his hair onto the floor in front of him—a contest he played constantly with anyone, even himself if no one wanted to compete.

Naturally, the meeting first tried to pin the blame on me—an outsider. But I'm not an artist for nothing. Next, they turned on the girl from the provinces, for it was she who broke off counting shoes to listen to a person who was not in her work unit, a person who just came into the shop like anyone who comes into the shop looking for shoes. She didn't seem to understand even when she was asked, 'Do you let the dust disturb your concentration when it blows in?' Instead, stupid girl, she began to cry. It was decided that she would henceforth be housed with Luka.

But that only solved the problem of the *maker* of the problem. The problem itself was still to be dealt with.

There were some in the meeting (those going grey at their temples) who just wanted the problem to go away, and were willing to do it the underhanded way. 'Sell him the shoe,' they advised.

Others recoiled from that idea, the very young and the oldest. 'What if we get caught?' one young woman asked. 'We will, surely,' an old woman said.

'He will, not us,' dandruff-head said, meaning me, and was nudged in the ribs by his middle-aged superior.

I didn't need *him* to tell *me*. The shoes in the window are there for their beauty, as is the painted sled that's in there now. They are not there to sell. If I allowed the shoes to be sold, where would I find shoes to put in the display?

Of course I could not sell a shoe from the window, I told the meeting. They are not mine to sell. They belong to the window.

'Then give him the shoe,' one voice said, I couldn't tell whose. The necks I expected would bend up and down, bent up and down enthusiastically, as none of their heads were mixed up in this business.

Luka laughed, which surprised me, as I had always thought she was ready to report me for something she might think she found. Suddenly she was on my side. 'Can't you just see this hero walking down the street, wearing a shoe from *our* window?' she said.

The cinema-scene that played in various minds at Luka's instigation produced titters, scowls, and paleness.

Next, the meeting turned to the topic of who this disturbing man could be:

A spy sent to see what we would do?

A person who was so uncultured that he had never been in a city, and thus had never seen shops? He has a strange accent, but then so many people in this city do.

After further fruitless speculation (the hungrier everyone got, the more peevish and argumentative the meeting became) a decision was finally reached. The problem of the one-legged man who wants to buy a shoe would be solved by myself, the most cultured and also the most lettered, by writing a Directive to Address Irregularities.

I wrote the Directive, and it properly addressed, I thought, every possible permutation of irregularity. I framed it and hung it behind the front counter, where it was admired and read out to those who could not read.

It explained that the stock in the shop was for sale.

It exhorted all workers to do their duty, and not be waylaid by people from outside the unit who would not have the unit's productivity as their goal, or might even be saboteurs.

It made clear the inalienable difference between the shop and the window. *Each to its purpose, and each to its needs.* (I would no more think of taking shoes from the SHOES shop to put in the window than I would steal a man's hair from his head, though his hair might look good under a hat in my CLOTHING window. His hair serves the man's head. The shoes in SHOES serve their inventory.)

The Directive went into finer detail than perhaps you have patience for. But by the time that the nail was banged into the wall and the Directive straightened, there was no fault in understanding amongst any of the workers in the unit, even the young girl who had never worn shoes till she came to the city, let alone seen a shop.

A state of peace and equilibrium reigned again.

I was at SHOES today, hanging shoes on a painted vine that sprouted a red shoe, a blue one with white laces, and a patent-leather boot, when an insistent knock on the door of the window broke my concentration and made me fumble the shoes, the precious shoes.

I knew before I opened the door, that it was *him.*

'I wish to buy that shoe,' he said, taking hold of the door and pulling it open. Not only that, but he insinuated his long body onto the base of the window floor and stretched out his long arm to point to the shoe he wanted. A left-foot shoe half hidden under the dropped patent-leather boot: a green shoe with yellow laces and a punched design along the toe. I leaned my body out over his, partly to push him back and partly to see what he was wearing: the same drab lace-up as every man who had bought shoes in this city for the past three years.

I pulled back into my window and stood upright. He stood upright also, supported by a cane in his left hand—a respectful distance from my window door.

He puffed out his chest to make sure I saw the stiffness of medals.

So this was to be a test of wills!

I fought in the Great War, too, though I was not, like him, a pensioner, if that was what he was. He was either that or something more sinister, as he clearly wanted to turn my life upside down.

I used the classic defence, which usually works: pointed disinterest. I went back to my work, shutting myself away from him.

He tapped on the door with his cane.

I called out: 'Luka, please ask for this hero's identity card. We will have to report him as an attemptive supply liberator.'

'Comrade,' I heard Luka say, and I could see without looking, that perpetual bubble of spit grow large and pop at the side of her mouth.

Then I heard Luka cry out some primitive peasant *Save me!* curse. The supply liberator must have had a shock of a card.

'Comrade window-dresser!' the man called. 'Come down, by order of the Ministry of the People's Welfare.'

I had known in my bones that he was a spy. Others would have wet their legs at the word *Ministry*, but I had nothing to fear.

My feet met the floor with a steadiness none of the SHOES work unit felt. They stood around comically rigid. But I had comported myself faultlessly throughout this trial.

The man leaned on the counter. Luka snatched the abacus out of his elbow's range. 'With the exception of'—and here he pointed with his cane to the couple of middle-aged men—'Unit SHOES, Hero Boulevard has performed with distinction.' He elaborated for a moment on the pride he felt in seeing a unit that—and he wiped a tear from his eyes, which brought tears to many.

He was not finished. *I am to be awarded another medal!* I wanted to sit at that announcement, I felt so weak.

The man from the Ministry continued. 'There is a need,' he said, 'for high-class shoes for heroes with one leg. At the moment, there is no unit detailed to carry out this function.'

That is true. There is the manufactory that makes shoes for windows. There are manufactories that make shoes for shops. But his Ministry had identified a need, as yet unfilled.

I therefore now announce to you what he announced to us at that moment that I can still feel, down to my toes: There will be a manufactory of high-class shoes for heroes of the left foot. Our unit will make those shoes, and I will design them. None of us has ever made shoes, and I certainly have not designed shoes before, but that has never stopped any worker, once there is a plan.

I am filled with joy, as this is recognition above my previous recognitions. I am drunk with joy. And so is all of my new work unit, except for a few middle-aged men. We shut SHOES to celebrate. The chair was dusted off for the esteemed posterior of our benefactor from the Ministry of the People's Welfare. I feel—I feel it still—a warmth of comradeship such as I have never felt with another. There is the unspoken promise between the Ministry man and myself (his eyes shone with approval towards me) that if this manufactory fulfils, there will be yet another manufactory established with myself as designer, for high-class shoes for the right foot.

In the glow of ruddy cheeks and shining eyes, bottles appeared from nowhere and glasses were filled. The first toast! We all raised our glasses, and the man from the Ministry inclined his glass with a little rakish tilt towards me . . .

The man from the Ministry proved to be a hero indeed. When the party was over, the SHOE unit members were as firm-legged as boiled turnips, but he took his leave, rising like an oak from his chair. He walked down the block and disappeared in the murk of a broken streetlight. Even with his cane, he walked with the tread of a true leader—a leader who that fine green shoe looked cobbled for, as soon as it met his foot.

~

Luckily, not every editor and publisher in the free world acts as if fiction were directed by a centrally planned economy, nor is every author fit to be assigned to a Work Unit. Therefore, to my editors and comrades in this volume, I raise a glass of homemade turnip plonk in celebration as a writer and *consumer* of these glorious products of the imagination, unfit for any Plan.

Anna Tambour

Pallas at Noon

Joy Marchand

Sing, O muse, of the death of Pallas by the sea.

Today, 4 a.m.

Chloe is up early to make the rolls. They're cinnamon raisin and she hopes they turn out like the ones pictured in *Good Housekeeping*. Into a heavy bowl, she sifts flour, salt from a terra cotta pig, sugar from a paper sack. She's wearing too many silk robes over too many silk nightgowns and her movements are stupid and slow. Sweat beading on her upper lip, her breath coming in gusts, she powders cinnamon with a mortar and pestle, plucks raisins from a screen on the windowsill. Everything by hand. Everything.

Dean's not awake yet and she's thankful because she needs more butter for the rolls and he has no tolerance for the hand-crank butter churn. Chloe's husband hates the chortle of the heavy cream splashing in the glass jar, hates the squeak of the crank. But she loves leaning against the granite countertop with the jar wedged in the crook of her arm, likes cycling the crank while the butterfat turns into a thick golden ribbon against the glass. She likes how the movement warms her beneath her heavily layered morning clothes until she feels damp, and small, and cocooned. Most of all, she likes the time it kills, this churning, grating, grinding, drying, washing, slicing. Work keeps her from floating away.

The rolls come out just like ones in the photograph. Dean eats them while looking at his notes, drinking the coffee percolated from freshly ground Sumatra. He offers sound bytes to fill the silence: two o'clock sales meeting, a machine presentation, the anticipated morning commute, his racquetball chops. By the way my darling, I used up the toilet tissue. Could you add it to the delivery order? Can you manage it today? How's the stutter, Clo?

N . . . n . . . n . . . not bad, she says. A shrug.

Then Dean is gone, and his rustling, clinking, paper-and-fork noises fade, and all that's left is a mouth print on a cup and a glossy smear of sugar on a bone china plate. The kitchen exhales, invigorated by silence and lemon furniture polish. A thesis, inspired by coffee smells, dish soap, and citrus oil, unfurls as she rinses the dishes. It weaves itself into the first line of a poem—holds for a moment—then unravels down the garbage disposal as the impossible catches her eye.

There are filthy fingerprints on the counter: tiny, sandy ovals made by tiny, sandy fingers—impossible marks in a fan shape on the freshly scrubbed surface. They must be a figment, Chloe thinks, a specter. There can be no marks since there is no child—has never been a child—in this barren house. With trembling hands, she erases the marks with an abrasive pad and a scatter of blue scouring powder, a pumice stone, a buffing rag, a pint of surface cleaner. A scrub brush, a steel wool pad, three capfuls of eye-stinging Mr. Clean.

When the counter is sterile, she starts on the floor.

Funeral Shroud

A recliner sits in the attic, positioned to catch the sunrise. Chloe lounged there on her last morning as a writer, with a yellow tablet and a ballpoint pen. Her jaw clenched tight, she sifted through her thoughts like a tired old woman searching a junk drawer for a thimble. She searched for a simple concept she could capture in ink on cheap yellow paper. Words came: *dusty drapes, grimy window, cardboard boxes, ready for the burn barrel.*

She abandoned the pen on the arm of the recliner and took up a sponge, slipping into a trance of tidying up as easily as one might slide into a tepid pool. The drapes went into a basket, joined by a pair of lap-throws and a dozen Christmas napkins. The mottled web of dirt on the attic window went into the fibers of a rag. Her anger went into a plastic bucket, to mingle with the gray-brown mop water.

While she sorted through the attic junk, the rhythmic potential of each item wafted upward like steam, opening her pores and tempting her palate with sultry iambic feet: *colored pencil, candy wrapper, crumpled yellow paper*. Then she was smiling, giddy with the possibilities—*O, flexible poetry!*—and it felt as if the curse on her work were about to be lifted. But when she stood to stretch, she noticed the boxes Dean had set aside for the burn barrel.

Expecting stacks of coupons and bundles of bank statements, she opened a carton and was startled by the blocks of static, the frenzied ant races. When her eyes focused, the furious black flecks coalesced into a pile of speckled composition books, titled in Dean's tiny copperplate. *Qualities of Light, Poems 400–450. The Sway of the Pendulum, Poems 451–500.*

The boxes were full of Dean's creative work, hundreds of sonnets inked in fine-tipped pen with the aid of an Ames lettering guide. The margins were packed with illustrations of fantastic machines, levers and gears and cogs. Beneath the books she found Dean's note-taking tackle, his steno pads, magazine clippings, newspaper articles, index cards. In the next box: a compass and protractor, French curves in three sizes, templates and drafting scales. In the last box: spools of kite string, bags of marbles, a conglomeration of magnets, a cup of bearings, a plastic baggie full of colored lenses, twists of piano wire, a shoebox brimming with mousetraps. Dean's materials, entombed in cardboard, stacked in a pile to be burned with the leaves, or set on the curb for city sanitation. His work. His thoughts. Dead dreams.

She left the funeral pyre as she'd found it and abandoned her own instruments on the arm of the recliner—yellow tablet and ballpoint pen, dictionary and pocket thesaurus. They remained there for years, lost and forgotten, gathering a shroud of dust pale as bone.

Today, 6 a.m.

The binoculars are titanium and fit in the palm of her hand. They are survivors of the attic purge, deemed useful for mistletoe spotting in the backyard tree line. Because they've been spared, she can crouch behind the curtain in the parlor and train them on the street like a scientist positioning the Hubble telescope. There is no dust in the lace curtain to mar the lenses, no grime on the windows to impede their function. Her view is immaculate.

At half past six Edie-Across-the-Street and Mister-Dave's-New-Wife open their doors to retrieve the morning paper. It is their habit to stand for a moment in their pink sponge curlers, newspapers under their arms, shouting things at one another that are meant to be pleasant. I see you got the *car* washed yesterday. I hear it's supposed to *rain* so you should see if he got a *rain coupon*. Oh, I told Dave to wait until tomorrow, *I really did*, but he couldn't wait *another minute*. You know how *men* get with their *cars*. Boy, don't I *ever*.

At quarter past seven The-Man-Who-Walks-with-the-Golf-Club sprinkles Cat Chow on his mat before heading out for his walk but The-Cat-with-the-Torn-Ear doesn't show up. Usually, the cat is there crunching kibble when the man returns from his shuffle, and they stop to converse about small things. Rrrrrrow-ow. That good, huh? Nnn-gow. Well, you know I can't afford the hoity-toity stuff. Brrrrrrr. The cat's absence leaves a hole in the fabric of the morning.

The last thing to check is the sign in Wanda-Next-Door's attic window. Chloe performs this operation from a window in the master suite because the attic has become a no-man's land. Evan Lee has gone off to college, and it is a more peaceful neighborhood these days without his gum-snapping girlfriends, and the squealing of tires as he came and went at all hours of the night. The For-Rent sign sits in Evan Lee's window like a disloyal sentry prepared to open the gates to some invading army. Shaky capital letters in black permanent marker—FOR RENT! ATTIC ROOM!! INQUIRE W/IN!!! The screaming statement is underlined, each word, twice.

Evan Lee's room does not have curtains. He has taken his rebel flags with him to Chico State. A quick scan of the room reveals white walls peppered with nail holes, closet doors that hang open with a cobwebby emptiness. Evan Lee has left his bed behind, the ancient headboard covered with stickers and pocketknife art. Gouged wood, words carved deeply in the grain, have always reminded her of letters carved in wet sand with a stick, words eaten in stages by the surf.

A sudden swell of black tide ripples across the white plush carpet of the master suite. The stench of rotting kelp drives her onto a window seat, where she huddles with her feet tucked up under the thick layers of her bulky clothing. The tide is impossible. It soaks the carpet, but it is and it isn't real. It wets the floor, yet leaves it dry as desert sand. Whenever this dark tide comes the giggling comes too, a watery, bubbling sound. To banish it, she has to scour something.

But the carpet is freshly shampooed, and cannot be made any cleaner. To quell the oceanic stink, she scurries across the bedroom and throws open the closet. A single robe sits on the rail among empty hangers. It is a quilted satin housecoat—too warm for the weather—but Chloe pulls it on over the other garments anyway, and finds that she's unable to button it up. Twisted layers of fabric bunch up underneath her armpits, but the weight of the coat soothes her. She stands, eyes closed, and banishes the phantom tide. Gone, the tide. Gone away, for now.

It's eight o'clock sharp when a van parks in front of the house next door. The driver sits in the idling vehicle, and examines the For-Rent sign with one ink-stained palm lifted like a shield to blot out the sun.

Murder Most Foul

The house boasts an arrangement of mission style furniture, red oak and red leather. These pieces are what Dean has always wanted, these upright, parallel objects that don't know how to cradle a person reading a good book. They are puzzle pieces, blocks of wood.

Years before the attic purge, Chloe was putting things in order one day, trying not to think about the letter sitting on the table, wet with her tears. Like a lion-tamer with one balky charge, Chloe was trying to make an addition to the library—a serious Stickley rocker—without disturbing the geometric precision of the rest. She knew where the rocker was supposed to go, but if placed there it would edge out her old recliner. So she fussed with it until Dean came home.

That recliner ruins the balance of the room, Clo, and the stuffing's coming out.

I p . . . puh-*hut* a slipcover on it. It's the same c . . . c . . . color as the up-HOL-stery. And the duh-RAPES.

See how it bunches up around the top? This cover's meant for a damned wing chair! We *agreed* the old recliner was going to the dump!

If we're going to duh-HUMP it, I need a trip to the wwww-woods.

Oh, Clo. Come here, sweetheart. Wipe your face.

SssssssTOP it. If I can't have the chair, I have to have suh . . . suh . . . something.

In a perfect world, we could spend our lives writing in the woods, but we're not kids anymore. I have to work. No, don't use your sleeve. A Kleenex. Here.

D . . . damn it, I duh . . . duh . . . duh . . . don't expect you to bbbbbbbBABYsit me. But I nuh . . . nuh . . . NEED . . . my *story chair*.

Well. Let's put it in the attic room. We'll finish the walls and put in a pellet stove. Your own little studio. How about it, Clo?

Later, while Chloe stood in the remodeled kitchen wearing her nightgown, her silk duster and fuzzy mules, scrubbing, peeling, chopping and braising, it was as if she were cooking dinner on a submarine tilted at a terminal angle. During Dean's monologue over five courses of Italian, she learned that the entire staff of Hammond Inc. had gone on a diet and henceforth Dean would only be eating things that were green: boiled kale, spinach pasta, seaweed soup, freshly shelled peas. Pistachio ice cream, for a treat.

You can whip it up in the ice cream maker. Hand crank, but it's no problem, right?

He'd been so reasonable about the recliner, and the wolves at Hammond could exert such dreadful pressure on him to toe the line, that she only smiled, threw her grocery list into the trash and pinned a new one on the refrigerator. When Dean kissed her goodnight and left her standing at the sink, she silently pictured his evening routine:

He would undress in increments, folding each item before

slipping it in the laundry chute. He would slide his round body into a Dior dressing gown and tie the sash in an elegant knot. He would look at his teeth, brush them hard enough to draw blood, and then floss, twice. He would check his hairline, and then his nose hair, patting anti-aging cream onto his crow's feet. He would set his alarm clock, slip into bed and lay his head on an ergonomic pillow.

Dean would not snore in the night.

Today, 8 a.m.

It might be a man or a woman who climbs out of the vehicle to pose like a matador in front of the neighbor's house. The figure is attenuated in the light, motionless inside a billowing white cotton shirt. Black hair ripples. The shoulders are squared, the head is raised high, and one hand is raised to shield the face from the sun. A curious little smile tugs at the lips, as if in response to some private absurdity.

Chloe shifts vantage points to track the stranger within Wanda-Next-Door's house, but the view from the parlor is obstructed by the rose arbors. Chloe stumbles from one room to the next, a fat bumblebee searching for a good place to land. But her heart can't take it, this pinging from portal to portal, and so despite the terror in her heart, she presses forth in her fluttering garments as if buffeted by a gale wind. She tugs open the attic trap door and pulls her ponderous bulk up the ladder.

Parked at the curb is a white van of indeterminate origin, its sides mottled with patches of gray auto putty. The plastic of one taillight has been replaced by a red cellophane gel, affixed with silver tape. On one window is a large vinyl decal with a pop-art interpretation of the *Birth of Venus*; through the adjacent window peers a face. It is smooth and motionless, the mouth a red Kool-Aid smear, the eyes cornflower blue. The face twists, gives an ugly, gap-toothed leer, and presses into the glass to do a blowfish—red lips stretching, cheeks puffed and quivering with air barely contained. Slithering from the pulsating orifice, the tongue probes the glass, undulating like an enormous slug in a mason jar.

The binoculars slide to the sill with the hollow thump of knuckles on a coffin lid. Chloe fumbles at the lenses, and strangles a sob. The white face, the searching tongue, the fingerprints on the sink—the images cling to her skin like plague germs, threatening to launch her on a death-march of scrubbing and scouring and disinfecting. She hauls the binoculars up to take one last look, but the leering face is gone.

Chloe scrabbles through a box of clothing marked for Goodwill, untangles an old necktie, and ratchets it down over her housecoat in a cumbersome double knot. The pressure crushes the breath from her lungs, and helps suppress the tears pooling in her eyes. She hitches a few breaths and refocuses the binoculars on the invasion. At forty minutes past eight, the stranger opens the doors of the van. There is no child inside, no ghosts or goblins, just a naked mattress, a kerosene lamp, and a heap of paint-spattered tarps. The stranger unloads a green duffel bag, a goose-neck lamp and a stool, a tackle box, a stack of frames and a TV tray made of rusty tin.

He—it—she (there's no reason to think it's a *she* but for an opinion Chloe has that Wanda-Next-Door would not rent to a *he*) *she* transports this equipment to the front porch in stages and when denied entry by the Lady of the Manor shifts them to the long drive, where the attic room can be accessed by a rough, wooden stair. She returns to the van for a folding easel, which she slings over her shoulder as if marching into battle.

Battleground

Dean and Chloe once lived in an apartment decorated with hand-me-down rugs and other furnishings they'd gleaned from flea markets and yard sales. Dean liked to say the sitting room was an ode to bad taste, that its timeless kitsch was a statement: macramé plant hangers, drapes of gingham, orange-crate tables and faded chintz sofas, all ringed with bookshelves done in fence slat and bricks. Grief was out of the question in that crazy room, even for Chloe, who spent hours curled up in the lopsided recliner analyzing rejection notices.

She was fiddling with a notice one day when Dean stormed in with three bags of groceries, a paycheck from Johnson-Williams-Brownell clenched in his teeth like a pirate's blade. His high GPA had earned him a sign-on bonus and he'd brought home three kinds of sugar, a mortar and pestle, a bag of flour, a can of shortening, a bag of lemons, a lemon zester and a pastry cutter. A bottle of vinegar, a box of eggs, and a rolling pin made of marble.

With a triumphant smile, he said his paycheck would change everything and she could take her time with the novel, dip back into poetry—or put the whole thing away for a while. Instead of living in the recliner scribbling all day she could do fun things, now that life no longer depended on her advances, which were infrequent and had never been generous.

Their college wardrobes and the crap in the living room could finally be replaced! Had she ever heard of Arts & Crafts? Not the hobby, the movement, silly girl. Such lines! Such precision and mathematical simplicity! They could go right away and select something nice. Did she like the *Good Housekeeping* cookbook? The recipes are a little complicated, but won't it be fun not to have to be so anxious? Just whisk up a meringue once a while?

Clo! Hey, Clo? Want to make a vinegar pie?

Don't cry, light of my life. I'll take care of you, always.

Today, 9 a.m.

She's holding the binoculars in one limp hand and she can't believe she's in the attic. This fusty old tomb, this mausoleum. With her eyes shut, she slides around obstacles as if walking on a tightrope. She translates the escape route with her slipper-covered toes and descends the ladder through the trap door, which she shuts with one sweaty hand. It's nine o'clock, Monday morning. It's nine, nine a.m., and time for the Weed Holocaust.

Because she won't go out front where the sky is too cerulean, too wide, Dean has installed a rock garden there. But in the back of the house, where fences and neighboring homes provide a comforting enclosure, there's an assortment of bulb flowers and blooming perennials that she must care for by hand. Tulip season is over, the bulbs have been retired, but there are still irises to thin, gladioli and hyacinths to stake, fifteen varieties of tea roses to spray for aphids.

She performs these duties in gardening clogs and her heavy house clothes, gauntlets and a beekeeper's veil. As she sways among the arbors, as unwieldy and slow as a hippopotamus, her skin hums. The open sky on her skin is so buoyant, so anti-gravitational, that without the layers she's certain she would soar into the clouds, ascending through the atmosphere into open space, where she would tumble, freeze-dried, for eternity.

"There you are." A voice comes from Wanda's side of the fence. There's a strange slice of face hovering over the slats: brow fierce, eyes dark. "I've been knocking."

Chloe panics. The garden gate is very far away. She can't move a muscle in that direction because that gate leads to the front yard where she can't bear to go. Another escape beckons—the door to the covered porch—but to access the porch she must scramble past the stranger. Trapped, she shrinks into a ball on the ground and says, "H . . . h . . . hello," to her hands.

"I have newspaper. Wanda says the boy threw it bad, and you won't come to get it." There is some sort of accent—Baltic? Greek? There is the smell of linseed oil, dark flash of black eyes, smear of indigo—a smile. "You are Mrs. Larroway, yes?"

Hot terror smells like crimson and vermilion; it crackles from the ends of Chloe's hair in scorching red filaments. It ripples like a backdraft along the surface of her skin, and all at once there is no earth, no gravity, no downward and no upward, only the sensation of the newspaper in her hand as Chloe explodes like a comet past the stranger, past the roses, over the porch, through the dining room, up through the trap door, and back into the attic, where she stands panting like a rabbit. In her clogs and beekeeper's hat, she stands in the eye of a cobweb storm. The newspaper is heavy in her hand, a double coupon edition.

Chloe is giddy. "Thuh . . . thuh . . ." she says, addressing the attic window, the shimmering glass, the yawning eye of Evan Lee's room. The For-Rent sign has been taken down.

"Thuh . . . thuh . . . thuh . . ." Chloe says, the corners of her mouth twitching, twisting.

She takes a step toward the window. And after a while, she takes another. And another, and yet another, until she can see the stranger peering through the fence.

"Thuh . . . thanks," Chloe whispers. Her breath fogs the dirty window. The dark head snaps up. The dark gaze penetrates the glass and skewers Chloe through the forehead.

The world turns into crystal. Chloe's heartbeats crash against her ribs, like the echo of waves battering the pilings of a pier. A memory comes of a little girl, frolicking, and around this dream child, insults drone and dip like angry hornets. There is the smell of salt. If Chloe tries very hard she can pretend the insults are just the sound of a gull flying low over the house, that the smell of the sea comes from the moist, hidden parts of her own body.

The air in the attic glistens, particulate.

Sparring Partner

Until her junior year in college, Chloe had avoided the library, dashing off pages of poetry while nestled deep in a lopsided recliner in the corner of her dorm room. After she fell for Dean Larroway (Applied Physics, Seat 26) she spent her nights on the library balcony, wedged against a magazine rack where she could secretly watch him work. The library was a marvel of steel and glass, and in the evening hours with the lights dimmed and the carrels quiet the overarching trees seemed to step inside, turning the reading room into a wild wood.

Dean spent his evenings in a study room building fabulous machines from balsa wood and string, piano wire and mirrors, prisms and shiny ball bearings. He sat and made detailed notes for each machine in a stenographer's pad. He used a lettering guide to carve long lines of text into a composition book—blocks of number-free copy that looked nothing like applied physics. He was an engineering student, but also a poet, his sonnets inspired by the mathematical splendor of the flashing, swaying, bobbing sculptures he built with hands as delicate as a girl's.

One night Dean's activities were discovered by a wandering pack of students. They circled him like hyenas, knocked down the delicate, swaying machine, scattered Dean's books and notes. They pushed Dean against the glass wall of the study room and took turns pretending to kiss him. They lectured him about "big boys' toys," cars, and airplanes, and trains and bridges, until they got bored with his lack of resistance and gave up. A whirlwind of hiking boots and denim, they spat in their hands, rubbed it in his hair, punched him in the arm and stalked off into the night.

Rumpled, bruised, flushed, Dean bent to pick up his broken machine.

Chloe folded a poem into a clunky paper airplane and flew it down to ping the windows of the study room. Startled, Dean looked around, took it up, unfurled it like a starving man peeling an orange. When he spotted her where she sat wedged like a mouse between magazine racks he smiled a shy, grateful smile. His eyes were the green of the overhanging wood.

It was love between them, then and thereafter. They sat together on the library balcony dreaming under the conifers and wide-reaching oaks. He complimented her work, and he didn't correct her stammer or finish her sentences. Happy to sit, Dean waited for her to express herself on her own time. When they finally touched, finally embraced, finally kissed, her undisciplined, impractical poems grew measured and majestic. Dean began to write epics as if he were the first man to fall in love with a beautiful woman. He cut a lock of her hair and made a braid—carried it in his pocket. Chloe fell, and fell, and fell. She lost herself, and was glad.

Dean could hear the heavenly music.

Today, 10 a.m.

Chloe is in the attic. Spiderwebs undulate with her breath like undersea vegetation. A delicate fuzz coats the surface of boxes and baskets like plankton and her writing tools are on the arms of the chair, sleeping under a shroud of powder. The room wants to be aired and scrubbed, to be arranged and alphabetized into submission. But Chloe drops into the recliner and watches dust spurt in a mushroom cloud. She sheds her clogs, strips off her gauntlets, hat and veil—hurls them into the boiling dust balls on the floor. Her heart, still giddy, sends blood to her limbs and a blush to her cheeks.

The window is hazy, but she wrenches it open and takes a breath of fresh air. Tucked into the recliner she can see signs of habitation in Evan Lee's room. Shirts are hanging in the closet. The goose-necked lamp is clamped to the nightstand. The easel is an origami crane with a tablet of newsprint in its beak. Red chalk, artist's gum, and sticks of charcoal are a jumble of kindling on the tin TV tray, waiting for the spark.

The artist approaches the easel with a stick of black chalk. She stands as if balanced on a precipice. A breeze from the open window ripples the paper, lifts her hair, toys with the hem of her white shirt. She closes her dark eyes, and her lips begin to move. The artist is summoning something from within, drawing the cloak of artistry around her, that veil of incandescent power. She stretches her arms, rolls her head to loosen her shoulder muscles, pulls her elbows across her chest one at a time, and then bounces lightly on the balls of her feet.

Hear me, she mouths. *Come to me, spirit.*

Three strokes hit the paper then the sheet is savaged from the pad. Others soon follow, to collect in a drift around the easel like crumpled gray snow. As she moves, her light cotton shirt flutters and undulates, collecting smears of charcoal at the cuffs and the hem. Lost in the work, the artist shrugs the garment away, baring a broad, strong back. She winds the cloth around her palm to use as an implement, her naked shoulders curved into the page. Eyes narrow and fierce, she smudges the paper with her thumbs, her wrists, her fingers. She swipes over the paper with elbows, forearms, clumps of wadded-up shirt. She leans into the tablet as a lover curves into an embrace. As the power of creation hits her, the artist tucks her dark head low and the strokes on the page become violent and wild. Her lips move and it's as if she is singing some ancient ballad as her marks impale the fibers of the page with lethal energy, crow's wing black, burnt crimson, bone white. Bright-eyed and gasping, she finishes the piece with a flourish. She brushes a wild strand of hair from her damp face and steps back to examine what her labor has wrought.

Without magnification, Chloe shouldn't be able to see the image, but it steps from the easel to stand at Evan Lee's windowsill. It is a little girl, pale, red-lipped and covered with beach sand. She stands in the window like a warrior, with a stick in her hand, a lance, a spear, a bright sword. Behind the girl is the massive, aquamarine curl of a wave, shot through with foam and strands of black kelp. In a shimmer of chalk dust, the warrior child waves her driftwood spear at Chloe and sticks out her little pink tongue. Then she's smiling, sharp nacreous teeth. Her hair flutters in the ocean breeze, crazy dandelion fluff. No longer a dread specter, a harbinger of cold aquatic death, she is a nixie, a sprite, a sandy-legged sylph.

Chloe bends toward the window, and scribbles a little to get the ink flowing from her pen. Words spill onto the dusty sheets, random, tumbling, breaching like porpoises over warm waves. As when she was crazy and young, her first disjointed attempts fall to the floor in a mad cascade of half-crumpled paper. Writing this topsy-turvy way, uninhibited, is like pulling the handle of a slot machine, again and again with blinking lights and caterwauling sirens: *Loss, loss, loss, win! Loss, loss, win! Jackpot! A winner! Fly!*

She isolates an image, adds another and another, and as the discarded pages pile up under the windowsill, an epic erupts and takes flight. Her pen hand dips and soars to keep pace with the words, climbing, banking, gliding on thermals, accompanied by a burbling that fills the room like a child's breath escaping water, but this time Chloe isn't driven to the disinfectant. She is uplifted up, up, up toward the receding storm clouds, "D . . . d . . . d . . . DONE!"

Triumphant, Chloe looks at the artist. With a gaze like volcanic glass, the artist releases the neck of the easel to lean naked against the windowsill, chin propped on her chalk-blackened elbows. She has no breasts, no nipples, no navel. Her skin is smooth caramel satin over muscle and bone. Like a priestess offering a blessing beneath a canopy of wild olive, she raises a hand, closes her eyes, and sings Chloe's newly penned verse:

> Young Pallas, daughter of Triton, and granddaughter of
> Ocean
> Was the beloved friend of Athene, Gray-Eyed goddess of war.
> Both girls loved a good skirmish, spear and javelin most of all
> And sadly, when they matured, all the crude nonsense started
> With "Mine's bigger than yours" and "It's quality not
> quantity."
> So, when Pallas raised her weapon, no doubt to prove a point
> She was struck down by accident to fall dead at Athene's feet.
> And grieved to the heart, Athene wrapped Pallas in the aegis
> The snake-cloak of protection, and placed her body in a
> shrine
> And bought her fixtures, and clothing and self-help books like
> "How to Forget Your Javelin, in Twenty-Eight Days or Less."
> And although in a tomb, Pallas wove macramé to pass the time,
> Learned to cook and to sew and to praise Athene's offerings.
> Growing strange and preoccupied, under the weight of her
> dread,
> She stuffed her ears full of wool, and bent to the sharp spindle
> Avoiding the call of the Deep.

Wolf Love

As a teenager in Venice Beach, Chloe wasn't afraid of the ocean and people and wide-open spaces. She spent long summer days in the sand scribbling poetry, waiting for boys to invite her into the surf. Befriending foreign boys was best because all languages were like oxygen, and she didn't stutter on foreign syllables. One summer she had many conquests. She gave four days of passion to a doe-eyed Argentinean, two days of frivolity to an apple-cheeked German, five days of tenderness to a studious Swede named Jan. The day Jan had to leave, Chloe ran home to her mother and wept tears of sand and salt.

Her mother had been shuffling notes with a screenwriter named Tinky all afternoon. She caught Chloe up in arms of warm cotton fluff and rolled her like a sausage in the scene-blocking cards until all of them including Tinky were pink and fizzy and giggling. Her mother told Chloe not to be sad. She said, Take heart, my little wild thing, for you were raised by wolves good and proper. Don't you know that wolves run in packs, and sing to the moon, until they find the One Wolf that makes them complete? Jan is certainly lovely—bless the moon and stars—but does he hear the heavenly music? Does he, Chloe-love?

Chloe pondered her mother's breathless question for the rest of the summer. She sat on the sharp rocks at Gideon's Point and ignored the bonfires and the hoots of her classmates. She was sick with emotions; love and fear battled inside her, war on an Olympian scale. But the fire that burns hot burns quickly, and in the last week before she went off to college, she smoldered like a banked ember in the depths of the recliner. She slept in the bright throne of creation that had not yet forgotten its purpose.

Today, 11 a.m.

Stricken, Chloe reads her poetry on the lips of a stranger. Her heart falters, and she presses against the arm of the recliner to keep from falling out the window. The artist smiles with a tired compassion, a battle-scarred veteran fresh from a deadly dance, still ankle-deep in the blood of a fallen companion. There is a moment of stillness, a moment of reflection, and then she motions. Sit on the windowsill. Pose for me. I will draw you.

Chloe stands motionless in the window, a gazelle paralyzed by the heat of a tiger's breath. She waits for slashing ivory teeth to end the meticulous diorama. Get it over with, cut my throat.

The artist reaches for her tools.

Wild Child

One afternoon, Chloe stood knock-kneed in her second-hand swimsuit and watched a gang of children build a sandcastle. There were three kids in the gang, two pale blond boys and a girl. They worked like golden fiends on the structure, but for all their frenzied scooping and dumping, the best they could do was a lopsided cone of sand. Unable to stop herself, Chloe sidled up and whispered to the boys about battlements, and moats and curtain walls. The stunning blonde sister tossed her silken hair over one shoulder and said, Look at that dumb girl. She's got a ratty hole in her bathing suit and her sandals don't match.

The stink of Chloe's fear excited the golden children. Twitching their little red beaks, they stalked her like scavengers. They made fun of her pale skin and her apricot-colored hair and her s . . . s . . . stutter most of all. Cawing, they snatched her packsack and tore it open, used her pencils like lawn darts and screamed her poems at one another, before twisting them into little ropes and flipping them into the surf. Then they fled the carnage, toward the blanket and umbrella fortress where their mother was reading a fashion magazine.

Chloe nudged her beach bag with her foot, and ran home. Unable to laugh it off, unable to cry, she was numb, mute, dead. Chloe's mother took her into the Story Chair and told her a good one about the day Chloe was born. Did you know you were born with a hole in your heart?

Mama, please.

Oh, I know what you're thinking. But there was a little hole—a real pinhole—right through the muscle of your heart. Even though it closed up when you were six, it still hurts. All your life you will pour things into this pinhole to ease the pain, the way you wiggle your tongue inside the empty tooth spot. As long as you keep your heart filled, you'll be blessed, Chloe-Bear. Promise me you'll fill it with magic and secrets and sunlight and ocean waves, and all the other things that hurt but also make you feel alive. Promise you'll do this. Forever and ever. Promise me.

Oh, I promise, Mama. I promise.

Today, Noon

The sun is streaming through the open window, drawing beads of sweat from deep within her body. Maybe the sweat comes from fear, or from tears trapped in the folds of the garments she uses to anchor herself. Her anxiety is receding. It's not as bad as it was when the artist first began to paint. But at eight minutes to noon, the heat is changing from prickly insect feet under her arms to a massive cowl of wet wool around her neck and shoulders.

A voice inside tells her that if she doesn't unwrap her sweating body soon, she might faint, strike her head. Die. Strangely, the idea of death is no longer comforting.

Nakedness has been a horror ever since she abandoned her tools on the reclining chair, and only in the shower, contained in that small, wet-pounding space, can she bear it. Whenever she's naked out in the open air, she feels rumpled and slack, although her muscles are still firm and her skin sleek. It's not the nakedness itself that disturbs her, but the buoyancy.

The artist waits with a long sable brush held lightly in her fingers. Her canvas has been prepared, the oils squeezed into mounds that glisten wetly against a sheet of rounded fiberboard. There's a glimmer in her dark gaze. Her expression is challenging, but loving, that of a teacher watching a favorite pupil. She could draw Chloe swaddled in bathrobes like circus tents, indeed she could, but instead she waits for the human being to emerge.

Chloe's hands are moist. They pat and pluck, and search her taut surfaces for access. She unfastens the necktie, her fingers trembling. The first thing to come off is the housecoat, size 32, and it hits the floor with a wet *fump*. The second item is a brocade bathrobe, size 18 (because it comes from a line that caters to women who like to consider themselves Rubenesque). The frog closures are satin, and they slip in her sweaty fingers. She shoves the bathrobe under the recliner with her foot. A third garment, cumbersome pink satin, drops to the floor with a rustle. With the release of each garment, her legs shake less, her hips ache less, and her heels seem to apply less pressure to the floor. Away drop three gabardine button-ups, sizes 18, 16 and 12. Next, two pairs of leggings and three pairs of tights, which she peels off and drapes over the arm of the chair like empty snakeskins. Off come two sweatshirts (sized 10) and two T-shirts (sized SM). Off comes a rumpled cashmere cardigan and a camisole edged in marabou, both dropping into the dust from light fingers. Dressed in a wisp of silk, Chloe teeters at the window. The sable brush caresses the underside of one lace-covered breast, the oil paint rolls across the curve of her hip, delineates the line of her thigh. All is terror. All is joy.

What would Dean think? Should she tell him how she stood bare to a stranger? Would his hands make that warding-off gesture? Would he call her a whore? Would he leave her? Should she go downstairs into the garden and behead the glads, the hyacinths, the fussy tea roses, before he comes home? Should she break all the dishes, smear all the windows with her sexual liquids, warn him somehow of her return to the Deep? Should she show him the wild child, that creature with the perforated heart, the beast she tamed and destroyed?

If she flies, will he fly with her?

Can he still hear the heavenly music?

Chloe looks across at the artist, and she hears the call of the sea. She looks at the brush, at the canvas, at the glistening oil paint, at the artist's moist, parted mouth, and Chloe's arms rise of their own accord to smooth the marks from her white skin. The crashing of the surf increases to a thunderous roar, and she tastes sea foam on her lips as she strips away the wisp of silk to stand naked at the window. The wood floor is as smooth as shell beneath her feet. She raises her hand to the artist, and she opens herself to Ocean.

Somewhere a clock strikes noon.

The Birth of Pallas

Chloe-Bear does not wear a bathing suit while she splashes in the waves. When her mother is not looking, she strips it from her body and flings it into the sand before plunging into the surf like a quicksilver fish. When she dives wearing the old patched suit, the sand tumbles down the neck and collects in a clump between her legs. This makes her itch, so little Chloe swims in her skin whenever she can get away with it.

Today she's playing dolphin, with much diving and breaching, and so the suit has to stay on the beach, where Mama is flipping through her notes like a crazy person. While Chloe-Bear dips and bobs in the warm waves, she wonders how much the little mermaid hated the prince because of the knives in her feet. She pretends to have a fish tail, and then a whale tail, and then flippers like a sea turtle, which is so funny she pees, but just a little. But it's the ocean, not the pool at the Y, so it's fine. Fish pee in the ocean all the time.

Her hair looks like carrots when it's wet, and that's fine. When she's done swimming, she's alone on the beach because it's Monday and it's not tourist season. She forgets all about her suit, and finds a long stick, because the rat's nest of her mother's gray hair rolling in the breeze makes her think of a poem. Naked, Chloe drags the stick along the edge of the surf where the sand is as wet and gray-brown as the belly of a seal. With her tongue hanging out, she writes a long poem in loopy letters, and dots all the i's with stars, even though that makes teachers mad. That kind of mad isn't the real kind of angry, especially when people like the words you write, with annoying little stars and everything.

When she finishes the poem Chloe signs her name in time to see the bubbly-white sea foam drag the first lines into the sea. After another surge of surf, the poem is gone, but it was kind of a dumb poem anyway, she thinks, so she takes a breath and lets the buoyancy take her. A wisp, a bit of beach fluff, Chloe drifts on a gust of salt wind, and her dragging toes leave long creases in the wet sand. Gathering the ocean spray around her like a cloak of invincibility she floats toward the far horizon, and then blasts off like a rocket into the high noon sun.

~

There has never been a boundary I didn't want to smudge. As a child, I wanted the ice cream with the gumballs stuck in it, and books with soft or crackly swatches of things to stroke. Later, I sculpted, played with geometric proofs, rode horses, acted in musicals, and read novels about kids who crossed into Faerie. In college, forced to choose a curriculum, I stumbled on classical studies and plunged my thumbs into a dozen pies. I gobbled ancient philosophy salted with classical mythology. I savored Roman art and architecture steeped in the pickling spice of three dead languages. When I wrote "Pallas at Noon," I meant to crack open Athene's myth and transform the stuff of epic poetry into personal prose. I stargazed with the telescope pointed the wrong way around, married poetry with physics, and wrote muses into the mop water. I wrote half of the story backward, and I had a blast.

Despite my best intentions, Chloe Larroway is not a boundary crosser. She is a boundary *sitter*—a boundary *watcher*. It's in Chloe's silent watching, I hope, that the borderlands in her smallish life are invaded, and her vast inner spaces illuminated.

Joy Marchand

Willow Pattern

Jon Singer

The plate in the display-case is worked in a lovely indigo underglaze. It is quite the darkest I have ever seen, and has the most saturated color; but the pattern is not as I recall it—the little faces of the lovers are fearful as they run across the bridge, their hands barely touching. Behind them the whip is held at a lower angle than the one I keep in memory, and there is no rope flying from its end. The rest of the scene is tautly still. Even the birds above the bridge seem locked into place, drawing the viewer's attention down to the figures below them.

The glaze on the rare Ming version in the next case is a soft buttery yellow, and makes it hard to see the pattern. There is, however, a button you can push for a special light to increase the contrast. When you do, you can see that the foliage is antique in appearance and that the reptilian heads of the creatures, as they turn toward you, are remarkably distinct; the more so, considering the usual slight looseness of the brushwork and the odd effect of the lighting. From time to time the case seems to fill with a thin fog.

I look at the greenish-black glaze of the plate on its stand. The stream is choked with weeds, and the house dilapidated. One of the birds falls from the sky, feathers everywhere, as the old man fires a warning shot. His face is grim. The lovers on this plate are in a panic, not even touching each other, flying headlong down the endless bridge toward the path they will never reach.

Here the glaze is palest sky-blue on a dark ground. Our experts have concluded that the figures are indeed aliens. Possibly they come from the far West, or they may be hairy people from the most Northern of the islands off the coast. They are, nonetheless, engaged in the statutory activities—scourging one another with whips, and casting their victim from the bridge onto the rocks below. The wind is rushing everywhere, and you can see their little hats in the sky, along with a few sickled leaves from the tree-ferns or cycads that almost obscure the low dwellings to either side of the bridge. The dusty texture of the glaze is singularly appropriate.

The glaze on the plate is red-brown. The figures are tumbling from the bridge into the stream, as if from the lightning-struck tower. It is hard to tell whether they are yet alive, or have been felled by the blasts from the shotgun—their faces are not visible, and their limbs, tossing randomly, give no clue. The face of the Father is almost obscured by the cloud of smoke billowing from the gun; but one eye, huge and bloodshot, protrudes through a gap . . . it is clear, from the positions and angles of the elements of the scene, that he has shot his daughter first.

This [disk] is the largest of its kind that we have yet recovered, and emits the most intense radiation from its glaze. The base material appears to be [granite?], some ten [untranslatable unit] thick, and has withstood repeated firings, possibly including one or more to test or anneal it before the glaze was applied. Some earlier units of this type, presumably made before the technique was fully developed, have cracked; this one, in contrast, is in splendid condition, with almost no flaking or spalling. It retains nearly all of its details, from glaze pattern to makers' insignia to the highly distinctive tooling marks in the surfaces of the rock, which are visible where there is no glaze cover. The inscription on the central boss of the underside translates: "It is estimated that [untranslatable, name] spent 17 [time unit indicating long cycles, possibly "years"] at the desk [?] and bench, toiling to conceive and produce this flawless record of the events of [untranslatable (Place-name?)]. [Name, honorific form] went on to produce only one further object of note before succumbing to [?] in the [untranslatable phrase] times of wanting."

The plate is still hot in my hands, its glaze ashen-gray. There are no leaves at all on the trees, and the bridge is missing, though I can see the bases or abutments on which it once stood. The house at the left side is canted at a crazy angle and will surely fall in the next windstorm. The ancient man sitting patiently in the doorway looks at me and then at the gun in his hand as he points it toward himself, but when he pulls the trigger nothing happens. He ran out of ammunition long ago. Presently he will try again, however, and perhaps this time it will work. The streambed is dry except for a few pools of mud, and the plate falls from my hand to the smoking earth as I try to inhale the thick acrid air. There is nothing more for us here; we have ruined it all.

A Great Idea (if such a thing comes to you) will fill your entire life. Almost nobody can sustain several; I don't seem to be capable of even one. Instead, perhaps partly as a result of my having so-called Attention Deficit Disorder, there's this huge swarm of little ideas flittering around in my head like butterflies and rarely alighting in one place for long. Two other possibly AD[H]D-related issues: I don't parse time in a linear manner and cannot plot worth a damn; and I am perhaps just a tiny bit Aspergerish, so I don't parse humans as well as I might. The net result is that I'm essentially incapable of writing fiction of a more standard or usual sort; in fact, I find it difficult to write fiction at all. The pieces that I do manage, at long intervals, to produce are typically shorter than 1,000 words. (I do write a certain amount of nonfiction.)

Jon Singer

Black Feather

K. Tempest Bradford

Exactly one year before she saw the raven, Brenna began to dream of flying. Every night for a year. Sometimes she was in a plane, sometimes she was in a bird, sometimes she was just herself—surrounded by sky, clouds, and too-thin-to-breathe air. In the dark, in the light, over cities and oceans and fields, she flew.

Then, on the twelfth day of the twelfth month, the dreams changed. They ended with a crash and fire and the feeling of falling. Most nights she almost didn't wake up in time.

Exactly one year from the night the dreams began, Brenna struggled out of sleep, the phantom smell of burning metal still in her nose. She reached out for Scott—he was not there. He was never there. He had never been there. She fell back onto her pillows and groaned. Another dream of flying, another reaching out for Scott. She wished she could stop doing both.

Brenna lived in Manhattan—a small, insignificant corner of it way at the very tip-top. On an island of concrete and glass and steel she had found the one place still mostly untouched. It had a lake and a forest and a hill she could climb without ever realizing how high she was at the top. From there everything seemed far away, not far down. Not like when you're in a building. Or falling from the sky.

She had lived by this park, this forest, for two months now. The apartment, her new apartment, paid up for the summer. A graduation gift from her mother.

That morning, while the sky was still pink and yellow, she went out and up the hill to the small meadow at the very top. She thought of it as *her* place.

It was there in that meadow, amongst the crumbling remains of benches and street lamps long abandoned to the regrowing wilderness, where she first met the raven. She was meditating under a large oak tree when she heard a raven's cry. It didn't register at first, and might not have ever, if it hadn't been so persistent. It didn't stop until she opened her eyes and saw it standing on a fallen tree trunk. One black raven. It had been a long time since she'd seen one. Not since England, when she put aside her fear of flying to follow Scott across an ocean. A year ago.

"Did you follow me?" she joked.

The raven looked right at her and cawed. It came back to her then, a rush of emotion and memory, half hidden, half forgotten. One warm day by the sea, looking back over the ocean toward New York, a raven standing out on the rocks, and her plea to him. *I want to fly. I want to fly and be free and go wherever and whenever... I want to fly!* She wanted it so badly that she felt her heart would break.

The feeling had overwhelmed her then and it overwhelmed her now. Here in the forest, an ocean between her and England, and she could still feel it. She found that she was crying. The raven's call echoed in her mind, but when she wiped the tears away he was gone. Gone without a sound—or had there been wings flapping? She turned to pick up her bag and saw a feather, long and shiny and black, lying on the rock by her side. A feather just for her.

She showed the feather to a friend. The psychic one.

"Feathers are powerful messages and special gifts," she said while Brenna absently shuffled a tarot deck. "Draw a card."

She drew the Hanged Man.

"Sacrifice."

"But of what?"

The next day she saw the raven again. He was staring at her through the bedroom window—the one with the view of the hill. She thought he was the only one, but soon there were two, then three. One day she saw them all. Twelve ravens, high up in the oak tree, watching over her.

~

She showed the feather to another friend. The non-psychic one.

"Crow's feather, you mean," she said.

"It is? How can you tell?" Brenna asked.

"Because we don't have ravens in New York, we have crows."

They called to her in her dreams. She heard them but couldn't find them. Their feathers littered the floor; long and shiny and black. She dreamed of flying through a forest of black trees and shiny ebon leaves, always following the raven's song. Six nights of this. Six nights of searching and never finding. Six nights of waking up sweaty with raven feathers in her hair.

On the seventh night the dream changed again. She found herself in a little wooden cabin, fire crackling in the hearth, twelve small beds along the hall. In the middle stood Brenna, wearing nothing but a man's white shirt.

The ravens called to her from outside, but she did not want to go. One by one they flew in through the open door. And in a moment, a blink, an instant, they were not ravens but young men. The youngest of all looked a lot like her.

"Who are you?" she asked.

"We are your brothers," one said.

"We died for you," said another.

The dream ended.

She ran into Scott (accidentally on purpose) in front of the building where he taught his summer course.

"So you live in Inwood now?" he asked as they walked toward his office.

"Yeah. Right by the forest."

"There are some interesting cave formations up there. Do you want to come explore them with me?"

"Sure, that'd be cool."

"Okay. Meet you by the baseball diamond at noon tomorrow."

He went into the building and was gone.

Brenna sighed. *Twenty-four hours. Yeah, I'll survive.*

~

On the eighth night she dreamed again. The cabin, again. This time the young men were already there.

"We're hungry," one said.

So she cooked them dinner.

They were each careful not to stain their white shirts.

The dream ended.

Scott took her up the hill to where the village Shorakapkok used to be at the base of a cliff—black rocks piled on one another, embedded in the soil, rising up and up and up farther than Brenna was willing to look.

"See up there?" Scott pointed. "An opening. Want to go take a look?"

"Uh . . ." She didn't want to admit that she'd always been afraid of heights.

Scott started making his way up, hopping from one large rock to another. *For an old guy, he certainly is spry.* He looked back at her.

She was torn. Should she go up? Risk being that high? If she slipped she had no wings to spread, to catch the air, to glide higher.

If she slipped and stumbled and fell she would die. She just knew it.

"Don't worry," he said. "I won't let you fall."

She carefully made her way to him, then went ahead, glancing back to make sure he was close.

He talked while they climbed. "This was an Algonquin village. You can still see some of their markings on the rocks."

She focused on climbing, taking her time—finding the footholds, the handholds, the way up.

"You're part Native American, aren't you?" he asked.

"Yeah, on my father's side."

She did not look down. She did not look up. She only climbed.

"And on your mother's?"

"Black and Irish."

They reached the shelf he'd pointed out. Brenna timidly

peeked over the edge and down to the bottom. She'd always been afraid of heights, but loved high places. She'd discovered this two summers before while rock climbing in Arizona. She'd been trying to impress a guy then, too.

"Did they really live in these caves?" she asked. The opening seemed awfully small to her.

"No, the caves were used for different purposes." He pulled an aluminum flashlight from his pocket and started to crawl in.

"You really should see this," he called back a moment after his legs had disappeared.

She poked her head into the opening—still dark, even with the faint glow of flashlight ahead. The cave, not much wider than she was, felt oppressive and smelled foreboding.

"Initiation rituals," Scott's voice bounced back to her. "Remember the Glastonbury Druids I discussed in class?"

She made some affirmative reply, but could barely breathe. The walls were pressing against her. The darkness was pushing her out. The flapping of wings. The call of ravens. Panicked, she scrambled backwards, catching herself just before falling off the shelf.

A while later Scott slid out, head first, and smiled reassuringly at her.

"No initiation for you today, huh?"

"I guess I'm just not ready." She smiled back.

Later, in her apartment, she showed the feather to Scott.

"It's not from a crow," he said.

"It's not?"

"No. Not a feather that big. That's definitely from a raven."

She stared at it.

"They're rarer than crows in New York, but not unheard of." He stared at her.

She invited him to stay longer. He declined.

On the ninth night, she dreamed again. The cabin, again. The young men were asleep. She went outside, into the forest, but there was nothing to see. In the garden behind the cabin, twelve lilies grew. She picked one for each brother.

The sound of wings. She looked up. They were ravens again, flying away.

The dream ended.

"It's a symbol. You have to find the meaning," her psychic friend said.

"It's nothing. You're overtired," her non-psychic friend said.

"Ravens are messengers from the otherworld. Someone there wants your attention," her psychic friend said.

"You probably ate too many tacos before bed," her non-psychic friend said.

"Past life regression." The psychiatrist spoke with authority.

It sounded like something her psychic friend would suggest.

"I assure you, I am serious," he said to the look on her face. "I've done them before and they've helped my patients every time."

She said she would try anything once. And if it didn't work, at least she'd get some sleep.

She lay on the couch listening to his words. She went back and back and back. Back along her life's path, growing younger with each breath. Back through high school, middle school, her first kiss, her first pitch, her first word, until she came to a place, comfortable, warm, familiar, red, the place just before birth, her mother's womb. Her arms wrapped around another, protecting him. She knows that she must hold on tight and never let go. She cannot lose him. But she is going back and back and back and his eyes open and his heart beats along with hers and he looks at her (I am your brother—I died for you) then the sound of wings.

She did not know when she began to scream, but she knew it took a long time for her to stop.

As a child she had desperately wanted a brother. She would try to adopt the neighborhood boys into her family. She would try to walk away with babies at the mall. Other girls her age had crushes and pretend boyfriends. She had pretend big brothers.

When she was nine her mother told her that she was a twin. She had had a brother in the womb with her, but for some reason he died in the eighth month. Her mother told Brenna that on the ultrasound pictures she seemed to be hugging him. The doctor advised her mother to give birth to both of them naturally. The labor was difficult. Brenna held on to her brother until the end—he was born first, though born dead.

Her parents had named him Benjamin. When she was twelve, her mother finally took her to see his grave. Beloved Son and Brother. After that, the thought of a brother only made her incredibly sad. She no longer wished for one. She pushed it out of her mind and forgot about it entirely. Intentionally. Until now.

She was reluctant to go to Scott. Lately he'd been quiet, restrained, uninterested. But she was desperate.

"The shrink didn't know what he was doing," Scott said.

"And you do?" she replied.

"Yes."

She believed him.

"Don't worry," he said. "I won't let you fall."

Again she went back and back and back, this time one hand in the physical world, safely tucked in Scott's, his voice guiding her back along the path of her life. She watched her life roll back and back and back like a movie on rewind, and when she came to the womb she was inside looking in, apart from the two small not-yet-people holding on to each other. The one that was not her opened his eyes (I am your brother—I love you) then the sound of wings.

She flew through the air, faster and faster and faster, flew back through her lives, each one freezing at one moment, a picture in her soul. She flew through them all until she came to the last one, the first one, and she could fly no more.

She is just a baby. They carry her out into the courtyard while they watch. Each son is led to the block, the oldest first, to have his head chopped off. And as the oldest falls, the next one becomes the oldest. Then he falls, then another, then another, until the twelfth son, the youngest who is now the oldest, is led to the block. He looks at her, his baby sister (I love you—I died for you) and he falls, too. She cries and cries. Her mother coos and cuddles. But there is no end to her crying.

"She cries for them," her mother says.

"She could not possibly understand," her father says.

She understands.

That night she didn't want to dream, didn't want to sleep. She lay in bed watching the stars roll across the sky like hieroglyphs holding all of the answers. Yet she could not read them. She looked over the pictures in her mind, the lives frozen. Twelve including this one, but not including the first. In each she saw a brother. In each he died.

She took the feather, her gift from the raven, and placed it beside her pillow. Her eyes drooped, then closed. She slipped into sleep, then into dreams.

She is flying. Back and back and back through her lives, frozen in place, until she comes to the first one and she can fly no more. So she speaks instead.

"Why are there twelve white shirts in the wash, Mother?" she asks the queen.

"Because they are not clean, Daughter," the queen answers with sadness. She has always been sad, even when she is happy.

"What soils them, Mother?"

"Blood."

The dream ended.

The next night she flew back again.

She is in a garden.

"Why does this plot have twelve lilies and nothing else, Mother?"

"Because nothing else will grow there, Daughter."

"Why is that?"

"Because that is where your brothers are buried."

The dream ended.

The next night she flew back again.

"Why are all my brothers dead, Mother?"

"Your father had them killed, Daughter."

"Why did he do that?"

"So you could have all the wealth and kingdom for yourself."

She asked Scott, "Are they dreams, or are they memories?"

"What's the difference?" was his enigmatic reply.

Brenna was starting to get frustrated.

"Try asking your dream what it wants you to understand."

That was a thought.

That afternoon, she lay in bed; too afraid to sleep, too depressed to rise. *So you could have all the wealth and kingdom for yourself.* How senseless.

A raven stared through her bedroom window. She mouthed to him, "I'm sorry."

That night she reluctantly slept again, dreamed again. This time she did not pick a destination, but she still ended up flying back and back and back until she could fly no more. She was running away and into the woods. She had to stop herself. Stop and think and ask . . . ask what?

"You're a very inquisitive child, aren't you?" A voice from above. She looked up. From a tree hung a man. He hung from one foot, upside down. He didn't seem at all affected by it. "Go ahead, ask me something. I know almost everything now."

"Why . . ."

". . . is the sky blue? . . . do fools fall in love? . . . do birds suddenly appear? You'll have to be more specific, my dear."

She was supposed to ask him about . . . about . . . "How . . ."

"Yes . . ."

"How can I bring my brothers back?"

"Ah! Now that is the question of the day, is it not? I could tell you—"

"Please tell me!"

"Oh, there are so many ways," the Hanging Man said. "You could sit in this tree and not speak a word for seven years. Maybe a handsome king would come by and make you his bride, hmm? Or, you could sew twelve brother-sized shirts. Or, you could convince the stars to give you their key to the glass mountain. You could do all of that. And more. In fact, you already have."

"When?"

"Before."

"Before?"

"In another time. In another world.

"In a fairy tale. In a myth.

"In the stories your mothers would tell."

Once upon a time there was a princess For a long time she didn't know that she had brothers **One day she overheard people talking** She was the one who had caused their misfortune *When night came she ran away and into the forest* I'm looking for my brothers **I'll keep walking as far as the sky is blue to find them** The way is hard, you won't be able to free them *The conditions are too hard* She went to the stars **You would have to remain silent for seven years** They were kind to her *You'd have to sew twelve little shirts for us* **Neither speak nor laugh** The morning star handed her the drumstick of a chicken *If you utter just a single word* You won't be able to open the glass mountain **Everything will be in vain** *All your work would be for naught*

The fragments danced in the corner of her mind's eye. But were they real memories, or the memories of dreams?

As if on cue, the Hanging Man said, "What's the difference?"

The flapping of wings. Twelve ravens perched in the tree—looking at her, watching over her.

"You say you want your brothers back? Here they are."

"They're birds," she said.

"They're ravens."

"Why?"

"Because they're dead."

The ravens began to call out to her. Calling and calling and calling. She covered her ears and closed her eyes and willed herself awake. Struggled up and up and up out of sleep. But the calling continued outside her bedroom window. Twelve ravens on the fire escape—calling to her.

Fly with us! Fly, fly, fly!

"I can't!" she yelled through the window. "I can't fly! I don't know how."

You're afraid, one said. Then the others. *You're afraid! You're afraid! You're afraid!*

"I am not afraid to fly!"

Afraid to die!

The phone rang. She jerked awake. The room was silent. She looked out the window—nothing there but the night. The phone rang again and she quickly picked it up.

"What?" she barked.

A short silence. "I'm sorry I woke you. I thought you'd appreciate it." Scott.

"How . . . how did you know?" She wasn't sure if she wanted the answer.

Another silence. "What are you afraid of, Brenna? Truly afraid of?"

She swallowed. On the other side of the window it was just becoming morning. The dark outline of the hill with the dark outline of the apartments with the dark outline of the bridge against the less dark of the sky.

"Falling," she finally said.

"Flying is nothing more than controlled falling," he replied.

There was a long silence.

"I'll call you later," he said, then hung up.

She couldn't fall back to sleep. She felt as though she'd done nothing but sleep. There was no sleep left in her, even in the cool light of dawn.

She slipped out of bed and got dressed in the semi-darkness. She went out the door, down the street, and into the forest. Halfway up the hill she came upon a little wooden cabin. It had never been there before. She went inside. On the table was a white shirt. She took it up and began to sew.

"There are many certainties in this world, Brenna," the Hanging Man said. He hung from nowhere, his head beside hers. His breath smelled of smoke. "One of them is that you will always complete the tasks that I give you. Without fail. No matter how hard or how many."

She could only regard him with a questioning gaze. She could not, must not, speak. This she knew.

"So what do you want now? Another twelve lives? Another twelve tries?"

She blinked, uncertain.

She finished the sleeve, the shirt was complete.

The dream ended.

She woke up in her bed. It was noon.

It was a dream . . .

She slipped out of bed and got dressed in the midday sun. She went out the door, down the street, and into the forest. Headed to her place at the top. To the tree. She pulled herself up into the branches, stepped out onto the limbs and looked down. It was surrounded by fire. She screamed.

"There are many certainties in this world, Brenna," the Hanging Man said. His hair kissed the flames, yet didn't seem at all affected by them. "One of them is that your brothers will never let you die."

The flames shot higher.

"They will always choose to die for you," he said.

"Why?"

"Because they love you. Because you are not ready."

"But I'm the reason they die!"

"No. You're the reason they live."

Ravens circled the tree, beating away flames with wings.

The Hanging Man spread his arms. "You completed the tasks. I granted your wish. Each brother lived a life equal to the one he would have had if not for you."

"Even Benjamin?"

"Even Benjamin."

"And if I wish again?"

"You will get the same. No more, no less."

Tips of wings ignited—black feathers scorched blacker. The ravens flapped fire, succumbing to the flames one by one.

"No!" She reached down into the fire.

"Death is inevitable. Whether you fear it or face it bravely."

The flames nearly consumed her.

The dream ended.

She woke up in her bed. It was almost evening.

It was . . .

The raven stared at her through the window. A white shirt hung from the doorknob.

She slipped out of bed and pulled the shirt from the knob. Held it close to her as sunlight seeped slowly from the sky.

"Okay," she said to herself. Then to the raven, "Okay."

She put on the shirt, then took the feather from her bedside and put it in her hair. Out the door, down the street, into the forest, up to the cliff. *The glass mountain.*

She began to climb. Taking her time—finding the footholds, the handholds, the way up. Higher and higher. The sun began to set. Higher and higher. The air began to mist. Higher and higher. She did not look down, she did not look up, she only climbed.

She reached the shelf, the mouth of the cave, took a deep breath and crawled inside. Deep into the darkness. The walls pressing in on her from every side. The darkness drawing her in, driving her forward, welcoming her to the end—the peak of the glass mountain.

Her brothers were there, waiting for her, in their white shirts. She ran to them, held them tight, and danced with each in turn. Then, one by one, they took off their shirts, the shirts she had sewn, and became ravens again. Flying in circles. Calling to her.

Flying is nothing more than controlled falling.

She stepped to the edge of the mountain, faced the setting sun, and nodded.

"Yes. I'm ready."

She fell forward from the edge, fell into the air. Her white shirt came apart at the seams, falling away from her as she turned, arms spread, wings spread, black, shiny fingers-feathers catching the wind, lifting her up and up and up as she joined the ravens, her brothers, in the sky. Flying into the sun, into the west. Flying home.

~

The first time I ever heard the word "interstitial" was at a WisCon panel discussion. It was, I believe, one of the first panels to introduce the concept of interstitiality as applied to art and writing. In response to a question I don't remember (probably about whether there can be interstitial artists as well as interstitial art), Ellen Kushner said that she didn't think that a *person* could be interstitial. I raised my hand and replied "I am." I have always felt in-between. In-between races, in-between sexual orientations, in-between cultures. I don't feel like I belong to any firm category, much as I and others have tried to stuff me into one or another. I don't know that this led me to write interstitial stories, but it certainly led me to write. Isn't that the cliché? The writer as outsider? I feel like a double agent. I have access to both "sides." Each time I sneak across the border I get more comfortable with the space in-between.

K. Tempest Bradford

A Drop of Raspberry

Csilla Kleinheincz

I woke suddenly. At one moment I was still sleeping the dream of the waters, swimming in and out of wakefulness like a sluggish fish, and then suddenly I was there in the lake bed, aware of the taste of the earth, the touch of the rough stones and the ticklish breeze, of my body rolling along, tastes, smells attacking me—and the pain.

The splash of the heavy body was still rippling on my surface. I could feel how the contours were outlined in me: a large man, his eyes open. He was blinking, and looking into me. I am sure he saw me as well.

He brought the awakening with him, and also the pain. His feelings were bitter, just like acid, and I shivered at the sight of him, as if a wind that precedes rain had blown over me.

Go, I told him, and I was upset. He must have jumped from one of the cliffs along the beach, but I could not look around to see if there were others as well nearby who might pull him out, because the blueness of the sky, the sun-yellow crowns of the trees suddenly hit my eyes, now more freshly than ever before. I grew dizzy, but maybe that was also because of the man.

Immense love, immense pain, so big that I could not bear it. I wanted to break out of the bed, to escape. I was alert, uncomprehending, and furious. All the drops in my body were protesting against wakefulness, but the pictures, the sounds, and the memories were spreading within me and were tingling all my bodily parts.

I tried to shut myself away from him, while he was slowly sinking down to the abyss. When I wanted to throw him up, he swam a few strokes farther down, and infused me with sparkling memory bubbles: a picture of a street, where he is running with someone's hot hand in his. A room, filled with heavy green smoke. Grasping, falling. A kiss at the brink of fear. A loose lock of hair, without a face or a body, only a blonde spiral, beautiful like a winter dawn.

With every bursting bubble I grew more and more awake, and something was stirring within me that should not have been there, not between the fish deep in the mud nor on the floating surface. Something that was only made clear by the stabbing pain.

Why? I asked him, and looked into his wide open eyes. *Why do you heap your burden upon me?*

His eyes were blue and sad; death was already summoning him.

He woke me up. Never mind with what, but he woke me up, and against that I could do nothing.

Sadness was shivering in my face; not my own, though mine now.

I broke out of myself, grabbed his shoulders and started to pull him upward. I knew that I would kill him, if I did not save him.

Before, I never felt sorry for the birds, never for the cold little life of the fish, the immense quantity of insects. I did not feel sorry for that girl who drowned in me many years ago—but this was different. He had done something to me.

I threw him on the shore, and crawled up next to him. He closed his eyes.

The burning pain vanished, but I brought the faint throbbing with me.

I looked down on him. We were panting for breath, both of us. I looked back on my lake-self, and sat up. The body, formed out of the memory of the long-dead girl, was obeying me. It was somewhat strange to be outside of myself, looking back on the mirror-like surface that was only just touched by the wind, passing by into the woods. I do not remember how I got up on the shore or when I broke in two.

Inside me the water was splashing silently, and that calmed me. I was still myself.

The man was coughing as if he were choking, his blonde hair stuck to his forehead. I saw the fear in his eyes, and quickly leaned over him, tasted his lips, and sniffed the water into my mouth. When he got mixed up with me, inside me, the pictures attacked me again. A girl with white gloves on the bed. A square, the clock up high, with little people hammering in it. Then a crying face, the feeling of someone stabbing me, where there is no wound. Choking where there is no lake. Emptiness.

"Why did you jump?"

"Why did you pull me out?" he asked with a hoarse voice, and then he sat up and looked at himself. He looked clumsy, crouching and soaking there.

They look so graceful when still in the water, I thought. *Out of it, they forget to move.*

"You will catch a cold," he said after a quick glance at me. "I left my coat somewhere around here." He stood up, wrung his shirt, and headed toward the trees. His coat was hanging neatly on one of them. I was watching the lake until he returned. The surface was sparkling, and a new feeling shook me.

"Nice, don't you think?" I asked, watching the play of the frills.

He stopped behind me.

"Yes, very nice." He placed the coat on my shoulders and helped me to put it on. It was warm, nicely soft.

I looked up at him.

"I'm Gabó," he said. "Thank you."

"I . . ." I looked at the lake, and recalled the girl, and the sounds that I had heard in the dreams. Steps, screams, stones playing ducks and drakes . . . "I am Tünde."

Once I found the name, it was easier. I turned back to him.

"Why did you jump?" I asked again.

"I would rather not tell you."

"It is my business as well," I said, and wanted to continue, *you woke me up*, but then he agreed with a stiff face.

"I think you're right, since you pulled me out."

He walked over to the shore and I followed him. The earth was muddy where I had licked it.

"I was here two years ago with my wife. That's when I asked her to marry me."

There was something in his voice that made me splash inside, possibly the acid memory of the pain. His eyes were red from the water and he was gazing ahead. However, I was sure that he was aware of my presence. Even though he was lost in the past, even though he had just escaped death, he knew I was there.

Only human beings can do this. We lakes, mountains, we forget everything that is not present, everything turns into a dream, a passing feeling. Light and characterless. But to be there, to be aware, only human beings can do that.

"We were here on the beach." He did not say more, and even though this memory did not wash over into me, I could see the blonde girl between the trees. And then he continued after all: "Today is the anniversary. She left with another guy two weeks ago."

Suddenly he crouched. He was shaking as if he had been hit by a storm, and I had to give him a hug, to be the bed for his waves. I waited, whispered, and my water spilled over. When I dried my face, his tears smudged over to my lips from my hands. His were salty.

"I'm sorry," he said, and then smiled. "I'm sorry, please would you mind giving me my handkerchief? There's a dry one in my coat."

In the end he was the one who pulled it out, because I could not find the opening of the pocket. He blew his nose, then pondered over something, and put it back.

"I'm so sorry," he said, and then looked at me. Already when he was floating around in me and white bubbles were surrounding him, already then I believed that he could see me. Even now it seemed that he saw my true self. "I don't know what you think about it."

"I am not angry, if that is what you are thinking. You woke me up, but I am not angry about it anymore."

"I'm not angry at you either, for pulling me out."

"You did not really want to die," I said suddenly, and closed my eyes. Pictures swam through the inner surface of my eyelids, just like fish. "You miss her, and no one can replace her, but you did not really want to die. It really is so . . . final."

The incredulous laughter got stuck in him.

"Who are you?" he asked.

"The lake."

"The lake?"

I made the skin on my arms do waves. The sarcastic smile froze on his lips.

"Please do it again!" he said hoarsely.

A wave ran through me. He could see how my body turned transparent, like a water column under the coat.

"Of course, this can't be for real," he said. I looked at him calmly, and waited.

Gabó pulled himself together at last. "I thought one shock was enough for a day. Please explain!"

I told him what I had seen. He filled in with the details, stuttering and jumping between the memories. His voice was warm while he spoke, even though I knew that talking was painful for him. The memories were like bubbles: he pushed them out of himself, so that he could sink into the cold unconsciousness.

As he was telling the story, as we were exchanging his memories between ourselves, slowly I tried to picture the woman he was missing. She was only present in his voice, in the flashing pictures, and I could not understand. Perhaps this was because she was not the one who had tried to drown in me, but Gabó. Him I understood: his pain was like December, when the memories of the warmth of autumn are still fresh, but spring is so far away that only the absence is present. Even hope hides away in the mud, just like the fish.

As we were standing there on the beach, evening fell. In the end he went silent. For a long time I only listened to his heartbeat, and neither he nor I thought or felt that we needed to talk.

When he finally spoke, it felt like it was only the evening wind that had spoken.

"I love her very much."

"I can feel it."

"I have to go."

He took his coat.

"You don't really need it, right?" he asked. "The coat I mean."

I shook my head.

"Now what? Shall I leave you here?"

"Can I let you go?" I replied, and smiled.

"Don't worry. There are no more lakes on the way home."

I spent some time looking at his back as he was leaving, and then I splashed back into the lake, and leaned back in myself, sinking into the deep dream of waters.

As soon as he put his hand in the water, I woke up. I recognized his touch, the stinging pain, and rose from the water. Sometimes I waited for a while, to make him wait for me, but I always turned up earlier than he would get bored waiting for me.

He brought unfamiliar smells with him. There was always a book in his pocket. He usually read it on the train, until he arrived at the forest. His coat was full of stories, and so was he. He always spoke about the other people's stories first, but then inevitably he would pass on to his own.

My water grew more and more salty as his tears got mixed up with it, although he cried less and less, and he spoke seldom of Anna nowadays. Sometimes we hiked in the woods, but most of our time we spent sitting on the beach. If it started raining, I melted back to my lake–self, because it was very difficult to keep my shape, and continued to converse with him from there.

This was different from sleeping the dream of the lakes, as if I had only just become my real self. The smells, the colors were sharp and sparkling, and I am sure that I would not have been able to dream Gabó up. Sometimes I recalled on the surface what I had seen, and we looked at the flight of the blackbirds again. Alone, I often replayed how I had pulled him out of the water.

I regretted that I did not remember them, as they were standing on my beach: Gabó putting the ring on her finger, and them kissing. I would have liked to have shown him, but at that time I did not know who he was, and human beings were only light or heavy steps on the green, quickly fading sounds between the trees of the forest.

With whatever hatred or anger he spoke of Anna, I am sure that he would have been happy about this: how had I seen them.

I did not even know. I was asleep then.

One day I asked him to take me to town. I was afraid and expectant about his world, which I had so far only experienced in a dead girl's memories as entangled pictures. But I felt that I had to know;

I could not know it only from his words. It was not enough.

As the train left the station in the forest, Gabó reassuringly touched my knee.

"Are you sure?"

"I would like to see where you live."

We talked so that I did not have to notice how the forest thinned out more and more behind the window, how the scenery grew duller and more grey each minute. Gabó spoke about the summer: the bird-catchers, whom he met frequently, the feeling when he could hold in his hand a bundle of feathers with a beating heart. He told jokes, put his arms around me so that I would not see the houses, but I escaped from his arms and gazed out.

The houses were large and colorless, the balconies just like fungus on the trunks of the trees. The city was unfamiliar and cold, not at all like among the smudged-out memories of the drowned girl. I thought that I would be able to handle it, but it was all larger, more grey than I had imagined.

I shivered.

"Come on, I'll take you somewhere where you will feel more at ease," Gabó said.

He took me to a tiny teahouse. There were pictures on the walls: lakes and mountains, sleeping and dreaming beautiful dreams.

"I live across." He pointed over to the other side of the square, through the window, at the brownish-grey block of houses. "I like this place."

I did not ask if he usually visited this place with Anna.

"Look!" He showed me a small menu card, but I gave it back to him. I could not read. "I'm sorry," he said. "I forgot. Sometimes I just forget that you could be something else as well as . . ."

"A human being?" I replied, smiling. "Sometimes even I forget. Sometimes the lake is the dream, and not the opposite."

"Wait, I'll choose one for you. . . . The Dream of the Earth." He looked at me. "No, in the end you'll turn into a pile of mud."

"I will splash you," I threatened him, and splashed a couple of drops on his nose from myself.

"Mate. Hmm. . . . You are my mate today, and tomorrow the

big-breasted blondes. Wings of Winds? Wind easing grass instead of diuretic tea?"

"Give it to me!" I reached out for the little menu card.

He pulled it away from me and laughed, his huge body shaking.

"But sweetheart, you can't even read!" he chuckled. It was true, and even though I was ashamed, I had to laugh with him.

"Never mind," I said, grabbing the card out of his hands, and just randomly pointed at one of the lines.

When he looked at it, he smiled at me warmly.

"You know what this is?"

I shook my head.

"It's called Forest Walk." He took my hands for a moment. "Your hands are cold."

"It is autumn," I said. "When winter comes, I will freeze."

I always had to remind him that I was not a true human being. He always forgot, and I was afraid that I would also forget. I was already far too awake, I knew too much about him. Sometimes I even kept my human shape in the lake; floating and with my hair spread across the water, I watched the sky.

The tea arrived. This was the first human drink that I had tried. The tastes of raspberry and wild strawberry were floating in my body. It was hot: the sip I had taken was beaming inside me, like the tiniest of suns.

"You're blushing," Gabó said quietly.

"It is the tea."

I drank the whole pot, steaming hot, as they do, and I enjoyed the heat spreading inside me.

"I have just drunk sunbeams."

"Come!" he said suddenly, and reached for his coat.

He paid, and then we went out into the street.

"Where are we going?"

"You said that you'd like to see where I live. Unless you mind."

We cut through the square. We were halfway there, when it started raining slowly. The drops melted into me, disappeared as they touched me. I accelerated my steps.

It was getting heavier, and suddenly I got scared. The water diluted me, started rippling inside me. I felt it was calling me.

"Gabó . . . I am going to fall apart . . ." I whispered. Drops in my hair, on my arms, I could not feel my borders anymore. I wanted to swallow the rain, so that I could swell into something huge. A wave ran through under my clothes.

"What's wrong?" he asked, frightened.

"Quickly!" The unfamiliar water wanted to erupt from inside me, but I was far too small to open up a dam.

It dissolved my contours.

Gabó grabbed me and brought me up to the flat.

I vaguely remember that we passed by closed doors, and then we were in the narrow hall. Gabó's strong arm held me. I could never evaluate his strength; he almost always splashed me apart. Now I was holding on to it.

He almost pushed me into the bathroom. I staggered, the rain filled me, and then I fell into the bathtub and lost my shape.

"Good heavens!" I heard Gabó's voice, and then I felt that something was pulling me downward. Darkness reached out for me and opened its gap.

Gabó's hand reached inside me, searched for something, and then I heard a pop, and the force was not pulling me down anymore. A rather big bit was missing from me, but the essence was still there. That much I could fill out.

"Tünde!" he shouted above me, his two hands stirring desperately inside me. He did not see that I was still there.

When I rose from the bathtub, he pulled me close. He was brutally pressing me, but on the other hand, I believe the reason he was holding on to me so hard was that he was afraid I would disappear too.

"I am here. You can relax . . . I am here," one of us said.

I became his lake. I was not sure that he knew. I believe he did, but he never let me know, and he possibly even tried to ignore it, because however much he depended on other people, he could not bear it if someone depended on him.

And I kept my mouth shut. If there was something I was really good at, it was that.

I tried to be awake as much as possible even without him, so that I could tell stories about forests, the hikers and the birds. The mountains, crowned by the trees, were ours, the fresh air too. The city and all the other people were lost in the distance. Only this was ours.

I did not speak to him about what it is like holding on to wakefulness, which meant the memory of him, his voice and his person. What it is like staring into the starry night or the foggy morning in solitude, when the owls are hooting, and the woodpeckers are pecking away. I did not tell him what it is like waiting and watching, scared, how the sun crawled lower in the sky each day. I did not tell him about what it is like being wakeful among the sleeping mountains.

I also did not say what it is like being alive, walking next to him, holding his hand, or being in his arms, until the shaking lessened.

We did not talk about a lot of things, at least not in words. But I believe standing close to each other, infused with each other's scent, is worth as much as talking.

The leaves had already fallen, and it took me great effort to ascend from the bed, my joints stiff. Gabó had to hold me for a long time under his coat, for me to become liquid and tepid again.

The mud of the road had been dug up by the jeeps of the forest rangers. There were neat piles of grey beech trunks on the side of the hill. Both of us climbed up them, and held onto each other not to fall down.

"I have reclaimed Anna's key," Gabó said on the top of the woodpile, and his ever-warm fingers held on to mine. His voice had an "I don't care" quality, but I do not believe that it was the same inside.

"What does it mean?"

"We're getting a divorce."

We looked into each other's eyes.

"I am sorry," I said, and although I did not know exactly what he meant, I could feel the importance of it from his glance. He had beautiful eyes, the color almost like me on a summer day.

"I know, honey."

We stayed silent for a while, and continued on the forest road.

"It would be so nice if you'd talk about yourself sometimes," he said suddenly.

"What shall I talk about?" I replied.

"Anything."

We reached the top of the hill, the wooden look-out.

"What shall I tell you? What it is like to dream? I am not aware of anything at the time, the sounds only reach me from afar. Fish swim around in me. In the summer I have ducks. I can feel when they eat, fly, dive, when they take their ducklings out on the lake for the first time . . ." I did not look back, but continued up the stairs. "Thousands die in me each summer. Thousands are born." I went silent, and Gabó hugged me from behind.

"When I am dreaming, I am not aware of anything. I do not wake up. I only am. Each life is a small wave on the surface that runs through and disappears on the beach. Now, however, everything has changed. Lakes do not usually think about what happens to the fish. They do not usually wake up. They do not really know anything about death, or suffering, or about love. They do not know anything." I was shaking.

"It was me, right?" he asked quietly. "I changed you."

I looked out on the naked forest, and the blue sky, where the clouds were lingering just like gossamer.

I wanted to talk about what was really important.

"I enjoy when you talk about yourself," I said finally. "You have lots of friends; all of them are interesting."

"You are the most important of them."

"And you are the most important being for me. I do not know why, but you are. If it were not so, you could not have woken me up."

"You did not know me then." He leaned on his elbows on the railing, next to me, and then he pulled away. "The urge always hits me, to jump into the deep," he said with deep and quiet horror in his voice.

I looked down, but I could only see the fallen leaves.

"Is this why you jumped in me?"

"No. For you, I fell," he chuckled.

I tickled him, until he laughed out loud.

"But really . . . why?"

"It seemed like a good idea. The lake was really lovely . . . you were lovely. And you know, there are times when a man gives up, even if he might regret it afterward. I am sorry. You must have thought me pitiful."

"No. I was angry. However, I did not think you pitiful. It is not pain that is pitiful."

"Then what?"

"The one who causes it," I said.

Gabó did not utter a word. He spoke with his silent sigh on my neck.

I could only just remember that I had seen a dream under the ice. This time it was not the thoughts of the bored fish that were streaming through me lazily; I could feel Gabó's warm hand. I was sleeping peacefully under the cover of the ice, and his thoughts were warming me.

Then the ice started breaking in spring. I was lying in my bed, sliding in and out of the dream as I have been doing for centuries, waiting for Gabó.

I could hardly feel his calling. When he dipped his hand in me, the old pain was only a faint, dull throbbing, and I had difficulty waking up.

"I thought you wouldn't come." Gabó straightened up, and held me close.

"I always come when you call for me."

"The other day you did not come."

Inside me there must have been a tiny splinter of ice left, because I felt cold. I did not wake up to Gabó?

"It was winter."

"But there was no ice anymore." It frightened me; I felt like disintegrating on the beach.

We sat down on our favorite log.

"Talk to me!" I said, and I was tense.

And Gabó spoke. About the split–up family at Christmas, the empty bed, about dark loneliness, about the fact that he had missed me. He was holding my hand all along, and I began to feel like I did in autumn. The long dream split up into pieces.

Gabó told me about books, poems—he once said that he would write one about me, but in the end nothing came of it—about the bird table in the garden at his parents' house.

And then with the same tone of voice as he spoke about the sparrows, he continued, "I've met a girl as well."

I smiled, because it was spring, and because there was nothing else I could do.

"We really understand each other. We have a lot in common. When we laugh, we're the only ones who exist. Can you understand that?"

I looked back at him. He was happy and sad at the same time.

"I am only a lake. But even I understand that."

"It's so good that finally I'm not alone." In his voice the amazement was still vibrating from the feeling of finding someone.

"I am glad," I said, and meant it.

Still, there was sadness between us, a peculiar gap that is present mainly when you are with someone that you really miss. I am a lake, and he is a human being. It is that simple.

When I saw him next, he was not alone. A slim, dark-haired girl was with him on the beach. Gabó's hand woke me up from the dream, but I did not get up; I stayed silently on the bed of rocks.

"Is the water cold?" the girl asked. She had a nice voice.

"Not that much," Gabó replied, and whispered down at me. "Are you there?"

I only shaped my face for him.

"Yes, I am here. I can see you." I looked over his shoulders. "I can see her."

"Don't you want to come out?"

I looked deep into his eyes.

"You are not really eager to see me out there."

He made such a torn face that I felt sorry for him.

"Listen! I am your lake. Always. . . . But now, return to her . . ." I reflected over it, and watched the waves as they reached the shore. "After that, come back on the beach and kiss her!"

"What?"

"What are you muttering?" the girl asked giggling, and stepped closer.

"Kiss her!" I said determined, and disappeared.

Gabó straightened up. It was not even his choice, it was the girl who embraced him first. I was watching them from the bed, and made the lights glitter at them. They were pretty together.

Gabó emerged from the embrace a little tensely, and then with a glance at me, he started to pull the girl away into the forest. *I will be back*, his eyes promised.

"Be good," I splashed after him quietly. I am not sure he heard it.

I waited until they left, and then I floated away relaxed and licked the shore where they had just stood.

I know that Gabó will return one day with or without the girl, and that he will put his hand in the water to wake me up. I think that I will sleep. Not out of spite or anger. The fact is that the pain is not strong enough any more to rouse me.

But I will make an effort. I would like to be conscious for as long as possible, watch the mountains, the lingering clouds. It would be good to hear the owls, however lonely the forest is.

And I would very much like it if they came to visit again. Now I know far too much to just sink back into the dream. I would like it if Gabó would look into me again, just as when he threw himself in me, and see himself and the girl on the beach.

I will be around much longer than the girl, or Gabó, or even the trees.

Lakes do not know about death, pain, or love. But inside me, a couple of tear drops and the taste of raspberry are circulating. That much I can feel. That much I know.

Translated from the Hungarian by Noémi Szelényi

~

Being between always came naturally to me. My mother brought Vietnamese stories, cuisine, and traditions with her, and I grew up listening to Hungarian songs and radio plays, reading European and Asian classics and Soviet science fiction with the same enthusiasm. Opening doors and peeking into other cultures, sciences, and arts is easy once you recognize the nature of your hunger. I opened as many doors in my short life as possible, and it took me some time to realize that I had wandered through the door of writing and made my home there.

I believe one of the curses of being a writer is that while you are, feel, and live, one part of you is always taking notes and making an inventory of everything: jokes, gestures, and the most intimate griefs alike. This part of you doesn't judge only by utility. It cannot be switched off. If you could switch it off, you couldn't be a writer. Once in a while a story is as much somebody else's as it is yours, and you must be careful, for you are opening a window on someone else's secrets. This is one of those stories.

Csilla Kleinheincz

The Utter Proximity of God

Michael J. DeLuca

Undoubtedly you have heard of Fecondita. It is the place to which Shakespeare refers when he speaks of the providence in a swallow's fall. Aquinas had only just seen it when he claimed God resides whole in all things and in each one.

Fecondita is a village in one of the valleys southwest of Torino, where God is actually present in every rock and tree, every beast, every dying swallow, every tawny, downy hair on the backs of your arms, every pore of the skin in the hollow of your collarbone. No, don't try to find it. Like the world into which we all have fallen—some hard enough to break bone—it is a place not found, but given. Be content that it exists, and no one else will find it either.

Fecondita has seen better days.

In Fecondita, swallows nest in the bathroom sinks of dead widows who forgot to close the windows before they drowned themselves from grief. In the bathtubs, munny grapes grow from the mould. A dozen widows who couldn't find the faith to die seclude themselves in a convent behind a hill, whispering rosaries with dry throats and refusing water. The forests resound with the off-key arias of a mad, drunken Sorcerer who never drinks and is not mad. All the fields but one lie fallow, filling up with whisper-weed and bramble.

And in that one still-tended field, the last two sane men in the village, Nico the simpleton and Giulio the cripple, dig their shoulders into the yoke and sweat right along with the cow, poor Grazia. With their help, the old beast plods across the dense earth, though her milky eyes bug out of her head, and beads of sweat like salty berries ripen on their brows. With all three of them heaving, the plow moves but slowly. It moves, until the cow keels over, dead.

"It's a sign from God!" cries Nico.

"A sign from God for what?" asks Giulio. "That you and I should quit being plowmen? I could have told you that without a sign. Help me up!"

"I didn't mean that," says Nico, pulling his brother out of the dirt. In the dent left by Giulio's body, dandelions are sprouting, though they plowed that furrow only a moment ago.

"What then?" asks Giulio, prodding the dead cow's flesh with the flat of his misshapen foot. "You think God wants us to play the martyr? To pick up the yoke and plow by ourselves? I should never have read you the *Lives of the Saints*. Get me my crutch!"

"That's not it either," says Nico, prying the wooden crutch from beneath Grazia's carcass, propping it under Giulio's arm.

"Then for God's sake, what?" shouts Giulio, raising a fist. "You think He is punishing us for not going off to war and dying noble, stupid deaths like all the others? You think this accursed field with its endless weeds and that forest full of deer that eat whatever we grow are not atonement enough?"

Nico cringes, covering his head, though Giulio doesn't really strike. "I think it is a sign from God that we should take a rest."

"Oh," says Giulio.

They sit on a toppled standing stone, one that has lain at the corner of the oxcart lane and the Roman Road to Torino ever since God first came to Fecondita. Each brother leans against the other. We float between them, on the back of a dandelion seed caught in an eddy of wind. God floats there too.

Over Nico's head, the campanile of the Convent of Our Lady Montimbanca rises above the hill. It strikes one o'clock, but they pulled the bell down years ago to melt it into bullets. So the only effect is a ripple in the air like that made by a drop in a puddle.

Through the crook of Giulio's crutch, the forest edge wriggles its hundred healthy limbs. It isn't taunting him, no. In fact, it is waving at us. But try telling Giulio that.

At last the berries of sweat stop rolling down their chests, and their breaths stop sounding quite so ragged.

"What the hell do we do, Nico?" Giulio asks. "We haven't got money for a new cow. If we did, we'd have to leave the village to buy one. And then we'd be killed in the war like everyone else.

God has it out for us, Nico. Poor Grazia. You and I can't even lift her out of the way."

"Does God really hate us, Giulio?"

"No," sighs Giulio. He pokes at his misshapen foot with the end of his crutch. "He did make you a fool, and me a cripple, so we couldn't join the army. He did save our lives. Though I don't know why."

"Then maybe He'll help us! You could go to the convent, and ask the nuns to pray God to send us a new cow!"

Giulio laughs. "I'm not going to ask the nuns anything, Nico. I already know what they'll say."

"What will they say, brother? Tell me."

"First, Mother Concetta will bring out her ruler. She'll say, 'Stupid boy, we taught you better,' and slap my wrist so hard it leaves a welt. Then Sister Traviata will kiss it. And lastly Sister Annunziata will remind me God's love doesn't work that way: if it did, their husbands would still be alive."

"But won't they pray for us, Giulio? Won't they pray for us just the same?"

"I suppose. We're still alive, after all. Their husbands have been dead for years. Who else have they to pray for?"

"Then it just might help! Like Mama says, you never know."

"I tell you what, brother. It isn't as though we've anything better to do. Why don't *you* go ask the nuns to pray for a new cow, and *I'll* go find the mad Sorcerer Sancto who lives in the forest, and get him to raise up Grazia from the dead. We'll see who helps us first: God or the Devil. Assuming we don't die of hunger before they do."

"The Sorcerer Sancto!" gasps Nico. "Not him! He nurses rat babies from his own demon teat, after our mama poisons their mama. That is why Mama can never get rid of the rats in our cellar. Or that is what she says, at least."

"Mama also says that God helps those who help themselves. And if that were the case, then why should poor Grazia keel over and die? But Mama has never met the Sorcerer. And neither have we. Which means he'll at least have something different to say. Even if he wants me to hit myself in the nose with a shovel and draw unholy runes in the blood, at least it will be something new."

Nico scratches his head. "You are wiser than I, older brother. You're probably right. But I think we had better ask Mama."

"You go," Giulio mutters.

God's dandelion seed floats on its way, and we with it, across the half-plowed field. Nico follows, hurrying up the oxcart path. Two swallows wing out of the woods, the same woods where the Sorcerer Sancto hides, each carrying a wild apple twice its size. The two birds disappear through the broken window of an empty farmhouse choked with munny vines and whisperweed, then emerge and flit back to the woods.

Apples often ripen out of season in Fecondita. The trick lies in finding the tree.

In the entryway to Signora Parrucca's kitchen, the smells of talc and perfumed hair pomade collide with the pungences of parmigiano and sweet peppers hung to dry. Pictures of her sons in mismatched frames line the rose-tiled walls. On our right against the ceiling smiles Tenente Colonello Ferdinando Marco Moresca Parrucca: blue-eyed, white-haired, and proud in his uniform. On our left, down by the floor, Nico and Giulio cringe from the flash. In between, were it God's will, we might count twenty-seven other pictures—but here comes Nico.

"Mama!" he calls, coming in the open door. "May I please have a bottle of beer, Mama? It's hot today!"

"Nicollino, trombini! Of course, if you ask so nice!" Signora Parrucca's voice floats up on a cool draft through the cellar door. She follows, wearing a yellow dress that makes her resemble a summer squash, and a glossy black wig half as tall as she is.

Nico takes a stool at the kitchen table. "Your favorite wig looks very fine today, Mama."

"Such a good boy." Signora Parrucca tousles Nico's hair, then brushes it back all out of place. She puts a brown bottle and a glass before him. "There."

"Thank you, Mama."

She sweeps out into the garden. Her voice comes through the

window. "Now tell me: what are you doing home so early? We need that field plowed! We can't live on beer and dried peppers all winter, you know."

Nico sips from the bottle. "Mama, I have bad news."

"Drink from the glass, young man!"

Nico winces and tips the bottle to pour.

Signora Parrucca swishes back in with a basket of peppers. "Bad news? Let's have it." She pats a stray hair back into her wig. She purses her big red lips into wrinkles.

He gulps. "Grazia keeled over and died in the field."

She drops the basket on the table. "WHAT?"

The bottle slips out of Nico's hands as he throws them up to ward off a blow. The glass tips over. Beer spills all over her dress.

"Bischero insensato!" Signora Parrucca cuffs her youngest son across the head. "Out of my sight. Go! Before I get the rolling pin."

Nico scurries out of reach. "But Mama, we need help! What should we do?"

"You'll just have to ask the Lord for help. I'm not going to clean up your messes the rest of your life. You're lucky twenty-eight of your brothers are dead, Nicollo, or I might not feel so bad about beating you senseless!"

"Giulio, Giulio! We were right! Mama says we must ask the Lord for help!" Nico runs up to the fallen stone and hugs his brother, who pushes and struggles to get away.

"Isn't that wonderful," says Giulio, freeing himself at last and fleeing several hobbling steps down the Roman Road.

"What do you think He will do?"

"God? I think He will cause the skies to open up and rain down yearling calves on all of our heads, and the roofs of all the houses will be staved in, and we will be blamed for it. And if we are lucky, by some miracle one may fall into a pond and survive. And assuming you and I and the calf and Mama all somehow live through the winter without any food, next year by this time the calf will be grown, and all four of us will be here again plowing the field. God willing."

"Really, Giulio? That doesn't sound so good."

"No, Nico, you fool. That was a joke. Go see the nuns. Sancto and I shall meet you here when the convent bell strikes four."

Munny grape vines thread the shut gates to the Convent of Our Lady Montimbanca. The rich, red fruit hangs heavy from the iron; the hinges strain to hold them. In a corner by the high brick wall, a few of the bars have fallen away. Nico ducks through; you and I and God walk at his heels, in the guise of a pregnant goat.

We find the sisters in the sanctuary. In shadow they kneel on bare stone, repeating Hail Marys and Our Fathers in voices hoarse as fraying rope to the rhythm of clicking beads. The stained-glass window over the altar casts the only light: a fluent blue that makes the room seem like the bottom of a lake, or a bathtub. The window shows the convent's patron, Montimbanca, preaching to the prisoners; the light would be brighter but for the vines climbing the window's other side.

"Reverend Mother," says Nico, kneeling beside her, "our cow Grazia died today. I have come to ask you and your sisters to pray God to send my family another, so that we may sow our field and grow food and survive through the winter."

"Shame on you, Nico."

Nico ducks to avoid another blow that never comes.

"Didn't you ever think God might have something more to do in this world plagued by war than worry about a single family that ought to be able to care for themselves? For seven years we have prayed God to protect this village, prayed on bruised knees with throats like parchment paper. For seven years, what good has it done? Look there, before the altar."

Through a crack in the stone floor, a white sunflower grows, indoors and without light. The goat is tempted to go over and eat it.

"He took our husbands. Every year He takes another of our sisters. Last year we brought the convent bathtub out into the garden and planted it with roses, because we realized even we, God's brides, could not resist its temptation. And in return for all our faith and pain, He gives a single flower. But do we stop praying?

No. God's works are not for us to understand, let alone a poor fool such as you."

Nico hangs his head. "I'm sorry, Reverend Mother. I didn't know."

"You are a fool, Nico, so I forgive you. You're lucky, though. Had your brother come instead, I would have had to fetch my ruler."

"Yes, Reverend Mother. Thank you."

"How is our little Giulio? We wish he would visit more often."

"Oh, he is well. Though he is worried because of poor Grazia, of course. He would have come with me, only just now he has gone to the forest to ask the mad Sorcerer Sancto to raise Grazia from the dead."

Mother Concetta grabs Nico by the ear, pinches hard, and doesn't let go. "Avenging angels of heaven defend our poor benighted village from the machinations of cripples and fools! Sisters! Sisters, please! For now our prayers will have to wait. We must go forth to drive out Satan. Sister Traviata, bring my yardstick."

In the forest of Fecondita, the Sorcerer Sancto lies asleep under an apple tree. He sleeps on the bare roots in only a loincloth, his arms flung up around his head, his ankles splayed. Dried mud streaks his face. Mosquitoes swarm him by the dozens. Giulio pokes him with a stick.

"Who are you?" the Sorcerer demands, awaking. He doesn't bother to swat at the bugs. After all, God is in them, too.

"I am Giulio Parrucca, from Fecondita."

"Ah, yes," I say, "the cripple. What are you doing here?" For yes, it is I, the Sorcerer Sancto, who write this. I did not say so before, for fear you would stop reading. It would not be the first time.

A deerfly lands on Giulio's cheek. God, who resides, if briefly, in the fly, feels the quake of Giulio's grimace. Then Giulio kills it.

"I came," says Giulio, "because I am tired of plowing and sowing. God gave me this useless leg, so I couldn't go to war. Instead I went to the convent to learn from the nuns. Among other impractical things, they imparted to me a love of reason, a healthy dislike for religion, an irrational terror of measuring implements, and an irresistible desire never to lay eyes on another nun for as long as I live. While I was there, I couldn't think of a worse existence. Then they let me out, and I became a plowman."

"I don't see what that has to do with me," I say.

The swallows have returned. They snap up the bugs that threaten to bite me; I help them to choose the best apples to take back to their nest.

"For three years I have sweated along with the cow," says Giulio. "Today the cow died. Though I know God has no wish to help me, but only to torment me and keep me from death, I choose to take it as a sign—a sign I should move on. I can think of only one profession worse than both plowing a field and learning from nuns, and that is yours. I am here, Signor Sancto, to become a mad Sorcerer. If you can prove that you possess powers gifted by Satan, then I shall become your apprentice."

The Sorcerer Sancto, who is me, laughs and laughs.

The swallows, startled, flitter away, nearly dropping their apples. A damp wind rises; storm clouds are on their way, the color of cannon-powder, booming like war. The forest shakes its hundred thousand healthy limbs in Giulio's face, without meaning to mock him, but Giulio wheels on his crutch and starts to limp away.

At last I stop laughing. I go after Giulio, and laying a hand on his shoulder, I ask, "How shall I prove my evil power?"

"Bring my family's dead cow back to life, so that Nico may sow my Mama's field and grow corn, and thus they'll survive through the winter."

What use has a mad holy man such as I for a faithless apprentice? No use at all. But God's will is easier shown than explained.

Seven years ago, when the war called the sons and husbands of Fecondita away to die, Giulio, Nico and I, Cecilio Sancto, stood in line with the rest. Giulio came because he wanted to fight. He hated Fecondita, and wished for nothing more than to escape and see the world. He wished it so hard he threw away his crutch. Nico came because his brothers did. I came to see what would happen. I wasn't a Sorcerer then, not yet—just a man of small faith and strong conviction.

Except for Giulio the cripple and Nico the simpleton, the army accepted into its doomed ranks every man of Fecondita, old or young, from twelve years of age to a hundred and twenty. They would have taken me. But when the sergeant reached my place in line, I wouldn't salute. I couldn't meet his eye. Like Giulio, I wanted to see the world. But I didn't want to have to kill or die to do it.

So I ran. I ran for the forest, as fast my two whole legs could go. The men of Fecondita laughed at my back. Even Giulio called me a coward.

The sergeant drew his pistol. He fired on me, a deserter. He would have killed me. But a dying swallow fell into the bullet's path, and I survived.

The soldiers came after me. But the forest of Fecondita, where God resides in every rock and leaf, did not betray me.

Thus did I become the mad, drunken Sorcerer Sancto, lonely, sober, and sane, who hides in the forest, seeing all and doing nothing, but somehow, by my power and God's will, protecting this village from harm.

Atop the fallen stone by the Roman Road, God and a ground squirrel sit cracking acorns. A summer storm rumbles overhead. The convent bell strikes four o'clock; four ripples spread across the field.

Along the Road from the north comes Mother Concetta, clutching her yardstick, dragging Nico by the ear. Twelve sisters march after her, saying Rosaries in rhythm with their steps.

From the forest to the south I, the Sorcerer Sancto, stride with a gait that eats up three yards at every step. Giulio hobbles gasping behind.

"There he is, sisters, the Demon!" cries Mother Concetta, letting go of Nico's ear at last to cross herself. "Oh, heavenly Father, defender of cripples and fools, please in your infinite mercy see your way to striking the evil, mad, drunken Sorcerer Sancto dead!"

Around the stinking corpse of Grazia three red foxes bow their heads—not praying, no, but feasting. Their coats gleam as bright as though Signora Parrucca had brushed them five times that very morning instead of her prized black wig.

Nico, his ear still quite purple and pulsing, runs to shoo them. The twelve nuns, hiking up their habits, hurry close behind. They form a ring in the fecund earth around the cow's corpse, linking their hands, except where Mother Concetta grips her yardstick.

I arrive in my loincloth and bow to the nuns. They shout prayers to God to strike me with a holy bolt.

Giulio hobbles up on his crutch with heaving breath, berries of sweat rolling down his chest. Nico waves hello.

"This cow smells rather ripe," I say. "Are you sure you want me to bring it to life?"

"No!" screech the nuns. "No, Giulio, don't let him! He is the servant of Satan!"

"Yes," wheezes Giulio, sinking down beside God on the fallen stone. The squirrel bites into the acorn's bitter meat and chitters.

I withdraw a small pouch from an unsanitary place among the limited folds of my garment. I open it up, and tip out some fine yellow powder into my palm. This I sprinkle on the corpse.

"What is that powder?" Giulio asks.

"Yellow curry," I say, "imported from Ind by my mother long ago."

"Is it magic?"

"No."

As the yellow curry settles, the dead cow's wrinkled, sagging flesh wrinkles and sags further still. Her bones crumble; her big, liquid eyes shrink away into dry dust and soon she's no more than a pile of earth. A thicket of thorns shoots up out of it, sprouting yellow roses.

"Dio mio!" the nuns exclaim, crossing themselves.

"A miracle!" cries Nico.

"What the hell good is that?" demands Giulio. "Now we'll just have to weed it again!"

"It's the best I can do," I try to explain.

"I knew it!" Giulio shouts. "He's a fraud! I knew from the start!"

"I am not," I protest. "I did as you asked: I brought her to life. Just not the same kind."

"You couldn't at least have made something to eat?"

"It's a matter of faith—of belief. I can only get roses." I admit I am not the greatest Sorcerer this village has seen. After all, Aquinas himself dwelt here for a time. But I do what I must.

"Ha!" cries Mother Concetta. "You see, you nasty boy? You mess around with God and the Devil, you see what you get!" She lifts her yardstick. Nico cringes. She slaps Giulio hard on the wrist.

"Ai!" wails Giulio. "God damn it!"

"Blasphemy!" Mother Concetta whacks him again.

Giulio covers his mouth with his arm. Huge tears roll down his cheeks.

Thunder rumbles over Fecondita. The first few drops of rain come down the size of pomegranates, smashing craters into the soft, black earth. The ground squirrel clamps its teeth on its nut and scurries off home—but God waits. So shall we.

"What are all of you doing there trampling my field?" A woman wearing a squash-yellow dress and a bright purple scarf on her head comes along the Roman Road from Torino, leading a giant black bull.

"Mama!" says Nico, running to give her a hug. "We are using the Sorcerer's magic curry to bring Grazia back to life!"

"Isn't that nice, Nico? But you see, we don't need Grazia anymore." The bull bellows greeting, nodding its blunted horns. "His name is Ferdinando. I bought him in Torino, with the money from selling my wig. So now you can all go home."

"Mama, your wig? But your wig was your favorite thing in the world!"

"I know, Nico." She pats his head. "But we needed a bull. And besides, I am getting too old for such things."

Giulio hobbles forward, cradling his wounded wrist to his chest. "You went to Torino? But Mama, the war! You weren't killed?"

"Does it look like I was killed, Giulio, you fool? The war is over. It has been for years."

Now the skies open up. The nuns shriek and run off towards the convent, whispering hosannas for fear of drowning. The swallows flit out of their bathroom window to swing the shutters closed. Ferdinando the bull grunts and pulls at his rope. Nico tries to shield his mother with his body.

"And now, my good boys," she announces, putting an arm around each, "I think we had better go home."

"Not yet!" I, the Sorcerer, shout, already soaking, holding my loincloth to keep it from slipping. A wrack of thunder tears the sky; the ground shudders as God protests on my behalf. "Not yet. Our bargain isn't finished, Giulio."

"And who is this?" asks Signora Parrucca.

"Mama, this is the Sorcerer Sancto."

"The Sorcerer! WHAT?" She drops the bull's rope, wrests Giulio's crutch from under his arm and advances, swinging. "Back! Back to your forest, before you get a black eye! Stay away from my boys. And quit helping my rats!"

"Moo," says Ferdinando, and lumbers away up the oxcart path.

"Wait, Mama!" Nico cries. "He isn't evil! He works miracles. See? He made these roses grow from Grazia's corpse."

"Well, in that case . . ." Signora Parrucca picks one. "How lovely! See how it matches my dress!" She tucks it behind her ear. "What's this he says about a bargain, Giulio?"

"I offered to be his apprentice, but he turned out a fraud and a coward. Give me my crutch. I'll hit him for you."

She cuffs him. "Insensato! Four years of school with those nuns, and now this. The next time I want a field plowed, I'm putting your brother in charge!" She pokes me with Giulio's stick. "What have you to say for all this?"

"Signora, I vowed to prove my power to bring Grazia back to life. This I have achieved."

"You have not!" shouts Giulio. The Signora shushes him.

"I vowed also that Nico would be able to sow your field and grow corn. This I have not."

"What do you mean, Stregoné Sancto? Of course he can sow the field. What do you think I bought Ferdinando for?"

"He can, with Ferdinando's help. But my wish is that he do more. Signora Parrucca, have you got any spices?"

She looks into the corners of her apron pocket. "Let's see. Some salt. Some ground pepper. What is this? Oregano?"

"Which do you like best, Nico?"

"The pepper, Sorcerer!"

"The pepper—give him a pinch of that. Careful not to wet it. Now, Nico. There is nothing magical or special about that pinch of pepper—save that God is in it, just as He is in this yellow curry, these raindrops, and every rock and tree, every munny-grape-filled bathtub, rat-infested cellar and empty campanile in all of Fecondita. Do you believe it?"

"Of course! God is everywhere! Everyone knows that!"

"Not everyone, Nico."

I make each of the others take a bit of spice. The Signora picks oregano. Giulio scowls and chooses the salt.

"Now sprinkle it over the field. You first, Signora."

She spills the oregano out of her fingers. Several budding dandelions at her feet shoot up into flower, then spill out into fuzzy balls of seed. A gust from the storm, and a thousand seeds burst into the air and scatter, each one then knocked to the earth by a falling drop of rain. A thousand little sprouts pop up across the field.

Signora Parucca covers her mouth. Giulio growls.

"Your turn, my apprentice."

Giulio scatters his salt. He grinds it into the dirt with the heel of his withered foot. Nothing happens. The weeds don't even wilt.

"You see? I told you He had it out for us, Nico." Giulio snatches his crutch from his mama and shakes it at the clouds. "If God *is* hiding in every rock and tree, it is only the better to laugh when we stumble over a root!"

Except for another rumble of thunder, God ignores him. I pat Giulio's shoulder, and say to his brother: "Now, Nico."

Nico throws his pinch of pepper in the air. It catches the storm wind just right, somehow dodging the raindrops, spreading wide across the last tilled field that remains in Fecondita, settling like ashes to the rich, black earth.

Now the ground really does begin to shake. Giulio drops his crutch. He and Signora Parrucca cling to each other to keep from falling. Ferdinando paws and snorts. I don't bother to resist, but fall on my back—and the long, green stalks of new corn that arise from the black, rumbling earth spring up around me, beneath me, lifting me into the air, as high as a man, then higher. Corn fills the field, all the way from the broken cobbles of the Roman Road to the packed earth of the oxcart path, from the forest edge with its hundred flailing limbs to the fallen standing stone. It grows so fast and thick that when Ferdinando charges, the shoots grow back even as he tramples them, and at last leave him caught, mooing forlornly, half a dozen feet above the ground. And Nico the Simpleton, now the Sorcerer, dances round and round it all, laughing like a drunken madman.

I laugh too—and not from madness. You see, it was not an apprentice that I sought, but a replacement.

On the morning after the rain, the drops of dew glisten like cherries on the fat husks of the corn. Giulio and I reach the end of the oxcart path and turn north, along the Roman Road that leads to Torino, and beyond it Milan, and Padova, and the rest of the world. We leave Fecondita as we would have wished seven years ago—not as soldiers, off to die, but as scholars, seekers of wisdom. God and a flock of swallows follow us almost to the border.

Giulio the cripple walks without a crutch; his brother Nico cured him. And I, mere Cecilio Sancto again, walk without fear—for I know the war is over, and Fecondita now has a greater protector. Nico is Sorcerer now.

And that, my friends, is the real reason why neither you nor I shall ever again find Fecondita. Unless it is his will.

Thank God for fools and cripples.

~

I wrote "The Utter Proximity of God" in the midst of a war between my ambitions and the expectations of genre, which occurred at the Odyssey

Fantasy Writing Workshop in 2005. The peace I found came from filling my head with early Calvino and late García Márquez. What was it about the magic realists? For me, they offered a way to bring back to the fantastic the experience of the sublime. The more "magical" a fiction becomes, the duller our capacity for wonder. Fantasies keep getting bigger; augmented reality encroaches on the real. I wanted a way to break that cycle. Magic realism gives me an escape: a less constricting set of tropes, in whose context the notion of parable doesn't seem quite so tired, and a fiction of ideas not so laughable: a means to find God, to find magic, in something as simple as a field of weeds.

Michael J. DeLuca

Alternate Anxieties

Karen Jordan Allen

mortal anxiety: anxiety based in the fear of death

mortal anxiety: anxiety rooted in/stemming from the uncertainty of life

rooted, stemming—significance of organic metaphors?

Possible Book Titles:
Mortal Anxiety by Katherine Smith
The Anxiety of Mortality by Katherine Smith

BIO (or introduction?)

Katherine Smith's life has been profoundly affected by mortal anxiety. She traces this back to the age of four, when the family beagle broke its leash while Katherine's mother was walking it. The dog ran in front of a dump truck and was flattened. The family got another dog, a docile and middle-aged shelter mutt, but thereafter Katherine gave herself the job of making sure the leash was in good repair and properly fastened before the dog got out the door. She didn't trust her mother, who had already proved herself incompetent in Katherine's eyes; she didn't trust her father, who claimed not to be a "dog person" and had grumbled about the new dog; and certainly her little brother, who was only one-and-a-half, couldn't be expected to keep the family dog safe. Thus Katherine appointed herself: She Who Makes Sure Bad Things Don't Happen.

But her anxiety was such that even when she grew old enough to walk the dog, she refused, because she did not think she could bear the pain if something happened to the dog while she was on the responsible end of the leash. Still, she inspected the leash and collar every time her mother (or father, or, later, her brother) took the dog for a walk. At least, she thought, if the dog gets away and gets hurt, it won't be my fault. I've done all I can.

This continued through a succession of family dogs.

mortal anxiety comes from:

1. the impossibility of knowing whether from moment to moment we (or our loved ones) shall continue to exist

—how can I relax and wash dishes, knowing that I could die any moment of a burst brain aneurysm, or that a stray undetected asteroid could kill me and most other life on Earth, or that one day the Earth will burn to cinders in the death throes of the Sun?

—note micro-concerns (personal death) vs. macro-concerns (fate of the Earth/Universe)

2. the impossibility of knowing when the simplest of daily choices (e.g. to leave the house at 4:04 instead of 4:03 or 4:05) is a life-or-death decision

—I could die in a car accident at the treacherous Outer Ave. blinking light at 4:08 that I might have missed at 4:07 or 4:09

—so how do I/we know when to leave the house? (consider relationship to agoraphobia)

Better title: *Living with Life's Great Impossibilities* by Katerina Smythe

could choice of title could be a life-or-death decision?

—I could get up from this chair now and fall down the stairs and break my neck, whereas if I ponder titles for five seconds longer I might successfully negotiate the stairs to make a cup of coffee

—likely both trips will be safe; 9,999 times out of 10,000, I won't fall, but who knows when that 10,000th time will be?

(opening chapter: "Lessons from a Dead Squirrel")
A TRUE ANECDOTE

One Thursday morning the squirrel with the broken tail, surely the same that frolicked for weeks in my back yard, dove under my Honda's right front tire as I hurried to Deer Run Community College to give a lecture on apocalypticism to my World Religions class. The squirrel met its personal apocalypse with a sickening thump. I said "oh!" in a pained voice, and glanced into my rear-view mirror, hoping that the gray lump on the pavement had suffered no mortal injury, and after a stunned moment would leap up and run into Mrs. Healy's lilac bushes. But no. I could see, even as they receded in the distance, four little paws, motionless, straight up in the air.

If only I had taken my usual route to work. Normally I pulled out from my driveway and turned right, but this morning a large semi-trailer had filled most of the street in that direction, and while I likely could have gotten by it, I decided instead to go left and around the block, and I was directly opposite my own house (though with three houses and their yards between) when the doomed squirrel threw itself under my radials.

The bright sunlight that had so lifted my spirits when I stepped out of the house suddenly fell flat and harsh, illuminating both happiness and tragedy with indifference. If I had taken my usual route, the squirrel would still be frolicking, I would still be smiling to the lively Haydn sonata playing on public radio, and all would be well in my world. At least as well as it ever was. But the event shadowed my day.

Just as the beagle's escape forever shadowed my life.

the eternal moment
the moment out of time
when the universe held its breath
when the universe stopped

definition of word to be coined: that pause identified only in retrospect, immediately before the life-altering/ending event, the point or fulcrum upon which all turns, before the phone call, the knock on the door, the breaking of the leash, the leap of a squirrel, when one feels certain that the disaster could have been averted had one just been alert enough to perceive that moment and turn it aside

BIO/INTRO cont'd.

Years later Katherine would awaken in the middle of the night, remembering the moment when the beagle strained at the leash, just before the leash snapped and the dog leapt away. That she could not go back and fix the leash, stop the disaster, change the story, seemed not only unfair but wrong—as if she had been shoved in error into a fake world, a counterfeit world, a world that was a mistake. Somewhere, somehow, she thought, the dog must still be alive and happy.

the alternate universe theory: in some science fiction (and some science), it is posited that events may have more than one outcome, with each outcome spinning off its own universe, so that millions of universes are generated each day; perhaps the squirrel with the broken tail and/or the flattened beagle frolic still in some of those universes

—equally possible: I lie dead, having noticed the squirrel a half-second earlier, twisted my steering wheel to avoid it, and rammed myself into a tree

am I *in* an "alternate" universe? alternate to what?

A DISTRACTION/DISLOCATION

Mother called, told me to sit down. "They" found a lump (I didn't even know she was going for her mammogram); "they're" going to do a biopsy. But it's small, don't worry, it's a long way from Maine to California, it would be expensive. Your father and brother and his wife are all here, they'll look after me, I'll be fine. (But what about me? I'm not fine with this at all, I want to be there. No, that's not true, I don't want to be there, I don't want to be in this universe. But if I have to be, I want to be there, not here, not alone, waiting.)

the moment: there it was, before I answered the phone, distracted, absorbed in making my coffee, contemplating my book

I might have turned it aside, but I missed it—

what if I determine to be alert to those moments, those fulcrum moments (ah! a name!), those pauses in existence before the universe bifurcates, and bifurcates again?

eternal bifurcations
eternal, infinite bifurcations

take this universe back, please, I would like another—

(chapter title: "The Fulcrum Moment")
ANOTHER MOMENT MISSED

At the Goodwill store the skirts are jammed so tightly I can hardly wedge my hand between them. The metal skirt clips on the hangers catch on one another, locking all the skirts into a long, solid row. I wonder who hangs them, how they think customers can possibly browse with pleasure when they risk physical injury just getting the damn clothes off the rack.

Irritated, but determined not to be defeated, I claw at the hangers with both hands and force open a few inches of space. I jam my elbow against the skirts on the left and check the size of one on the right, a pretty thing of peach-colored chiffon. Yes, a 10. Just the thing to match a jacket I found here last week.

Then I see the blood well up under a flap of skin on my right index finger. It oozes out, trickles down my nail, and hangs perilously, a swelling crimson droplet.

With my other hand I dig in my pocket for a tissue. I catch the blood just as it falls. The peach-colored chiffon is saved.

In my mental rearview mirror, I glimpse again—belatedly—the moment, the fulcrum moment when in frustration and impatience I grabbed the hangers—not a mortal moment, but still. In another universe, I am already in the dressing room trying the skirt on.

I check to see if I left flesh or blood on the metal skirt clips. No, but the clips are discolored, rusty. Thoreau's brother died of tetanus after cutting himself with a rusty razor. I try to remember whether my tetanus booster is up-to-date. With a free-flowing wound like this, the danger is minimal. But what a bizarre and banal death that would be.

In another universe—

Perhaps a mortal moment, after all.

therapeutic value of the alternate universe theory:

—a sophisticated illusion (?) to help us manage the pain of uncertainty/finality

—helpful only if we believe we can choose the "better" universe (or does just the vision of, say, the squirrel still frolicking *somewhere* ease our pain?)

—not a defense against the eventuality of death, unless we posit universes of impossibly old people (and squirrels and beagles)

but mortal anxiety ≠ anxiety about death

—the "good" death, quiet in bed at ninety or one hundred, that one is "ready" for (at least some have said they are ready); that death does not inspire mortal anxiety

—the young death, the accidental death, the "wrong" death that comes before we are finished, before we even know who we are; and the impossibility of foreseeing and avoiding that death, of controlling the terms of our existence—

New title: *Mortal Anxiety and the Alternate Universe* by E. K. Smythe (would appeal to multiple markets: psychology, philosophy, science, science fiction; the cover needn't tell that E. K. is a woman—if that matters)

BIO/INTRO, cont'd.

Mortal, or existential, anxiety destroyed Katherine's marriage of five years to "Steve." He knew of her anxiety when he married her but neither thought that it would come between them and having a family. "Steve" dreamed of becoming a father. At first Katherine wanted children, too, despite her terror of taking on responsibility for their safety (if she couldn't trust herself with a dog—then a child?). Then their friends "Bridget" and "Dennis" lost their infant son to the flu. Every year a few, very few children succumb unpredictably to influenza; theirs was one. Katherine had never seen such intense grief. She kept waiting for time to bring healing, but it didn't. "Bridget" sank into depression. "Dennis" sought distraction in an affair. They divorced. "Bridget" moved in with her parents and spent her spare time drinking.

A bottomless well of anxiety opened up in Katherine's heart. How would she ever survive such a horrendous loss? She knew that people did, that not everyone destroyed themselves or their marriages. Some families circled, like wagons, embracing each other until they could move on. But could she?

"Steve" mourned the loss of his friends' child, even tried to help them patch up their marriage. He spoke with Katherine of the risk of that awful pain, the risk of loving as a parent loves. Still, his longing to be a parent survived his contemplation of the risk. Katherine admired his bravery but could not find it in herself. "Steve" finally left. Now he has a new wife and a six-month-old son. He is happy. Katherine is glad he is happy. But when she contemplates having her own children she falls back into that terrible well of anxiety and only by promising herself childlessness forever can she pull herself out.

how can I with words open up that bottomless well?

perhaps I should keep it covered and let those who can maintain their illusions keep them

or is it the well itself that offers a way into other universes?

(chapter title: "Creating the Alternate Universe/s")
A TEST SITUATION

My mother awaits—hence I await—the biopsy results. I go online to check prices to fly to California. Then I realize this is the ideal test situation. How many universes can I create, spin off, as I make my reservations? I select "search by price" for a Boston–LA flight and am rewarded with a plethora of possibilities. Overwhelmed, I should say. Which airline? Which day? Which flight? My life will turn out differently depending on the choice—perhaps only a little differently, perhaps a lot. Perhaps end. But I cannot tell unless I peer into those other universes.

I select a date at random, choose another a week later, look for a flight leaving neither too early nor too late. I take it all the way up to "Click to buy ticket" and my hand freezes over the computer. This is it, a fulcrum moment, I can buy or not.

And even if I buy, I can go or not.

Which life, which universe do I choose? To buy this ticket, go on this flight? To buy this ticket, then choose later whether to go or not? To start over?

I hold my hand motionless, letting my thoughts pour into the moment and fill it, nudging me into this universe or that. Or at least opening a tiny window, a hatch, into other possible universes, so that I know what I am choosing.

The universes close up tight.

Tell me, God, tell me what to do.

God, as usual, is silent. Or not there.

segue to: "God and Mortal Anxiety"

—are there universes in which God is, and universes in which He/She is not? or universes with many Gods? or one God for many universes?

—religious people have been found to be happier, less depressed, less anxious; check research

—is it the belief in God as such, or the existential certainty that accompanies such belief, that relieves anxiety?

—atheists are likewise certain; are they less anxious?

—agnostics, the uncertain, the know-nots: if uncertainty breeds anxiety, then anxiety must trail them like a hungry dog

(yet more) BIO/INTRO

Because Katherine teaches religion, her students—and others—assume her to be a religious person. She is a religious person in the sense that the deep questions of life concern her greatly, and she seeks the subjective responses of religion and philosophy, not just the objective answers of science. But so far her studies have shed no light on the question of God. Despite—or perhaps because of—years of religious study, Katherine finds herself a thoroughgoing agnostic. Faith in God and the prospect of heaven, being unreal to her, can neither comfort her nor calm her anxiety.

could it be belief in heaven, rather than spiritual certainty or belief in God, that relieves mortal anxiety?

—heaven: a kind of alternate universe accessible primarily through death, perhaps also through trance or vision

—carrying heavy moral weight (unlike most other alternate universes)

—pre-existent to this universe? i.e. not a result of bifurcations of it or of universes preceding; or perhaps a very early bifurcation

but a universe accessible by death is not therapeutically useful when the interior aim is to *avoid* untimely death

ways other than death to access alternate universes:

—inward: meditation, hypnosis, trance, aided by fasting, drugs, pain

—outward: specialized technology (not yet known), travel at a particular speed or direction, key geographical points/gateways, transitional objects

is *belief* in the alternate universe necessary to reach it (as perhaps to reach heaven)?

—then the agnostic is doomed; neither science nor theology can save her

(unless in writing this book I find a way—)

~

AN OUTSIDE TRIP

Despite Katherine's anxieties, she persists in the belief that only total immersion in the vagaries of life will eventually bring security. She knows she thinks too much. To get out of her head, out of her anxieties, she goes to the supermarket. Instead of imagining the universes that may be splitting off as she chooses to take this road instead of that, this parking space instead of that, this shopping cart instead of that, she focuses on the tastes she plans to bring home: mango, pineapple, strawberries. Plain first, then with vanilla yogurt, then whipped with a little sugar and spice into an East Indian lassi.

Her mouth waters.

The man in front of her in the checkout line has a basket full of hamburger, a dozen packages. None have been put into a protective plastic bag, although these are provided in the meat section. When Katherine buys hamburger, she pulls a plastic bag over her hand like a glove, picks up the package of meat, then pulls the bag back up, never touching the original plastic wrap packaging. Who knows, a little juice might have dripped out, a little meat spilled, bacteria-filled, contaminated.

Katherine has never contracted food poisoning at home.

She watches the man load the hamburger onto the conveyor belt, notices the wet spot underneath when he shifts the packages to make room for more, a crumb of red that might have oozed out of the plastic-wrap. She looks at her mango and pineapple (there were no strawberries today). Alternate universes spin before her: Despite the hamburger, nothing happens, she washes everything thoroughly and stays well. Or she has a touch of food poisoning, recovers. Or she dies of a new modern virulent form of E. coli. Or—

She excuses herself from the line, mumbling something about a forgotten item. But she forgot nothing. On the contrary, she remembers too much. She heads for another line, stops in her tracks. Who's to say the customer three or four places ahead of her, already in the parking lot, didn't leave the cashier's hands and the conveyor belt already contaminated?

She decides to go back to the produce department for plastic bags for her fruit. Then she spots a cashier spritzing her station with disinfectant, wiping everything down, switching on the light that says the lane is open. Katherine scurries over, stepping in front of a slow old man with a package of pork chops. She smiles apologetically; he nods and his eyes twinkle. She puts the mango and pineapple onto a conveyor belt, which still glistens with disinfectant. She will wash them before cutting them up, before closing her mouth around their incomparable sweetness. But she feels confident that even if the washing is not perfect, the fruit will not sicken her in this universe she has chosen/created.

If she gets sick, it will not be her fault. She has done what she can.

creating the secure universe: the aspiration of the mortally anxious

their ritual objects: plastic bags, helmets, antibacterial sprays, locks, alarms, sensors, diagnostic tests, seatbelts, organic foods, insurance policies

limits on creation of the "safe" universe:

—ability to choose universes by taking precautions is limited to hazards which can be foreseen and prevented

—for unforeseen/unforeseeable events, the only chance to choose lies in catching that moment, the fulcrum moment

—but *how* to access other universes through that moment?

A REAL TEST

The phone rings. Katherine puts down the fork with mango still skewered upon it, reaches for the phone, pauses with her hand extended. She senses her mother at the other end of the line, tries to picture her face: relieved? devastated? worried but hopeful? This is it, the moment, she feels it, she *knows* it. How does she turn it aside? By never answering the phone? By answering in this moment rather than the next, by waiting another ring? By closing her eyes and taking some inward turn in her mind? By clicking her heels, turning left three times, saying "abracadabra"?

She sweats, she fights tears, but she cannot move her mind/self/reality into position to leap/fall/dissolve from this universe into another. She feels herself toppling into the well of anxiety, but rallies and lifts the phone. Hello.

Hello. Her mother's voice is strained. She wastes no time. "It" is malignant. She will have surgery right away. The doctor is hopeful. But—

Katherine watches the moment recede in her rearview mental mirror, feels herself sitting at the bifurcation of universes—they split and split again into a great cauliflower-like fractal of possibilities, of realities—innumerable universes exploding from the moment and mushrooming up and out (those organic metaphors again) in great clouds.

In which universe does her mother die soon, die later, respond to treatment, not respond, go into remission, experience a complete cure?

Katherine hangs onto the phone, the tips of her fingers whiten. She wishes she could reach out and grab onto the "good" universes, let them pull her along and her mother with her, into a place where squirrels still frolic and beagles play and, if she cannot avoid all pain, at least she can exercise some choice about which pain to experience and which to let go.

But the universes slip from her hands like so many silken cords. She clings to the one that remains, praying, with all that is within her, that this is the right one, the one where she belongs, and that the pain will not be more than she—than I—can bear.

~

I've never thought to call myself "interstitial" (until now), but I have always felt caught between sometimes conflicting identities: am I poet or scientist, country girl or academic, mystic or naturalist, Midwesterner or Yankee? To add to my bewilderment, I tend to feel greater affinity for the world in which I am not; back home in Indiana I feel like a New Englander, but in Maine I'm aware of my lingering Midwesternisms. So I'm always more or less out of place—except when I am in nature, and when I write.

My writing grows from yet another experience of incongruity—the sense of life as a constant juxtaposition of the bizarre and the taken-for-granted. My own experience leans to the bizarre, not because my life has been bizarre in any usual sense, but because I find existence essentially incredible. Perhaps the inability to take things (such as existence) for granted is one of the roots of anxiety—but also of imagination.

As for "Alternate Anxieties," I owe its existence to an unlucky squirrel, who died in the manner described. I was left to ponder the enormous consequences of seemingly trivial choices. Thus, a story.

Karen Jordan Allen

Burning Beard:
The Dreams and Visions of Joseph ben Jacob, Lord Viceroy of Egypt

Rachel Pollack

"There was a young Hebrew in the prison, a slave of the captain of the guard. We told him our dreams and he interpreted them."
—*Genesis* 41:12

"Why did you repay good with evil? This is the cup from which my lord drinks, and which he uses for divination."
—*Genesis* 44:5

"If a Man Sees Himself in a Dream

killing an ox:	Good. It means the removal of the dreamer's enemies.
writing on a palette:	Good. It means the establishment of the dreamer's office.
uncovering his backside:	Bad. It means the dreamer will become an orphan."

—Excerpts from Egyptian Dream Book, found on *recto*, or back side, of a papyrus from the 19th Dynasty.

In the last month of his life, when his runaway liver has all but eaten his body, Lord Joseph orders his slave to set his flimsy frame upright, like the sacred pillar of the God Osiris in the annual festival of rebirth. Joseph has other things on his mind, however, than his journey to the next world. He has his servant dress him as a Phoenician trader, and then two bearers carry him alone to the dream house behind the temple of Thoth, God of magic, science, writing, celestial navigation, swindlers, gamblers, and dreams. Joseph braces himself against the red column on the outside of the building, then enters with as firm a step as he can. The two interpreters who come to him strike him as hacks, their beards unkempt, their hair dirty, their makeup cracked and sloppy, and their long coats—

It hardly matters that the coats are torn in places, bare in others. Just the sight of those swirls of color floods Joseph's heart with memory. He sees his childhood dream as if he has just woken up from it. The court magicians in their magnificent coats lined up before Pharaoh. The Burning Beard and his brother shouting their demands. The sticks that changed into snakes. And he remembers the coat his mother made for him, the start of all his troubles. And the way he screamed when Judah and Gad tore it off him and drenched it in the blood of some poor ibex they'd caught in one of their traps.

Startled, Joseph realizes the interpreters are speaking to him. "Sir," they say, "how may we serve you?"

"As you see," Joseph says, "I am an old man, on the edge of death. Lately my dreams have troubled me. And where better to seek answers than in Luxor, so renowned for dreamers?" The two smile. Joseph says, "Of course, I would have preferred the interpretations of your famous Joseph—" He watches them wince. "—but I am only a merchant, and I am sure Lord Joseph speaks only to princes."

The younger of the two, a man about thirty with slicked down hair says, "Well, he's sick, you know. And there are those who say the Pharaoh's publicity people exaggerate his powers." He adds, with a wave of his hand, "One lucky guess, years ago . . ."

"Tell me," Joseph says, his voice lower, "is he really a Hebrew? I've heard that, but I find it hard to believe."

In a voice even lower, the young one says "Not only a Hebrew, but a slave. It's true. They plucked him out of prison."

Joseph feigns shock and a slight disgust. "Egypt is certainly more sophisticated than Phoenicia," he says. "In Tyre our slaves sweat for us, not the other way around."

The other stares at the stone cut floor. "Yes," he says. "Well, the Viceroy is old, and things change."

Quickly, the older one says "Why don't you tell us your dreams?"

"Lately, they've been very—I guess vivid is the best word. Just last night I dreamed I was sailing all alone down a river."

"Ah, good," the older one says. "A sign of wealth to come."

"It had better come soon, or I won't have much use for it. But to continue— I climbed the mast—"

"Wonderful. Your God will bear you aloft with renewed health and good fortune."

Joseph notices their eyes on the purse he carries on his belt. He goes on, "When I came down I became very hungry and ate the first thing I saw, which only afterwards I realized was the offal of animals. I haven't dared to tell anyone of this. Surely this is some omen of destruction."

"Oh no," the younger one jumps in. "In fact, it ensures prosperity."

"Really?" Joseph says. "Then what a lucky dream. Every turn a good omen." He smiles, remembering the fun he had making up the silly dream out of their lists. But the smile fades. He says, "Maybe you can do another one. Actually, this dream has come to me several times in my life." They nod. Joseph knows that the dream books place great emphasis on recurrence. After all, he thinks, if a dream is important enough to come back, maybe the interpreters can charge double.

He closes his eyes for a moment, sighs. When he looks at them again he sees them through a yellow haze of sickness. He begins, "I dream of a man. Very large and frightening. Strangely, his beard appears all on fire."

He can see them race through their catalogues in their minds. Finally the old one says "Umm, good. It means you will achieve authority in your home."

Joseph says, "But the man is not me."

The young one says, "That doesn't matter."

"I see. Then I'll continue. This man, who dresses as a shepherd but was once a prince, appears before Pharaoh. He demands that Pharaoh surrender to him a vast horde of Pharaoh's subjects." He pauses, but now there is no answer. They look confused. Joseph continues "When the mob follow the man he promises them paradise, but instead leads them into the desert."

"A bad sign?" the old one says tentatively.

Joseph says, "They clamor for food, of course, but instead he leaves them to climb a mountain. And there, in the clouds, he writes a book. He writes it on stone and sheepskin. The history of the world, he calls it. The history and all its laws."

Now there is silence. "Can you help me?" Joseph says. "Should I fear or hope?" The two just stand there. Finally, so tired he can hardly move, Joseph drops the purse on a painted stone table and leaves the temple.

Ten-year-old Joseph wants to open a school for diviners. "Prophecy, dreams interpreted, plan for the future," his announcements will say. And under a portrait of him, "Lord Joseph, Reader and Advisor." Reuben, his oldest brother, shakes his head in disgust. Small flecks of mud fly out of his beard and into Poppa Jacob's lentils. Reuben says, "What does that mean, reader and advisor? Since when do you know how to read?"

Joseph blushes. "I'm going to learn," he says. Over Reuben's laugh he adds quickly, "Anyway, when I see the future, that's a kind of reading. The dreams and the pictures I see in the wine. That's just like reading."

Reuben snorts his disgust. To their father he says, "If you'd make him do some decent work he wouldn't act this way."

Rachel is about to say something but Joseph looks at her with his please-mother-I-can-handle-this-myself look. He says, "Divining is work. Didn't that Phoenician woman give me a basket of pomegranates for finding her cat?"

Under his breath, Reuben mutters, "*Rotten* pomegranates. And why would anyone want a cat, for Yah's sake?"

But Joseph ignores him. He can see he's got the old man's attention. "And we can sell things," he adds. "Open a shop."

"A shop?" Jacob says. His nostrils flare slightly in alarm.

"Sure," Joseph says, not noticing his mother's signal to stop. "When people study with me they'll need equipment. Colored coats, cups to pour the wine, even books. I can write instruction books. 'The Interpretation of Dreams.' That's when I learn to read, of course."

Jacob spits on the rug, an act that makes Rachel turn her face. "We are not merchants," he says. "Dammit, maybe your brothers are right." He ignores his wife's stagy whisper "Half brothers," and goes on, "Maybe you need to get your fingers in some sheep, slap some mud on that pretty face of yours."

Before Joseph can make it worse Rachel covers his mouth and pulls him outside.

Over the laughter of the brothers, Judah yells, "Goodbye, *Lord* Joseph. See you in the sheep dung!"

Rachel makes sure Joseph wraps his coat around him against the desert's bite. Even under the thin light of the stars, the waves of color flicker as if alive. What wonderful dreams this boy has, she thinks. She remembers the morning he demanded the coat. Needed it for his work, he said. Leah's brats tried to stop it being made, of course, but Rachel won. Just like always. She says, "Those loudmouths. How dare they laugh at you? You *are* a lord. A true prince compared to them."

But Joseph pays her no attention. Instead, he stares at the planets, Venus and Jupiter, as bright as fire, hanging from the skin of a half-dead Moon. Images fall from them, as if from holes in the storage house of night.

He sees a lion, a great beast, except it changes, becomes a cub, its fur a wave of light. Seraphs come down, those fake men with the leathery wings that Joseph's father saw in his dream climbing up and down that ladder to heaven and never thought to shout at them, "Why don't you just fly?" The seraphs place a crown like a baby sun on the lion's head. And then they just fly away, as if they have done their job. *No*, Joseph wants to scream at them, *don't leave me*. For already he can see them. The wild dogs. They climb up from holes in the Earth, they cover the lion, tear holes in his skin, spit into his eyes.

Joseph slams his own eyes with the heels of his hands. The trick works, for suddenly he becomes aware of his mother beside him, her worry a bright mark on her face as she wipes a drop of spit from his open mouth. Vaguely, he pushes her hand away. Now the tail comes, he thinks. The bit of clean information after the torrent of pictures. Just as his brothers begin to leave their father's grand tent, it hits Joseph, so hard he staggers backward. They want to kill him. If they could, they would tie him to a rock and slit him open, the way his great-grandfather Abraham tried to kill Grandpa Isaac, and even struggled against the—seraph?—that held his hand and shouted in his ear to stop, stop, it was over, Yah had changed His mind. And yet, in all the terror, Joseph can't help but smirk, for he realizes something further. Reuben, *Reuben*, will stop them.

"What are you laughing at?" Reuben says as he marches past, and it's all Joseph can do not to really laugh, for it almost doesn't matter, scary as it is. He knows something about them that they don't even know themselves. And doesn't that make him their lord?

Mostly Joseph divines from dreams, but sometimes the cup shows him what he needs to know. His mother gave him the cup when he was five. She'd ordered it made two years before, when their travels took them past the old woman who kept the kiln outside Luz. Rachel had had her own dream of how it should look, with rainbow swirls in the glaze, and four knobs of different colors. It took a long time but she made Jacob wait, despite the older boys' complaints, until the potter finished it. And then Rachel put it aside until the ceremony by the fire, when Joseph's first haircut would turn him from a wild animal (one who secretly still sucked at his mother) into a human. Rachel couldn't attend—yet another boys-only event—but they came and told her what happened—how he whooped it up, jumping and waving his arms like a cross between a monkey and a bat, how his hair made the fire flare so that Jacob had to yank the child back to keep him from getting scorched. And then how Joseph quieted when his father gave him the cup, how he purred over it like a girl, how his father poured the wine. But instead of drinking Joseph just stared at it, stared and made a noise like a nightmare, and might have flung it away if Jacob hadn't grabbed hold of him (a salvation Jacob later regretted) and forced him to drink the wine so they could end the ceremony.

It took Rachel a long time to get Joseph to tell her what he'd seen. Darkness, he said finally. Darkness over all the world, thicker than smoke. And a hand in the dark sky, a finger outstretched, reaching, reaching, stroking invisible foreheads. He heard cries, he said, shrieks and wails in the blackness. Then light came—and everywhere, in every home, from palace to shack, women held their dead children against their bodies. "I'm not going to die, am I?" Joseph asked her.

"No, no, darling, it's not for you, it's for someone else. The bad people. Don't worry, sweetie, it's not for you." Joseph cried and cried while his mother held him and kissed the torn remnants of his hair.

As much as they make fun of him, as much as they complain to Jacob about his airs and his lack of work, the brothers will sometimes sneak into his tent, after they think everyone has fallen asleep. "Can you find my staff?" they'll say, or "Who's this Ugarit girl Pop's got lined up for me? Is she good-looking? Can she keep her mouth shut?" The wives come even more often, scurrying along the path as if anyone who saw them would mistake them for rabbits. "Tell me it's going to be a boy," they say, "Please, he'll kill me if it's another girl," as if the diviner can control something like that, as if events are at the mercy of the diviner, and not the other way around.

At first, Joseph soaks in their secret devotions. When Zebulon ridicules him, Joseph looks him in the eye, as if to say, "Put on a good show, big brother, because you know and I know what you think about after dark, under your sheepskin." Or maybe he'll just finger the colored stone Zeb gave him as a bribe not to say anything. But after a while he wishes they'd leave him alone. He even pretends to sleep, but they just grab him by the shoulder. Worst of all are the ones who offer themselves to him, not just the wives, but sometimes the brothers too, pretending it's something Joseph is longing for. Do they do it just to reward him, or because they really desire him, or because they think of it as some kind of magic that will change a bad prediction? Joseph tries to find the answer in his cup, or a dream, but the wine and the night remain as blank as his brothers' faces. He can see the fate of entire tribes but not the motives of his own brothers. Maybe there are no motives. Maybe people do things for no reason at all.

~

And Joseph himself? Why does he do it? Just to know things other people don't? To make himself better than his brothers? Because he can? Because he can't stop himself? As a child he loves the excitement, that lick of fire that sometimes becomes a whip. Later, especially the last days in Egypt, he wishes it would end. His body can't take the shock, his mind can't take the knowledge. He prays, he sacrifices goats stolen from the palace herd and smuggled into the desert. No use. The visions keep coming, wanted or not.

Only near the very end of his life does he get an answer. The half burnt goat sends up a shimmer of light that Joseph stares at, hypnotized, so that he doesn't hear the desert roar, or see the swirl of sand that marks a storm until it literally slaps him in the face. He cowers down and covers himself as best he can, and wonders if he will die here so that no one will ever find his body. Maybe his family will think Yah just sucked him up into heaven, too impatient to wait for Joseph to die. In the midst of it all, he hears it. The Voice. An actual voice! High pitched, somewhere between a man and a woman, it shouts at him out of the whirlwind. "Do you think I do this for *you?* I opened secrets for you because I *needed* you. I will close them when I close them!"

The fact is, Joseph is no fool. By his final years, he's known for a long time that Yah has used him. He doesn't like that this bothers him, but it does. A messenger, he tells himself. A filler. A bridge between his father and the other one, the Burning Beard. He knows exactly what people will think over the millennia. Jacob will get ranked as the last patriarch (the only real patriarch, Joseph thinks, the only one to pump out enough boys to found a nation), the other one the Great Leader. And Joseph? A clever bureaucrat. A nice guy who lured his family to Egypt and left them there to get into trouble.

He considers writing his own story. "The Life of Joseph ben Jacob, Lord Viceroy of Egypt." But what good would it do? A fire would incinerate the papyrus, or a desert lion would claw it to shreds, or maybe a freak flood would wash away the hieroglyphs. By whatever means, Yah would make sure no one would ever see it. The Beard is the writer, after all. God's scribe.

~

Some things Joseph knows from the ripples and colors of the wine. Others require a dream. He first sees the man he calls "the Beard" in a dream. Joseph is eight, a spindly brat with a squeaky voice. He's had a bad evening, swatted by Simeon for a trick he'd played on Levi. In despair that no one loves him, he drinks down a whole cup of wine from the flask his mother has given him. The cup falls with a thud on the dirt floor of his tent as he instantly falls down asleep.

At first, he sees only the flame. It fills his dream like floodwaters hitting a dry riverbed. Finally, Joseph and the fire separate so that he can see it as a blaze on a man's face. No, not the face, the beard. The man has thick eyebrows and thin hair and sad eyes and a beard bushier than Reuben's, except the beard is on fire! The flames roar all about the face and neck, yet somehow never seem to hurt him. They don't even seem to consume anything; his beard always stays the same. Later in life, in countless dreams, Joseph will study this man and the inferno on his face. He will wonder if maybe the fire is an illusion—the man's a master magician, after all—or a trick of the desert light (except it looks the same inside Pharaoh's palace). And he will wonder why no one ever seems to notice it, not the Pharaoh, not the Beard's self-serving brother, not the whiny mob that follows him through the desert. In that first time, however, the fiery beard scares him so much he can only hide in the corner of his dream, hardly even aware that the man stands on a dark mountain scorched by lightning, and talks to the clouds.

Joseph doesn't like this man. He doesn't like his haughty pretension of modesty, the I'm-just-a-poor-shepherd routine. He detests the man's willingness to slaughter hordes of his own people just for the sake of discipline. He dislikes his speeches that go on for hours and hours, in that thick slurry voice, always with the same message, obey, obey, obey. Joseph distrusts the man's total lack of humor, his equal lack of respect for women. Can't he see that his sister controls the waters, so that without her to make the rocks sweat they would all die of thirst? As far as Joseph can tell, the mob would have done a lot better if they had followed the sister and not the Beard. Joseph thinks of her as his proper heir as leader of the Hebrews. But then, he has to admit, he always did like women better.

Most of all, Joseph detests the Beard's penchant for self-punishment. The way he lies down in the dirt, cutting his face on the pebbles, the way he'll swear off sex but won't give his wife permission to take anyone else. And what about his hunger strikes that go on for days and days, as if Yah can't stand the smell of food on a man's breath? It might not bother Joseph so much if the man wasn't such a role model for his people. *Joseph's* people. Doesn't the man know that Joseph saved his family—the mob's ancestors, after all—and all of Egypt from starvation just a few generations before? It was Joseph who explained Pharaoh's dream of the seven fat cows and the seven lean ones, Joseph who took over Egypt's food storage systems during the seven good years, building up the stocks for the seven years of famine. It was Joseph who took in his family and fed them so the tribes could survive. Doesn't the Beard know all this? He claims to know everything, doesn't he? The man who talks to Yah. How dare he denounce food? How *dare* he?

Some dreams come so quickly they seem to pounce on him the moment he closes his eyes. Others lie in wait all night until they seize him just before he plans to wake up. The dream of the coat comes that way. Joseph has fidgeted in his sleep for hours, flinging out his arm as if trying to push something away. And then at dawn, just as Reuben and Judah and Issachar and Zebulon are gulping down stony bread on their way to the sheep, their little brother dreams once more of the Burning Beard. He sees the Beard stride into the biggest room Joseph has ever seen. Stone columns thicker than Jacob's ancient ram hold up a roof higher than the Moon. The Beard comes with his brother, who has slicked down his hair and oiled his beard, and wears a silver plate around his neck, obviously more aware than the Beard of how you dress when you appear before a king. Or maybe the Beard has deliberately crafted his appearance, his torn muddy robe, his matted hair, as either contempt for the Pharaoh or a declaration of his own humility.

"Look at me, I'm just a country bumpkin, a simple shepherd on an errand for God." Later, in other dreams, Joseph will learn just how staged this act is from the man who grew up as Pharaoh's adopted son. Now, however, the dreaming boy knows only the gleam of the throne room and the scowl of the invader.

The brothers speak together. Though Joseph cannot follow any of it (he will not learn Egyptian for another twenty years) he understands that the Beard has something wrong with his speech so that silver-plate needs to interpret for him. Whatever they say, it certainly bothers the king, who shouts at them and holds up some gold bauble like a protection against the evil eye. The Beard says something to his brother, who strangely throws his shepherd's staff on the floor. Have they surrendered? But no, it's a trick, and a pretty good one, because the *stick* surrenders its rigidity and becomes a snake!

Asleep, Joseph still shivers under his sheepskin. The king, however, shouts something at one of his toadies who then rushes away, to return a moment later with a whole squad of magicians in the most amazing coats Joseph has ever seen. For Joseph the rest of the dream slides by in a blur—the king's magicians turn their sticks into snakes too only to have silver-plate's snake gobble them up like a basket of honeycakes—because he cannot take his dream eyes off those coats. Panels of linen overlaid with braids of wool, every piece a different color, and hung with charms and talismans of stone and metal. *I want that*, the dream Joseph thinks to himself, and "I've got to have that" he says out loud the moment he wakes up.

He begins his campaign that very day, whining and posturing and even refusing to eat (later, he will blame the Beard for this fasting, as if his dreams infected him) until he wins over first his mother and then at last his father. With Jacob on his side, Joseph can ignore the complaints of his brothers, who claim it makes Joseph look like "a Hittite whore."

Joseph doesn't try for the talismans. Jacob probably could afford it, but Joseph knows his limits. Besides, it's the coat he cares about, all the colors, even more swirls than his cup of dreams. The day he gets it he struts all about the camp, the sides of it held open like the fan of a peacock—or maybe like a foolish baboon who does not know enough to protect his chest from his enemies.

That same night, Joseph dreams of the coat soaked in blood.

Joseph's dream power comes from his mother. "All power comes from mothers," Rachel tells him, and thereby sets aside the story Jacob likes, that Yah taught dream interpretation to Adam, who taught it to Seth, who taught it to Noah, whose animals dreamed every night on the boat, only to lose the knack when they walked down the ramp back onto the sodden earth. "Listen to me," Rachel whispers, "you think great men like Adam spent their time with dreams? It was Eve. And she didn't learn it from God, she learned it from the serpent. She bit into the apple and snipped off the head of a worm. And that's when people started to dream."

Joseph's worst moment comes in prison. He sits on his tailbone with his legs drawn up and his arms around his knees, trying to let as little of his body as possible touch the mud and slime of the floor. He's tried so hard, it's so unfair. No matter what terrible tricks Yah played on him—his brothers' hatred, his coat taken from him and streaked with blood—he's done his best, he's accepted it, really he has. And now this! And all because he tried to do something right. When your master's wife wants to screw you you're supposed to say no, right? Isn't that what Yah teaches (not that it's ever stopped Jacob, but that's not the point). And instead of a reward he has to sit in garbage and eat worse.

Something touches Joseph's sleeve. He screams and jerks back, certain it's a rat. But when he opens his eyes he sees two men not much older than himself. They wear linen and their hair is curled, signs they've fallen from a high place. "Please," one says. "You're the Hebrew who interprets dreams, aren't you? Will you help us? Please?"

"No," Joseph says. "Go away, leave me alone." And yet, he feels a certain tug of pleasure that his reputation as Potiphar's dream speaker has followed him into hell. He tries to ignore them, but they just stand there, looking so desperate, that finally he says, "Oh all right. Tell me your dreams."

The one who goes first announces that he was Pharaoh's chief wine steward before the court gossips slid him into jail. He tells Joseph, "In my dream I saw— I was in a garden. It was nighttime, I think. I looked up high and saw three branches. They began to bud. Blossoms shot forth. There were three ripe grapes. Suddenly, Pharaoh's cup was in my hand. Or maybe it was there before, I'm not sure. I squeezed the grapes in my hand. I poured the juice into the cup. I gave it to Pharaoh. He was just there and I gave it to him and he drank it."

Joseph rolls his eyes. This is not exactly a great mystery, he thinks. He says "All right, here's the meaning. In three days Pharaoh will lift up your head. He will examine your case and restore you to your office. You'll be safe from this filth and back in the palace. Congratulations."

The man claps his hands. "Blessed Mother Isis!" he cries. "Thank you!" He bends down to kiss Joseph's knees but Joseph pulls his legs even closer to his chest.

"Just promise me something," Joseph says. "When you're back pouring wine for Pharaoh, remember me? Tell him I don't deserve this."

"Oh yes," the man says, and claps his hands again.

"Now me," the other one says. He kneels down before Joseph and says, "In my dream I'm walking in the street behind the palace. There are three baskets on top of my head. Two of them are filled with white bread, but the one on top holds all the lovely things I bake for Pharaoh. Cakes shaped like Horus, a spelt bun like the belly of Hathor. Just as I'm thinking about how much the king will like them, birds come and pluck them away." He laughs, as if he's told a joke. "Right out of the basket. Now," he says, "tell me the meaning."

Joseph stares at him. He stares and stares at the man's eager face. *Why has Yah done this to me?* he thinks, but even that last shred of self-pity drains out of him, washed away in horror at such pathetic innocence.

"Go on, go on," the man insists.

Can he fake it? Joseph wonders. He tries to think of some story but his mind jams. He can't escape. Yah has set the truth on him like a pack of dogs. In a cracked whisper he says "In three days Pharaoh shall lift your head from your shoulders. He will hang you from a tree and the birds will eat your body."

The baker doesn't scream, only makes a noise deep in his chest. "Oh Gods," he says, "help me. Help me, please."

Joseph is stunned. No anger, no hate. No demands to change it or make it go away or even to think again. Just that trust. Without thought, Joseph wraps his arms around the man like a mother. "I'm sorry," he says, "I'm so sorry."

Joseph will stay two years in the prison before Pharaoh will dream a dream not found anywhere in the catalogues, and his wine steward, hearing of lean cows and fat cows, will remember the man he had promised not to forget. In all those months, Joseph will think of that empty promise only three or four times. But he will see the face of the baker every morning, before he opens his eyes.

People at court sometimes joke about the Viceroy's clay cup. Childish, they call it. Primitive. Hebrew. Visitors from Kush or Mesopotamia look shocked when they see him raise it in honor of Pharaoh's health. Their advance men, whose job it is to know all the gossip, whisper to them that Lord Joseph uses this cup to divine the future. Perhaps he sees visions in the wine, they say. Or perhaps—these are the views of the more scientifically minded—some impurity in the clay flakes off into the liquid and induces heightened states of awareness. The visitors shake their heads. That's all well and good, they say. He saved Egypt from famine, after all. But why does he drink from it in public?

During long dinners the Viceroy, like other men, will sometimes pause to swirl his barley wine, or else just stare blankly into his cup. At such times, all conversation, all breathing, stops, until Lord Joseph once more lifts up his eyes and makes some bland comment.

The princes, the courtiers, and the slaves all agree. The God Thoth visits Joseph at night, when together they discuss the secrets of the universe. A bright light leaks under the door of the Viceroy's bedchamber, and sometimes an alert slave will hear the flutter of Thoth's wings. And sometimes, they say, Thoth himself becomes the student, silent with wonder as Joseph teaches him secrets beyond the knowledge of Gods.

The boy Joseph curls himself up in the pit where his brothers have thrown him. Frozen in the desert night without his coat, he clutches the one treasure they didn't take from him, the cup his mother gave him, which he keeps always in a pouch on a cord around his waist. What will it be? A lion, a scorpion, a snake? Instead, before Judah and Simeon come back to sell him as a slave, a deep sleep takes him. He does not know it, but Yah has covered him with a foul smell that will drive away the beasts, for now is the time to dream. Joseph sees himself standing before a dark sky, with his arms out and his face lifted. A crown appears on his head. The crown becomes light, pure light that spreads through his body—his forehead, his mouth, his shoulders, all the way to his fingertips, light that streams out of him, through his heart and his lungs, even his entrails, if he shits he shits light, his penis ejaculates light, the muscles and bones of his legs pure light, his toes on fire with light. Joseph tries to cry out, but light rivers from his mouth.

And then it shatters. Broken light, broken Joseph splashes through the world, becomes darkness, becomes dust, becomes bodies and rock, light encased in darkness and bodies. And letters. Letters that fall from the sky, like drops of black flame.

Joseph wakes to the hands of the slave traders dragging him up from the dirt.

Does the Beard dream? Does the fire on his face allow him even to sleep? Or does he spend so much time chatting with Yah, punishing slackers, and writing, writing, writing, that he looks at dreams, and even the future, as a hobby for children and weak minds? After all, what does the Beard care about the future? He has his book. For him, time ends with the final letter.

When his brothers bully him, when they throw mud on his coat or trip him so he falls on pebbles sharp enough to splash his coat with blood, Joseph just wants to get back at them. In Jacob's tent one night he decides to make up a prophecy. "Listen, everybody," he announces, "I had a dream. Last night. A really good one." They roll their eyes or make faces but no one stops him. They don't want to believe in him, but they do. "Here it is," he says gleefully. "All of us were out in the fields binding sheaves. We stepped back from them, but my sheaf stood upright and all yours bowed down to it." He smiles. "What do you think?"

Silence. No one wants to look at anyone. At last, Reuben says "Since when do you ever go out and bind sheaves?" Inside their laughter, Joseph hears the whisper of fear.

That night, a dream comes to him. The Sun, the Moon, and eleven stars all bow down to him. He wakes up more scared than elated. He should keep it to himself, he knows. He's already got them mad; who knows what they'll do if he pushes this one at them? He pours some water into his cup from the gourd his mother's handmaids fill for him. Before he can drink, however, he sees in the bubbles everything that will follow—how the dream will provoke his brothers, how he will become a slave in Egypt, how he will rise to viceroy so that his family and in fact all Egypt will bow to him. It will not last, he sees. Their descendants will all become slaves, only to get free once more and stumble through the desert for forty years, *forty years*, before they can get back to their homeland. The vision doesn't last. Startled, he spills the water, and the details spill from his brain. And yet he knows now that everything leads to something else, that all his actions serve some secret purpose known only to Yah. Is it all just tricks, then? Do Yah's schemes ever come to an end?

He can stop it, he knows. All he has to do is never tell anyone the dream. Doesn't Grandpa Isaac claim God gives all of us free will? (He remembers his father whisper, "All except my brother Esau. He's too stupid.") If Joseph just keeps silent, the whole routine can never get started.

That afternoon, Zebulon kicks him and he blurts out, "You think you're so strong? I dreamed that the Sun and Moon and eleven stars all bowed down to me. That's right, eleven. What do you think of that?"

Joseph is old now, facing the blank door of death. He has blessed his children and his grandchildren and their children. Soon, he knows, the embalmers will suck out his brains, squirt the "blood of Thoth" into his body, wrap him in bandages, and encase him in stone. He wonders—if his descendants really do leave Egypt, will they find him and drag him along with them?

At the foot of his bed lies a wool and linen coat painted in swirls of color. Joseph has no idea how it got there. By the size of it it looks made for a boy, or maybe a shrunken old man. Next to the bed, on a little stand, sits his cup, as bright as the coat. He has told his slave to fill it with wine, though Joseph knows he lacks the strength to lift it, let alone pour it down his throat.

When he dies, will he see Rachel and Jacob? Or has he waited so long they've grown impatient and wandered off somewhere where he will never find them? He is alone now. The doctors and the magicians, his family, his servants, he's ordered them all away, and to his surprise they have listened. He wants more than anything to stay awake, so he can feel his soul, his *ka*, as the Egyptians call it, rattle around inside his body until it finds the way out. He tells himself that he's read all the papyruses, the "books of the dead," and wants to find out for himself. But he knows the real reason to stay awake. He doesn't want any more dreams. As always, however, Yah makes His own plans.

In his dream, Joseph sees the Burning Beard one more time. With his face even more of a blaze than usual, he and his brother accost Pharaoh in the early morning, when Pharaoh goes down to wash in the Nile. Joseph watches them argue, but all he can hear is a roar. Now the brother raises his staff, he strikes the water—and the Nile turns to blood! Joseph shouts but does not wake up. All over Egypt, he sees, water has turned to blood, not just the river but the streams and the reservoirs and even the wells. For days it goes on, with the old, the young, and the weak dying of thirst. Finally the water returns.

Only—frogs return with it. The entire Nile swarms with them. Soon they cover people's tables, their food, their bodies. And still more horrors follow. The brother strikes the dust and lice spring forth. Wild beasts roar in from the desert.

Joseph twists in agony, but Yah will not release him. He sees both brothers take fistfuls of furnace ash and throw them into the sky. A wind blows the ash over all the people of Egypt, and where it touches the skin, boils erupt. Now the Beard lifts his arms to the sky and hail kills every creature unfortunate enough to be standing outside. As if he has not done enough he spreads his hands at night and calls up an east wind to bring swarms of locusts. They eat whatever crops the hail has left standing. *No*, Joseph cries. *I saved these people from famine. Don't do this.* He can only watch as the Beard lifts his hand and pulls down three days of darkness.

And then—and then—when the darkness lifts, the firstborn of every woman and animal, from Pharaoh's wives and handmaids to the simplest farm slave who could never affect political decisions in any way, even the cows and the sheep and the chickens, the firstborn of every one of them falls down dead.

Just at the moment of waking up, Joseph sees that the finger of death has spared certain houses, those marked with a smear of lamb's blood. The Hebrews. Yah and the Beard have saved the Hebrews. Joseph's people. But aren't the Egyptians Joseph's people as well? And didn't he bring the Hebrews to Egypt? If all this carnage comes because the Hebrews have lived in Egypt, *is it all Joseph's fault?*

He wakes up choking. For the first time in days, his eyes find the strength to weep. He wishes he could get up and kneel by the bed, but since he cannot he prays on his back. "Please," he whispers. "I have never asked You for anything. Not really. Now I am begging You. Make me wrong. Make this one dream false. Make all my powers a lie. Take my gift and wipe it from the world. Do anything, *anything*, but please, *please, make me wrong.*"

But he knows it will not happen. He is Joseph ben Jacob, Lord Viceroy of dreams. And he has never made a wrong prediction in his life.

~

Joseph is my favorite character in the Bible—smart, gentle, non-violent, and a diviner, a seer. Stories about him and Moses are often pious and mawkish, based on Joseph's supposed longing to have his bones brought to the Promised Land, and Moses' dedication in doing that. In my vision,

Joseph loves Egypt and is horrified by Moses, and even more horrified by God, who is willing to kill vast numbers of innocent people just to make a point. The story blends the midrash tradition—fictions based on Biblical characters and moments—with modern slang and attitudes, Egyptian dream practices, references to Freud and so on. It is one of my two or three favorites among my own stories.

Rachel Pollack

Rats

Veronica Schanoes

What I am about to tell you is a fairy tale and so it is constantly repeating. Little Red Riding Hood is always setting off through the forest to visit her granny. Cinderella is always trying on a glass slipper. Just so, this story is constantly reenacting itself. Otherwise, Cinderella becomes just another tired old queen with a palace full of pretty dresses, abusing the servants when the fireplaces haven't been properly cleaned, embroiled in a love-hate relationship with the paparazzi. Beauty and Beast become yet another wealthy, good-looking couple. They are only themselves in the story and so they only exist in the story. We know Little Red Riding Hood only as the girl in the red cloak carrying her basket through the forest. Who is she during the dog days of summer? How can we pick her out of the mob of little girls in bathing suits and jellies running through the sprinkler in Tompkins Square Park? Is she the one who has cut her foot open on the broken beer bottle? Or is she the one with the translucent green water gun?

Just so, you will know these characters by their story. As with all fairy tales, even new ones, you may well recognize the story. The shape of it will feel right. This feeling is a lie. All stories are lies, because stories have beginnings, middles, and endings, narrative arcs in which the end is the fitting and only mate for the beginning—yes, that's right, we think upon closing the book. Yes, that's the way. Yes, it had to happen like that. Yes.

But life is not like that—there is no narrative causality, there is no foreshadowing, no narrative tone or subtly tuned metaphor to warn us about what is coming. And when somebody dies, it is not tragic, not inevitably brought on as fitting end, not a fabulous disaster. It is stupid. And it hurts. It's not all right, Mommy! sobbed a little girl in the playground who had skinned her knee, whose mother was patting her and lying to her, telling her that it was all right. It's not all right, it hurts! she said. I was there. I heard her say it. She was right.

But this is a fairy tale and so it is a lie, perhaps one that makes the stupidity hurt a little less, or perhaps a little more. You must not expect it to be realistic. Now read on. . . .

Once upon a time.

Once upon a time, there was a man and a woman, young and very much in love, living in the suburbs of Philadelphia. Now, they very much enjoyed living in the suburbs and unlike me and perhaps you as well, they did not at all regret their distance from the graffiti and traffic, the pulsing hot energy, the concrete harmonic wave reaction of the city. But happy as they were with each other and their home, there was one source of pain and emptiness that seemed to grow every time they looked into each other's eyes, and that was because they were childless. The house was quiet and always remained neat as a shot of bourbon. Neither husband nor wife ever had to stay at home nursing a child through a flu—neither of them ever knew what the current bug going around was. They never stayed up having serious discussions about orthodonture or the rising cost of college tuition, and because of this, their hearts ached.

"Oh," said the woman. "If only we had a child to love, who would kiss us and smile, and burn with youth as we fade into old age."

"Oh," the man would reply. "If only we had a child to love, who would laugh and dance, and remember our stories and family long after we can no longer."

And so they passed their days. Together they knelt as they visited the oracles of doctors' offices; together they left sacrifices and offerings at the altars of fertility clinics. And still from sunup to sundown, they saw their faces reflected only in the mirrors of their quiet house, and those faces were growing older and sadder with each glance.

One day, though, as the woman was driving back from the supermarket with the trunk of the station wagon, bought when they were first married and filled with dewy hope for a family, laden with unnaturally bright, unhealthily glossy fruits, vegetables, and even meat, she felt a certain quickening in her womb as she drove over a pothole, and she knew by the bruised strawberries she unpacked from the car that at last their prayers were answered and she was pregnant. When she told her husband he was as delighted as she and they went to great lengths to ensure the health and future happiness of their baby.

But even as the woman visited doctors, she and her husband knew the four shadows were lurking behind, waiting, and would come whether invited or not, so finally they invited the four to visit them. It was a lovely Saturday morning and the woman served homemade rugelach while the four shadows bestowed gifts on the child growing in her mother's womb.

"She will have an ear for music," said the first, putting two raspberry rugelach into its mouth at once.

"She will be brave and adventurous," said the second, stuffing three or four chocolate rugelach into its pockets to eat later.

But the third was not so kindly inclined—if you know this story, you know that there is always one. But contrary to what you may have heard, it was invited just as much as the others were, because while pain and evil cannot be kept out, they cannot come in without consent. In any case, there is always one. This is the way the story goes.

"She shall be beautiful and bold—adventurous and have a passion for music and all that," said the third. "But my gift to your child is pain. This child shall suffer and she will not understand why; she will be in pain and there will be no rest for her; she will suffer and suffer and she will always be alone in her suffering, world without end." The third scowled and threw a piece of raisin rugelach across the room. Some people are like that. Shadows too. The rugelach fell into a potted plant.

Sometimes cruelty cannot help itself, even when it has been placated with an invitation and excellent homemade pastry, and then what can you do?

You can do this: you can turn for help to the fourth shadow, who is not strong enough to break the evil spell—it never is, you know; if it were, there would be no story—but it can, perhaps, amend it.

So as the man and woman sat in shock, but perhaps not as much shock as they might have been had they never heard the story themselves, the fourth approached the woman, who had crossed her hands protectively over her womb.

"Now, my dear," it began, spraying crumbs from the six apricot rugelach it was eating. "Uncross your hands—it looks ill-bred and it does no good, you know. What's done is done, and I cannot undo it: you must bite the bullet and play the cards you're dealt. My gift is this: your daughter, on her seventeenth birthday, will prick herself on a needle and find a—a respite, you might say—and after she has done that, she will be able to rest, and eventually she will be wakened by a kiss, a lover's kiss, and she will never be lonely again."

And the soon-to-be parents had to be content with that.

After the woman gave birth to her daughter she studied the baby anxiously for signs of suffering, but the baby just lay, small, limp, and sweating in her arms, with a cap of black fuzz like velvet covering her head. She didn't cry, and hadn't, even when the doctor had smacked her, partially out of genuine concern for this quiet, unresponsive, barely baby, and partially out of habit, and partially because he liked to hit babies. She just lay in her mother's arms with her eyes squeezed shut, looking so white and soft that her mother named her Lily.

Lily could not tolerate her mother's milk—she could nurse only a little while before vomiting. She kept her eyes shut all day, as if even a little light burned her painfully. After she was home for a few days, she began to cry, and then she cried continuously and loudly, no matter how recently she had been fed or changed. She could only sleep for an hour at a time and she screamed otherwise, as though she were trying to drown out some other more distressing noise.

One afternoon, when Lily was a toddler, her mother laid her down for a nap and after ten or fifteen minutes dropped the baby-raising book she was reading in a panic. Lily's crying had stopped suddenly, and when her mother looked into her room, there was Lily smashing her own head against the wall, over and over, with a look of relief on her two-year-old face. When her mother rushed to stop her, she started screaming again, and she screamed all the while her mother was washing the blood off the wall.

She had night terrors and terrors in the bright sunshine and very few friends. She continued to hit her head against the wall. She tried to hit herself with a hammer and when she was prevented from doing so she laid about her, smashing her mother's hand. When her mother went to the emergency room to have her hand set and put in a cast the nurses clucked their tongues and told each other what a monster her husband must be.

When she got home she found Lily curled in a ball under the dining-room table, gibbering with fear of rats, of which there were none, and she would allow only her mother to speak to her.

Lily did love music. She snuck out of the house late at night and got rides into the city to see bands play, and she loved her father's recordings of Bach and Chopin as well. Back when she was three or four, Chopin had been the only thing that could get her to lie down and sleep. Chopin and phenobarbital. She wrote long reviews of new records for her school paper which were cut for reasons of space. As she got older, she got better and better at forcing the burning gnawing rats under her skin on the people around her. But she still felt alone because they could just walk away from her but she could not rip her way out of her skin her brain her breath although she tried so hard, more than once, but her mother caught her, put her back together, sewed her up, every single time, but not once could she clean Lily so well that she didn't feel the corrosion and corruption sliding through her veins, her lymph nodes, her brain, so that she didn't feel the rats burrowing through her body.

Lily ran away to New York City when she was sixteen and a half and in what her parents loathed, she found a kind of peace, in the neon lights and phantasmagoric graffiti that blotted out what was in her eyes and especially in the loud noises and the hard fast beats coming from CBGB that drowned out the rats clawing through her brain much better than her own screaming ever had, it was like banging her head against the wall from the inside. She knew there was something wrong with her—she talked to other people who loved the bands she saw because the fast and loud young and snotty sound wired them, jolted them full of electricity and sparks, but

Lily just sped naturally and all she wanted was to make it stop.

On her seventeenth birthday, Lily went home with a skinny man who played bass and shot heroin. Lily watched him cook the powder in some water over his lighter and stuck her arm out. "Show me how," she told him.

"You have easy veins," he told her, because her veins were large and close to the surface of her skin, fat and filled with rats. They showed with shimmering clarity, veiled only by the fleshy paper of her lily white skin.

He shot her up and just after the needle came away from her skin—it stopped. It really stopped, not just the rat-pain that she knew about, but the black tarpits of her thinking and feeling—they stopped too. It stopped, and God, it felt so good and free that she didn't mind the puking, it even felt fine, because everything else had stopped, and she could finally get some sleep, some real sleep.

The next morning she woke up and felt like shit again. And it was worse, because for a while she'd felt fine. Just fine.

We should all get to feel just fine sometimes.

So Lily found some kind of respite on a needle's tip and the marks it left were less obvious than the old dull hard scars on her wrists that she rubbed raw when she needed a fix. She worked as a stripper, using feathers, black gloves, and fetish boots to hide all kinds of scars, and sometimes in a midtown brothel. So she was often flush, and if she was still a holy terror, a mindfuck and a half, now she was flush, and had some calmer periods and a social circle, even if they did sometimes ignore her. She wrote pieces on music for underground papers, and once every two weeks her mother came to visit and bought her groceries and took her out to lunch and apologized when she threw cutlery at waiters and worried and worried over how thin Lily was becoming.

You can't stay high all the time, but you can try.

Lily knew she was getting thin. She would stare in the mirror and not see herself, and when she could put the rats to sleep she wasn't quite sure who she was or how she would know who she was.

Who are you? asked the caterpillar, drawing on his hookah. Keep your temper.

The rats were eating her from the inside out and she was dissolving, she was real only under her mother's eyes—the power of her mother's gaze held her bones together even as her ligaments and skin slowly liquefied, dissipating in a soft-focus movie dissolve.

Dissolve.

Fade in. We are in London with Lily, far enough away from her mother that she could dissolve entirely. Lily had heard that there was something happening in London, something that could shut down the banging slamming violence in her skull even better than the noise at CBs, some kind of annihilation.

There was.

Look at Lily at the Roxy, if you can recognize her. Can you find her? She is in the bathroom, shooting herself up with heroin and water from the toilet. She is out front sitting by the stage, sitting on the stage, sitting at the bar, throwing herself against the wall so violently that she breaks her own nose. The rats are still following her, snapping and snarling at anybody who comes near, and when nobody comes near, they turn on themselves, begin to eat themselves, gnaw on their own soft bellies.

Can you recognize Lily? When her face and form began to dissolve in the mirror, she panicked and knew she had to take some drastic action before she blinked and found only a mass of rats where her reflection should be, a feeding frenzy. In London the colors were bright like the sun when you have a hangover, so bright it hurt to look at them. The clothing was made to be noticed, to cause people to shrink back and flinch away. Lily wanted to look like that. She bleached her hair from chestnut brown to white blonde and left dark roots showing. She back-combed it so a frizzy mess stood out around her head like a halo: Saint Lily, Our Lady of the Rats. She drew large black circles around both eyes, coloring them in carefully. She outlined her lips even more carefully, and the shine on them is blinding. Her black clothing was covered in bright chrome like a 1950s car.

She was visible then. She could see herself when she looked in the mirror, bright and blonde, outlined in black. Covered in rats.

Her mother thought she looked like a corpse.

Everyone can see her now, everyone who matters, anyway. She is out and about and she is sleeping with the young man playing bass, well, posing with the bass, on stage. He is wearing tight black jeans, no shirt, and a gold lamé jacket. He is a year older than she. Neither of them is out of their teens. They are children. Despite everything, their skin looks new and shiny.

She had been frightened of him the first time they met. Now she was visible, but that came with a certain price as well. Usually the rats kept everyone at arm's length if that close, so that no matter how desperately she threw herself at people they shied away. They knew enough to be frightened by the rats, even if they couldn't see them, even if they didn't know they were there. They told themselves, told each other that they avoided her because she was nasty, the most horrible person in the world, a liar, a selfish bitch, and she was, she knew she was, but really they were afraid of the rats.

But the rats stood aside when Chris came near. They drew back at his approach, casting their eyes down and to the side as if embarrassed by their own abated ferocity. There was something familiar about him, but Lily was too confused by the rats' unusual behavior to think much about what it was. Chris was slight with skin so pale that Lily longed to bruise him and watch the spreading purple, skin that had sharp lines etched into it by smoke and sleeplessness, and zits all over his face. One of them was infected. When he spoke she could barely understand him, his voice was so deep and the vowels so impenetrable.

When she shot him up he said it was his first time but she knew better from the way he brought his sweet blue veins up so that they almost floated above the surface of his sheer skin. When they fucked later that night she could tell that it was his first time.

Lily didn't have much curiosity left—it hurt too much to be awake and she tried to dull herself as much as possible. But while they were kissing for the first time she felt a chill that startled her into wakening and she looked over his shoulder and saw what was so familiar about her Chris (she knew he was hers and she his now). Over his shoulder she saw his rats—just a few, younger than hers, but growing and mating and soon the two of them would be locked together, breaking skin with needles and teeth, surrounded by flocks of rats that could no longer be distinguished or separated out, just a sea of lashing tails and sharp teeth and clutching claws. But she wouldn't be alone, he would see them too, and he wouldn't be alone, she would see them too, their children, their parents, their rats.

Do you recognize this story yet? Perhaps you've seen the T-shirts on every summer camp kid on St. Marks Place as they fantasize about desperation and hope that self-destruction holds some kind of romance.

Do you recognize this story yet? Perhaps you've read bits of interviews here and there: she was nauseating, she was the most horrible person in the world, she was a curse, a dark plague sent to London on purpose to destroy us, she turned him into a sex slave, she destroyed him, say the middle-aged men and occasional women who look back twenty-five years at a schizophrenic teenage girl with a personality disorder shooting junk—because here and now we still haven't figured out a way to make that kind of illness bearable—who'd wanted to die since she was ten because she hurt so much, and what they see is a frenzied harpy. She destroyed him.

And her? What about her?

Can we not weep for her?

Look again at those photographs and home movies and look at how young they were. Shiny. Not old enough ever to have worried about lines on her face, or knees that ached with the damp, or white hairs—every ache and twinge is a fucking blessing and don't you forget it.

Do you recognize this story yet?

Don't you already know what happens next?

Kiss kiss kiss fun fun lies. Yes oh yes we're having fun. I'm so happy!

Kiss kiss kiss fight fight fight. He hit her and she wore sunglasses at night. She trashed his mother's apartment. He left her and turned back at the train station. He was running by the time he got back to the squat they had been sharing—he had a vision of Lily sprawled on the floor dying—not alone, please, anything but alone. He lifted her head up onto his lap; her heart was beating still but her lips were turning blue. His mum had been a nurse and he knew how to make her breathe again.

Kiss.

On tour with the band, away from Lily, he became a spitting wire, destroying rooms, grabbing pretty girls from the audience, shitting all over them, smashing himself against any edge he could find, carving his skin so that he became a pustule of snot and blood and shit and cum where oh where was his Lily Lily I love you.

The band broke up. He could fuck up but he couldn't play. They moved to New York and bopped around Alphabet City. They tried methadone and they needed so much they stopped bothering and anyway methadone only stopped the craving for heroin; it didn't give her any respite. When they were flush they spent money like it was going out of style, on smack, on makeup, on clothing, on presents for each other.

She bought him a knife.

If there is a knife in the story, somebody will have to get stabbed by the end.

Lily knows that she can't stand much more of this, much more of herself, much more of her jonesing, much more of the endless days trapped in a gray room in a gray city, and even though it's all gray the city still hurts her eyes, it's a kind of neon gray. The effort it takes just to open her eyes in the morning (afternoon), just to get dressed is too much and if she could feel desire any more, if she could want anything, all she would want would be to stop fighting, stop moving, to sink back and let herself blur and dissolve under warm blankets.

But the smack-sickness shakes her down and she has to move.

Even her rats are weak, she can see. They are staggering and puking. Sometimes they half-heartedly bite one another. She wants to die, but her Chris takes too good care of her, except when he hits her, for that to happen.

When they were curled up together under the covers back in London, which is already acquiring the coloring of a home in her quietly bleeding memory, Lily had asked Chris how much he loved her. More than air, he said. More than smack. Would you douse yourself in gasoline and set yourself on fire if I needed you to? she asked. Yes, he said. Would you set me on fire if I needed you to? she asked. Not that, he said. I love you, I couldn't live without you, don't, don't, don't leave me alone. Not that. Anything but alone.

The regular chant of lovers.

If I needed you to? she pressed. Wouldn't you do it if I needed you to?

He couldn't. He wouldn't.

Then you don't really love me at all, she told him, if you don't love me enough to help me when I need it.

So he had to say yes. And he had to promise.

Now, in piercing gray New York City she puts the knife in his hand and reminds him of his promise. He pushes her away. No. But he doesn't drop the knife. Perhaps he's forgotten to. She reminds him again and somehow she finds energy and drive she hasn't had in months to scream and berate and plead in a voice like fingernails on a blackboard. She hits him with his bass and scratches at his sores. A man keeps his promises, she tells him. A real man isn't scared of blood.

She winds up shaking and crying to herself on the bathroom floor when Chris comes in, takes her head on his lap and stabs her in the gut, wrenching the knife up towards her breasts. He goes on stabbing and sawing and stroking her forehead until she stops breathing.

The last things she sees are the expression of blank, loving concern on his face and the rats swarming in as her blood spreads across the bathroom tiles.

He watches the rats gnaw on the soft flesh of her stomach and crawl through her body in triumph until finally he watches them lie down and die, exposing their little bellies to the ceiling. The next morning, he remembers nothing.

The police find him sitting bolt upright in bed, staring straight ahead, with the knife next to him. They take Lily away in a body bag. No more kisses.

He is dying now, he thinks. Her absence is slowly draining his blood away. His rats are all dead and their corpses appear everywhere he looks.

You know the rest of the story. He dies a month later of an overdose procured for him by his mother. Why are you still reading? What are you waiting for? The kiss? But he kissed her already, don't you remember? And she woke up, and afterward she was never alone.

They were children, you know. And there still are children in pain and they continue to die and for the people who love them that is not romantic. Their parents and friends don't know what is going to happen ahead of time. They have no narrator. When these children die, all that is left is a blank, an absence, and friends and parents lose the ability to see in color. The future takes on a different shape and they go into shock, staring into space for hours. They walk out into traffic and they don't see the trucks, don't hear the horns. A mist lifts and they find that they have pinned the messenger to the wall by his throat. They find themselves calling out names on streets in the dead of night. Walking up the block becomes too hard and they turn back. They can't hear the doctor's voice.

Death is not romantic; it is not exciting; it is no poignant closure and it has no narrative causality. There are even now teenagers—children—slicing themselves and collapsing their veins and refusing to eat because the alternative is worse, and their deaths will not be a story. Instead there will be an empty place in the future where their lives would have been. Death has no narrative arc and no dignity, and now you can silkscreen these two kids' pictures on your fucking T-shirt.

~

> "Yesterday I thought I was a crud. Then I saw the Sex Pistols, and I became a king."—Joe Strummer, 1976

Punk rock saved my life when I needed it most. The Clash—Joe Strummer in particular—made me feel powerful, like there was lightning in my blood, and I don't think I'm the only one, though I guess I don't care if I am. But nothing works for everybody; punk rock wasn't enough to save Nancy Spungen's life, and it wasn't enough to save Sid Vicious either. I wrote "Rats" because I was angry with the way the recent coffee-table histories of punk seem to have no problem with demonizing a dead, mentally ill, teenage girl. This story is about what it means to grieve for the suffering of a thoroughly unpleasant, even hateful, person (it's easier when you've never had to deal with her personally, of course).

"Rats" is at war with the idea of Story even while it uses the most traditional narrative conventions. Its main character is a girl about whom nobody, myself included, has a good word to say, so it can take place only between the lines of what people *do* say. Those tensions make the story interstitial: it is tearing itself apart in order to lay bare the violence inherent in the very notion of Story. "Rats" invokes recent history, and then peels it back to reveal the magical thinking that is truer to experience than realism ever can be—the rats in the walls.

Veronica Schanoes

Climbing Redemption Mountain

Mikal Trimm

When Pa died, it was generally agreed that he might not make it to the happy side of the Afterlife. He just hadn't been sweet enough to tip the scales the right way.

"Friends, we have a soul here in grave need of intervention. The journey to Salvation comes at a price, and our Brother Lemuel Task is a few dollars short of the fare."

So said Reverend Samuels, and the rest of the congregation nodded in response.

Cole and me sat in our pew, heads bowed, lips moving, and tried not to squirm. We knew what was coming and prayer wasn't going to change things.

"Brother Task needs to travel the long, hard road, friends. He needs to go up Redemption Mountain. Can I get an *amen*?"

"Amen!" our neighbors chanted.

Amen, and amen, and damn y'all to Hell, Cole whispered, his face going gray under the tan.

I just sat there, picturing the Mountain.

We wrapped Pa up good and tight in real linen, and Maisy Reynolds painted a bunch of Paradise scenes on his wrappings. She really knew her Bible, and Pa's body could've been displayed at one of them fancy museums in France or Germany or New York. There was Moses as a baby in his basket, and David with his guitar, and a whole lot of saints and prophets with long beards and long faces. Mary was there, too, right there where the cloth bunched up around Pa's nethers.

Mary looked kind of like Maisy. Not sure what that meant.

The whole town came out to build the Heaven-Cart. Darby Wheelwright and Jamie Cooper and Kurt Smithy—even old Burly Mason, who didn't really have anything to do with the cart but lent moral support by yelling at people a lot and pointing.

Ladies brought basket lunches and lemonade, and the little ones ran around the fields playing *Soul-Catcher* or *Bear-the-Cross*, just like Cole and me did back before Mama died.

Course, Mama never went up Redemption Mountain. Her soul's done gone.

Pa was another story.

The Heaven-cart looked like a big beer barrel tipped over sideways. No tap, no lid. Two big wheels with heavy wooden spokes and thick iron rims, and two padded handles up front, so the folks pulling the cargo wouldn't get blisters.

Pa went into the open top of the barrel. Me and Cole took up the handles, taking a minute to settle the leather pads on our shoulders.

Reverend Samuels gave the send-off speech, speaking the words like they were new-born.

"'The road is narrow, and few there are who follow it.' Thus saith the Lord." *Amen.* "'Treat thy neighbor as thyself.' Thus saith the Lord." *Amen, Brother, amen.* "'We are all brothers and sisters under the eyes of God,' thus saith the Lord." *Amen, amen, amen, Brother.* "'Your neighbor is your brother or your sister; we are all family in His eyes.' Thus saith the Lord." *Amenamenamen.* "'Forgive your brothers and sisters, your *family*, a thousand times and a thousand times again.' Thus saith the Lord."

A hush.

"'And help them carry their burdens, as you would want them to help you.'"

"Thus. Saith. The Lord!"

The folks answered so loud they could've shook the floor out of Paradise itself.

"Heard it all before." Cole kept wiggling around, like he was already pulling the cart. He spat on his hands and gripped his handle, like that would do some good.

"You ain't never hauled a Heaven-cart, Cole. I can't even remember the last time we built one."

Cole shrugged his shoulders, finding the most comfortable place to let the handle rest. "Still heard it all before. Reverend-talk.

Lots of words that don't mean nothin'."

"They're *Book-words*, little brother. Don't ever forget that."

Cole found his spot, lifted his side of the Heaven-cart. " 'Less you learned to read since this morning, *big brother*, you don't know no more'n I do." He nodded toward Reverend Samuels, spat. "Neither does he."

"You saying you don't believe? You gonna go heretic on us?" I hadn't even grabbed my handle yet, and Cole already had my dander up.

"I'm sayin', shut up and pull."

We started up Redemption Mountain, Pa behind us and a long hard road ahead.

Maisy Reynolds ran up and planted a quick kiss on my cheek. "You get this man to the top, Ben. You make sure he gets saved. For m— for your dead ma's sake."

Then she was gone, back with the rest, and I wondered why she cared so much.

Cole lurched forward, and I grabbed and pulled just to keep from being run over.

Shouts and prayers echoed from the valley. Hard to tell which was which.

I never really noticed how much bigger Cole was than me until we started pulling that cart up the mountain.

Two years younger than me, and he outweighed me by twenty pounds at least, all of it muscle. Taller, too, not by much, but enough so it counted, especially when I was trying to match my step with his and keep the handle in a comfortable spot on my shoulder.

So while he trudged along with his cart-handle in an easy notch next to his collarbone, I pushed my legs harder to keep up, and the handle on my side kept hitting me in the same spot, *thwack, thwack*, until I could feel the blisters forming across my neck and shoulder.

I knew I couldn't say a word, though. I was the older brother. I was the *man*. We were taking Pa to Eternity, and I had to be strong.

We walked for hours, hauling Pa's body along a well-worn

path. The rise stayed even, but I could tell we weren't making a lot of progress to the top.

"How long you think this'll take? No one ever mentions it, you know? Like they're not sure or something."

Cole plodded along, not even turning his head when he answered me. "Don't know. Don't care. Takes as long as it takes."

"Ain't you even curious? C'mon, Cole, it's been a long time since anyone we know's done this. Don't you think about what's up there?"

Cole stopped dead. My handle slid off my shoulder, and I felt the cart try to twist sideways. I grabbed hard on the raw wood knob at the end, splinters ramming into my palm.

"I don't want to think, Ben. I just want to get this damn rig up the mountain and drop it off. Don't care who was here before, don't care who'll be here after." Cole took a deep breath, readjusted his hold on the cart, and spat a thick glob right next to my shoe. "Any more questions?"

I took the hint. *Shut up and pull.*

Right after we started up again, the blisters popped.

I hardly even noticed.

The trail got rougher. The wagon shook and moaned, and I wondered if Pa's soul was beating the slats trying to get out. The wheels went off-balance, pitted by rocks and roots, and even Cole grunted under the strain of pulling the thing along.

Then we hit a nasty switchback that took us around an old, weathered oak and a jagged crack in the rock itself. We fretted with the cart for near an hour, nursing the wheels around roots and wedges of rock, finally able to get the rig facing up the slope again—

—and they were everywhere.

Heaven-carts. No two alike, big and small, different woods, shapes, wheels. Sitting there abandoned, some near whole, others just skeletons. Ribs of wood, rims of rust. They slumped together on either side of the path—the *end* of the path—crippled and forgotten.

Like Pa, almost. Like his gray old soul.

"Why are these all here?" I kept staring at the wrecks of carts, couldn't move to save my life. Pa's Heaven-cart got heavier, and I felt the pain shoot across my raw shoulder until Cole lifted the handle off me and pushed me away.

"Looks like the carts only make it this far." Cole didn't spare me a glance. He just looked further up-mountain, whistling between his teeth.

I finally quit tallying the wagons and saw what Cole saw—no path, no way for a cart or even a horse to pass. Just broken rock and dried-up shrubs and a long, rough climb to the top.

"We gotta *carry* him?"

I turned to look at Cole, but he'd already moved on, checking out the other wagons.

"Don't suppose that's necessary, Ben."

"What's that mean?"

"Means," Cole said, tugging a length of yellowed linen from one of the abandoned carts, "this looks like the end of the line, big brother."

Something rattled when he pulled the cloth, and toe-bones spilled out and bounced across the path.

Everything spun, and I sat down hard beside Pa's Heaven-cart. I might've even passed out for a minute—I saw the little demon-spots you see when the Devil steals your breath. My ears buzzed with a swarm or two of bees.

I heard Mama's voice, way back in the distance, talking about planting seeds . . .

Then Cole slapped me upside the head, just like Pa used to do when I got lost in there, and it all came back.

"Let's take a look in those wagons, Cole. That alright with you?"

Cole shook his head, then helped me stand up again.

Lot of the carts was empty.

Lots more weren't.

I looked inside the rotting Heaven-carts. Bones and cloth, sometimes even skin like leather holding the pieces together. A God-damned mess, and I wasn't cursing when I said it.

Cole snickered when I blasphemed. "Don't think God had

nothin' to do with this. Just looks like a lot of folk don't care much about redemption. Leastwise, not 'less it's their own."

"Pa doesn't deserve this. Don't know who these folks were," and I turned a circle, arms up, taking in all the unsaved dead, "but Pa ain't staying here. He's taking the narrow path."

"Fine. You want to carry him first?"

I looked around at all the abandoned carts, and all I could think of was Ma. She always had some use for everything, no matter how old and worn. She used to say it was a sin to waste anything, even if it was broken.

Rope and wood, canvas and linen—this place wasn't a graveyard, not if you looked at it like Ma would've.

"Give me some help, little brother, and we won't have to carry him at all."

For one of the few times in his life, Cole didn't give me any backtalk.

The trail was there, if you looked real hard.

Me and Cole pulled Pa behind us on a makeshift stretcher. We'd put pieces together, a bit of frayed rope here, some canvas from an old cart there, couple of cart-handles, even some linen from one of the old skeletons. Cole got that—I figured we could use it, but I couldn't make myself unwrap the bones. I wanted to try and bolt some wheels on there, but we couldn't make a new shaft, so we wound up just dragging the contraption behind us.

Still, it was better than having to carry Pa's stiff body.

Besides Pa, the only things we took from our own Heaven-cart were our water-skins and some wrapped vittles, mostly hardtack and waxed cheese. Some folks had thrown prayer-beads and luck-wreaths in the cart with Pa, but we figured we didn't need to carry anything we didn't have to.

Good thing, too. The way up got harder and harder, and sometimes me and Cole had to pick up Pa's stretcher and balance him over our heads to make it through a tight turn. My arms hated me, and even Cole trembled whenever we got the chance to put Pa down.

We hit a nice flat expanse, and Pa went down without us even trying to agree about it. The sky turned purple while we caught our breath, and the air got chillier. My clothes clung to my body, wet with sweat and colder by the minute. Pa's body, tethered to the stretcher by fraying ropes, looked too solid in its wrappings, like a petrified log.

No heavier than the weight of the Cross, as Ma used to remind us when we complained about hard tasks.

Cole flopped on the ground spread-eagle, eyes closed and breathing rough.

"That's it for today, Ben. We ain't making the top any time soon, and I need some food and rest. My back don't like Pa much right about now."

I wanted to argue some, but truth was I couldn't take another step. Cole was bigger than me, stronger, and he probably could've gone another mile or two, but I figured he was giving me an out.

That's what I figured, anyway. Been wrong before, will be again.

Just not about Cole.

Baby?

Mama's talking. *I hear you, Ma.*

Don't be afraid, son. You're on the right path. I think your Daddy's calling . . .

"Ben."

Even the moon had drifted off. "What's wrong? Pa move or something?"

"Why are you doing this?"

I remembered Ma's voice from the dream, but the words got lost when I opened my eyes. Cole sat by the remains of our campfire, staring at me. I don't think he'd slept a wink since we settled down for the night.

"What, sleeping? Snoring?"

"You know what I mean."

I could barely make out Pa's body at the edge of the embers' glow, out of reach of stray sparks. "Yeah, I know what you mean. I just don't know what you're askin'. Why are *you* doing it?"

Cole shrugged, looked out past Pa into the darkness. "'Cause you are, I guess. Don't really have a choice, comes down to it."

"You always got a choice, Cole. If nobody ever had choices, we'd all be pure good or pure evil, no two ways about it. There wouldn't be no need for Redemption Mountain, 'cause we'd know where people were goin' when they died, no question."

"That's Reverend-talk again. You might as well go join the church-school and learn to read, way you go on."

I didn't like the way Cole was talking. Scared me some, truth to tell. "That ain't just talk, Cole. We all learn right from wrong sooner or later. Pa just . . ."

"Pa just didn't know how to tell the difference?" Cole pulled up close to me, watching my face, his eyes glimmering with ember-sparks.

"Don't do that, Cole. Don't pretend you know what I was thinkin'. Pa had a hard time of things, is all."

"He beat us, Ben. He drank and carried on something fierce. Just 'cause he never killed nobody or run off with someone's wife or stole from his neighbors, that don't make him worth savin'."

I didn't want to listen to this anymore. Pa was Pa. *Our* Pa, our flesh, our blood. "If he wasn't worth tryin' to save, why you think Ma married him in the first place?"

Cole laughed, but it was a Devil-laugh, dark and nasty, filled with secrets. "Pa always said you was a mama's boy, Ben. You know that? Nope, guess you wouldn't. He only told me, times when we was in the fields workin' and you was starin' off into space like you do. He'd say, 'Cole, I want you to look good and hard at your brother. That's what happens when you let a woman have too much time in a boy's life. I done failed Ben, but you ain't goin' down that same road. I promise you that, son, I surely swear it.'"

"You're lyin', Cole. You want me to hate Pa and give up tryin' to save his soul." But Cole's voice even sounded like Pa's when he told me all that, and I knew Pa'd probably said it. I knew Cole got beat lots more than me, too, back before Ma died.

Once she was gone it all evened out.

Cole quit smiling. He lay back down and closed his fire-touched eyes.

"Yeah. I'm lyin'. Go back to sleep."

"Cole, I—"

"But think about this, big brother. If Pa was so great, if he wasn't just a mean old *sumbitch* . . ." Cole's voice got soft as the crackling embers, but I heard him, heard him inside where the words kept burning long after he said them.

". . . then why did Ma kill herself?"

Cole slept after that. I stayed up, looking into the red glow of the dying fire and searching for Ma's face in the ashes.

I don't know when I fell asleep, but when I woke up Cole was gone. Took the food, all the water-skins but one, and left me there sleeping. Didn't even bother to leave me the flint-stone.

Don't know where he planned on going. Back down the mountain? What would he tell the folks back home? He got tired and left? Pa wasn't worth it?

I died on the way?

The fire was dead-cold, and the fog was up. The sun snuck some rays around the mountain, but I couldn't make out much more than ghost-shapes dancing around me. I thought about all those bodies left behind in the Heaven-carts, and all the souls trapped here, never able to reach the end of their journey.

They stood there in the mist. They *were* the mist.

I heard their voices. No words, just moans and whispers, like they wanted me to help them all but they didn't know how to ask proper. Lots of lost folk, praying for someone to come take them up the mountain.

Maybe I heard Pa's voice out there. Maybe he needed to tell me something—

Lord, oh Lord, I forgot about Pa's body.

I ignored the voices best I could, and the mist finally died off in the morning light.

Pa's body lay there, his fine linen wrappings sliced up and flapping in the breeze. I saw his skin peeking out through the deepest cuts, gray and all dried-up, like something a snake left behind. Cole left Pa's head covered—guess maybe even my little brother didn't have the guts to look at Pa when he did this.

Pa's wrapped head rested on a pile of broken sticks, torn canvas, and frayed rope. Took me a full minute before I figured out what Cole had done.

The stretcher.

Cole took Pa's last chance for making Redemption and turned it into a pillow. I swear I heard Cole's voice, deep and nasty like it was last night.

Sleep real good now, Pa. Don't say I never done nothin' for you.

I wondered how I could've slept through the noise. Wondered if maybe I'd heard something in my sleep and decided not to wake up on purpose.

And all them other voices came back right about then, saying one word, over and over.

No, no, no, no, no . . .

Make a man outta you yet, boy.

I carried Pa over my left shoulder for a while, 'till I felt something dripping down my chest, warm and sticky.

Wasn't Pa's blood, he was nice and dry. Don't know what they do to bodies before the trip up Redemption, but Pa didn't seep or drip or smell. I thought he was heavy when we started out, but a grown man should've weighed more than Pa did, all said and done.

The blood was mine. I just forgot what I was doing and used my cart-shoulder. All those broke blisters got rubbed raw and started bleeding.

Moved the body, kept on walking. Pa wasn't so heavy after all, now I'd put my mind to it.

Pebbles shifted under my feet, like to broke my toes more than once. I learned to walk careful, get a good footing before I took another step. Roots that looked to be strong enough to break Redemption's face until I grabbed at them tore out of crannies with one half-assed tug. Deer-trails petered out before they hit water.

Redemption Mountain was making fun of me.

C'mon, boy. Show me your ma didn't take all the piss and vinegar out of you. Keep on climbin', boy. Prove your brother wrong.

I kept on climbing.

Put some back into it, boy! Prove you got somethin' between your legs 'sides skeeter bites! Show me what you got hangin' in your sack!

Rock and scraggly bush, then no roots or branches at all, just crags and shale and a long blank face of mountain . . .

Wrong way, boy! Ain't you got no sense? Go back down and hit this damn mountain where it counts. Watch the ground, find the trail, work boy work boy work work work—

My feet hit more loose gravel and I fell over, Pa's weight dragging me down so fast I couldn't even try to balance myself. I landed on my knees first, felt a sharp pain and heard bone snap, and twisted toward the hard face of the mountain, trying to save Pa and me together.

Something tore across my back, a knife cutting a canyon down my spine. I waited for the fall down Redemption.

And I just lay there. Hard rock under me, Pa's body stiff and cold on top of me. My knees played dead and my back screamed with pure burning hurt, but I didn't feel like I broke anything inside.

I shoved Pa off, slow and careful. Something under me rolled around like kindling.

I managed to pull myself up, hugging the face of the mountain for all I was worth.

Bones.

Scattered around my feet, strung together with tatters of rotted cloth bindings. Lots of the bones were broke, and I saw fresh blood on some of them, my blood, dripping down a rib here or a leg there, like they was trying to come alive again.

Pa rested there in the pile, waiting to join up with his kin, knee-bone to cheek-bone, spine to ribcage. My knees felt like vine-rot melons and my spine wanted to tear away and head off to a better place.

Pa looked comfortable.

I stood there and laughed, thinking of Cole and Pa and all them folk down at the foot of the mountain.

'Cause, see, someone made it this far. Not everybody gave up with the carts.

That was pretty much it for the day. I fell down by Pa's body and slept with him, there between the bones.

I dreamed about Mama . . .

Coming in from the fields, me and Cole and Pa tired and sweaty and aching, ready for dinner, ready for the hot-sweet smell of Ma's cooking, and Pa lights up first, his nose working faster than his body ever did.

He runs, hits the back porch, slams through the dutch-door before me and Cole even know something's wrong, and—

No.

Coming in from the fields, me and Cole and Pa tired and sweaty and—

No.

Coming in from the fields—

No, and no, and no again, and the dream keeps playing over and over and I know it's wrong, it ain't true, it's a lie in my head that don't do nobody no good but me.

Want to wake up now. Can I wake up now? Pa's getting mighty lonely, he needs to get up that mountain and be with the rest of the redeemed . . .

Ma's voice. Remember, child. The path won't be easier if you pave it with lies.

I come in from the fields. Been stuck in my head again, and Pa slapped me and cussed me all day, but I just kept slipping away.

"Go on home, boy. You ain't no good to anybody like that. Me and your brother'll finish up here, you see if you can help your Mama with dinner."

"Do some girl's *work," I heard Cole snigger, but Pa slapped Cole harder than he slapped me and Cole shut up fast.*

Skip-skip, *the dream jerks around. Ma's not on the porch shelling peas.* Skip-skip, *and the kitchen stove's cold, no fire lit, much less banked.* Skip-skip, *and I'm out of the house, calling for Ma, ain't no place she'd be but* home, *and now I'm soaked and aching, looking for Ma, looking and looking for Ma Ma Ma—*

Skip. Skip. *Lord oh Lord, please let me skip this—*

—But there I am in the barn, wondering if some critter got in there

and spooked one of the milk-cows, and I hear a bat squeaking, but it's broad daylight, can't be a bat—

Don't look up, Ben. Just a dream. Wakey wakey, Ben-my-baby, *like Ma used to say. God damn you if you look up—*

Ma stares at me, hanging from the rafters, her face purple and swollen, her tongue big as a cow's, thrusting out between her black lips . . .

Just couldn't see the Light anymore, baby. *Ma's voice, sweet and soft, talking from that dead mouth.*

You see it though, baby-mine. You see it more than I ever did.

Wakey wakey, c'mon, Ben . . .

You just follow the path, honey. You keep going. Ain't none of us lost yet . . .

And Ma stares at me with those cloudy eyes, and I sit there and cry until Pa and Cole come home.

Morning came, and aches and hunger and tiredness and fear, all one big package, tied up in torn bandages, glittering with frost.

Took me three tries to get Pa settled again. My knees stretched the cloth of my jeans they was so swelled up, but like I figured, nothing was broke, Lord be praised. My back throbbed, gashed raw by a jagged edge of Redemption rock.

I wanted to guzzle water to make up for the hollow place in my stomach, but I managed to take just a trickle, knowing that whatever was left in the skin might be all I'd get.

Pa felt heavy again. Redemption Mountain looked tall enough to reach Heaven itself. My legs trembled like a newborn colt's. *Goin' down's a lot easier than goin' up, big brother.* Cole's voice, whispering his Devil-talk in my ear.

Then Pa on my back, telling me *you go, boy. You just put one foot down then the other and quit thinkin' so goldarned much! And mind the path!*

One foot in front of the other. No thinking about pain or hunger or anything else but the end of the trail.

Redemption.

~

Couldn't help thinking, whatever Pa might've wanted. Had to keep my head full of noise just to drown out the pain and hunger and plain cussed tiredness.

So I kept walking, and I listened.

Cole asks why Ma killed herself, Pa says keep on walkin' boy, Ma says she lost the Light, Maisy Reynolds paints her picture on Pa and tells me to save him for Ma's sake, Reverend Samuels says—

Dead end, I missed a turn somewhere, and there's no way to go forward, so I go back, back, looking for the true path to the top.

—Maisy says save him for my sake, no no, for your dead Ma's sake, that's it, and Reverend Samuels tells us that taking your own life is the one unforgivable sin, you're turning your back on God and His wisdom, you're giving up on Eternity, so no Heaven-cart for Elspeth Task, God-have-mercy-on-our-Sister's-damned-soul—

Sip of water, glance at the setting sun, prayer for time and strength.

—Cole says Pa says Ma says Reverend-talk Mary's face staring at me from Pa's shriveled loins—

The mountain gave me a flat spot and I fell down, Pa covering me like the bony hand of Death.

Ma, your son's comin' to you.

And Ma's voice, the only dream I had left, *Not lookin' for my son, Ben. Just bring me my husband.*

I woke up with the sun drifting over the mountain. Pa lay there, his wrappings brown and gray from dirt, an ugly bundle of sin.

Cole said something about Pa. *He drank and carried on somethin' fierce . . .*

Yep. You ain't lying, Cole, he did.

Just 'cause he never run off with someone's wife . . .

Nope, he never did that either, little brother.

'Course, Maisy Reynolds never got married.

Pa jumped in. *Don't you be thinkin', boy. Don't you try to find sin when you ain't got no proof.*

Ma's face, black lips and all, Pa. Ain't that proof?

And Ma, always Ma, taking his side. *Ben-my-baby, Ben-my-strong-young-man, you don't know the truth, honey. You ain't the judge, you ain't a Reverend, and you can't ever be God.*

Not fair, Ma, not after what he done to you!

Wake up, son. Just 'cause you see the sun don't mean your eyes are open.

I cried. Just sat there, not much water left in my skin, and bawled like a baby. *I'm hungry, Ma, and I'm cold, and I'm tired, and this mountain don't ever end, it just keeps growing like that Tower of Babel, and I want to go home now. Can I go home now, Ma? Pa? Cole? Won't somebody answer me?*

And the morning mists showed up again, crying just like me, but all they could say was *no, no, no, no, no . . .*

Paths and paths and paths, looping back on themselves, taking switchbacks right when I thought they was going straight to the top. Didn't care 'bout food anymore, nor water, and I was so full of pain that it felt right.

I fell over so many times I learned to roll as I fell, letting Pa's body hit first. He finally caved in, his ribs flat up against his backbone. Nothing between them, no innards to squash out. No soul to lose.

The mountain already had that.

Take it back, boy. You're the only one who can.

Couldn't even tell whose voice that was. They all got mixed up together, somewhere along the trail.

When I finally saw the peak, I barely knew why I was there. Pa's body curled around me, his old bones broke and loose in his bindings. If Cole'd done a better job of slashing the linens, Pa'd be scattered across the face of Redemption by now, just more bones for someone else to trip on.

If anyone else ever made it this far.

There weren't no more paths, just this one spot, a ledge barely big enough for me to let Pa down on without worrying he might roll back off the mountain.

And, almost touching distance from the top of Redemption, a wall of stone, maybe ten feet high, with just enough crags that I could probably climb it, given time to rest between handholds.

By myself. Long as I left Pa where he lay.

Ten feet. Maybe twelve, hard to say. If I had a rope, I could climb up and pull Pa after me. It could work, long as I had a rope.

Pa's linens barely kept him whole. A few threads held him in his skin, and I blessed Cole for not having enough time to do the job right, but no way could I try to unravel any of that mess and make a rope. Pa'd just go to pieces, considering the state of his body and all.

Cole hadn't messed with Pa's head, though.

I didn't want to see his face, Lord no. But I figured I could get ten feet of strong, tight-wove linen if I wanted it bad enough.

If I wanted it.

Ma? Is it worth it? Did he do things to you? Did he push you into the barn, put your head in the noose, even though he wasn't there in the flesh?

No answer from Ma. Didn't really expect one. Sometimes you're just left alone.

I turned Pa over on his stomach, found a good place to start, and gathered the cloth.

Cole didn't leave me no knife, so I had to make a knot somewhere around Pa's shoulders, right where Cole cut the linen up. I tied the other end of Pa's wrappings around my waist.

I never knew a head was so big. I had ten feet of winding-sheet and some to spare.

I checked the knots and climbed those last few feet. It was slow going. When I finally reached the top of Redemption, my fingers was raw as my back. I wanted to take a quick look at the top. I wanted to see where I'd brought us, me and Pa. I felt a pain around my waist, like Pa was tugging at the reins.

I just kept walking. The linen rope strained around my hips. I took a couple steps back, real easy, and the line loosed up some. I tried to breathe. Tried again. Couldn't feel nothing but the empty inside me, my stomach, my lungs, my heart.

Wasn't nothing atop Redemption Mountain but a short, bare stretch of flat rock.

No bones, no rotted cloth, no sign anybody ever made it up here before, ever.

I had to make myself go back to the ledge. The mist was rising again, and I could barely see Pa's poor broke body down below.

Sorry, Pa. I'm bringin' you up here, don't matter what it takes, but I ain't sure you'll be likin' it much.

I laid myself down on the edge of Redemption and reeled Pa in.

When Pa came over the top, he was facing me, hanging from the cloth rope, and for just a flash of time I saw Ma, hanging from the rafters of the barn, her face swelled up, her lips black and near-bursting.

Let him go. Just let Pa fall back down the mountain. Ain't nobody ever gonna know, Ben. You did all you could for him—now let the mountain take him for good.

I almost did it. Almost shifted my butt and scrunched the rolls of cloth out from under me, slipped the tied loop off and let Pa fly back down Redemption, scattering his mean old bones down the mountain while he fell.

And Maisy Reynolds whispered in my mind, not like Ma or Pa, where it felt like they talked right in my ear, but just a memory buzzing around, looking for the right time to get heard.

You get this man to the top, Ben. You make sure he gets saved. For my sake. For your dead ma's sake.

For your sake.

I knew she never said it that way, but it was there in the whisper. Maisy-Mary, her drawings all sliced up now, still giving me mysteries, even up here.

I dragged Pa over the edge of Redemption, turned his face away, and cried until the sun set.

You done good, boy.

Maybe I was sleeping. Too hungry and tired to do much more than that, so maybe.

The mist came up the side of the mountain, thick and pale, a Lamb-of-God white fog from below. Like Redemption burned down there somewhere, throwing off all the dead-weight on the mountain in big puffs of smoke.

I saw faces, heard voices, felt dry touches of old, dead folk across my skin. *Lost for so long,* they told me. *Lost and looking for home.* They all just kept rising past me, straight up from Redemption, until there wasn't any mist left up there.

Pa's voice again, *you done real, real good,* and Ma in there somewhere, not her voice, so much, but just a hint of Ma's soul, there with Pa, nodding her head and smiling behind him.

Seemed like she was saying something about leaving.

Go home, Ben. Go home, my fine, fine man.

I picked up Pa's body, all the loose pieces that used to be this big strong man. He didn't weigh more than a whisper now, no more than the voices that used to clutter my head. I took him right to the middle of Redemption Mountain, laid him out so the sun would shine on him whenever it rose over Redemption's narrow peak.

Then I found a path down Redemption. Didn't have no food, barely any water, and I was tired as God on the sixth day. I didn't care a whit.

Redemption Mountain was empty now. Souls all flown away, going wherever they deserved to end up, I suppose.

But that didn't mean there wasn't nobody left to save.

It sure wasn't going to be an easy path down, but I owed Maisy Reynolds a story, and maybe even a chance at redemption.

~

I don't set out to write stories that exist outside of comfortable genre boundaries. Take "Climbing Redemption Mountain," for example. I'm pretty sure I intended to write a straightforward fantasy story: start with an unusual way of attending to the dead, do a little world-building around it, and *voilà*—fantasy!

Then the little voice in my head (the "let's really screw with this" voice), said, *How 'bout we make this some weird variation on Christianity. You don't see* that *much these days . . .*

I listened.

This is what happens when you grow up as a voracious reader, and "genre" is only a word you confused with "gender" as a wee child. On my bookshelves, right at this moment, Peter Straub kisses John Steinbeck; Kurt Vonnegut canoodles with Joseph Wambaugh; Gregory Maguire peers at George R. R. Martin's backside; and I don't even want to think about what Elmore Leonard, John D. MacDonald, Richard Matheson, and Julian May are doing to each other.

Oh, wait. I get it.

They're busy gettin' all *interstitial*.

And I'm one of their many, many children.

Mikal Trimm

Timothy

Colin Greenland

On the side of the hill the last of the daylight is almost gone. The hedges are solid black ramparts, shielding the houses from the path. Behind the hedges the windows are yellow with electricity.

It is a warm, still night. The front door of one of the houses is open. On the doorstep stands a woman in a nightdress calling a cat.

'Timothy!'

The light of the house is behind her. Through the thin white cloth her form is clear as can be. She is small and slender. She is not aware of her display.

'Timothy, Timothy.'

Outside the little box of a front garden a shadow in human shape moves at an angle across the road. It is a man running on tiptoe, like a dancer making a silent entrance. It is not clear where he has come from: whether up by the path, like an honest pedestrian, or from behind a tree where he has been standing for some time, watching.

The woman's name is Leanne. She is also at this moment on tiptoe, on her front doorstep, scanning the hedges. She has not seen the shadow.

Deftly the man slips his hand over the gate. He dabs at the latch with his fingertips.

Leanne is startled. There is someone coming in the gate, someone she doesn't know.

She shades her eyes with her hand, trying to see his face. 'Yes?' she says. 'Can I help you?' Her voice is high with tension.

'You called me,' says the man. His voice is quiet too, self-assured. 'I'm Timothy,' he says.

Leanne laughs, flustered. 'Timothy's our cat!' she says.

'That's right,' says the man again. 'I'm Timothy.' He lifts his arms out to the side. 'I was a cat, until last night. This morning I woke up like this.'

He looks down at himself, and up again at her.

Timothy is a black cat. The young man is white, but he is dressed all in black: black turtleneck, black trousers, black shoes. His hair is clean, long and dark; his face smooth, capable, like the face of a young doctor in a hospital drama.

Leanne moves to step back inside and shut the front door on him, but somehow he slips under her arm and into the hall. He scampers around the corner and down the stairs. It is almost as if he knows the way.

'Excuse me!' says Leanne loudly. She leaves the front door open and goes after him.

Already he is in the kitchen. When she comes marching in, he is running around the far side of the table, on his way to the basket chair, the chair Timothy always chooses.

She heads him off. He goes gliding around the room, running his hands along her worktops.

'Are you out of your mind?' she says.

'No,' he answers simply. 'Just out of my body.'

What does he want? Is it a joke? She could laugh at his impudence.

He seems quite uninterested in her feelings. He picks up a spoon and sniffs it.

Leanne rallies. 'Put that down! Out you go!'

The young man puts his head on one side, looking at the spoon. 'You called me in,' he says blandly.

Leanne feels warm. She can feel her cheeks going pink.

'So your name's Timothy,' she says.

'It's the name you gave me,' he says. His tone is mildly accusing. Now he is investigating the tin opener.

Leanne folds her arms. It is a joke, and a thin one. She will turn it on him before she turns him out.

'Very well, then,' she says. 'If you're Timothy, what's my name?'

The man raises his eyebrows. 'I haven't the slightest idea,' he says. He presses his thumbnail between his two front teeth. 'Is that an awful disappointment?'

He lowers his head and comes trotting towards her.

Leanne gathers the breast of her nightdress in her hand. It is an automatic gesture, the gesture of someone clutching a jacket closed, to protect themselves. Leanne is not wearing a jacket. The fabric of the nightdress tightens across her breasts, showing their shape still more clearly.

'Stay away,' she warns; and he does. He veers off, to the other side of the kitchen table. He backs into the basket chair, drawing his knees up.

'The only name we ever really notice is our own,' he tells Leanne. 'And then only when food comes after it.'

He speaks without arrogance or irony. He speaks like an aristocrat, precluding any denial.

Tucked beneath him on the faded old appliqué cushion, his feet are small and neat, in black slip-ons. The shoes look thin, not suitable for walking the streets.

Leanne's feet are bare. She is all bare, but for the nightdress.

'Did I say sit down?' she asks.

Her visitor does not get up. 'Many times,' he says.

She hardens her voice. She feels a ripple of anticipatory resentment in her diaphragm, as if some delicate fancy is about to be betrayed.

'You're a friend of Howard's, I suppose.'

'Howard,' he repeats. He knows he has heard the word before. 'Yes: Howard. Your mate.'

She hides a smile. Howard would not like that.

'Well, you're a bold one. I suppose you're after a bed for the night.'

He meets her eye. 'Of course,' he says. 'Aren't you?'

Timothy will sleep on their bed, when he can. Howard objects, especially when he starts to wash himself. He is Leanne's cat, Timothy: one of her domestic responsibilities, like any other. Howard makes her put him out. By morning he always finds his way back in.

'Bed is a very fluid concept to a cat,' says the man in black. 'There are places to sleep,' he says, 'and places not to.' He flexes one hand backwards at the wrist. 'Places to stretch; and places to run; and places to sit very quietly, staring at nothing.'

He lifts his head towards her, smiling, as if pleased with his nonsense. He twists his head round over his shoulder and yawns, soundlessly. His mouth opens wide. His teeth look human enough, though, the glimpse she has of them.

'Places to hunt.'

Her face flushes again. She is alone in the house on the side of the hill, wrapped around with the night; hedged about with privacy.

If she ran outside and screamed, in a minute Nonnie and Jack next door would be out. Mrs Mandelbaum from the other side in her dressing gown, she would love a drama, an occasion for calling the police.

The police.

In a minute, thinks Leanne, a lot can happen.

She notices for the first time the muscles of his thighs.

She leans on the table, steadying herself. She takes a good look at him. His tight black garb and slip-on shoes make her think of an actor. Is this a performance? A little drama, improvised, for an audience of one?

She looks into his eyes. They are green. His pupils are not slits, but round as tunnels, with who knows what waiting at the other end.

Behind him the little window over the draining board is still open. Above the drying crockery, the curtain stirs.

She says: 'What colour are the curtains, then? Tell me that, if you're Timothy.'

He doesn't even try to sneak a look. 'I never saw colours before this morning,' he tells her. 'Nice, aren't they?'

She makes a hard line of her mouth and a fist of her hand.

'It's dogs that don't see colours! Dogs, not cats!'

She hears herself. She sounds like a child in the playground, accusing another child of breaking the rules of a game.

'Dogs and cats,' says the young man. 'And fish and birds and cows. You know that, don't you?'

She makes herself speak coldly.

'Well, this is all quite hilarious, I'm sure, but it's time you were going.'

'Going?' he says. 'I've only just got in.'

She strides to the fridge and opens it violently. She pulls out a half-empty tin of cat food and empties it into a dish. She dumps the dish on the table in front of the intruder and stands back, folding her arms again.

He looks at it. He shakes his head, as at some marvel. 'That's just the way I remember it . . .'

'Well?' she says. 'Aren't you going to eat it?'

'It won't do now,' he says. 'I'm not a cat now, am I?'

She shakes her head, in her turn. 'I don't know the word for what you are.'

'Well, I'm not a cat,' he says, almost rudely. 'Do I look like a cat?' He jumps up, swivelling his hips, showing her his bottom. 'Do you see my fine tail? Mm?'

Now he has gone too far. She snatches up the rolling pin and bustles around the table brandishing it like a cartoon housewife.

'Get out! Out!'

He is too quick for her. He springs backwards out of the chair. Turning in the air like an acrobat, he lands on the edge of the draining board. There he pauses the merest instant, legs braced; then jumps again, up onto the windowsill. He balances there, squeezed against the lintel. The curtain flutters around him. With a twist of his shoulders he is through the gap and gone; with not a dish rattled, not a teaspoon disturbed.

The kitchen is silent and empty. There is no sound from the garden. The white and yellow curtain blows in the evening breeze.

Leanne puts down the rolling pin. She puts Timothy's food bowl on the newspaper behind the back door, next to his water bowl. She takes the chair from the end of the table and stands on it, as she does every night at this season, to shut the little window before she goes to bed.

Tonight, as she sometimes does, she looks out into the darkness. Against the light of the neighbours' windows she sees the silhouettes of her rhododendrons, the bobbled spires of her hollyhocks. There is nothing untoward out there.

When Howard comes home Leanne is in bed, reading a magazine. Howard is finishing a limp sandwich in a cellophane wrapper. He kisses his wife on the cheek. His breath smells of cheese and pickle.

She asks him: 'How was your day, dear?'

She watches him answer. She sees him, fatigued, remote, mouthing his reply like a fish blowing bubbles. The bubbles burst on the surface of the moment and are gone, leaving not the least trace in her mind. His very dullness is soothing, she realises, not for the first time. Her tumbled heart grows quiet.

She turns the light out, but for a long while she cannot sleep. She thinks about the young man in black. The nerve of him.

She smiles into the secret dark.

Of the cat Timothy there is no sign.

All next day Timothy stays away.

In the evening Leanne eats a ready meal in front of the television, a chicken breast with asparagus. She drinks a glass of Muscadet. The television pelts her with events: national events, foreign events, events in the realms of business and sport. A duchess shakes hands with the director of a ballet company. A man with a blanket over his head is bundled into a police car.

Leanne picks up Sunday's paper and starts the crossword. In the grid of squares she enters the names of an Italian city and a tool used by carpenters. Then she gets up and goes into the kitchen.

She slices a banana in a bowl and adds some yogurt. She eats it standing at the kitchen table. Then she does the washing up, slowly and conscientiously.

It is not yet seven. Leanne takes the bottle out of the fridge and pours herself a second glass of wine. She takes a sip. The wine tastes cold and stony. She carries her glass upstairs and starts to run a bath.

The bedroom window looks onto the front garden. The grass is parched. There has been no rain all month. In the street the low sun lights the parked cars. A couple arrive, walking slowly, close together. They get in one of the cars and drive away.

Leanne takes off her shirt.

The evening breeze stirs the leaves of the trees.

Leanne unhooks her skirt. She lowers the zip.

Downstairs, bright music and applause spill from the television.

Leanne takes off her underwear. She stands in front of the full-length mirror. She spreads her hands on her ribs, fingers wide.

She remembers seeing Timothy one day playing on the lawn. He was prancing, stiff-legged, darting at something that seemed, when he lifted his paw, to be attached to his claws. It was struggling.

The moment she stepped outside, without seeming to notice her, he had made a sudden gathering motion with his head and all his limbs. It was too slight, too contained, to be called a pounce. He lay couched in the grass, immediately and completely at ease.

Only then did he turn and look at her.

His face was rigid, imperious. His eyes were slits of absolute authority.

Leanne runs her hands up over the shallow curves of her breasts. She draws her forefingers along under her nipples.

In the bath, Leanne lies breathing scented sandalwood oil, for calming thoughts. She hears laughter from the television, entertaining the empty drawing room.

She lies a long time in the bath. Her muscles relax. Distantly, she hears the doors of cars and houses open and close. Somewhere a phone rings, a dozen times, then falls silent.

Leanne dries herself and puts on her nightdress. She brushes her hair. She finds her wine, grown tepid and slightly harsh. She finishes it and takes the empty glass downstairs.

In the kitchen the food she emptied into Timothy's bowl is still there, untouched, turning dull. The water in his water bowl is evaporating. Its surface looks thick. Leanne can see the dust that lies on it.

Outside it is dark now, except for the streetlights.

She opens the front door and stands on the doorstep and calls, as before.

'Timothy?'

Her nightdress stirs around her knees.

'Timothy!'

Nothing moves. There is no sign of her cat, or of anyone else.

Leanne goes back inside. Her hand is on the latch to close the door.

Something moves, in the garden. She feels a hot spasm of shock, like heartburn. There is something there, something large, on the grass.

'Timothy?'

Everything is still.

Leanne steps outside. She crouches down, trying to see what it is.

Out of the darkness, the man in black comes jumping lightly towards her.

She freezes.

He stands over her, inside her dark enclosure of hedges.

'Is it you again?' she says.

The yellow streetlights mock their meeting.

The silhouette sketches a bow. Tonight he does not speak. Tonight he is wearing an elegant black mask.

Leanne puts her hand to her mouth, stifling a small cry. All day she has been thinking about him. Now he is here, she runs away, indoors.

He leaps onto the step.

She holds the door between them like a shield.

He tips his head around it, enquiringly.

The mask is made of black velvet. From the top rise two sculpted triangular ears. Over his nose is a patch of silky black. On either side of it is a spray of short silvery whiskers.

'That's new,' says Leanne. She tries to laugh, but her voice shakes. The mask is a threat. It frightens her.

Her visitor capers on the step. She dreads that he will turn around and show he has acquired a tail too, of wire wrapped in plush.

He lifts his chin.

She remembers Timothy on the lawn, guarding his prey.

'Go away,' she whispers fiercely.

He dances on the spot. He is not going. She must get him inside before Mrs Mandelbaum's curtains start to twitch.

The mask makes everything impossible. What if it isn't the same man? What if this one is a burglar, come for a sack of candlesticks and spoons? Leanne stands frozen, irresolute.

The man in the black mask sidles in the half-open door. He presses himself to the wallpaper. Her eyes fixed on him, with nerveless fingers Leanne turns the door handle and the milled knob of the lock together, so the door will close without a sound.

She can see his green eyes now, through the eyeholes of his mask. They are close enough to kiss. He smells of the night; of the spicy pavements, the cooling lawns.

'Look at you,' she says softly, scoldingly.

He rubs the back of one wrist over the top of his head, brushing one of the velvet ears. She wants to touch them. She will not give him the satisfaction.

She is being foolish.

'Come in,' she says. 'Come in here.'

She takes him in the drawing room. The television is still on. It shows a studio audience laughing and clapping. The man in the cat mask seems wary. He paces an arc around the set, keeping his eye on it.

Leanne closes the door.

The picture on the television changes. Now there are two men on a stage, smiling hectically. One of them speaks, the other throws back his head and laughs. Behind them pink lights flash off and on.

The man in the mask crouches on the floor with his hands between his knees. He holds his head back, watching the screen suspiciously.

Leanne is unnerved. 'I'll put it off,' she says.

He ignores her.

She searches for the remote control. It eludes her. She picks up the newspaper, puts it down again. The braying inanity seems to scour her eardrums.

She finds the remote down the side of the couch cushions. She points it, and presses the button.

The television goes blank, falls silent.

The man on the floor arches his back. He licks his shoulder.

The silence is worse than the television. The abandoned crossword puzzle accuses her, evidence of the deficiency of her personality.

'Do you do crosswords?' she asks him. 'I haven't the patience.'

Her visitor gets up and starts to prowl. He examines the terrain of the drawing room the way last night he examined the kitchen. She feels insulted; inadequate; too tired to think.

'I'll get you a drink,' she says.

The man springs up into Howard's chair. He squats there facing her, knees bent, back straight. His penis is erect, perfectly visible through the tight soft cloth of his trousers.

Leanne prickles with gooseflesh. She is suddenly conscious of her nightwear.

'I'm just going to fetch a cardigan,' she says.

At that, he jumps down and comes frisking towards her again.

This time she says nothing. She lets him reach her. When he does, she shuts her eyes and opens her mouth. A small, tight noise escapes her.

The man in the cat mask rubs his head against her breasts.

Leanne opens her eyes. She looks at the whiskers on his mask. They are made of the finest silver wire, sewn on with the tiniest, neatest stitches. The man's own chin is clean shaven.

Leanne realises she has stopped breathing.

In the stillness they hear the sound of the front gate opening.

The intruder bristles. He starts, as if to dash out of the room.

'No.' Leanne finds she is holding him by the shoulder, restraining him. She can feel every muscle in his body taut, humming.

The key slides into the lock. The front door shudders open.

'Darling?'

It is Howard.

Leanne does not answer. She and the man in the mask stand together, motionless.

Her husband's footsteps go past the drawing room, to the foot of the stairs.

'Are you in bed?'

Now they move towards the kitchen.

Leanne breaks away from her accomplice. She goes out of the room, shutting the door behind her, and walks firmly towards the kitchen.

'Hello, darling,' she calls.

Howard is already turning round, coming back. He glances at her, past her into the hall, as if suspecting something. He accepts a kiss on the cheek.

'I was just watching some television,' she says.

'What's on?' Howard asks. Clearly he fancies some distraction himself.

'Nothing, really,' says his wife. 'Just some stupid thing.'

Howard starts back up the hall away from her, towards the drawing room.

Leanne raises her voice. 'Are you hungry?' she says. 'Can I get you something?'

Her husband walks on, muttering a refusal. It is as if the word television is a spell to draw him. Leanne curses herself for speaking it.

He opens the door of the drawing room, and goes in.

She hurries in there after him.

He is alone. He has picked up the remote control and is turning the television on.

The curtains are closed; the windows too.

On the screen, a sultry woman gloats over shampoo. Howard changes the channel. A butterfly sits on a leaf. Reverently, a man's voice describes its habits.

Howard continues to change channels. Unable to look anywhere else, Leanne wills her heart to beat and her lungs to breathe as she watches the screen.

Under a tree, two men discuss variations in arboriculture. A muscular builder in a yellow safety helmet points at a half-constructed house. A bald vicar winks, and bites into a bar of chocolate.

'How was your day?' Leanne hears herself ask.

'Fucking awful.'

Howard leans over the back of the couch to pick up the discarded newspaper. He starts leafing through it.

Leanne stands there in her bare feet. She holds the neck of her nightdress tightly.

'What's that?'

Her husband is pointing at something on the floor.

It is something small, made of material. It is crumpled black velvet, with hints of blue along its folds.

Leanne picks it up and crushes it in her hand. She holds it behind her back, like something she is ashamed of.

'I do wish you could learn not to scatter your clothes all over the house,' she hears her husband say. 'You never know when I might be bringing someone home.'

She hears herself apologising. She hears him saying: 'This whole place could do with tidying up.'

He does not ask about the cat, which is still missing.

In bed she remembers how her visitor looked in the garden. He had bowed to her, courtly and grave. Puss in Boots. She smiles.

She slips her hand under her pillow, to touch the mask.

She falls asleep, and dreams she is in a place of tall rocks, where the ground is running with water. There are other people there, somewhere: she can hear them talking. She knows she is supposed to be with them. She searches among the rocks, but she cannot find them.

It is the third night. On the side of the hill the darkness lies like a blanket. The houses wait behind their hedges, their windows like yellow staring eyes.

The air is hot and heavy. On the main road, the traffic growls.

The front door of the house is open. On the doorstep stands the woman, calling his name.

The hallway gapes behind her like an open throat. The light is on. He cannot see her face.

He springs once more onto the path.

She does not react. She wears her dressing gown, tightly belted. Her body is tense with something, some conviction or displeasure.

There is something strange about her tonight. Something about her face.

She has his mask on.

He throws back his head and sings to the zenith of the night, a long, high, wavering note.

'Quiet!' she says. Her voice is deep now as his is high.

She makes fists of her hands. She places them on her hips.

He prowls back and forth.

'Come on, then, Timothy,' she says. 'Come on. Come on, then. Good boy.'

She steps back into the hallway. She walks backwards, her hands on her sash.

He starts to croon again. He feels the sound, hard and stinging in the back of his throat.

'Ah, Timothy . . .'

With a clumsy gesture, the woman opens her gown. Underneath, she is naked, smooth and pink. At her crotch she bears one small, ridiculous tuft of fur.

'Timothy . . .'

He leaps the step.

Her gown flaps like the wings of a stricken bird. Is she trying to pull it back on?

He plunges after her into the dining room. Inside, it is dark. He swipes the gown from her shoulder.

She claps her hand to her shoulder and gasps, long and hard.

He presses her back against the dinner table. A vase of flowers rocks.

He nuzzles her under the chin. The smell of her is rich, fresh, salty.

She pushes his head away, roughly, her hand against the side of his face.

He ducks under her hand. There are red lines on her shoulder where his claws caught her, tiny beads of red blood on her pink skin. He nips her neck with his teeth.

She reaches for the back of his head and pulls him away by the hair.

The room pulsates. The furniture shouts at him.

She puts her lips to his ear. 'Upstairs,' she says.

He resists. He barely recognises the word.

Places to sleep and places to hunt . . .

He tries to grasp her with fingers suddenly unfamiliar. She wriggles. She bolts for the stairs, hauling her dressing gown like a broken tail. She laughs, breathless and high.

He gives chase. Pink skin flickers between the banisters as she stumbles upstairs. Her bare bottom flashes round the corner of the landing.

He bounds up after her, three steps at a time.

She is in the bedroom. She has the dressing gown on again, though she is making no attempt to close it. She poses provocatively, leaning back on the bed. One foot is stretched out towards him, the other leg drawn up. The fingers of her right hand toy with the tuft of fur.

He springs upon her. Fiercely he nuzzles her neck. She wraps her arms around his back. His nostrils fill with the musk of her desire.

Still she stops, pulling back a moment. She holds very still on the bed as he writhes upon her body.

'This is all wrong, Timothy,' she says.

She pauses while his racing heart beats four times, while he tries to pin her hips between his knees.

She slips one hand suddenly beneath him, palm up. She caresses the length of the erection that strains the tight fabric of his trousers.

'Cats don't wear clothes . . .'

She rubs her breasts against his shirt.

He mauls them with his hands. She gasps again, and arches her back. He tries to bite her mask. Her eyes stare from it, penetrating him.

She twists onto her belly, crawls away across the bed. Her elbows dent the duvet.

He grabs her ankle. He paws at his clothes, forgetting buttons and zips.

'Wait,' she says. 'Shh. Wait. Wait.'

She comes to him again and strips him. She purrs in her throat as she releases the firm weight of his penis. He thrusts it between her legs, shoving blindly.

'No no no,' she says. 'Wait. Wait. Here.'

She goes up on all fours. She looks at him over her shoulder. The dressing gown covers her. She reaches behind her, and tosses it up over her back.

The pink cleft smiles at him.

His nails squeeze her ribs as he enters her from behind. He snarls. He is hot and hard.

She snarls, echoing him, replying. She is soft and wet.

She smells like fish.

The pair mate like beasts, pounding the bed against the wall. Cries threaten the suburban night. A lamp goes over and the bulb smashes. In their lounge Nonnie frowns at Jack, who raises his eyebrows. Mrs Mandelbaum tuts and turns up the volume on her television.

Howard comes in to find Leanne fast asleep on top of the bed, naked. The bed is a mess. What on earth can she have been doing? She has even managed to knock her bedside lamp over. He goes to pick it up, sees the broken glass, and decides, sourly, to leave it for the morning.

His wife's skin glows dimly in the streetlight that filters through the curtains. Howard lays a hand on her abdomen. She does not stir. Though the window is open, there is a strange, rank smell in the room.

In the morning at a quarter to seven Leanne wakes. She wakes like a young child, suddenly and completely, feeling refreshed.

She turns her head. Howard lies beside her as always, solid and unmoving. He is frowning in his sleep. His mouth is open.

Leanne feels a weight lying on her feet. She lifts herself on one elbow to see.

'Timothy?' she says.

It is the cat, returned at last. He has found his way onto the bed, as usual. There he lies, curled up, fast asleep.

His mistress reaches one hand down to fondle behind his ear. She wonders what it is he dreams of.

Walking home once, years ago, on a warm summer night, I passed a house where the front door was open. A woman stood outside calling a name, a masculine name. I'm not sure the name was Timothy, in fact; but whatever it was, I assumed it was the name of her cat.

As someone constantly bewildered by the world, and by the confidence with which everyone else professes to understand what goes on, I habitually mistrust my assumptions. Nothing and no one I've encountered has ever been quite what I expected beforehand. People are taller, shorter, nicer, nastier. Lovers turn into scorpions, frogs into princes. I don't see any reason to imagine that will ever change. So I'm always ready to make an imaginative leap. Like many people with a taste for the fantastic, I feel more at home with the improbable.

So then, walking on between the trees and over the hill, I thought to myself, Why should it be a cat? What if it isn't? Or what if the name she's calling turns out to be the name of something else, someone else? What if someone answers the summons and is not at all who she was expecting?

Colin Greenland

Hunger

Vandana Singh

She woke up early as usual. The apartment, with its plump sofas like sleeping walruses, the pictures on the walls slightly and mysteriously askew, pale light from the windows glinting off yesterday's glasses she'd forgotten on the coffee table—the apartment seemed as though it had been traveling through alien universes all night and had only now landed in this universe, cautiously letting in the unfamiliar air. Outside the birds were stirring, parakeets in the neem trees, mynahs strutting on the roadsides, their calls mingling with the beep beep beep of a car backing in the parking area below.

How strange everything was! In the dream last night it had been the most natural thing in the world to be dancing with a tree, to be nibbling gently at the red fruit hanging from its branches as they swayed. Vikas hadn't been with her in that dream, and she had felt slightly guilty dancing with someone else, even in a dream, even if that someone had been a tree that could walk. But it had seemed so natural, so familiar, that in that moment she'd been convinced, finally, that she had found her home planet. And just as she'd started feeling at home, her eyes had opened, and there she was, lying in a strange bed next to a strange beast that she slowly recognized as her very dear husband, Vikas.

And where have *you* been? she wanted to ask him, but he was asleep. If she told him her dream he would laugh and threaten to find a shrink. Not for you, Divya, he would say, but for me. He liked to say that she was beyond redemption, reading those trashy science fiction novels. But sometimes she wanted to ask him quite seriously how to explain the way she felt in the mornings: that even the most familiar thing felt strange, that she had to—almost—learn the world anew. Try explaining that! she said to Vikas's imaginary shrink.

Their daughter lay asleep in her room, curled like an embryo among the sheets. She was twelve today, there was going to be a big party, what was she, Divya, doing, standing in the doorway of the child's room, thinking about alien universes! The child herself—how much longer a child? So strange, so different from the squalling, wrinkled little creature she had first held in her arms twelve years ago! Her face still so young, so innocent, and yet on the inside she was developing layers, convolutions; she was becoming someone that Divya as yet did not know. Divya sighed and went out of the room, drifting through the apartment, touching and straightening things as though to make sure they were there, they were fine. She picked up the glasses from the coffee table and went into the kitchen, which (being on the northwest side of the apartment) was still in darkness. With the usual trepidation she turned on the light.

As light flooded the room, mice fled to dark corners. Divya stepped gingerly in. The kitchen was never hers at night but belonged, for that duration, to the denizens of another world. There were cockroach cocktail parties and mouse reunions, and (in the monsoons) conferences of lost frogs. In the kitchen sink, the nali-ka-kida, the drain insects, whatever they were, waited hopefully for darkness, waving their feelers. None of the other creatures—mice and muskrats and frogs—bothered Divya like the cockroaches and nali-ka-kida. But it unnerved her that she had somehow, quite unknowingly, surrendered ownership of the kitchen at night.

She put the glasses noisily in the sink. Kallu the crow flew down to the windowsill from the neem tree outside, and cawed at her. His presence was a relief. She gave him a piece of the paratha that she had been saving up from last night to eat later. The parathas were fat, stuffed with spiced potatoes and peas, the best that the cook Damyanti had ever made. For a moment Divya wanted desperately to curl up in bed with the parathas and a book with a title like *The Aliens of Malgudi* or *Antariksh ki Yatra*. The day stretched before her, rife with impossibilities—to get all that food cooked, the whole house cleaned, and then to entertain the families of Vikas's colleagues without a faux pas . . . It simply couldn't be done. She wasn't made for such things—she was from another planet, where you danced with trees and ate parathas and read trashy science fiction novels.

But it had to be done. "Take me with you, Kallu," she told the crow, but he only cawed sardonically at her and flew heavily off. She sighed and began to wash the glasses. If only Vikas hadn't gotten that big promotion, she thought, feeling guilty for thinking so. Now he was junior vice-president, which was not at all as exciting as a president of vices ought to be—and they had to move amongst the upper echelons of the company, VPs and CEOs, whose houses were completely air-conditioned and windows all shut, so that mice and cockroaches and frogs would have to line up and come in at the main entrance, with the permission of the doorkeeper, like everybody else. The most innocent of things, like children's birthdays, were now minor political extravaganzas with the women all made up, clinking with expensive jewelry, sniping gently at each other while calling each other "darling," and the men talking on like robots about stocks and shares.

She went to the back door and found the newspaper on the landing. As she straightened she smelled it—a stench rolling down from the top of the stairs. The pungent, sharp, stale odor of urine.

The old man was responsible for the smell. He lived on the top landing, which was little used because it led to the rooftop terrace. Divya looked at the door of the servants' flat. It was shut tight. So was the door of the apartment opposite hers, where the morose and silent Mr. Kapadia lived. She took a deep breath and knocked loudly on the servant quarter door, where Ranu, Mr. Kapadia's cook, lived with her husband.

The woman herself opened the door. She turned her nose up at the smell.

"All right, all right," she spat, before Divya could say a word. She turned and yelled for her husband. "Wash the stairs, you lazy lout, that good-for-nothing fellow has wet his bed again!" She looked at Divya, hands on hips, nostrils flared.

"Satisfied?"

"Why don't you let the old man use the bathroom in the night?" Divya said angrily. "The poor fellow is your father-in-law—treat him with some respect! And listen, make sure the stairs stay clean all day. We have people coming over!"

In answer Ranu slammed the door. Divya went back into the house, feeling sick. She wondered if the old fellow was ill again. She let him run little errands for her, like getting the milk from the milk booth in the mornings, for which she would give him a little money or food. He was a small, thin, emaciated, bird-like man, with a slurred speech that had resulted from some disease of his middle age. Sometimes he would tell her stories of his bygone days and she would nod at intervals although she hardly understood any of it, except a word here or there, like bicycle, or river, or tomato chutney, which, put together, made no sense at all. In her more fanciful moments she had thought that perhaps the old fellow was an alien, speaking to her in an exotic tongue or in code, delivering a message that she had to try to decipher. But he was just an old man down on his luck, with no place to go but the nest of rags at the top of the stairs, subject always to the whims and frightful temper of his daughter-in-law. Divya resolved that later on she would find out if the fellow had fallen ill. He hadn't come by yesterday for the milk. She would have to send Vikas to the milk booth today.

Divya was hungry.

She had been cleaning all morning and had skipped lunch. By the afternoon, the house was sparkling. She hadn't known what to do with most of the things that they had accumulated—the piles of books on the floor all over the house, the loose photographs on every surface like schools of dead fish, the magazines sliding off stacks in the bathroom. But she had found in herself unexpected reserves of cunning—she'd hidden piles of books behind the beds in the bedrooms, given the magazines to the kabari man without asking Vikas if he wanted to keep any of them, collected the photos and put them in a plastic bag in the clothes cupboard. The cleaning woman, who was lazier than a street dog in the sun, loved parties and had worked with great enthusiasm to make the floors shine, knowing that some of the good food would come her way later on.

Late afternoon, Divya was standing in front of the stove, stirring the matar-paneer. There was sweat gathering on her forehead, under the hairline, and steam rising off the big karhai as the peas bubbled in their sauce of onions, ginger, tomatoes, cumin and coriander. Big chunks of paneer like white barges in the gravy, and the aroma! The aroma was enough to make the head swim. Divya had never been so hungry, and was regretting not having had lunch. She was paying for it now: her stomach rumbled, her mouth watered, she felt faint with desire. It should have been easy to munch something while cooking.

But the fact was that she was afraid of the cook. Damyanti was a small, stern woman who stood no nonsense from her employers. She took great pride in her creations and had, Divya thought, an unreasonable code of conduct: you did not eat before your guests, you did not filch from the serving dishes, and there was no need to taste the food unless you wanted to insult the cook. Damyanti had already scolded her once for trying to throw away the carrot-tops.

"You've left so much of the carrots on this, I can easily take it home and put it in a sabzi; and the greens can go to Karan's cow. Don't you know what happens to those who waste food?"

The reason Damyanti could bully her employers and get away with it was because her cooking was sublime. The fact that she had condescended to stay and cook for much of the afternoon meant that Divya was, by tacit agreement, completely under her thumb.

"What happens?" Divya asked, trying to sound unconcerned.

"People who waste food end up being reborn as nali-ka-kidas," said Damyanti, setting hot onion pakoras into a cloth-lined serving dish. Divya shivered. Imagine that, having those horrible, long feelers, living in dark drains, emerging at night to eat the leavings of others!

The matar-paneer was done; Damyanti was setting up the big dekchi for the rice, putting in the ghee, the cardamom, a cinnamon stick, cloves. It smelled like heaven. Divya clutched the wall with one hand. The thought occurred to her that she should let the party go to hell, dismiss Damyanti and sit on the kitchen floor, surrounded by vats of fragrant dishes, and fall upon them in a frenzy. She collected herself. Maybe she should simply go get the parathas she had been saving in the fridge. They would taste divine, even cold. She had surely never been so hungry as now!

But Damyanti (coming to get the dhania leaves) caught her at the fridge, with her hand clutching a piece of paratha halfway to her mouth.

"Chee chee!" she said. "Don't you know what happens to the woman who eats during cooking? Do you want to make all the food jootha?"

Divya never found out what terrible fate would have resulted from her almost-lapse because at that precise moment Vikas came in with the cake, laughing and trying to fend Charu off because she wanted to see what it looked like. Divya had to put the parathas back and make room in the fridge for the enormous cake. Vikas touched Divya's disheveled hair as she turned away—she suppressed a desire to bite his hand.

"Are you going to face the guests like this, Divu? They'll be here in an hour! Go dress!"

"I have to get the chholey cooking," she said irritably, following Damyanti into the kitchen. There was a knock on the back door.

"I'll see who it is!" Charu said, flying off resplendent in a new blue dress, happy because the cake was her favorite kind, triple chocolate. Divya went back into the kitchen, got the other karhai on the stove, put in the oil and the spices and the onions. When Damyanti's back was turned for half a second she popped a piece of paneer into her mouth from the dish of matar-paneer, and burnt her mouth. She could hear Charu talking to someone at the door, running into the house and back to the door again; she heard the soft, hesitant, mangled words of the old man upstairs. So he was up and about, the old fraud! Pissing in his bed, stinking up the stairs, giving her a headache first thing in the morning! And she had had to get the milk herself earlier, because Vikas had to go out to get the drinks! Tears welled up in her eyes. If only she could eat something! How absurd this was, to be afraid to eat in your own house!

She was about to purloin another piece of paneer, burnt mouth or no, when Vikas came in.

"Divya, you'll never believe what I saw in our room! A mouse!

Really, when will you stop feeding every living creature in the area! They think our house is a hotel! And we have all these people coming . . . where did you put the rat poison?"

He had gotten it last week, a small blue vial of death that she hadn't been able to bring herself to use. It stood on the highest shelf in their bathroom.

"It wasn't there," he said when she told him this. "Divya, really!"

He knew she didn't like using the poison, but the traps they had used hadn't worked either. Vikas had taken the traps to the park every morning and let the mice out, but they had wasted no time in returning. Stricter measures had been called for.

What Divya remembered was this: she was ten years old, and had been visiting an aunt's house in the summer. It was an old bungalow, ridden with denizens of all kinds, including an army of mice. Her uncle had set poisoned food all over the house and killed off the army. Divya had a vivid memory of the tiny corpses, their bodies twisted with the final agony, all over the house. Then, a day or two later, there had been the smell in her room, which had finally been traced to a nest behind the big wooden cupboard. Twelve baby mice, pink and hairless, had died of starvation after the adults had been killed. All the time Divya had been reading her mystery books and sipping her lemonade, those babies had been dying slowly. She had cried for days.

"Vikas, this is no time to be setting out rat poison," she said, but he was already distracted by the pakoras. "Smells good," he said wistfully, leaning over the glass-covered dish.

Before Divya could utter a word, Damyanti had put two pakoras and some tamarind chutney on a plate and handed it to him, all the while smiling approvingly as Vikas ate. Divya stared at him, and then at her, speechless with indignation.

"But . . ." she started to say, when she heard the fridge door open and shut and there was Charu walking past the kitchen door in her blue dress, holding Divya's precious parathas in her hand.

In an instant she was in front of her daughter, confronting her, snatching the parathas away. She stared at Charu, breathless with anger.

"What are you doing with my parathas?"

Charu stared back, eyes wide with confusion.

"I was just giving it to the old man, he said he was hungry, Ma..."

There was a roaring in Divya's ears. She felt momentarily dizzy.

"Tell him we can't spare any," she said, more harshly than she had intended. "Don't you have better things to do? Where are the presents you were wrapping for your friends? Did you get enough for the other children, too?"

An expression she could not identify flickered over the child's face. Divya knew Charu was not happy about the other children, the strangers who would be coming to the party. Apart from Charu's three friends there would be a fourteen-year-old boy, the nephew of Vikas's new boss, Mr. Lamba, and an eleven-year-old girl, daughter of the Pathanias. But all that—the sulks and protestations—had been over and done with, or so Divya thought. She saw the tears rise in Charu's eyes.

"It's my birthday," the child said, fiercely. "You're not supposed to scold me on my birthday!"

At that moment Divya was aware that certain knots had come into being in the smooth tapestry of her life, knots she would not necessarily know how to untangle, but there was Vikas calling out that the Chaturvedis were already here, and Charu was already at the door, talking to the old man. Damyanti took the parathas from Divya's limp fingers and pushed her, not ungently, in the direction of the bedroom.

"Get ready for your guests, I'll do the chholey," she said, and Divya went to change her sari and wash her face and put on some lipstick, feeling dazed, feeling as though something momentous had happened or was about to happen. The book she was reading, *The Aliens of Malgudi*, lay on the dressing table; she stared wistfully at the lurid cover, with the spaceship and the buxom space-bandit Viraa. The plot had to do with Viraa discovering aliens disguised as humans, living in the town of Malgudi. They were from some planet light-years away. Divya wondered how she was going to survive.

As for the Chaturvedis, she should have remembered from the gossip that they always came at least half an hour early, possibly because Mrs. Chaturvedi—an inveterate gossip and interlocutor—liked to have her victims to herself before the others came.

The party was in full swing. Divya dashed from kitchen to drawing room, from guest to guest, until the world became a blur of silk sarees and lipsticked mouths opening and closing, the clink of glasses; the flow of myriad streams of conversations, none of which made any sense to her. In the kitchen she took a moment to wipe her brow. Just then Mrs. Lamba loomed large in the kitchen doorway, resplendent in green silk.

"My dear, what a lot of trouble! Look at you, all sweating! You should have got the whole thing catered. I will give you my caterer's telephone number. He does some very nice European-style hors d'oeuvres . . ."

"Aha, but, Mrs. Lamba, you must try these pakoras . . ." Mrs. Raman said brightly, munching away behind her. Mrs. Lamba condescended to nibble at one.

"Not bad," she said in a surprised tone. Damyanti, wiping the serving dish for the chholey, glared at her.

Vikas came in wanting more glasses. There weren't enough at the bar. The Saikias and the Bhosles were here. And where was the fruit juice for the children?

Over the next hour or so, Divya caught a few glimpses of her daughter. Charu wouldn't look at her. The girl's laugh was higher than usual—she was in the middle of her little circle of friends. At the periphery were the eleven-year-old daughter of the Pathanias and the fourteen-year-old nephew of the Lambas. Divya went over to make sure they weren't feeling left out. No, Charu was nothing if not kind-hearted—she had served birthday cake to everyone, and now the two had been invited to play a computer game in Charu's room along with the inner circle of friends, and they were all trooping off together. The Lambas' nephew looked frankly bored; the Ramans' daughter cast a despairing glance at her parents as she left the room.

So much unhappiness, Divya thought suddenly. She was feeling better, with some pakoras in her stomach, but now a wave of anguish swept through her. She looked at the women, clustered together, their face paint standing out garishly in the light. It was one of those moments when everyone had run out of conversation at the same time, like actors taking a break from their roles. Mrs. Lamba's fleshy face looked haggard, Mrs. Raman's, nervous. In that moment she had a sudden shock of recognition, a fellow-feeling she could not explain. Then Mrs. Chaturvedi leaned toward Mrs. Lamba with a conspiratorial look, and the buzz of conversation resumed. What were they hatching now? Whose reputation was being built up, or destroyed? By contrast the men seemed less sinister, talking in loud voices about the latest financial news—they were like little puppets, moving and twitching to order, while the women, with Mrs. Lamba at the center, controlled the strings. Why had Divya had that sudden moment of empathy with the women—no, empathy was too strong a word—but why she had felt what she felt, she did not know.

She had a sudden longing for the days when Vikas was still a junior manager in the company and birthdays, and life itself, were less complicated. Then, she could ensure everyone's happiness. Charu could be comforted with a hug. But look at her now, with that veil over her eyes, taking a tray of soda to her room for her friends. She didn't like the way I snapped at her, Divya thought. On her birthday too! She's getting all sensitive and dignified now. Every year she steps away from me, one step. Two steps. And look at Vikas! He looked the genial host, pouring the drinks, laughing at Mr. Lamba's jokes, but she could see the strain on his face. Her poor Vikas, growing up, growing old. Worried about creating the right impression. The old Vikas had enjoyed making cartoons of his superiors, shared jokes with her about how stupid office politics was. She felt sorry for him, having to laugh at those jokes of Mr. Lamba.

What was the point of it all?

As the evening wore on, she knew that she had achieved some degree of success. Damyanti had left around the middle of the evening and she had managed the serving of the dinner mostly on her own, with some help from Mrs. Bhosle and Mrs. Raman, two ladies on the outer perimeter of Mrs. Lamba's circle. Whether it was Damyanti's cooking or whether Mrs. Lamba had been feeling indulgent, she felt as though she had passed some kind of test, that she had crossed an invisible barrier and was now one of Them. She didn't like it, didn't like pretending to like it. She wasn't as good at acting as the other women. But for Vikas . . . she looked across at him, and he raised his head and met her gaze, and in his look was relief and humor and the reassurance that the evening would soon be over . . . yes, she would do it for him. At least for another half an hour, or however long it took for the last glasses to be set down, the last goodbyes said.

Then she heard a child scream.

The children had been running around, playing some kind of crazy game, after having sat still through dinner. The Lambas' nephew, Ajeet, had started them on it, Divya thought, against Charu's wishes. But he had the authority of being fourteen and having traveled all over the world with his parents (his speech was peppered with references to London and New York and Sydney), and he was already beginning to develop an air of studied cynicism, a man of the world. Divya could sense Charu being pulled in, and repelled, and pulled in, and repelled, and had suffered for her daughter, who still would not look at her. She wanted to tell her that the world wouldn't care for her hurt feelings, that she needed to be stronger and less vulnerable to everyday hurts if she were to survive; she wanted to tell her that the kind of men that grew from boys like Ajeet were bad news, all preening, fake charm and pretended indifference . . . look at him, manipulating the younger ones just because he was bored and wanted whatever entertainment the situation had to offer . . .

In the split second after the scream Divya established that it was not her Charu, and that the sound came from outside the apartment, from the vicinity of the back door. She was already moving toward it, and so was Vikas, and Mrs. Pathania, whose daughter it was who had screamed. At the back door she saw that the children were clustered at the top of the stairs that led to the terrace; there was a faint smell in the air, not urine. The landing was very quiet, with only one light burning over the stairway, and the servants' quarter door (she noted as she ran up the stairs) was locked.

The children moved aside to let her see; Mrs. Pathania's daughter was already half-falling down the stairs into her mother's arms. What Divya saw was the old man curled up in a nest of rags, clutching his throat with both hands, quite dead. His hooked nose, protruding from his too-thin face, gave him the appearance of a strange bird; his heavy-lidded eyes were open and staring at some alien vista she could not imagine. At the same time she was aware that Vikas was gently ushering the children down the stairs, and the Lambas were coming up to look. She started to say:

"He's sick, poor man, I'll get the doctor," for the sake of the children, but the boy Ajeet interrupted her.

"He's dead," he said scornfully. He gave her a defiant half-grin. "I kicked his foot, so I know."

At the precise moment before the Lambas reached the landing, Divya saw two things: the piece of paper in the dead man's hand, and the blue vial of rat poison standing quite close to his ragged pillow. In that instant she had swooped down and gathered both items, covering them with the pallu of her sari. She turned to face the Lambas. Mrs. Lamba gave a high-pitched cry and fell against her husband, who, not being built to handle the weight, tottered against the wall. Mrs. Bhosle took over, muttering words of comfort and calling for brandy, giving Divya an unexpectedly sympathetic look. Mr. Lamba drew himself up to his full height. Divya noticed that the tip of his nose was quite pale.

"What is the meaning of this! Who is this fellow?"

"The father-in-law of my neighbor's servant," Divya said. "They don't feed him—"

"I don't care who he is," Mr. Lamba said. "How can you tolerate having riffraff living in your building? The man could be dangerous! Or have a disease! Like AIDS!"

Mrs. Lamba shook herself loose from Mrs. Bhosle's grip. She pointed an accusing finger at Divya.

"What will I tell my sister when she gets back from London! Her son has been subjected to this . . . this unspeakable sight! The poor boy! And you call yourself a hostess! Wife of a vice-president!"

She turned to the other guests standing in shocked silence on the steps.

"Let us leave this horrible place . . . these . . . people," she said. "They have no standards." She turned to Divya, shook a finger in her face. "Never have I been so insulted in all my life!"

Divya looked from the dead body of the man to the upturned faces. Mrs. Bhosle shook her head, but nobody said anything to contradict Mrs. Lamba.

"Yes, please leave," Divya said firmly. Charu had begun to sob against her father's chest. Poor Vikas—he looked completely shocked. Mrs. Bhosle and Mrs. Raman helped everyone find purses and shawls, and then ushered them all out. Divya did not say any goodbyes except to thank Mrs. Bhosle and Mrs. Raman for their help. Already, as the party was going down the stairs, she could hear Mrs. Chaturvedi's high, whining voice, eagerly discussing the incident. The ladies would feast off it for many parties and dinners to come.

While they waited for the police to arrive, Charu cried against her mother's shoulder, her sobs shaking her whole body. Divya could do nothing but hold her. Waves of guilt washed over her. If only she could go back to that moment in time, when the old man had knocked on the door and Charu had been taking the parathas to him! Perhaps the parathas would not have saved him (the damned things were still in the fridge)—but who could tell? The poor man, to die like that! It wasn't fair—to raise your son and grow old, and be turned out to starve . . . Nor was it fair that she, Divya, was to be punished for one moment of carelessness, one instant where she had forgotten the right thing to do—and that this oversight should carry so much weight that it outweighed all her earlier acts of kindness to the old man, the giving of food, and the chance to earn a little money and respectability. Had none of that counted for anything? Would she now have to tiptoe through the world, watching for any lapse, any moment of forgetfulness? If the punishment was to be hers alone, she could bear it—but how cruel of the world, to punish a child instead: Charu in her new blue dress, who had learned on the day she turned twelve that Death lived in the world, and in time it would devour everyone she loved. And that it was possible to die alone and unloved. How does a child of twelve recover from that?

That moment . . . she kept returning to it in her mind. If only she hadn't been so hungry at the time! If Damyanti hadn't given Vikas those pakoras, or if Vikas hadn't been asking her about the rat poison . . .

The rat poison. A cold terror swept over Divya. How had the rat poison gotten to the old man's bedside?

She heard Vikas pacing to and fro in the drawing room, waiting for the police.

She had put the blue vial back on the bathroom shelf, behind the shampoo. The little square of stiff paper that had been in the dead man's hand she had put in the little dresser drawer where she kept her jewelry. It was a black and white picture—she hadn't had time to look at it properly. Now she made Charu sip some water.

"He was an old man, Charu," Divya said. "He was ill. Nothing we could have done would have saved him."

And so we lie to our children, she thought bitterly.

Charu choked on the water, coughed.

"He said the rats were running all over him at night . . ."

Divya held her breath. "Did you give him the rat poison?"

Charu nodded. "He said the rats were really big and he was afraid of getting bitten . . ."

Divya steadied herself, patted the child's hair.

"Listen, Charu, what you did was fine, but I don't want you to mention it to anyone. All right? Don't say anything about what the old man said or what you did. Let Papa and me talk to the policemen."

Charu's eyes went wide.

"Oh mama, do you think . . . oh, do you think . . ."

"No, no, child, quiet now. Everything is going to be fine."

Two policemen came, took notes, banged on the servants' door and on Mr. Kapadia's as well, but there was no answer. It was Saturday and Ranu and her husband were out—if Mr. Kapadia was in, he didn't care. The policemen didn't seem to care either. They nodded when Divya talked about how Ranu and her family had neglected the old man, but shrugged when she asked if they would be brought to task.

"If we launched an investigation each time some old fellow dies of starvation, we would be overwhelmed," said one. They got up and left the family to the silence, the splendid ruins of the birthday party.

During a visit to the bathroom, Divya got a chance to look at the picture the old man had been holding when he died. It was a black-and-white photo, creased with age, and it was nearly impossible to make out whose picture it was. Divya would look at it many times in the next few months and wonder if the person was a woman or an animal or something entirely different.

Divya slept next to Charu that night, something she had not done in many years. They both slept fitfully. Divya felt sorry for Vikas, tossing alone in the big bed in the next room. It would soon be time to worry about what would happen to his job. How strange that their fates should be tied to one old man whom nobody had known, whose speech nobody had understood (except for Charu—she realized, with a shock, that Charu must have been able to understand him to carry out his last request). Simply by dying, the old man would change their daughter's view of the world, and affect Vikas's career and the delicate network of social connections and links in which he existed, and change Divya herself in ways that she was yet to discover. She wondered what the old fellow had been trying to tell her these past years, in his broken voice; she should have listened more closely. She should have . . . she should have . . .

The old man lay in the center of her whirling thoughts like an enigma. Some of the tears she wept that night were for him, but as sleep slowly came to her she realized that she had never known his name.

In the weeks and months that followed, Vikas gave up his job, changed companies and began to plan a move to a different apartment in a different part of town. His new job was not as prestigious or as well-paying as the old one had been, and Divya could tell that he was unhappy. He began to play around with an old hobby, photography, disappearing for hours sometimes on weekends, and coming back to plunge himself in the darkroom he had set up in a storeroom in the flat. He refused to talk about the terrible incident, which bothered Divya because before this she had been able to talk to him about everything. Charu had the resilience of youth; she appeared to recover quite quickly, although her school performance suffered in the months following the incident. But Divya could tell that something had changed within the child. There was a sadness about her eyes that Divya could sense even when Charu was laughing with her friends. Charu had always been a soft-hearted girl, but after the incident she could no longer bear any kind of cruelty, nor could she, as a consequence, watch the news without tears. Divya worried how Charu would live in the world, whether she would learn to adapt enough to survive its horrors. She feared also that Charu blamed her for the whole thing, but apart from the inevitable distancing that growth brings, there was no indication of this. There were times when the girl would come upon her mother and give her a fierce, deep hug for no reason at all, and Divya felt Charu was trying to tell her something in some other language, and that she was able to comprehend it in that other language as well.

But the change in Divya herself was perhaps the most peculiar. She had, like most mothers, always been sensitive to the needs of those she loved, but now she was able to anticipate them even before there was any evidence of them. She knew, for instance, that Charu would have her period tomorrow, and that the cramps would be bad; consequently she refused to let Charu go to school that day. She knew in the morning if Vikas was going to have a bad day at work, and when Kallu the crow landed on her kitchen window with an injured wing, she knew it before he had alighted.

When she went out, however, the gift or curse that had been left for her by the old man's death took its strangest form. When she looked upon the faces of strangers they appeared to her like aliens, like the open mouths of birds, crying their need. But most clearly she could sense those who were hungry, whether they were schoolchildren who had forgotten their lunch or beggars under the bridge, or the boot-boy at the corner, or the emaciated girl sweeping the dusty street in front of the municipal building. Even in the great tide of humanity that thronged the pavements, amidst busy officegoers and college students with cellphones, or in the shadows of the high-rises and luxury apartment blocks, she could sense the hungry and forgotten, great masses of them, living like cockroaches in the cracks and interstices of the new old city. Their open mouths, gaping and horrific with need, at first frightened her, but then she began to carry about with her a few parathas, which she handed out to the hungry without a word, in the hope that the keening chorus of despair that nobody but she was able to hear would lessen a little. Although this didn't happen, she found herself unable to stop handing out parathas to the needy. Meanwhile she continued to read her science fiction novels because, more than ever, they seemed to reflect her own realization of the utter strangeness of the world. Slowly the understanding came to her that these stories were trying to tell her a great truth in a very convoluted way, that they were all in some kind of code, designed to deceive the literary snob and waylay the careless reader. And that this great truth, which she would spend her life unraveling, was centered around the notion that you did not have to go to the stars to find aliens or to measure distances between people in light-years.

I grew up in New Delhi, and when I was about fifteen we lived in an apartment that was part of a 4-plex, like the one in the story. There really was an old man who lived on top of the stairs, who was turned out and left to starve by his son and daughter-in-law. That memory has been with me for years, like fruit ripening on a tree, waiting to be plucked and thus to become the core of a story. The story is not really autobiographical because the part of it that actually happened is such a small fraction of the whole thing. Most of the stories I write are like this, based on a memory or an image that becomes transformed by the imagination into something I couldn't have predicted when I wrote the first sentence. That's one of the reasons I write: to find out what happens at the end.

Vandana Singh

A Map of the Everywhere

Matthew Cheney

Alfred worked in the sewer fields because all the other jobs he'd held had disappointed him. He was easily given to disappointment. A few days after his seventh birthday, his parents had stopped talking to each other, and soon they used only the smallest possible words with him, often communicating purely through grunts and snorts. Aching for more variety and another way to live, he apprenticed himself to a clockmaker when he was fifteen, but never quite learned the craft before running off to work for a potter, then a civil engineer, then a mason.

None of these jobs held his interest for long; he showed no talent for them, and though he disliked making decisions, he found the one decision that came naturally to him was the decision to move on. When he was twenty-two, he entered a mountain monastery, but he discovered his faith was thin, slippery, and easy to lose, and he found the daily routine of prayers and flagellations left many scars. He moved on to join the nomadic coffee pickers who wandered past the monastery every few days shouting out obscenities at the monks, who, legend had it, had once refused to pray for a picker who had plummeted to his death after reaching for a bean dangling off the side of a cliff.

Alfred enjoyed his time with the coffee pickers, enjoyed their ribald humor and earthy wisdom, but the constant exposure to coffee kept him from getting much sleep, and after a few sleepless years he found himself wandering farther and farther away from his colleagues in search of beans to pick, until one day he realized he'd lost his way and wandered all the way back to the city.

He did not want to be in the city, and so he walked down street after street, but the streets only led to other streets, all of which seemed to lead back to each other. He asked pedestrians for directions, but only one spoke to him, a small old woman with eyes obscured by a grey-green gauze of film. "Get yourself a shovel and dig," the woman said, then snorted dryly and blew a cloud of dust from her nose. Alfred would have been annoyed and distressed if he weren't so exhausted, but he did not have the strength to offer any response. He stumbled down a blind alley, curled up amidst a pile of outdated computer components dumped behind a pet shop, and fell asleep. He dreamed of roads leading toward treeless hills where wind scarred the soil and a grey moon cast shadows that looked like ancient pictograms written across the landscape.

When he woke, Alfred discovered he had been loaded into the back of a large pickup truck along with the computer components. He ran his hands over acoustic couplers, memory cards, logic boards, monitors with sentences burned into their glass, and bulky CPUs sporting little metal labels saying, "Made in China."

Soon the truck came to a stop at a junkyard. A plump man with a scraggly grey beard and a missing eye asked him who he was and why he was in the back of the truck. Alfred said he was looking for work, and the man said there was no work at the junkyard, but the sewer fields a few miles in that direction were always looking for workers with nowhere else to go, and Alfred thanked the man and began walking down the road.

He was still far from the sewer fields when he heard the clanks and groans of the refinery. Soon he could see the massive pipes and smokestacks silhouetted on the horizon, and then he saw the fields, the broad expanse of brown-black sewage oozing from the side of the road to the farthest horizon. He had heard about the sewer fields, heard terrible stories of the people who toiled in them, sorting through the waves of excrement in search of objects and materials that would please the field owners. Workers who were lucky could make quite a lot of money, it was said, but Alfred had never met anyone who knew a lucky worker—at least one whose luck had held out long enough to be enjoyed. Instead, he heard tales of Jack's friend Franco, who got sucked up into the refinery engines and turned to smoke and ash, or Rosa's Uncle Hans, who drowned in the sewage, or the ghosts that spoke in ways no one understood.

Alfred, it turned out, was neither lucky nor unlucky, which is the best fate for a field worker. After only a few days in the fields, standing in chest-high sewage with a yellow plastic colander the foreman had given him on the first day, he stopped noticing the stench, stopped retching and puking, stopped thinking that at any moment he would collapse and end up like Franco or Uncle Hans. By the beginning of the second week, the refinery's gasps and screams and hums calmed him as he worked, lulled him into a pleasant state of half-dreaming, his mind lost in images of roads and of the words for roads, images that lasted just long enough to be erased as his hands held the colander and sifted through the sewage.

At first, Alfred spent his nights sleeping on the edge of the fields. He could have joined one of the camps of workers farther out, but by the time the sun set, he was too tired to talk. He ate the roots and vegetables that grew plentifully near the fields, and enjoyed his solitude. It required no prayers or self-abuse, and it gave him time to think about the strange visions that filled his daydreams: visions of lollipop-shaped children and old men with mouths full of coins and cuckoo clocks that held midnight rituals to sacrifice pocket watches to the gods. He had never had such visions before. Before, the monotony of daily work would lull him into a blind and mindless state, letting time drift through him without notice.

One night, Alfred woke to the sound of whispers. A pair of gauzy eyes stared down at him from a face as craggled as the moon. "This is where I have come to dig," the voice (little more than a breeze) said from dusty lips.

Alfred stood up. He could not tell if it was a man or woman in front of him, wrapped in shreds of plastic, leaning on a rusty shovel. "What are you digging?" Alfred said.

"A hole," the creature replied.

"Why?" Alfred said.

The creature paused for a moment to consider the question, then said, "I must dig a hole to China."

Alfred tended toward grumpiness whenever he was woken in the middle of the night. He said, "Look, I already have enough surrealism in my life, and I really don't have the patience for more. Would you please explain to me why you have to be exactly here, exactly now, doing exactly this?"

The creature spoke of pecuniary canons of taste, the conservation of archaic traits, modern survivals of prowess, and the belief in luck. Alfred didn't listen closely. The voice slipped more and more toward silence as the creature stood there, sweeping loose gravel with the shovel, until the voice disappeared in the scrape of rock and dirt against metal. Alfred feared that the creature was crying and not able to make a sound or shed a tear, its voice hollowed out, its ducts gone dry. Alfred shuddered. He walked away.

As the first bits of sunlight slipped over the horizon, Alfred stopped walking and looked out across the shadowy plains of the sewer fields, where he saw workers already sifting through it all and foremen riding motorized sleds from one worker to the next to note who had collected what and to prod them on with lectures about empowerment and the good life. Alfred fell to his knees, ready to pray for salvation, but then he remembered that he had lost his faith and lost his way, and so he clawed at the damp soil in search of something he could not name, hoping his luck might reveal itself if he just jostled the topography a bit, but he found only some berries. They were sweet and made him smile.

Behind him, Alfred heard soft footsteps. He turned around. Three creatures with gauzy eyes, craggled faces, and dusty lips, all wearing shreds of plastic, all leaning on shovels, stood staring at him. "You must dig a hole to China," one of the creatures whispered.

"I was digging for faith or direction," Alfred replied. "I have no interest in China. I couldn't even find it on a map."

"Then you have need of a cartographer," another of the creatures said. "I have known many cartographers."

"They are a strange breed, cartographers," another of the creatures said.

"They live in hovels and garrets," another of the creatures said. "They seldom shave."

"I have to go to work soon," Alfred said. "I need to find some more berries before I starve to death or start to eat the dirt. Excuse me—" He began to walk away, but the three creatures stood in front of him.

One of the creatures said, "The conventional scheme of decent living calls for a considerable exercise of the earlier barbaric traits."

One of the creatures said, "We are the scars of wounding words."

All three of the creatures thrust their shovels into the ground. Each pulled up a pile of dirt and held it in front of Alfred. "Choose wisely," one of the creatures said.

Before he could think about what he was doing or why, Alfred reached into the pile of dirt in the shovel of the creature to his left, and from the dirt he pulled a grey business card with a name and address printed on it. He flicked the dirt off the card with his finger and read what was written there:

GÜNTHER P. LOPEZ
cartographer and mime
17 Gough Square, Lichfield

When he looked up from the card, Alfred for a moment thought the creatures had disappeared, but then he saw that they had positioned themselves along the side of the road with their backs to him, and they had commenced digging to China.

At that moment, Alfred realized the dawn had turned to day and he was late for work. He could not pull his eyes from the spectacle of the creatures at the side of the road. He was entranced by their gnomic greyness, his imagination inspired to build entire lives for them, lost lives—families discarded for the sake of indeterminate destinies, memories forgotten in quests that the years whittled down to simple syllables and empty gestures. Alfred pressed his fingers into his eyes. The creatures did not turn around. "Please . . ." he said, but they continued digging. Fury rose in his chest, he clenched his teeth, he tried to keep his feet from moving, but within a moment he had become so unwitted that he could not escape his old habit of moving on, and he ran and ran down the road.

It was, for a very long time, a straight road, utterly without curves or even indentations, basically a berm raised in the midst of the sewer sea, but after many monotonous miles, kilometers, and versts of unvarying straightness, the road curved, swerved, dived, and diverged into a web of tributaries radiating from a point, all labeled with flimsy metal signs indicating avenues and boulevards, lanes and highways, turnpikes, beltways, thoroughfares, underpasses, boreens, detours, post roads, and main drags.

By now, Alfred's anxieties had barnacled themselves to other possibilities, worrying him about where to go and what to do there or here or wherever he ended up, but he remembered the card of the cartographer and it eased his mind, giving him one direction to look for: Lichfield.

Alfred wandered down Lichfield Lane, going on the assumption that such a lane might lead to Lichfield, and for once his assumption proved correct. He emerged from the tree-lined lane in a small town with dirt streets and narrow wooden buildings raised on stilts. "Why the stilts?" he asked an old woman sitting in a rocking chair up on the porch of a supply shop for rocket scientists.

"Better circulation!" the woman yelled down at him, apparently assuming he was hard of hearing. Alfred was about to reply, but before he could issue any words, the woman got out of her rocking chair, fired up a jetpack, and flew off into the clouds drifting across the blue and summery sky.

It did not take Alfred long to locate Günther Lopez, whose office towered high above everything else in Lichfield. Not only were its stilts taller than any others, but it was the only lighthouse in town, although why a town so far from the ocean would need a lighthouse at all was (and remained) a mystery to Alfred.

"Ahoy!" Alfred called up to the lighthouse. "Günther Lopez!"

After a moment, a man with a bright white, clean-shaven face and sensitive green eyes peeked out of an open window toward the top of the lighthouse tower and called out, "Wie ist das Wetter heute?"

"Excuse me?"

"No creo en los signos del zodíaco!"

"I am in need of a cartographer," Alfred said.

Lopez held his hands to his face and suddenly his entire countenance erupted with a bright, idiotic smile. He gestured for Alfred to ascend the iron stairs spiralling around one of the stilts.

The inside of the lighthouse was spare, a single round room with brightly-colored plastic chairs and a large glass table in the center. At the far side, a bookcase sprouted rolls of maps.

Lopez greeted Alfred by pretending to shake hands with him from across the room. Alfred watched with growing frustration as the man carried on a lively, silent conversation with himself. Finally, Alfred said, "Shi-gatsu ni Amerika e kaerimasu!"

Lopez froze when he heard the words. His face sank like wet clay. "How did you know?" he said quietly.

"How did I know what?"

"Don't be coy. My mother's ancestry is a precious secret to me. I had no idea anyone else knew she was Finnish."

"I have come here with a purpose," Alfred said. "I am allergic to non sequiturs, and I can already feel my nose stuffing up. Please, can we talk cartography?"

"Upland planetable rectification alidade bathymetry hachure monoscopic isopleth!" Lopez screamed, then fell to the floor, where he gasped and panted with great élan.

Alfred turned away so that Lopez would not see the tears welling in his eyes. This road, too, had led to nothing. The muscles in his back tensed, whipping memories across his skin.

From the vantage of the lighthouse tower, Alfred looked down at a clearing in the middle of a dense forest. On a rock in the clearing sat a man who rested his head in his hands. While the cartographer continued to chatter behind him, Alfred stared at the man, wondering if what he saw were alive or, instead, a particularly skilled sculpture. The answer came when the man glanced up at the lighthouse. Sorrow-laden eyes, indisputably alive, met Alfred's own eyes for one blink before the head returned to the hands.

Without looking back, Alfred climbed down the spiral stairs and walked away from Lichfield toward the forest. He trudged through the undergrowth and between the trees, pushing his way into the lightless woods. When darkness engulfed him he saw a sparkle of light coming from the clearing at the far side, and he made his way toward it.

The man still sat on the rock. Alfred looked at him and felt compassion growing in his heart. He wanted to speak, to offer words of consolation or sympathy or hope, but language seemed suddenly too blunt, too barbed, too barbaric. Gently, tentatively, he set his hand on the man's neck. The skin was soft and warm. The man turned and looked at Alfred. He had a dark face with a prominent nose and small green eyes, their whites crackled red, having run out of tears.

"I'm looking for a cartographer," Alfred whispered.

"My mother is a cartographer," the man said. "Her office is in the lighthouse. Her name is Günther Lopez. She is insane, but she is a good cartographer."

"She's not the kind of cartographer I need," Alfred said, but he wasn't sure why he said this or how he knew it was true, and so he decided to tell a story: "I once spent some time with a civil engineer, surveying places to put new roads and buildings, but I could not make the compass work and I could not draw straight lines. He stopped talking to me and would scream when anyone said my name. He accused me of being a poet, and he said that I would ruin him."

The man nodded. "When I was younger," he said, "I told my mother I didn't know where to go or how to get there, and she said she would draw me a map, because she hated to see me in pain. I followed the map to the edge of the world, and when I got there, all I found was silence. I wrote a play, because I thought that might alleviate the silence. It didn't help. When I dragged myself home, my friends stole the play and read it to each other and after they woke up they said well at least I'd learned to amuse myself."

Alfred leaned down and kissed the man. "My name is Zachary," the man said.

Zachary and Alfred sat together in the woods until the sun went down and the stars came up and the sky filled with old ladies wearing jetpacks, out for an evening flight. Zachary whispered words from his play into Alfred's ear, and Alfred laughed many times, amused.

Here is the last speech in Zachary's play:

> **ZEUS:** Tales from the unpublished autobiography of Zeus, god of everything, part one. Ahemmm. When I was just a wee little deity, crawling about in some ethereal nook or cranny, I found a map of the Everywhere, and I studied this map until the stars went out for the night. When light returned, the map was gone. No one could tell me where it went. I was lost, destined not so much to wander as to stumble from point to point, thing to thing, and where to where. Forever finding hosts of theres, never finding a single here. Waiting, always, for the stars to go out again, and for my map to find me, to press itself against my skin in the momentary darkness.

By the clocks, it was tomorrow when they left the woods, and even the clearing was dark. The forest itself was so dense as to be more than dark, to be the very antithesis of sight, but Alfred and Zachary had four other senses left, and used them well to touch and hear and taste and smell their way back to Lichfield.

"Can we go anywhere other than the lighthouse?" Alfred asked. "I'm not sure I'm up for another encounter with . . ."

"My mother won't be there now," Zachary said. "She goes home at night, because the light bothers her."

Alfred looked up and saw a thick bolt of light swirling through the sky from the top of the lighthouse. It caught clouds and moondust in its journey from one side of the night to another, illuminating the way for the ghosts of unmoored boats potentially floating lost across the land.

Alfred said, "Let's go there then," and so they did.

In the round room in the center of the light, Zachary showed Alfred map after map: maps of fertile and infertile lands, maps of entangled roads, maps of divided continents and lonely islands, maps demonstrating the movement of authoritarian medical discourse from urban centers to rural outlands. "This is her favorite," Zachary said, pulling a small vellum map from the bookcase and unrolling it with care and respect on the glass table.

Alfred scrutinized the map, but did not know what it showed. The outlines of areas looked like towns of some sort, with hills and rivers between some of them. But none of the words made any sense to him. "What is it all?" he asked. He pointed to words: *gynecomastia, feminae barbatae, androtrichia, androglottia, gynophysia . . .*

"She said it was a map of the states of desire. Or maybe disappointment. I don't remember. I've never been able to understand it, myself, but I find it entrancing, nonetheless."

After looking at the maps, they lay together on the wooden floor and let the light spin around them. Zachary told Alfred about his father, a linguist, and how he was certain it was his father who drove his mother mad, filling her with words she could not mime, an entire ungesturable grammar. His father died in an act of conjugation soon after Zachary was born. Alfred told Zachary about his own parents, his father who had always regretted not dying in a war, his mother who became an architect after years spent studying accounting. He spoke of his apprenticeships and of his time in the monastery and his life with the coffee pickers and in the sewer fields, and he said he had come to Lichfield to find Günther Lopez because foreigners in plastic rags had whispered it would be best for him, and so he'd run down yet another road, and arrived here at this place that seemed to him more vivid and specific than any other he'd encountered, though he could not say how or why, and the mystery of it all pleased him and helped him feel, for now, alive.

Zachary said he had once had an older brother who was somewhat simple-minded, who got what jobs he could here and there depending on the season, now and then collecting some money from the worst sorts of labor, now and then stealing some pennies from their mother, but he seldom came home and mostly slept in barns and stables. Eventually, someone turned him over to the authorities, because someone had seen him in the clearing in the forest with a young girl, and the young girl had given him some caresses, the sort of caresses he had seen other men his age receive from girls not much older than this one, and that he himself had received when the bigger boys from town made him play the game they all called "curdled milk." The authorities brought Zachary's brother to a judge, and the judge indicted him and then turned him over to the care of a doctor, and the doctor gave the boy to other doctors, specialists, who asked Zachary's brother many questions and then wrote up a report that was published in a well-known journal. They measured his brainpan, they studied his facial bone structure, they inspected his anatomy to find degeneracy, and they made him talk and talk about his thoughts and ideas, his inclinations, his habits, his feelings. In the end, in terms only lawyers could understand, the judge pronounced Zachary's brother not guilty, but the doctors kept him for themselves. "He is still with them," Zachary said, "in their asylum, but we are told we cannot talk about it, that he no longer exists and never existed. I heard boys in the schoolhouse trying to tell the story, and the schoolmaster told them to watch their language and never talk about these things ever again, or they, too, would end up like my brother."

Alfred kissed Zachary's cheek. They lay side-by-side in silence. Zachary began to unbutton Alfred's shirt, but Alfred pushed his hand away. "Not while there is light," Alfred said.

"Why not?"

"My skin will repulse you," Alfred said. "It was ruined by the lash and by the sewer fields, by every place that I have lived and every person I have known."

Zachary looked into Alfred's eyes and smiled and kissed him, then continued to unbutton his shirt. Alfred began to object again, but stopped, and soon Zachary ran his hand gently over Alfred's chest and back, feeling the landscape of welts and scars, while Alfred sobbed. Zachary removed his own shirt, revealing smooth and perfect skin, a blank world. He pulled off his trousers and underpants, and Alfred did the same, and they lay together in the very center of the room, arms and legs entwined, breaths intermingling, skin against skin, while the lighthouse light swung around them, reaching out through the unmapped darkness to the stars.

Just before morning, a breeze blew through the room, and all the maps on the table, and many of the maps from the bookcase, danced into the air and settled on Alfred and Zachary's bodies. The sight might have horrified Zachary's mother, who prided herself on the care and organization she devoted to her maps, but she didn't come to the office in the lighthouse until the afternoon, because in the morning she woke from a dream of Zachary's brother with the sudden knowledge of how to reach the asylum, and so that morning she walked to the other end of Lichfield Lane to a perfectly square building made from obsidian bricks, and she spoke to an army of doctors and demanded that her son be released to her, and he was. The moment she saw her son, his mother began to unwrap the plastic the doctors had bound him with. She wiped his eyes and scrubbed his face and gave him water to bring back his voice, which, after years of breathing medical dust, had all but gone away. His skin was hard as sun-baked clay, but it softened slightly beneath her touch.

Zachary and Alfred spent the morning cleaning up the room and teasing each other, and by the time Günther Lopez arrived with Zachary's brother, the maps seemed to be unruffled and unbreezed.

"This is Muriuki," Günther Lopez said. "He is your brother."

Muriuki was a short, plump man with a bald head, perfectly round eyes, and exactly the same nose as Zachary. Günther Lopez said, "I am going to teach him to make puppets. We will be a family again. I will perform as a mime and cartographer, and you and Muriuki will put on a puppet show, and we will all be happy and world famous."

Zachary said, "Mother, this is Alfred. He and I are moving on from here and we will never return."

Günther Lopez said, "Well, wait till we get some puppets made. We can't leave until then."

Zachary held Alfred's hand and led him toward the door. "Goodbye," Zachary said to Muriuki.

"I'm sorry we didn't get to spend more time together," Muriuki said.

"You're welcome to come with us if you want," Alfred said.

"No," Muriuki said, "I think our mother needs me. But I'll send you postcards."

"Where will you send the postcards to?" Zachary said.

"The moon, of course," Muriuki said, his eyes wide, serious, and poetic. "He'll see you, wherever you go, and he'll write my words into your dreams."

Zachary and Alfred climbed down the spiral stairs and walked slowly through the town, letting each building inspire imaginary memories for them of where they might have first caught a glimpse of each other and where they might have first touched hands and where they might have first watched a movie together and where they might have first kissed.

As they passed a diner in an abandoned boxcar, Zachary said to Alfred, "You're too thin!"

Alfred said, "It's been a long time since I had anything to eat."

"We must eat!" Zachary said, and he led Alfred into the diner. They sat in a booth with wooden seats and a marble table. A waiter dressed in a tattered tuxedo brought them menus written on fig leaves and told them the special of the day was broiled anaphora. Zachary ordered a peanut butter sandwich and a cup of coffee. Alfred ordered a garden salad and a tofu burger.

"I've decided to become a vegetarian," Alfred said.

"I've been a vegetarian for a long time," Zachary said. "I don't like to hurt animals. They know more about the world than we do, but the knowledge disappears when they die."

"I just like being a member of minority cultures," Alfred said.

After they finished their food, Alfred said, "Where should we go from here?"

"I don't know," Zachary said. "We left all the maps back at the lighthouse. If you want, we can just sit here and look into each other's eyes forever."

Alfred blushed and bowed his head. "I can't stop moving," he said. "My life is a picaresque story."

Zachary put a finger under Alfred's chin and lifted his head. "But you're in a love story now."

"It can't last," Alfred said.

"Why not?"

"They never do."

"Some love stories are timeless," Zachary said.

"We'll fight. We'll misunderstand each other. We'll hurt each other's feelings with careless comments and selfish moments. We'll get old and wrinkled and sick. We'll fall out of love. I'd rather just keep walking . . ." He stood up, but Zachary stood in his way.

"Let's dance," Zachary said.

"There's no music."

The waiter pressed a button on the face of a cuckoo clock in a corner of the diner and the sound of a tinkly waltz filled the air.

Alfred said, "I'm a terrible dancer."

Zachary put his arms around him and began moving in time to the music.

At first, Alfred couldn't figure out where to put his feet, and he stepped on Zachary's toes and once even nearly fell over. But soon they were moving gracefully, their left hands clasped together and their right arms wrapped around each other's bodies, and they giggled and whispered, and while they danced the waiter carried all of the tables and seats outside, leaving the diner empty except for the music and the two dancers, who swung around and around, laughing and kissing and resting their heads on each other's shoulders. As dusk turned the entire world grey except for a warm yellow light inside the boxcar, Alfred and Zachary finally stopped dancing, and when they looked outside they saw a crowd of people sitting in the chairs there, watching them, a crowd of people dressed in rags of old plastic, their faces craggled and lips dusty, their eyes lively with childlike joy, and the sound of their applause carried through the night to the lighthouse (where Günther Lopez was trying to show Muriuki how to make puppets from paper clips) and then on and on to the sewer fields and to the junkyard and the pet shop and the monastery, where the coffee pickers stopped shouting obscenities at the monks just long enough to hear the strange sound filling the air, and the monks briefly ceased whipping themselves and praying, and somewhere even farther away Alfred's mother stopped designing a skyscraper and his father stopped looking at pictures in a book about war, and though they were too far away to hear the sound of the applause, they knew something had changed in the world.

Alfred and Zachary bowed to their audience and giggled with a bit of embarrassment, a bit of exhaustion. As the audience continued to applaud, the two men dashed out the back door of the diner and away, running through the dark until they collapsed together in a soggy ravine, where they slept through all of the day and most of the night. When they woke, they stood up stiffly, brushed off their clothes, and continued walking, hand in hand, Zachary humming a waltz and Alfred trying to remember some prayers. They would wander together through many more nights and days, and now and then they would utter occasional harsh words to each other, now and then one would withdraw or another would be selfish, now and then they would disagree about which road to follow or which restaurant to beg a meal from, but through it all they continued to talk to each other, to fight back disappointment together, and nearly every day brought a laugh or two, and they looked forward to reaching old age, when perhaps they might settle down somewhere and draw a map of where they'd been and what they'd seen, but for now, walking through the world, the last thing either Zachary or Alfred wanted was a map.

Today the only labels I like for what I write are *Wishes* and *Exorcisms*. Sometimes the two labels overlap, like searchlights finding each other in a dark sky.

A few months before he died in 1904, Anton Chekhov wrote to his wife, an actress in Moscow. He was forty-four years old, living in Yalta, and in the last stages of tuberculosis, a disease he had suffered from for almost half his life, a disease that had claimed his brother, Nikolai, in 1889. He wrote, "You ask: What is life? That's just like asking: What is a carrot? A carrot is a carrot, and that's all we know."

I want my stories to be like life, which means I want them to be like carrots, which means each story is a story, and that's all we know.

Matthew Cheney

Emblemata
(reciting the Heart Sutra)

Léa Silhol

There is no ignorance,
and no end to ignorance,
no old age, no death,
no release from old age and death.
No suffering,
no cause of suffering,
no end of suffering,
no path to reach the end of suffering.

—Prajna Paramita Hrdaya Sutra

Pages from the travel notebook of Alexandre Iacovleff

Bâmiyân, 1931
Rupam (form)

We left Bayreuth on the fourth of April, and have traveled almost continuously ever since. The landscapes roll past us, and I sway rhythmically, jounced by the vibration of the awkward, hybrid half-track vehicles. It has taken us a month and a half to reach the Afghan frontier, to cross the border that separated us from this "land of piety and purity" where we are by no means sure we are welcome.

But the Orient is a paradox, a trickster. Instead of the difficulties we anticipated, of minutely examined passports and visas, we have received a welcome out of the Arabian Nights. After the rifles of Islam Kaleh and the unscalable walls, we have been unexpectedly greeted with hospitable offerings of dates, almond paste, and pistachios. Steel and sweetmeats. Georges Le Fevre wrote in his notebook about this "land where legend says every inhabitant's life-partner is his rifle, and the traveler must always assume that he is being aimed at." Aimed at, yes, and straight for the heart, by steel or by sugar. The human climate here is as uncertain, as volatile as the rough country we explore. To explore: It's the primary object of the Citroën Yellow Cruise, and I, a man of images, have joined the expedition to explore this country with lines, to immortalize the route with brush and pencils. . . . No roads, no maps; fighting in the north; in between, an uncertain welcome.

Outside the port of Islam Kaleh, the inhabitants react unpredictably: indifferent, excited, or amazed by the slow passage of our half-tracks. My eyelashes are laden with grains of sand; my hand aches at not being able to preserve everything I see.

At Herat, where the roads to India and the Occident meet, the covered market is immobilized in time, crystallized, with all the gestures and movement of a way of life unchanged for centuries. We are in the midst of history, in a past sewn with golden thread and perfumed with spices.

Outside the city, the governor has had a house made ready for us. Another unexpected welcome. We're told to make ourselves at home. We are receiving a slow, patient introduction to Afghani courtesy, to its sugar and its steel. Here, even some of the children who smile at us sling a Mauser in a bandolier over one shoulder.

On the road, in the vistas around us, the beauty of the light falls on an unbearable contrast of landscapes. Under our feet, the land is harsher than the desert. High above us rise peaks crowned with mountain snow. Between them hang suspended mirage-like cities of cool shadow and vibrant colors, more enervating than perfume: hospitable, but forbidden, displaying their beauty to us without letting us touch more than the edges of their veils. Farther down the road we travel, farther, walled between the vigilant, indolent guards who line our route and the excessive pomp with which we are greeted. Step by step, until we reach the heights, the pinnacle of all these preparations for our bewitchment. The apotheosis.

Mokour.

Seven thousand kilometers from our comfortable West, we are ushered into palatial luxury.

"You are much expected."

And, to demonstrate, days of feasting.

To show us its face, proud Afghanistan summons to Mokour a troop of warrior-dancers. The men have the savage beauty of their earth, and its paradoxes. Bracelets by the dozens on their arms, gazelle eyes veiled with black antimony.

Their hair, partly or wholly unbound, whips their wild faces. Their eyes are cast down, self-absorbed. They display themselves, they guard themselves, proud, immodest, unaccepted and unaccepting, pivoting about themselves. Some dance holding their rifles, others bare-handed; the two are the same. Beside me, amazed and admiring, Georges makes phrases: they spring from the earth like savage flowers, he says. As for myself, I think they are like flames. Wanting to draw them, my hand cannot follow them to the extremes of motion at which they fling themselves. I feel alienated, heavy, caught within my culture, which can no longer create such a thing as this, this dance of absolutes between ecstasy and defiance that only these warriors can embody.

They have come from far away to display themselves to us and defy us, and once they are done, they leave; they have done what they had to. One of them, leaving, smiles at me and glances at my notebook. I have tried to draw him and had no more success than with the others. Perhaps he is smiling in victory. "Can you comprehend us or represent us? Capture and halt our motion?" perhaps his eyes say; perhaps not.

This is the pride of these men, to dance not for us but for themselves. Above all they danced because they are what they are, and we are merely passersby. We are their guests, but strangers. The welcome they offer is what they decided they should give us, a debt of honor that they recognize they owe, and recognize themselves by owing. Only Islam affirms its pride with such an odalisque's elegance.

We ford four rivers; it's half adventure, half clown show. The land is wild, the inhabitants charming. We reach Kabul at the beginning of the summer. Kabul, paradox of paradoxes, fragmented between abortive modern projects and the millennial layers of its history. Our convoy passes, slow, silent, stupefied, between the buildings of a city within a city, built and then capriciously abandoned. Already dead. Practice work, an attempt to see if the modern world was worth anything, the abortive dream of an outdated king. He wanted to construct a second Paris on the Afghan earth; the earth voted no.

The saying is that the king was guilty of trying, in one reign, to make changes that take lifetimes. He broke rhythm, and was condemned to exile.

After dead modern Kabul, old Kabul is like an explicit message, immutable and alive.

After the khans, we meet the current king and his ministers. Hospitable, but guarded. We are welcomed as strangers, but we do not belong to this land.

We continue on the road toward the west.

And we find ourselves at the valley of Bâmiyân.

From the veranda of a villa someone has lent us, in the gigantically scaled landscape spread out before me, I see for the first time the cliff pierced by the colossal niches of the great Buddhas. They are fifty meters high, dominating everything.

Impossible for us not to approach them; impossible not to enter the pass of the Hindu Kush and climb into the grottoes excavated in the "pure and pious country" before there was an Afghanistan.

Higher and higher I climb, until I stand on the very head of the Enlightened One.

There I have to sit down, to bring out my sketchpad. To preserve on paper the paintings that are disappearing from the vault.

From far away, but too close, I hear Hackin explaining that the Muslims who now live here consider these Buddhist images heretical. They regularly tar them and set them on fire; sometimes they shoot at them. So many are already lost, he says.

When the others leave, I remain. I feel an oppressive urgency, as if to leave without drawing everything, saving everything on paper, would be to admit in advance that these centuries-old paintings will soon be lost to the world.

I feel here the ardor of a thousand convinced and patient hands, the spirit of a million prayers. I owe them equal ardor, equal spirit. I copy the designs I hope to make immortal, but my hand wanders away into scribbling marginal notes, powerless to re-create everything, because I cannot comprehend it.

Behind me, someone laughs.

I turn.

A silhouette against a radiant sky: his voice comes to me first.

"You stay here for hours, Frenchman. Aren't you dizzy? And what do you write there? . . . You are anxious to 'decipher the flight of supple and vivid lines over the surface eaten by time and wounded by fanatics' rifle fire'?"

He's quoting my notes. He laughs again. And this time I see him more clearly.

"What are you drawing? What are you stalking? Ah . . . their smiles . . ."

He keeps behind me, a little to my right, standing on the head of the great Buddha. (How can he read over my shoulder from where he is?) His arms are crossed, he's still laughing, without mockery but with great amusement.

He's standing right at the edge of the abyss, closer than I am to falling. He leans slightly backward, as if to expose the planes of his face to the wind that touches his back. He wears copper earrings and a long dagger at his belt. He looks like the dancer who smiled at me in Mokour. Perhaps it's the same man, I don't know. They all looked alike in the dance, even the most savage of them, the one I tried in vain to draw, who seemed the incarnation of all of them.

He looks at me, smiling.

It is the same man.

His eyes are no longer ringed with kohl, nor his hair unbound. But his look is still impossible to mistake.

And seeing him, with the volplane of the Afghan countryside behind him, I tell myself that this is how a man should exist, the place where he should be. Unafraid of the height, perpetually and irrationally defying gravity and himself. Turning his back on the abyss through not fear but pride: as sure of himself as a lion in his territory, and his territory is the world.

"How brave you are, Frenchman, to climb so high, to the very forehead of the ancient gods. To get closer to them, to walk on them, to find—what?"

"To find out."

" 'Find out'?"

He laughs again, a little more loudly.

"What they're hiding. Their faces. Their smiles."

"You think they hide something? Or they *know* something? Perhaps . . ."

For a moment he presents his profile to the wind, his eyes half-closed. His smile is not that of the Buddhas, but something in him is like them.

He throws me an amused side glance, then slowly, deliberately, turns and fades into the shadow of the arch.

His smile is like a courtesan's, inviting and challenging at once. But he has promised nothing. And if he's making me a proposition, it's something other than the obvious, something all the more tempting because I don't know what it is.

I gather up my sketchbook and pencils and follow him.

Below, in the bowl of the valley, two horses are standing. He is already astride one waiting for me. I mount the other and follow him without questioning. Sometimes, to become closer to something, one must put a distance between oneself and it and be silent. Each act of apprenticeship is half will, half submission.

We ride. It's some time before my unknown man speaks.

Sunyata (emptiness)

"Do you know the Heart Sutra? No? Once in my journeying, I met a man who walked alone, though he had many followers. He possessed nothing, although he had seen and possessed everything that was futile and essential. He wished to gain nothing, to keep nothing, to give nothing away, though his followers thought he did. I told him I had lost all my old life; I was questioning the value of my endless future when my world had been destroyed and only I remained alive. He smiled and told me I had never had anything. Not even myself. No eye, no ear, no nose or tongue. No body, no thought. No *self.* No form. He told me that to travel to emptiness, one must start out from form. And he smiled again. You who like smiles, do you want me to explain what was the form of that smile? Yes? All right, first you must *see*."

He dismounts; I imitate him. He leans down and picks up something from the powdery earth. He holds out the palm of his hand toward me, and I see a plaster medallion shining white through its encrustations of dirt.

"The Greeks, they called these Emblemata."

I pick carefully at the object, rub it gently to disengage an astonishingly pure face.

"Little images of deities. Some think, because these works look simple, not important, they were sketches made by student artists. The soil of Gandhara is sown with them still. They show the spirits, the divinities, the procession of Dionysus, often. Maenads, Silenus. . . . You know them?"

"A little."

"For the people of those times, the gods were everywhere. Later, in more 'civilized' eras, artists would paint big and little kings, and even bankers' wives and their own mistresses. But in those barbaric times artists immortalized almost nothing but the gods. Men had proud hearts; they wanted nothing less than Olympus. Of course, they were actually representing concepts, making them in stone or on the breakable skin of vases; they were modeling the essence of this world using the materials of this world. Sculptors know you have to slap the clay or strike the marble so that the idea can emerge. Strike and slap . . . It's the same to shape the spirit, eh?" He laughs. "So, still, often, sculptors are barbarous. They take for a time the imprint of the gods, or the primary impulses that the gods incarnated. They betray the gods less than painters do. The beings who chisel at the hard matter of the world extract its essence; painters, who make colors flow and dance at the end of a brush, merely impress their visions on the world.

"The men of Attica knew that. Their gods, they found them everywhere. Now they're dead or silent; there's nothing left of them but traces, like the Emblemata scattered on this ground. Laughable. A bit of fragile plaster. All the same, that's all there is.

"At least on the surface—Ah, but only on the surface.

"The Greeks who came here with Alexander left enormous ruins behind. Dust, fires, invasions buried them; but they're still here, underneath this parched once-fertile skin of earth. For more than a century, the French have been searching for them, patiently, curiously. They like that, Frenchmen, to study the ancient forms. And ancient they are. Old, serious, heavy. Only the little things, the light unimportant things, rise again to the surface, alone, like these plaster shells where someone has sketched the profile of a god.

"Some people, you know how it is, they see nothing but the lessons one can learn from an ancient object: its materials, its motifs, its form. Fewer see the great importance of this little thing."

"Which is?"

"*How* it came to be. One man's hand modeled this, and then disappeared. His civilization became ashes, the wind blew it away, and he was forgotten, the man and his art and his passage through this world. But, later, other artists came here and found these chips of yesterday. They rubbed the balls of their thumbs over the lines; they saw the faces of the Greek gods, Apollo's cold perfection, the satyrs' grimaces; and they didn't need a French archeologist to recognize gods. They just didn't know the names; they depended on nothing but their artists' eyes. And the faces of the Buddhas these artists made emerged from the stone of Gandhara with Apollo's profile. With all that and more: the straight nose, the long eyelids, the folds of the drapery, but without the Occidental divinities' cold posing; because the Buddha is Blessed, he wants to smile. His smile has blossomed. The sculptures have freed it from its encrustations. And the Buddhas show their radiant faces to the world, to fascinate you.

"That is form. The explication, and what your eye sees. The form of the smile, but *not* the smile.

"Because the smile cannot be understood unless you accept that form is emptiness."

I raise my eyebrows. "Emptiness?"

"Oh, the problems you make for yourself, Iacovleff! When you draw, where's the form of what you're drawing? Is it there, on your sketch pad? No, you know it isn't."

He taps my forehead with stiff fingers.

"It's there. When you put marks on the paper, that's only the way you're explaining the form to yourself, by pretending to show it to others. While you think you're battling impermanence, you're subscribing to it. You're uselessly trying to immortalize a particular form. You want to seize it, comprehend it. But form doesn't exist and you can't draw emptiness. So you artists are never satisfied with your work.

"The potter who makes a bowl creates it with a function in mind, a use. If the bowl fits its use, if it can serve in a tavern or a palace, it's a good bowl and the potter can be satisfied. Making it beautiful, that's between the potter and himself, as long as its beauty doesn't take away from its function. But what you do is nothing but an attempt to give form to the world because you sense its emptiness. You think you can show the form of the world, but on the contrary, aren't you fighting to invent it?"

"Are you saying my work is useless? Is that where we're going?"

"No. What you do is not a work, it's an intention. Intention is not useless, but just more complex than a work that can be submitted to examination. No, what you do isn't useless. Because form is nothing else than emptiness, but emptiness is nothing else than form."

"Then what are you trying to explain to me? That your Sutra has a firm foundation?"

"A Sutra isn't explained. It is transmitted, and some people understand it and receive it into themselves, open themselves to it, and some don't. Those who experience its truth suffer, because it's terrible to accept that everything around us, everything that causes all our joys and sorrows, is illusion. Beauty and suffering, love and pain, and our very selves: all illusion. Nothingness. But it's exactly because our spirits rebel, because we *can't* detach ourselves from these concepts of beauty and suffering and self, that proves there's a truth for us to understand.

"But a Sutra can't be explained. I'm not explaining it to you, I'm reciting it. It happens that you're here and are listening. The demonstration of a Sutra is the world, Frenchman. It's everything that you see now around us. Me, I'm just reciting."

He looks at me out of the corner of his eye, provocatively. Something in me revolts against what he says, but I don't know how to tell him; so my anger turns on him.

"I'm no *Frenchman*, stop calling me that. I'm Russian, if I have to be anything."

He bursts out laughing. His laugh is loud, raucous, long and joyful. He wipes his eyes.

"Finally! I thought you'd never dare. No, you're not Russian. You were born in Russia, you left your country for Paris; you're not Russian and you're not French. You're a *foreigner*. Why do you suppose I chose you to speak to? I'm a foreigner like you, a passerby, a voyager, an exile; you see me as the symbol of what the natives are, but I come from 'outside,' like you. One must come from 'outside' to be able to take that step from outside to the center, and to wear the mask without which there is no revelation. I came here as a *xenos*. I asked for hospitality, and it was given to me."

"Who are you? You know too much about everything to be what you pretended to be."

"You try to solve my mystery the way you approach anything that is *other*. You want to learn what I know about the Buddhas' smile by studying what I am; but you haven't understood that what I *am* means nothing. I am nothing. I am a moment in your life. A mask over emptiness.—Don't get angry, *Russian*. I like to amuse myself, but I don't mean you harm.—Don't ask who I am, ask who you are. Who is Alexandre Iacovleff? Brown hair? Raised eyebrows? A hand that draws? A foot, a hand, a face . . . *or any other part of the human body*." He laughs. "Shakespeare had a phrase for everything. 'What's Montague? What's in a name?' Without a name, are you not still yourself? And if you do need a name, would you keep Iacovleff, or Alexandre? Be careful if you keep only Alexandre, though your first name is the more personal of your names. For another Alexander came here once. He did wonders. He conquered, he built, on his way toward the incredible Indies. And he returned broken, sorrowful, betrayed. Are you that Alexander, returned to Gandhara? Are you another Alexander? Or no Alexander at all?"

I want to laugh myself. "All that and nothing."

"Yes. Nothing and all that."

And he laughs unaffectedly. Not like a Buddha, but like a trickster warrior who has momentarily put down his weapons.

"Is there a reason to laugh about it?"

"Oh, you never get tired of looking for a reason. Is that really what you want to look for? All right. Look. You see this land all the way to the horizon, bare, dry, but it wasn't always that way. A long time ago, these valleys were rolling and green. When Genghis Khan came, he destroyed the inhabitants' painstaking work, the vital and fragile reservoirs. What they say about him is true, you know? Where he passed, the grass never grew again. So many peoples before him, so many dynasties. The Bactrians, Darius, Alexander, the Scythians, so many others, and now the Muslims whom you blame for firing off their rifles . . . They have all fought, conquered, and built; built and built again; and, even if they don't want to, they have all *inherited* layers of ancient forms, geological strata of forms. The profiles of the Emblemata have given their faces to the Blessed but also their versos to the Bactrians' coins. Inheritance is a difficult job, stranger. It means living on the hinge between past and present; in a past that isn't even yours, that can be hatefully greater than you. A past of other architectures, languages, arts. Other gods.

"So many gods, so many different gods! Zoroaster, and all the Persian deities, and Zeus and his turbulent crew, and more, and more, and the Buddha whom Ashoka chose, and now the One True God of Mohammed. Which one is the rightful one, and which one hasn't borrowed a few of his predecessors' traits, thanks to his worshippers? For good and evil, human perceptions are part of the form of the layers. Yesterday sacred, tomorrow profane; yesterday revered, tomorrow profaned; because men change their minds to defy the changeableness of the world. Men seek eternity, and they think they achieve it by burying what preceded them. By burying it, by destroying it. Living on the hinge is dangerous if you don't accept change; you pinch your fingers.

"And the sand comes. It transforms everything. People think it erases everything, destroys everything, but it links everything, it transforms everything. It's men who destroy and deny, when they can. And when it's impossible to destroy, they appropriate, which is at least preferable. And everything is changed and destroyed, and everything remains. You perceive only one layer of the strata, the present, of this land, of yourself, of myself. Because you have not accepted that sensation, perception, intention, consciousness . . .that they're all the void."

He contemplates the horizon for a moment, dreaming, almost grave, then turns back.

"You're still reciting the sutra."

"Yes. Come, night is falling, it'll be cold. We'll make a fire and have some tea."

Parasamgate (beyond)

Behind us the horizon is scarlet. My guide cradles his little terracotta bowl. I have lighted my pipe and he's rolled himself a ragged cigarette perfumed with spices. Between us the fire burns, small but fierce. Light between us; around us, the dark.

"Tell me the rest of it," I say.

"Ask me a question. Questions get me started."

"If our names are unimportant, why not tell me yours?"

"A good question," he laughs, "I didn't expect it. If you need a name to help you remember my form, call me Tunkun. In the Uzbek language, it means night and day, one thing and the other, or the space between them. It's the name I have here, now. But what's your real question?"

"What are you?"

"Ah . . . But what do you think I am, if I'm not a warrior who is much more well-informed than you expected?"

"You are a being of the desert—a Djinn."

"A Djinn?" He laughs. "No. I'm not one of that ancient race. I come from another, less subtle and less frank, a race that has codified and ruled this world for too long not to see its power fail from its own contradictions. But you're right, I have a great deal in common with those spirits of the burning winds of the desert. Fire, for one."

He passes his hand over the flames and they lean toward him.

"*I love the fire*," he quotes teasingly, "*and the fire loves me.*" He laughs. "Excuse me, I love a good phrase, I love all the arts of men! The Djinns and I, yes, both born of fire. But they are entirely fire, at home where they live, may the dust of time spare them! Me, I'm not so direct. I was designed twisted. Halfway between fire and cold, day and night, white and black. A foreigner. I told you."

"But you're not a man."

"Excuse me?" He raises an amused eyebrow.

"Not a mortal man. You are older, more powerful. A sort of genius loci. A . . . god?"

He sighs.

"What does it matter what I am? I'll tell you what I saw, if it helps you. Long before Alexander, I came here, along the silk thread that leads to the Orient, fleeing my madness and paying my debts. They say I had a chariot drawn by leopards and many kinds of exotic creatures followed me. True. False. My followers were with me, yes. But here, in these once-fertile lands, I felt alone, as if spread between the angles of the world. Here, it's the part of the map where men should engrave a compass rose. A crossroad, a cross, a star. A mark and a marked spot: where so many tides have turned and turned, so many dynasties and creatures; so many invasions and crimes perpetuated again and again, so many cities that rose and fell, so many blindly transmitted strata of the past . . .

"A meeting place, fugitive, ephemeral, a place that geography didn't intend to endure.

"A crossroads, historians call this place; and that's true. But if a crossroads is a point of convergence and fusion, it's equally a breaking point. The one doesn't exist without the other. At a crossroads, which my people, like yours, have always recognized as a place of danger and power, the certainty of the path breaks down, feet stumble; for a moment one stops, one contemplates one's choices, one conjures gods.

"Here, at this junction and breaking point, there was beauty. The beauty of fusion, of melding, of the melting pot. *Better* made from combinations of *good*. But also negation, denial, utter violence, stupidity.

"Everything seems so set, so fixed now, but that is a dangerous illusion. Everything is movement. This fixedness is nothing but the brightness of the desert, which hides the unstoppable movement of the dunes. Destruction, believe me, is more powerful than any melting pot. Rifle-stocks across the noses of your Buddhas, that's the crossroads at work. There has been beauty here; but beneath it, always, there's hatred. Here men marry art to art and create a mingled beauty; but not forever, never forever. And who's to blame? The Muslims; the northern pillagers; Genghis Khan; your countrymen, the Russians, who one day will import here the tyranny of the proletariat? Even the French, who began their excavations by disemboweling the stupas 'to see what was underneath'? Who's guilty? Men, time, life, the world? All of these, and none. It's not important.

"Because yesterday, today, tomorrow all exist together, for those who know how to see. Because all things, which are by nature emptiness, have neither beginning nor end.

"Listen. I have told you what was and I will tell you what will be. Your French compatriots will find the Alexandria they're looking for. They've excavated patiently but they'll find it by luck. A few years from now—in a time you won't see, because you aren't long for this world—a shah out hunting will see the capital of a column rising like a vision from bare ground. He will talk about his vision, and the French, less mystical than he, will dig. And they will find Ay Khanum, the royal capital. They will uncover its endless ramparts, the towers of its citadel, its enormous palace, its theatre and its sanctuaries. They will walk in Alexander's footsteps and prove their theories. And doubtless some of them will weep with joy at the miraculous mingled beauty of Greece and the Orient. *Better* born from two *goods*. There, in the north, at Ay Khanum.

"At Begram and at Peshawar, they will find the treasure of treasures: sublime works in glass, Hellenistic bronzes, perfume-flasks, unbelievable Indian plaquettes. Emblemata by the hundreds. They will find the crossroads within the crossroads: face to face, Athenas with the curves of sacred dancers and Buddhas more beautiful than the ones you have seen here. Angels and devils born of the crossroads; the world will be struck with amazement. Some of these treasures will remain here, some will be taken to foreign countries; and only the stolen and the exiles will survive. Because the sand will blow. There will be war and destruction. The City of the Moon Lady, Ay Khanum, so recently returned to the surface of the earth, will be sacked and raped. The museum will be pillaged. And the great Buddhas of Bâmiyân themselves, which have stood for so many centuries, will fall under blows struck in the name of younger and fiercer gods. No one will see this plain from where we have seen it, standing on the head of a patient Enlightened One, climbing to understand better, tracing a new path in the weave of this crossroads, adding to the millions of threads the improbable and unimportant thread of our encounter.

"Stranger, you're pale. I am too, perhaps. No need. These things are emptiness. They neither begin nor end, they are neither vicious nor pure, not perfect nor broken. They cannot be those things, or become them. Never, in any time, in any place."

He says this, but his eyes are grave, and his mouth has a crease I haven't seen before. He sighs and is silent a moment. I respect this pause in the mourning that he does not allow himself. When he turns back toward me, his voice is infinitely calm.

"I met the man they call the Awakened One. I loved him, even though his lesson was difficult and painful. And still . . . To take the lesson into oneself, one must be willing to see everything, all these eras at once. The greatness, the falls, the heights, the pillage. Even to accept, as he told me, that these statues will fall, and what he taught will count for nothing.

"Will Ay Khanum be more beautiful tomorrow, for having been excavated and exhibited? Was she more beautiful yesterday, when burnt offerings were made at the foot of monumental Zeus? Is she less grand for being underground today? Is she even real? More real in the sunlight, or underground? Real because she was built by the exalted hands of man? When those hands will have destroyed the Buddhas, what shall we say to ourselves? That it's a terrible loss, that we're horrified by the stupidity that lost us the beauty of Apollo's meeting with Siddhartha? Should you and I be glad because we saw them with our own eyes, while their beauty lasted? And you, stranger, who have already cried over their wounds, should it console you that you have preserved their image for the future?"

I have trouble answering him. My voice sounds dry when I speak.

"If I accept what you tell me, no, I won't feel any of that. Because, since they have existed, they cannot be destroyed. Because, never having existed, they have never been drawn. They do not exist. They are forever."

He smiles at me still, but his eyes are somber.

"Yes, Iacovleff. Yes. And now you are reciting the Heart Sutra yourself. And now you understand why they are smiling, the Bodhisattvas and the blessed ones of Gandhara, smiling that secret smile that comprehends everything and never alters. And the eyes, too, stranger. Haven't you seen their eyes? Half-closed, because *they* know in advance, and admit, what is going to happen. They know the emptiness of everything, including themselves and what they have left behind them.

"It is the echo of the Zen master's answer to his pupil: 'What do you do when you encounter the Buddha in your path? Kill him.' Even ultimate wisdom must be abandoned as one more illusion.

"It's here, you see, at the crossroads of all things, that the last lesson of impermanence had to be learned. The emptiness of form, the form of emptiness.

"And here I returned, after Alexander and all his conquests. Without a chariot, without leopards, without honor or escort. To sit in front of an old friend, like an obsolete and outworn god who takes off his sandals and becomes a follower of another god, one wiser and infinitely more humorous, who has understood and accepted that we all wear out, gods though we were.

"In the end, at the crossroads, we are all caught in the hinge of time.

"To recite the hard lesson of the Heart Sutra.

"No eye, no ear, no nose, no tongue, no body, no mind, no self. No Alexandre."

I repeat after him, one step behind his smile, "No Alexandre."

And he replies, one beat behind me, "No Dionysus. And you know, don't you, where this logically leads us, once we've accepted the emptiness of all things; do you know why the Buddhas smile?"

He turns away and says, softly, "No created thing, no knowledge, no ignorance. No destruction of any created thing, no limit to knowledge, no end to ignorance. No Four Noble Truths, no, neither suffering, nor cause of suffering, nor Path to reach the end of suffering. No old age and death, no cure for old age and death. No salvation, nor exile from salvation.

"No gods.

"No Buddha."

And he repeats, and it seems to me that his voice trembles, "No Buddha.

"Ga-te, ga-te, para-gate para-samgate bodhi-svaha.

"Sleep, stranger, sleep. The night has come and I have finished talking. Sleep . . ."

I stretch out on the ground, still warm from the sun of the vanished day, and his voice cradles me, my eyelids become heavy. In the darkness I see the incandescent end of his cigarette, glowing in the rhythm of his rising and falling breath. And I think I hear him murmuring, from farther and farther away,

Gone, gone, gone beyond, gone completely beyond . . .

In the morning my eyes are full of grit. The dawn is cold. I tell myself my guide will have disappeared, as men do so often when they can't face the morning after a night of confidences. But he is there, brewing tea over the feeble campfire. He has the unruly look of those who have not slept and have counted too many stars. He must read my thoughts, for he says:

"Yes, once men met me only for a day, between the rising and the setting sun. The given length of time, the rule: one day, 'the life of a mayfly,' they used to say. Once, when I was a god. No more."

He smiles like a man and not a god. Like a friend, perhaps.

"I'll take you back, Alexandre."

I accept his tea and his silence. We follow the road back without a word, and at the foot of the great Buddha, we part ways. He has finished talking. And, if I have understood him correctly, I haven't much time to learn the lesson.

I don't tell him goodbye. There is no beginning, he told me, and no end. So I don't say goodbye. I don't say . . .
anything.

Svaha (all is well)
15 June—on the road to India

I draw, and I erase.

And draw, and erase.

And the page doesn't change, in spite of the traces of the work I have destroyed.

And the page takes no account of the spoiled sketches, nor of the ones that would have earned me riches and glory, and a ridiculous immortality.

The page treats success and failure with the same passivity. I forget them myself, and neither re-invoke nor reject them.

I draw, and I erase myself.

In spite of myself, I have sketched out my twilight encounter, as if I am a man who is measuring what he still needs to do. Not to meditate on it or transmit it, but because one day, perhaps, at the very end, I will feel the need of a form in front of which I can sit. As if I were sitting in front of an old friend, waiting with him until the clocks stop. Until the Void finally imposes itself, and the All that it also is. The Beyond, where we must go.

I have sketched the form, not of a god, but of a man. I know its emptiness. I have learned too from him that one can indulge illusions, if one recognizes them for illusions.

I erase. I do not erase. The emptiness is there even when the form endures.

I smile, calm and tranquil, while the convoy rolls.

I draw the people at the side of the road, and the buildings.

I do not draw the smile of the Blessed of Gandhara.

Not any more; no longer.

The Heart Sutra is not explained. It is only recited.

Translated from the French by Sarah Smith

~

When I was a kid, I wanted to become an archeologist. I liked to dig in old cultures, languages, and layers of soil. I discovered Buddhism when I was 15, and was fascinated *because* my mind was revolted by the concept. When your inner self reacts so strongly, there must be something to investigate! The Buddhas of Gandhara were the depictions I loved above all. I have regretted being a writer sometimes, because of the joy it must be to unearth these wonders. But now, looking closely into the alchemy of art, I come to see writing as akin to archeology. You dig, traverse, connect and reveal, delve for buried truths. And to achieve this, you must use yourself as an interface. The destruction of the Buddhas of Afghanistan was for me a wound, a loss, a face-off with anger, a sheer impossibility to understand that I had to transmute and decipher. I did this as an archeologist-writer, delving into this event though cracks in history and the inability of strangers to convene: looking for the truth of the crossroads, and how to deal with it. I did this by reciting the Heart Sutra. It's the hardest of all, and thus my favorite one.

Léa Silhol

When It Rains, You'd Better Get Out of Ulga

Adrián Ferrero

You probably know that every wave we trace, with hands or feet or fingers or toes or legs or knees or elbows or abdomen, depicts a message for someone in this space, or in a coming time that for now we may ignore. For example: When I soak my toes like beards in a stream in the land of Ulga, this will be a sending that will affect—years, months, and centuries later—the way the coward Dudú drinks his milk. But this occurred or will occur (depending how you see it) far later than the events that I'm about to narrate.

The land of Ulga is a vast domain, as large as many mountains bound together. That being so, is it a mountainous country? No, not at all. It is high, like the mountains, but there are no peaks. It is as long as those rivers which rise and fall, which come and go, but without contours. Imagine the opposite of a vast sea, without deserts. Ulga's contours have a different physiognomy: that of its waters. Waters which gently descend, plentiful and indulgent with its inhabitants and tourists; waters which recline against the banks of its rivers and unfurl into cascades and waterfalls.

The land of Ulga has 527,306 watercourses, of which we can count rivers, lakes, lagoons, brooks, seas, oceans, aquifers, geysers, swamps, pools, ponds, little rivers, dikes, hot springs, marshes, rapids, waterfalls, and streams, many streams crossing everywhere.

Just as Ulga is rich in waters, so also are the activities of its inhabitants. Every inhabitant of Ulga knows how to swim. Every inhabitant of Ulga knows how to drink from a crystal glass. Every inhabitant of Ulga bathes four or five times a day. Ulga is almost all water. But Ulga also has earth, firm as a rock and as hard as a riverbed.

The customs of Ulga's men and women didn't change much from generation to generation. They always did the same thing, more or less, despite being a stubborn, studious people. Their traditions passed from fathers to sons, from sons to grandchildren, from grandchildren to great-grandchildren, from great-grandchildren to great-great-grandchildren, from great-great-grandchildren to great-great-great-grandchildren and so on that way.

The blood of Ulga's inhabitants was mixed with that of its older denizens, a people of large boats and comfortable, old dresses. They came from the sea, from the immemorial glaciers, from the caverns close to the immemorial glaciers. They climbed the ice floes and wallowed over the frozen stone, playing at licking the rigid surface and drinking it in big mouthfuls.

As noted earlier, the messages of Ulga's first inhabitants had begun to reach its final inhabitants. While the coward Dudú drank his milk, the honey he dripped into his glass made great whirlpools which foretold the inconceivable. Dudú knew but didn't say. An augury of storms, and the death of eighty newborns under the full moon.

The night the stranger arrived in Ulga, all the goats bleated, all at once. All the moths crashed into lamps. The hogs tore down the corrals of their sties and two ewes gave birth to five-legged lambs.

The stranger didn't reveal his identity. He stopped at the inn by the White Lake. He asked for nothing but a spartan meal. But drink he did, taking long swallows from transparent bottles filled with fresh water. He washed his face with milk. He slept the whole night. It isn't known what he dreamed of. Some say he dreamt all the dreams of the whole humanity since the dawn of the world. I can't confirm that. It's a lot of time and a lot of memory. He was a powerful man. It could have been true.

The following day the stranger opened the curtains of his room, searched for a woman, and lay with her until nightfall. He supped on green vegetables of very few colors. He drank pure spring water and slept until the morning of the following day.

Today is Tuesday, and the stranger has breakfasted without saying a word. He has taken his clothes and walked the distance remaining to the center of Ulga. The stranger has looked in the village, has not spoken to the people, except once: he asked for directions to the Bamboo River. He arrived there. He sat on the riverbanks. He looked out for a long time. Before the daylight faded, he wrote something in his notebook with the yellow cover. Before leaving he told a passing shepherd without waiting for greeting: "The river doesn't say, but what it says is that the flood of the seas will come from the Heavens."

The shepherd remembered what he had heard. He went with his goats. The stranger never told anyone what he had written. But I'll tell you what his journal said:

From the waves of the sea came the first men with three-feathered hats in boats with figureheads at their prows. They were brought by a sarcophagus with sails and great loads of clay. The end is filled with silence. You can't talk with your mouth full of water.

They began to say many things about the stranger. That he came to steal secrets. That he was a smuggler. That he sold brown and white women. That he didn't want to die. That he came to die. That he loved a woman in the country of Begonias. That he would never, ever say what he had come to do. Silence feeds the circulation of words, their swelling-up and coursing-over.

One day he told them: "My name is Dikon."

But he didn't say anything else. Ulga's inhabitants knew, thanks to the shepherds, that Dikon had come to write what the seas and oceans said, and what the lakes and rivers, what the banks and shores along everything that ran a course had to say.

Everything that runs along a course might be of blood or of water or of sap or of juice. Everything that runs goes towards some place and comes from some place else: this murmuring has something to say.

Evidently Dikon was searching for a way by which to regain a flow, a gliding, the brush of a watercourse, the magic of a slope, the voice of a sound blue or green or white or chalk. All of the colors of those which could be water.

Another day Dikon sat by a waterfall of an intense sky blue color. Sky blue because the water splashed against stone and the sun gave it a fresh and very sweet clarity. Sky blue like Dula's eyes in winter while looking at reindeer. Sky blue like the stains left by the candies Jalim chewed beside the fire. Dikon watched and watched and listened and listened. Water is something to look at, but also, and before all else, something that must be listened to. In the end, it is something to be touched.

Dikon listened to the waterfall's musings. Its sound entered very deep inside his ears, it entered and swirled, turning around and around, it entered and left and entered again. As if something stirred it and spun it and swallowed everything one thought about, even those thoughts kept unshared. At last, Dikon saw the waves that went from one end to the other and continued on towards some destination, who knows where, maybe the end of the world, or the origin-place, or the place of greatest unknown. The water carried many things: dirty clothes, a secret from Milan, the astonished eyes of the Simelas, the last cry and sigh of a couple, the flame of an extinguished matchstick, an oak leaf, many insects—anything, in fact, that might fit into the coursing water. And finally, Dikon wasn't content to watch and listen; he wanted to touch what he had heard and seen. He came close to the shore, extended a hand, then a forefinger, he sank it in, palpated the surface, submerged the hand entirely, then the arm . . . quite soon the water was up to his throat. Soaking wet, spun round and round in a gasping whirlpool, he returned to the shore and sat in the sun. In the land of Ulga, the sun shines brighter whenever someone emerges from water; its radiance becomes incomparably smooth and sparkling.

Dikon wrote this in his journal, once dry: *Whatever I write wouldn't suffice to pronounce the name I was told today, when the sun flamed as a myriad of red suns. I didn't dream it. The name was sun, earth, air, axis, center . . . and a word that now I can't remember. And it was the most important one! I'm afraid. Endings always frighten me. Especially if they come from on high.* Dikon's gaze was as deep as the ocean bottom. Dudú, who had met him once at a bend in the road (precisely at a junction), was heard to say afterwards that he had seen a storm, like a falling curtain of water as he looked into those eyes. The truth of it was, a great many speculations were set forth about Dikon's life. Dudú defended him before the tribe. He argued that a look as clear and diaphanous as a current of water was proof of his honesty. Not a person to be distrusted. The others laughed, ha ha ha, and Dudú didn't say another word.

Every night at the tavern of Ulga, the entertainment of choice was to eat truffles and trade news about who had sighted the stranger (no one called him Dikon, even though they all knew his name)—in what region, near which river or stream, and what he had been doing.

Lar, the man with curly white hair who liked to eat pickled gherkins, admitted that he had spied on him once from behind some ferns. White over white, hair over spines, he had watched Dikon sitting for a very long time along the water. Dikon sat in peace, ears pricked at every sound, and finally flung himself, fully dressed, into the water. Spinning and spinning, carried along by the obstinate current, Dikon returned to earth two kilometers further near the border with Jaspur, where the people of Lapas dwelled. Curious to know Dikon's destination, Lar had observed his journey down the river and his ascent towards the earth. The stranger had stretched in the sun like a caterpillar, yawned eight times, and finally returned upstream against the current to his point of origin. Dried, renewed, and tanned by the sun, the stranger had taken up a feather and written many strange words in his journal. Then he took a breath and fell into a very deep coma.

Simurg told a different story. That he had seen the stranger at some blue springs. Dikon had undressed in the mist and bathed there casually until sunset. Then he had dressed languidly, drunk from a bottle of clear water, and lain down to sleep with his stomach full of milk. Later he started a fire and wrote many words or drawings (Simurg wasn't sure) by its light. And then he had left by the same way he came, along one of those trails without beginning or end.

Lampebo spoke last. He said that he had seen Dikon swimming in the Lake of the Three Names. The stranger had studied the heavens, as if waiting for a ciphered message. He had watched the waters, then dove into their depths and emerged half an hour later—long after Lampebo had taken him for drowned—carrying something in his arms. What it was, or how, or where he carried it, Lampebo didn't know. But he knew that Dikon was laden with the Truth. And that was the last time that anyone saw Dikon in Ulga.

The Council reviewed the particulars, pondered long over the accounts, but did not come to any conclusions. Partly because the inhabitants of Ulga don't think very hard. Or partly because everything in Ulga is simplified, like water. Partly because the people live secluded lives and don't argue much. Partly because everything is largely decided ahead of time. The Council resolved to wait, attentive, and see if the stranger reappeared. The information was uncertain and improbable. Like the rains that threatened to fall over Ulga.

Dudú drank his milk with honey; he saw something in this unrest. On the next day he left Ulga, on a caravan with his sister and the rest of the family. No one ever heard of them again. In their exodus, they left behind only the walls of their homestead, four nets, a machete, and the contents of two wine bottles, spilled in a fountain. A letter had arrived.

What follows is excerpted from the journal of Dikon, which I found floating in this vastness of water, within a box hermetically sealed with paraffin and seals of wax. The seventh seal broke when the moon departed and I read the following:

Journal of Dikon.

In the Fifth Day of the Calendar of Ur.

My gods signaled it. The water doesn't lie; I repeat what they ask of me. The water will announce what awaits us. Death—the greatest catastrophe in Ulga's history. I write these words to a handful. The sea will be high, very high, almost to where the skies are now. And I, I who am below, shall swim for those who deliver the backwards waterfall. If the sea should fall on our heads, what good to swim? To navigate a boat? Ulga's delivery. This is my last entry. The one they ordered me to leave. It's what I read in the water, what the waters dictate to me; the words I hear, in any case, in their gushing.

The water told me:

"The goats will die and the milk of a thousand nannies will feed the future. It's now I have to write. The water tells the truth."

The water also told me:

"Don't be afraid. Water bites but also warns. Tell it in your words, after listening to the course of all the seas arriving at this stream and turning to return."

The water concluded:

"If the journal survives, those who come from the future will know—why Ulga is a great sea carrying so many things adrift. If they call it a flood, let them call it that. Only salt will remain."

The last ice floe melted and the water said "Go" and in that moment, I closed my journal with the yellow cover.

I could speculate that this was Ulga once, that this water carrying me towards the future now, towards the north, is cruel and subduing. Dikon sealed the box with everything the sea and current told him. The water isn't mute. The water doesn't run. The water tells many things. Not everyone can hear it and transcribe and translate its intentions. I think a lot aboard. I won't lie. Today it is night already and I can't see a thing, so I'll try to listen to the water. Perhaps it will announce another sea, another sky, another drought. Let it talk.

—To Angélica Gorodischer, for the duration of a universe

Translated from the Spanish by Edo Mor

~

I like to think that literature, rather than being something, is first and foremost a way of looking, a way of living, a way of being in the world. It does not resemble the gaze of a mortal being but the faceted gaze of a fly—and why not?—the gaze of bluebottles, those brightly colored insects made of a golden green that stick themselves to anything they find tempting. Don't we writers adhere to language, to certain objects, beings or sensations, avid to take from them what we like or find suitable?

My short story and Ulga's country were written on a rainy evening. My wife Paulina was expecting our daughter Emilia, who is now five and who first pronounced a magical word to me: "papá." Her eyes, from her mother's amniotic depths, looked at me or gave shape to that watery gaze which soaks the story and, who knows, perhaps it was that same liquid and fluid current what brought her to my shore, like the foam of an ocean not yet mapped.

Adrián Ferrero

Queen of the Butterfly Kingdom

Holly Phillips

The woman from the embassy called again this morning, as she does every morning. The negotiations are continuing, she said. They had not been apprised of any changes.

Changes, I said. I was deeply impressed by her choice of word; but then, I am always intrigued by people's private lexicons. Of course I knew she meant "changes in the situation," but that only meant there were no fresh rumors of torture, no dead men displayed for the evening news. Change. Well, yes, injury is change. Death is certainly change.

We'll let you know as soon as we hear anything new, she said.

Don't let your life stop, was my distant mother's advice. Another phone call, messages from another world, the real world of home. Carry on, my mother said. Carry on as best you can.

I stood in this borrowed kitchen, the glazed tiles cold beneath my feet, Ryan's blue terrycloth robe cinched around my waist, my teacup cooling in my hand. I wanted to think about the word "changes." I wanted to let it carve new pathways through the erosion patterns in my brain, and why not? I'm a writer. I would never say, Words are my life, because that is too extravagant, too grandiose, but it is secretly true. My vocation is to turn the nothing of dreams into books on the shelves. Magic! See me build my castles in the air! But my bare feet were cold, and I decided my mother was right. I made a fresh cup of tea and carried it up the many stairs of this narrow city house to the attic that the absent owners converted to a children's playroom, and that I have in my turn made into a kind of office. My desk is an old door propped across two piles of banker's boxes full of the manuscripts and contracts I couldn't bear to leave behind. I turned on the laptop and without checking my email (there is no cable connection up here) I opened a new document in Word.

The white screen, the blank page. This is the novel I came here to write. No, no. I came here because I am in love, but this is the novel I could not write at home.

I had to get up again and go down three flights to the living room where a pile of Ryan's mail waits for him to come back—come home, I almost said. I always compose in manuscript format, it's so much easier than reformatting later, but I find the intricacies of this foreign address impossible to remember. I went back upstairs and typed it in at the top left-hand corner of the screen, then keyed down a few spaces and typed the title.

Queen of the Butterfly Kingdom

Then I looked at it again, and tried it with a "The" at the beginning, but no. Too definite. There's something dreamy about it the other way.

Queen of the Butterfly Kingdom

A few more spaces down, and I typed Chapter One.

And then, after a while, I got up and went down two flights to shower and put on some clothes.

Like other cities, this one is composed of hidden neighborhoods—neighborhoods, that is, that look like undifferentiated city to the unaccustomed small-town eye. I have been exploring since we first arrived, although Ryan teased me, calling me a scaredy-cat and a hick Canuck. I didn't mind. On the one hand, I was feeling cat-like then, slinking close to the walls with my sides sucked in, somewhat inclined to growl; and on the other hand I loved the sound of those words snapped together like a couple of birch twigs brittle with ice. Hick Canuck. At an embassy dinner he whispered it in my ear to make me laugh, his voice two soft puffs of air against my neck, like kernels of corn exploding. Hick Canuck. Especially delicious since, by the standards of this ancient country, so was everybody at the table, from the Ambassador on down.

But what Ryan didn't see, being busy with briefings even before the team left with the special envoy, was how, like a cat, I expanded my territory in cautious circles. I hate to hurry these things. It seemed rash to venture out into the streets and the stores—the buses! My God!—before I even knew how the light switches worked, the telephone, the stove. I mean "know" in the intimate sense, the habitual sense that does not even register the smells and sounds of home. When I am a foreigner, I am an explorer, continually amazed at tourists who can simply visit a place like this. Eventually, though, I discovered the side streets and main streets, the children's parks and the botanical parks and the jogging trails, the street with the bakeries, the street with the hardware stores, the street with the whores. Neighborhoods are such subtle things here I had to watch which way the neighbors turned when they left their doors, which way they came from with their string bags full of food. I thought that if I bought a string bag and filled it at the right butcher's shop and wine store I would cease to be a stranger, or at least a foreigner, but it hasn't worked out that way. At home the bus drivers wave even when I'm not catching the bus, the café owner teases me if I don't get my usual decaf latté with no foam. Here I don't know how to ask for no foam, and though I go to the neighborhood café they have yet to notice that I always scrape it off with my spoon.

At least when I go at the quiet time after lunch I can sit at my regular table. Not the one in the window, it's too big for one person, but the one against the wall just down from the window corner. Today I came too early, however, and had to sit at a table in back. As I struggled through my order (I have memorized the words, but they still come out of my mouth as sounds) I consoled myself with the thought that really, there is no café in the world where a writer can't open her notebook and sit, pen in hand, entirely at home.

I opened my notebook, and sat, pen in hand.

A drop of rain fell on the page, blurring the forgotten words of last week. *Keep it fresh and strange*, the notebook said. I couldn't remember what "it" was. Something from the novel. Magic? Love? More raindrops fell, spattering on the tabletop, pinging off the saucer beneath my glass.

"Lady, you are so far out of your place I could not find you."

I looked up to see the rainbird perched like a crow on the back of an empty chair.

"You found me," I pointed out. "Here you are."

"And here *you* are." The rainbird spread his arms in a gesture at the café, the waiters, the hissing espresso machine. Crystal droplets scattered from his feathers like shining beads from a broken necklace. "I wonder why, when you have all the worlds and time."

I ducked my head and smoothed the damp-rippled page. His black glass eyes were hard to meet. "Where would you have me go?"

"'Go,' lady? You are the center. To you the worlds bend like glass in the rain."

As he spoke more rain fell, a pattering that mingled with the roar and sigh of steam, like liquid consonants in a whispered hiss. What language did they speak? I did not know, and then I did: it was the poetry of the grass that bowed towards my chair, an invisible meadow sketched out in the gleam of spiderwebs and dew. The waiter walked by, oblivious, and the grass laughed and danced aside.

"Come, lady. We are here." The rainbird leaned forward on his perch, his hands between his knees, avid as a boy. "Give us your tale."

"I have no stories in me," I said sadly. "The only one I know these days is out there in the real world somewhere, unfinished, out of reach."

He tossed his head and snapped his beak in annoyance. I thought I saw a bright fragment of a severed wing fall to the floor, but when I looked, the floor was carpeted in a moss of jewels, beads of dew catching the light and colors of the busy street outside.

"Lady," the rainbird said, "that story is not worthy of you. Are you not the hero, the villain, the mystery, the queen? In *that* story you barely figure. You have made yourself an afterthought, a figment, a shadow by the fireless hearth. As far as you are concerned, *that* story is no story at all."

I sat in sullen silence. He was talking about Ryan's story, Ryan's captivity, Ryan's peril. What he was talking about was no story at all. It was my life. Mine, and Ryan's, for as long as Ryan lived.

"Listen, lady." The rainbird was coaxing now. "Spin your own tale. Spin *our* tale, yours and mine. Come away with me, come back to your true place. Come home."

While he spoke the elegant grasses moved around me, draping

me in shining cobwebs, winding me a cloak of rain-gemmed strands. In every droplet there shone a story, as round and complete as a world, and in every story shone my face crowned in flames or petals or thorns.

My face, but not Ryan's. However hard I looked, the only story he figured in was his own.

"Come home," the rainbird said, and when I echoed him, "Home," I felt the shining strands drawn across my mouth and nose, not a cloak but a muffling shroud. "Am I supposed to bury myself in my dreams?"

"Not bury," said the rainbird. "Live!"

But as I sat there, pen in hand, life was wearing chains many miles to the east.

"Even an empty hearth can make a story," I said. I closed my notebook, paid my tab, and left without another word.

Morning again, still no news, and I climbed up to the attic to make another attempt at work. Once there, however, I discovered I had failed to save yesterday's aborted beginning, and I had to open a new document. And then, of course, I had to go back downstairs to the living room for an envelope with this address on it, and then it occurred to me to wonder if I should be using this address on my manuscripts at all. Even if Ryan—

Even if Ryan comes back, this posting was only supposed to be for two years. Where will I be when it comes time to discuss the book with an editor? I needed to call my agent, there were so many things I should have discussed with her before I left. It all happened so quickly, and now here I am, where morning is the middle of the night back home. Email, I thought, but the only connection is in Ryan's office, and I just— How can I explain myself to you? It wasn't the pain of missing him while sitting in his space, the space he hasn't even had a chance to make his own. It was the outrageousness, the sheer humiliating cliché of being the woman who felt the pain, the woman who had been left behind. I can't escape the pain, but surely I can escape the cliché? Suddenly my mother was the wisest person I knew. Waiting, after all, is still a kind of life.

So I went out for food. Shopping is surprisingly painless, even for someone who is effectively a deaf-mute. Everything has a price on it, or on its shelf, and for all the weirdnesses and seemingly perverse and willful oddities of this foreign land, the cash registers still show an electronic total and the bills are all numbered in their corners just as you would expect. I do prefer fresh food, however; not only for the usual reasons, but because this alien packaging can be deceptive. Ryan and I had been eating breakfast cereal for a week when he came home laughing from a reception to say he had been served our cereal with bits of sausage and mustard perched on the little squares. I had the dreadful sense that he had told our mistake to his fellow guests, who would have laughed and offered up dumb foreigner stories of their own. I should have laughed, too, but I was overcome by that wretched playground feeling of having innocently worn the wrong tights, the wrong backpack, the wrong brand of shoes to school. What's got into you? Ryan asked me, but his voice was tender, tinged with a kind of wonder. To myself, having published a scant handful of books, I am barely a writer, but to Ryan I am an artist and therefore mysterious, even a little exalted. Where do you go? he asks me when he catches me dreaming. Where were you just now? I am too shy to answer honestly. My books are public, my airy castles open for daily tours, but my imagination is still as secret as a locked bedroom door. Read my next book, I say, and he promises me he will.

I walked back from the shops with the handle of my string bag cutting into my fingers, and looked up outside the house to notice, almost simultaneously, the fresh post-rain light slipping under the hem of the clouds and the officious Mercedes parked illegally at the curb. The driver's door was swinging open (perhaps the movement that had caught my eye) and Alain Bernard climbed out into the narrow street. Alain is fairly young and fairly important, and he had something to do with Ryan's appointment to the envoy's staff. I don't know the details. They might be friends, but then again, they might not.

This, of course, was not what I thought when Alain climbed out of the car. You can guess what I did think. Or can you? I'm not sure you can call it thinking, it's more like the floor of your mind giving way, like a sudden shove out of a mental window, so your heart takes flight and your stomach plummets. Alain took an urgent step toward me and I dropped my bag, loosing a single orange into the street. I wanted to fend him off, to go away, to pretend I hadn't seen him, but even in that dreadful moment the writer in me was thinking how inadequate that single orange was. In the movie version of my life it would have been a dozen oranges cascading over the blackened bricks, leaping and rolling, caroming off the curb in an extravagant emotional collapse. But what does a woman living alone, a woman who can barely force herself to swallow past the loneliness and fear, want with a dozen oranges? I bought exactly two, and one was still peering out at me through the string bars of its cage.

Oh, God! No, don't think it, it's nothing like that, there's no bad news! Alain, who read everything in that single wobbling orange, snatched up the fruit and then snatched up me, holding me tight against his double-breasted diplomatic wool while he cursed himself in both official languages, his feet awkwardly straddled across the fallen bag. This was very dramatic but I'm not really fond of drama outside of books. I stiffened like an offended cat and after a moment Alain let me go.

Jesus, he said, I'm such an asshole. I just came to see how you are.

I'm fine, I told him. I should have also told him he wasn't an asshole, which he isn't, but I did not. I bent and gathered my suddenly pitiful bag from between his polished black toes and held it mutely open like a beggar's cup to receive the escaped orange. He dropped it in with a precise movement of finger and thumb, and that picture—his hand with its watch and starched cuff, my white, nail-bitten fingers, the orange—looked like another frame from the same movie, the kind of image that makes the instructor hit pause and say to her class, Now what is the director trying to say with this shot? To which I say, God knows. Me, I've always written for my characters and let theme take care of itself.

Alain followed me down the area stairs and in by the basement door. Thanks to my mother's advice I wasn't embarrassed by a dirty kitchen: no depressed sink full of dishes, no distractedly unswept floor. I put the groceries away and filled the kettle, but Alain said I looked like I needed a drink. Taking this to mean he wanted one, I led him upstairs to the living room where Ryan keeps a supply. I will drink for pleasure but not for comfort, and the afternoon whiskey tasted like medicine.

You haven't called me, Alain said. Tell me how you've been.

I've been waiting, I said.

I look at this and think how cold I must have sounded to poor Alain, who after all has better things to do in this crisis than hold a hostage's girlfriend's hand—at least, I hope to God he has better things to do. Are we all just waiting, waiting, waiting? This is my faith: that somewhere, men and women who have known Ryan far longer than I, who have worked with him in situations exactly as crucial and frightening as this one, are talking, pleading, promising, blustering, threatening, using every psychological trick and political strategy to bring him and the others home. And yet here is Alain, drinking Ryan's whiskey and looking at me with an intense, intimate, questioning pain in his eyes. Shall I tell you my secret thought? I am not vain. I swear I am not, I may never recover from the astonishment of Ryan's declaration of love—for me! of all people!—and yet, fairly or not, I can't help but question the source of Alain's concern. He has always watched me too closely, with too much tension around his eyes. But how would I know? Maybe what I see there isn't wanting, but guilt. He was still calling himself names when he left. I locked the door behind him, went up all those stairs, and turned the computer on. To hell with the address. I typed the title, spaced down, and once again tapped out Chapter One.

Morning. The same phone call, the same woman, the same lack of news. No news is good news, the koan of cynical times. For an instant after I hung up the telephone I wanted, I desired, I longed to be with Ryan, wherever he is. Let me wear the blindfold and the chains, let me sit in the dark, in the icy water of the flooded cell. Only let me be there instead of here, like this, thinking this, alone. But then I had to laugh, for Ryan was probably longing just as powerfully, and infinitely more sensibly, to be here with me. I toasted a piece of bread I knew I wouldn't eat and sat with the plate between my elbows and my teacup pressed against my chin. Ryan and I usually share a pot of coffee in the morning, but these days the caffeine sends unbearable twitches down my nerves. I can't tell you now all the things I thought sitting at the table this morning, but I know my mind circled a long, long way before it looped back to the city, the house, the novel waiting unwritten upstairs.

The kitchen only has windows looking out on the skinny garden in back. Gardens are important here. This one is very tasteful, with clean, patterned bricks and shade-loving plants, and right now all the beds are full of narcissus and crocus, their watercolor hues freshly painted by the rain. At home there is snow on the ground, but here we have flowers and new leaves on the trees. After a while I pulled my notebook out of the bag that had been sitting on the counter since yesterday, and just then I saw the first flicker of movement at the top of the garden wall. Just a pale flash at first, as if someone in the lane had tossed a bit of burning trash into the yard. But no: the paleness clung, and doubled itself, and became two paws. The rest of the intruder followed in swift installments, an elbow, a head and foreleg, a torso and a tail, until a cat entire dropped down into the bushes at the foot of the wall.

Tiger, tiger, burning bright. The rain striped his orange sides with sullen smoke. He shook himself, irritable with damp, and stood upright, a cat-man with flowing robes and a turban that was all fringe and flame. He fussed with the set of his coat as he stalked fastidiously through the shaggy grass of the lawn toward my door. His knock was an impatient tattoo. I opened cautiously, thinking of the varnished doorframe and the dark timbers of the ceiling.

"Madame." He bowed himself inside, his clothes rustling like starched silk. He wore a scent like sandalwood and burning cedar. I don't know what he smelled when he sniffed the air. "You have had a visitor."

He spoke as if he had a right to be offended, which put my hackles up. "Alain. A friend."

"If he were a friend he would know better than to interrupt you at your work."

"I was not working."

"Why not?"

I made an exasperated gesture, already fed up with his peremptory air. He changed his manner, bowed and rubbed his furry cheek against my hand.

"Madame. Don't scold me, I beg you. I think only of you."

Threads of smoke and steam rose about him, heady with the scent of dreams. The mutter of the rain outside blurred into the drowsy murmur of flames.

"I won't scold," I said, seduced by his warmth. "But—"

"Say me no buts. Only hear me out, I pray." The firecat sat opposite me in Ryan's chair, and smoke wove itself into braids and wreaths about the table and the room. "I ask for nothing, I have no needs and no desires. I do not ask for comfort, and I do not hunger for the food laid out for another man's return. But lady, others do. Let me protect you. Let me hide you away—"

"From what?" I said. I made my tone sharp enough to cut through the insinuating strands of smoke that stroked my face.

The firecat smiled. "Why, lady, from these interruptions and intrusions, these visitors and telephone calls, these newspapers and—"

"And this real world?"

"Real? Is your absent lover more real than I?"

"Ryan is real." If I had not been surprised I would not have felt such dismay. My voice was hoarse, my hands curled into fists. "Ryan is real."

"More real than I? What is he but a memory, an invention, a dream? What do you have of him but an echo in your skull—and what, then, am I? Do you call me less than that?"

"He is real," I said again, and as if I could make it true by saying it: "He is alive. He is more alive than you ever were."

The firecat stood and loomed over me, his paws on the table, flames flickering up from the wood like tiny, incandescent wings. "I will show you what is real," he purred. "I will show you what is real and what is not. I will show you just how real, and how unreal, *you* are, for a start."

But before he could, the silence of that tall, narrow, empty house was shattered by the telephone.

Don't drop anything, Alain said, it's only me.

He wanted to take me out to dinner. You need to get out, he said, as if he had found me huddled in a broom closet, soft as a mushroom, pale as a fish in a cave. The trouble is that as wrong as Alain was, he was also right. I am tender and sad. But he was winkling me out of my shell like a raccoon with a snail, and I could not summon the strength of will to say no, even though I knew how it would be. Alain trying to alleviate my loneliness, and me knowing it is impossible. My loneliness has too specific a cause, it requires too specific a cure.

This evening, not knowing where Alain was taking me, I dressed in what I persist in thinking of as my grown-up clothes—clothes in silk and wool, clothes I bought new. To be honest with you, though I look good in them, I don't like them much. When I wear them I feel as though they are also wearing me. As Ryan says, I prefer clothes that have been beaten into submission before I put them on.

Oh, let me laugh, let me laugh. If black humor isn't funny at midnight, when should it be? But having thought that phrase, having permitted entry to those words, "beaten" and "submission," they became a hammer and chisel carving a bloody path of empathy across the inside of my skin. I wanted to tell Ryan, Hold fast to your integrity; if you have to, you can afford to let your dignity go. But is that true? Or is that just the writer in me wanting to be wise?

If Ryan were a character in a book I was writing, I would peel him like an onion. I would strip away a layer of him for every succeeding stage of his capture and confinement, make him denser, simpler, truer—smaller—for every door he is dragged through, every narrower, darker, harder cell he inhabits, until he is so small and pure he can slip through the bars of his cage, the keyhole of his door. I would leave his captors bewildered, humbled by their own powerlessness and by the weakness of their fortress keep that keeps nothing of worth, all the treasure flown, thin and light and free as a butterfly on the warming breeze.

And as a writer, I would not do it gently. If Ryan were an invention of mine I would be cruel to him, even savage. His layers of humor, temper, affection, fear would be stripped away—I would strip them away—like layers of skin. I would pare him down to the delicate framework of bone, all the vulnerable leverage points of his being exposed. God, it's too easy to think of ways to torture a human being. I can come up with dozens without effort, it's as if they wait, a noisome crowd of tallow-sweated men, leaning against some unmarked door in the mind. Why is it so easy? Is it only my own fear, the inevitable recognition of my own body's mortal tenderness? Or do we all have a storeroom of horrors in our minds? Perhaps it is only a part of our human legacy, a psychic equivalent to the rusted iron maidens they display in the museums here. Ryan and I saw several of these displays when he played the tourist with me before he was called away. He, too, will have a store of horrors pressing against the doors of his mind. If he were a character of mine, we would share those horrors, neither of us truly alone in the dark as I wrote the story of his ordeal. At least he would have me, even if I were the author of his pain.

At least I would have my victim, him.

Alain arrived with a smile hung across the face of his worry and took me to a restaurant so quiet and civilized it was like a Victorian library. The waiters whispered in French and Alain answered in his earthy Gaspesian drawl, which made me smile. We really are all hicks beneath the wool. We are the children of loggers and trappers and cowboys, the grandchildren of the intrepid or disgraceful younger sons, and we are sometimes childlike, I think, in this subtle and sinister ancient world. We are all explorers here. We are voyageurs, and we are Iroquois in the royal court, where the racks are kept well-oiled and ready for use. We'll get them back, Alain said, but I can't help but wonder if this is another case of arrows vs. guns.

This morning the telephone did not ring.

I feel as though I have become a character in a novel—or less even than that: a painted icon traced out in tarnished gold. I am Woman Who Waits By Phone. Did I sleep through the ring? I wasn't asleep, I could chart for you the course of my night hour by hour, tell you to the minute the time the garbage truck rumbled by, to the minute when the natural light first overtook the light from the streetlamp outside. I did not sleep—yet, did I dream I was awake? I know I did not, but somehow the knowledge cannot touch my doubt. And then getting up—did the jangling springs of this antique bed drown the electronic burble of the modern phone? did the water thundering into the sink? the growl of the kettle working itself up to a boil? On every other day since Ryan left, the telephone's ring has burst into the house and rummaged through the air of every room, invasive as a policeman or a thief, yet this morning it might have been drowned by the windy rush of air into my lungs.

I did all the predictable things: checked the dial tone twice, checked that the handset was in its cradle three times, started to call the embassy and stopped. How many times? I don't remember. *Don't tie up the line* joined forces with *Don't ask for news if you are afraid of what you might hear* to weigh me down with chains. I wanted to call. I wanted to shower and dress and go out for coffee as if this were just another day of waiting. How is this different? Because I have not been told that I am still in suspense. I am in suspension about my own suspense. I might be falling and not even know. I find that this is perhaps not unendurable—and is this the real human tragedy, that so little is unendurable? Or is it that we so often have no choice but to endure?—nevertheless, I also find I cannot do anything *but* endure. It is I who have been stripped to the bone. Without skin I am cold, without muscles I am immobile, without nerves I am numb. I sit in this last, smallest, darkest cell, this cell without a window or a door, this cell without even cracks in its walls, and I am at the end of my inventions. They sit outside the door, powerless and mute. I have carried myself into the dead heart of the maze, and here I sit still alone, waiting to become so small, so light, so close to nothing that I can evaporate into the air. Waiting. The only sound is the sound my blood makes as it marches past my ears. Waiting.

When the telephone finally rings, it clamors like a bugle, loud enough to shake down the walls. This house is two hundred and eighty years old, and bricks and timbers, floorboards and chimney-pots that have stood for longer than my country has had a name are crumbling around my ears. Dust stops up my throat and burns my eyes so that I am blind with tears. There is light, but I cannot see; air, but I cannot breathe. I grope through the crumbs of brick and splinters of oak until I touch the smooth anachronistic plastic of the phone.

It rings again and lightning flashes through the bones of my hand. Dust glows blue and an ominous ruddy smoke-shadow hovers over the jackdaw piles of shattered beams. I lift the receiver to my ear.

"Hello," I say, my voice harsh with dust. "Hello?"

An unfamiliar voice with a familiar accent says my name.

"Yes," I say, a husk of a word.

"Please hold."

Hold? There is nothing beneath my feet, I am dangling over a void at the end of this telephone cord, of course I hold! The receiver clicks and hums, and then static bursts over me like a storm of bees.

"Go ahead," says a voice as distant as the moon.

Thinking the voice is speaking to me, I say, "Hello?" and so I miss a word or two, perhaps my name.

"Is this thing working? Hello? Are you there?"

Ryan, rescued, is shouting at me from God knows where, a helicopter, a submarine, the far side of the moon.

"I'm here," I say. "I'm here. When are you coming home?"

And suddenly the air is full, not of dust, but of wings.

~

I wrote this story in one great and glorious rush when I was visiting Ottawa, my nation's capital and a city that is older by a couple of centuries than my western hometown. I don't have a laptop so I was writing by hand in my notebook, which I haven't done regularly for years. Writing on the computer is my job and the product is (hopefully) destined for public exposure—still creative, still personally meaningful, but certainly the beginning of a communication with the world. Writing "Queen of the Butterfly Kingdom" by hand seemed to draw out a much more intimate and inward voice than is usual for me, and perhaps it drew more of me into the character, too. The questions raised by the story have certainly always interested me in a very personal way. Where lies the intersection between the inner, imaginative life and that outer life even a writer has to live? How do they interact, the stories we live and the stories we dream? And is the one any more real than the other in the end?

Holly Phillips

A Dirge for Prester John

Catherynne M. Valente

I. The Habitation of the Blessed

We carried him down to the river.

It churned: basalt, granite, marble, quartz—sandstone, limestone, soapstone. Alabaster against obsidian, flint against agate. Eddies of jasper slipped by, swirls of schist, carbuncle and chrysolite, slate, beryl, and a sound like shoulders breaking.

Fortunatus the Gryphon carried the body on his broad and fur-fringed back—how his wings were upraised like banners, gold and red and bright! Behind his snapping tail followed the wailing lamia twelve by twelve, molting their iridescent skins in grief.

Behind them came shrieking hyena and crocodiles with their great black eyes streaming tears of milk and blood.

Even still behind these came lowing tigers, their colors banked, and in their ranks monopods wrapped in high black stockings, carrying birch-bark cages filled with green-thoraxed crickets singing out their dirges.

The red and the white lions dragged their manes in the dust; centaurs buried their faces in blue-veined hands.

The peacocks closed the blue-green eyes of their tails.

The soft-nosed mules threw up their heads in broken-throated braying.

The panthers stumbled to their black and muscled knees, licking the soil from their tears.

On camels rode the cyclops holding out into the night lanterns which hung like rolling, bloodshot eyes, and farther in the procession came white bears, elephants, satyrs playing mourn-slashed pipes, pygmies beating ape-skin drums, giants whose staves drew great furrows in the road, and the dervish-spinning cannibal choir, their pale teeth gleaming.

Behind these flew low the four flame-winged phoenix, last of their race.

And after all of these, feet bare on the sand, skirts banded thick and blue about her waist, eyes cast downward, walked Hagia of the Blemmyae, who tells this tale.

II. The First Moveable Sphere

When we first found him, he was face-down in the pepper-fields, his skin blazed to a cracked and blistered scarlet, his hair sparse as thirsty grass.

The pygmies wanted to eat him. He must have been strong to have wandered this far, from whatever strange country—they should have the right to bisect his liver and take the strength, wet and dripping, into their tribe.

The red lion, Hadulph, nosed his maimed feet, and snuffled at his dark clothes.

"He smells of salt water and pressed flour," he announced, "and he who smells of pressed flour knows the taste of baked bread, and he who knows the taste of baked bread is civilized, and we do not eat the civilized, unless they are already dead and related to us, which is a matter of religion and none of anyone's business."

I looked down at his shape between the black and red pepper plants, in their long rows like a chessboard. It looked like the end of a game to me: I stood over the toppled kingpiece, a big-shouldered knight who has managed, in her jagged L-shaped steps, to finally make forward progress. I rubbed the soft and empty space above my collarbone—like a fontanel, it is silky and pulsating, a mesh of shadow and meat under the skin, never quite closed, and each Blemmye finds their own way with it, but often we are caught, deep in thought, stroking the place where our head is not. I stroked it then, considering the flotsam that the desert wind had washed onto our hard black peppercorns like the sands of a beach.

"He is wretched, like a baby, wrinkled and prone and motherless. Take him to the al-Qasr, and iron him out until he is smooth," I said quietly, and the pygmies grumbled, gnashing their tattooed teeth.

Hadulph took the stranger on his broad and rosy back, where the fur bristles between his great shoulder blades, and that is how Presbyter Johannes came into our lives on the back of one beast, and left on the back of another.

III. The Crystalline Heaven

Behind the ivory-and-amethyst pillars of the al-Qasr, which he insisted we rename the Basilica of St. Thomas, I sat with my hands demurely in my lap, fingering Hadulph's flame-colored tail. We sat in rows like children—the pygmies picked at their ears, the phoenix ran sticks of cinnamon through their beaks, carving it for their nests, the monopods relaxed on their backs, wide feet thrust overhead, each toe ringed with silver and emerald. Grisalba, a lamia with a tail like water running over moss, combed her long black hair, looking bored.

John the Priest tried not to look at me. His hair had grown back, but it was white, whiter than a man his age should own.

I told him once while he ran his tongue over the small of my back that the sun had taken all his blood, and left him with nothing in his veins but light.

He, ever the good teacher, tried to make eye contact with each of us in turn, but he could not look at my eyes, he could not look down to the full curve of my high, sun-brown breasts, and the green eyes that stared calmly from their tips under a thick fringe of lashes. I blinked often, to interrupt his droning, and he tried to look only at where my head might be if I were a woman.

A-ve.

He repeated these words as if they had any meaning for us, sounding each syllable. We did not like Latin. It sat on our tongues like an old orange, sweet-sour and rind-ridden.

A. Ve.

A-ve Ma-ri-a.

A. Ve. Mari. A.

Grisalba yawned and picked at her tail, lazily slapping its tip against the chalcedony floor. Hadulph chuckled and bit into the consonants like elbow joints.

A-ve Ma-ri-a gra-ti-a ple-na. Ti like she. Ple like play. She plays, gratia plena, Maria plays, ave Maria gratia plena.

A. Ve. Mari. A. Gra. Tea. A. Plea. Na.

"I wonder what his sweat tastes like?" Grisalba murmured in my ear. I grinned, but he could not chide me, for that would mean glancing down past my nipple-eyes to the mouth-which-is-a-navel, and he would not risk it.

No, no. She plays. She; play. Shall we try the Pater Noster instead then?

Pa. Tear. No. Star.

IV. Saturn, Cold and Dry

The strange man lay on one of the fallen pillars in the central hall of the al-Qasr—the smooth tower of violet stone had crashed to the floor one day while the quarter-moon market bustled in the portico—tile-shards of gold and splinters of ebony came tumbling after it, and we could all see the stars through the hole it made, like coins dropped into the hand of heaven. A brace of tigers looked up from arguing with a two-faced apothecary about whether she should be allowed to sell the powdered testicles of greater feline castrati as aphrodisiacs; the lamia paused in their venom-dance; I placed an arm beneath my breasts and lifted my eyes from the scribe-work before me to the ceiling. We all looked back and forth from the fallen pillar to the hole in the roof, up and down, up and down: work to sky to ruined architecture.

Of things that exist, some exist by nature, some from other causes, I had copied out from one greenish sheet of pepper-leaf paper to another. *Animals and their variegated parts exist, and the plants and the simple bodies exist, and we say that these and the like exist by nature.*

The pillar had chipped its complex torus, and bitten into the onyx floor.

All the things mentioned present a feature in which they differ from things which are constituted by art. Each of them has within itself a principle of stationariness (in respect of place, or of growth and decrease, or by way of alteration).

The constellation of Taurus-in-Extremis, the Slaughtered Cow, could be seen winking through the broken wood, and ebony dust drifted down on a soft breeze off of the river.

Even motion can be called a kind of stationariness if it is compulsive and unending, as in the motion of the gryphon's heart or the bamboo's growth. On the other hand, a bed or a coat or anything else of that sort, insofar as it is a product of art, has innate impulses to change.

Rich black earth had spurted up around the ruptured floor. The pillar's belly was swathed in it.

As an indication of this, take the well-known Antinoë's Experiment: if you plant a bed and the rotting wood and the worm-bitten sheets in the deep earth, it will certainly and with the hesitation of no more than a season, which is to say no more than an ear of corn or a stalk of barley, send up shoots.

I could just glimpse the edge of the sardis-snake which guarded the entrance of the al-Qasr, ensuring that no folk who are not lamia and thereby licensed, could bring poison under its roof. Behind it and far off, the Cricket-star flickered as if in chirruping song.

A bed-tree would come up out of the fertile land, its fruit four-postered, and its leaves would unfurl as green pillows, and its stalk would be a deep cushion on which any hermit might rest. It is art which changes, which evolves, and nature which is stationary.

The quarter-moon market gave a collective shrug and went about itself, stepping over the purple column and leaving it where it had fallen—wasn't it better, the cyclops murmured, to let a little light in, and have a nice place to stretch one's feet? I glanced back at my thrice-copied treatise, tiresome as all secondhand treatises are, and finished the page.

However, since this experiment may be repeated with bamboo or gryphon or meta-collinarum or trilobite, perhaps it is fairer to say that animals and their parts, plants and simple bodies are artifice, brother to the bed and the coat, and that nature is constituted only in the substance in which these things may be buried—that is to say, soil and water, and no more.

~

By the time we laid the stranger out on the pillar, it had grown over with phlox and kudzu and lavender and pepperwort, and we rested his battered head on a thatch of banana leaves. He moaned and retched like a sailor coughing up the sea, and I held him while he wracked himself clean. It was past the fishing hour when his eyes slitted open and his moth-voice rasped:

"Thomas, I came searching for Thomas and his tomb, the Apostle, where is the Apostle?"

Hadulph and I exchanged glances. "What is an Apostle?" the lion said.

V. Jupiter, Hot and Moist

We lay down on the altar that is a throne that was a sacrificial mound before the al-Qasr was the Basilica, and when we woke, the nave that was the portico was full of roses and partridges and orthodox hymns, and peacocks lay sleeping on my shoulders. Their blue heads pressed on me like bruises: the pulse of their throats, the witness of their tails.

"Say it," he said. He sat me on the ivory chair and knelt at my knees, the beauty that all supplicants possess sitting full and shining on his thick features. He closed his kiss over my navel-mouth and his tears were like new wax. "Say it," he whispered.

The ivory chair is long; it curls at its ends into arm-rests in the shape of ram's horns, severed from the sea-goat when the first caravan settled in this endless valley, the first enclave of bird and monopod and gryphon and cricket and phoenix and pygmy—and blemmye. And they camped on the beach-head and pulled from the sea with their silver spears a fatted kid, and ate the fat of its tail sizzling from the driftwood fire, and in time those first horns were affixed to the long chaise which became a sacrificial plank which became an altar which became a throne which became my pillow as his weight pressed the small of my back against the cold ivory—

"Please," he said, and wept, for he had tried not to, tried not to brush his palm against my eyelid, tried not to run his fingers across the teeth in my belly, tried not to glance at the soft place where my head is not. He had tried not to lift me onto the nacreous chair, and tried not to enter me like a postulant sliding his hands into the reliquary to grip the dry bone. *Virginity confers strength*, he had said. *It is the pearl which purchases paradise.*

I had led him to the edge of the river which churns basalt against schist, and showed him the trick with the bed—but I had used my favorite lapis-and-opal ring. I moved his hand as I would a child's, digging the furrow by moonlight and the river's din, placing the ring in the earth, covering it with moist, warm soil. *Wait*, I had said, *till the pepper blooms black, and you will see what paradise I can purchase at the price of a ring.*

We waited; I learned my Latin declensions: *rosa, rosae, rosae, rosam, rosā.* The pepper harvest piled up black and red fruits; the stalks withered; the snows came and went again. *Rex. Regis. Regi. Regem. Regē.*

I took him to the river which churns agate against marble and showed him the thing we had made: a sapling, whose stem was of silver, whose leaves curled deep and blue, lapis dark as eyes, veined in quartz flaws. Tiny fruits of white opal hung glittering from its slender branches, and the moon washed it in christening light. *This is hell*, he quavered, as I stroked the jeweled tree. It seemed to shrink from him in shame. I touched his face, his unyielding neck; I wrenched his head towards me, and he stared into the eyes that blink from my breasts, the cobalt leaves peeking around my ribs like the heads of curious peacocks. *At the ends of the earth is paradise; look around you, the earth is nowhere to be seen,* I had whispered, *and I do not need pearls.*

As if his hand was dragged through the night by a hook of bone, he had touched the place where my head is not, the soft and pulsing shadowy absence, the skin stretched and taut, and beneath our tree of blue stone he had spilled his seed into me for the first time—it seemed safer than to spill it into the ground.

"Say it, please, Hagia, say it," he cried, and the muscles of his neck strained in his cry, and I held his face in my hands, and his tears rolled over my knuckles, and I sung quietly under him, and my voice filled the empty choir:

Ave Maria, gratia plena, dominus tecum. Benedicta tu in mulieribus—

VI. Mars, Hot and Dry

Fortunatus clawed the sand of our crumbling amphitheater, with the nations of our nation gathered—as much as the nations are inclined to gather, which is to say lazily and without much intent of discussing anything. He was nervous; the color in his tail was low and banked, and his throat dry. The hulking beast did not love speaking, and he loved less that his size bought him respect he did not feel he had earned. So everyone listened, and he hated them for listening.

"I think," he began, his beak glittering gold in the glare of the sun, "that we ought to make him king."

"Why?" shouted Grisalba, trying to wrangle a slab of honeycomb with her sister, who had thought she was invited to a festival, and not a makeshift parliament. "When Abibas the Mule-King died, we planted him and if we have any disputes we take it to the mule-tree and it's been as good a government as you could ask for."

Fortunatus frowned, and the glare went out of his gold. "Abibas has dropped his leaves and it has been far too long since he gave us any velvet-nosed fruit on which to hang the hopes of primogeniture. The Priest will not be partial—there are no other creatures like him among us, no faction for him to favor. And," the gryphon cast his yellow eyes to the sand, speaking softly—yet the amphitheater did its work, and not one of us failed to hear him, "he must be lonely. There is no one here for him, no one of his kind who understands his passion for the Ap-oss-el, no one to speak his snarled language and look him in the eye without reflecting their own strangeness back to him. I pity him—do you not?"

"He will make us convert!" cried the monopods, snapping their garters in consternation. "He will make the al-Qasr into a church and we will all crawl around begging forgiveness for who knows what!"

Fortunatus shrugged his great, shaggy shoulders. "And when Gamaliel the Phoenix was queen, she called the al-Qasr an aerie, and set it aflame every hundred years. We rebuilt it, and called it what we pleased. This is the way of government. That is the way of the governed. How can he ask for more than she did? Besides, it is a lonely thing to be king, and he is the loneliest of us."

I held a long green canopy over my torso with both hands to keep out the sun; a pair of rooks alighted on it, and their weight dragged the warm cloth to my shoulders. I said nothing, but scowled and practiced my verbs silently.

Regno, regnas, regnat. Regnamus, regnatis, regnant.

I reign, you reign, he or she reigns over.

VII. The Sun, Benevolent Gold

"My name is John."

His blistered lips were watered, and he had not yet noticed that I held him in my arms, propped against the breasts he would call demonic and unnatural. He had not yet called us all demons, succubi, *inferni*—he only asked for bread, and more water.

He had not yet screamed when Hadulph spoke, or trembled when the crickets chirped in iambic rhymes. He had not yet called us all damned, demanded tribute to kings we had never heard of, forbade anyone not made in God's image to touch his flesh.

He had not yet castigated us for our ignorance of the Trinity, or preached the virgin birth in our mating season. He had not yet searched the lowlands for a fig tree we ought not to touch, or gibbered in the antechamber, broken by our calm and curious gazes, which we fixed on our pet day and night, waiting for him to perform some new and interesting trick.

He had not yet dried his tears, and seen how the al-Qasr was not unlike a Basilica, and how the giants were not unlike Nephilim, and how Hadulph was not unlike the avatar of St. Mark, and the valley of our nations was not unlike Eden. He had not yet decided that all of the creatures of the world were not unlike holy things—except for the blemmyae, except for me, whose ugliness could not be borne by any sacred sight. He had not yet called us his mission, and followed Grisalba home trying to explain transubstantiation, which she, being the niece of a cannibal-dervish, understood well enough, but pretended to misconstrue so that he would follow her home.

He had not yet called her a whore and tried to make her do penance with a taper in each hand. She had not yet sunk her teeth into his cheek, and sent him purpled and pustulant back to Hadulph.

Hadulph had not yet licked him clean, roughly and patiently, as cats will, and called him his errant cub. He had not yet fallen asleep against the scarlet haunch of the lion.

He had not yet retreated into the al-Qasr to study our natures and embrace humility, ashamed of his pronouncements and his pride. I had not yet brought him barley-bread and black wine, or watched over him through three fevers, or showed him, when he despaired, how my collarbone opens into a sliver of skin like clouds stretched over a loom.

He had not yet come crawling through the dark, shame-scalded, to hear my belly speak, and read to him from the green pepper-papyrus of my daily calligraphy, just to hear the way I said my vowels. He had not yet said that my accent sounded of seraphim.

"My name is John," he said, "I . . . I think I have become lost."

VIII. Venus, Cold and Moist

The long bones are found in the limbs, and each consists of a body or shaft and two extremities. The body, or diaphysis, is cylindrical, with a central cavity termed the medullary canal.

The Presbyter cloistered: cross-sections of satyr and blemmye are spread out on a low desk of sethym wood, the male blemmye with limbs outstretched, encircled with diagrammatic symbols as though he is pinioned to a wheel, showing the compact perfection of his four extremities, which correspond to the elements. The satyr was bent double, clutching her hooves, a goat-haired ouroboros.

"Please concentrate, John," begs Fortunatus, his conscripted tutor. "If you do not learn our anatomies how will you live among us? How will you help portion the harvest if you do not know that the phoenix require cassia and cardamom for their nests, while the satyr cannot eat the pepper plants that the rest of us prize? How will you build, brick upon brick, if you do not know that the blemmye orient their houses in clusters of four, facing outward, while the monopods have no houses at all, but lie beneath their own feet, like mice beneath toadstools? How will you sell your goods at the quarter-moon market if you do not know that the lamia especially love honeycomb still clung with lethargic bees, while the dervishes eat nothing but their dead?"

"Where I come from, all men have the same shape," says the Presbyter, his eyes bloodshot from reading, unwilling to acknowledge the scribe, best of his own *discipuli*, who translates each of the illuminated anatomicals into Latin so that he will believe them true—for he has told them that Latin is the language of truth, and the vulgar tongues the dialects of lies.

"That is a sad country, and you should give thanks to your God that you need not return there, where every face is another's twin," the gryphon says with a long sigh.

"All the same I long for it, and wish myself there, where nothing is strange," John murmurs to himself, and stares past me to the long, candle-thin windows. His hair still shows scalp in patches, but the scalp itself is not so scorched and peeling as it has been. He shakes himself from dreams of Jerusalem and looks at the wheel of flesh before him.

"I do not understand the blemmyae," he announces, without turning his head to me. "They carry their faces in their chests and have no head—I suppose the brain is just behind the heart then, in the chest cavity—but how," the Priest blushes, and shifts in his seat so that it will be clear that he does not address the indecorous question to me, "how would she nurse a child, Fortunatus?"

The gryphon twitches his wings—once, twice.
"Why, she would but weep."

IX. Mercury, Lined with Quicksilver

I admit it was I who showed him the mirror.

We think nothing of it—it is only a mirror, and we are not vain. Rastno the Glassblower made it soon after the al-Qasr was erected, and it was hung up in the portico before the pillar fell, draped in damask, for its visions were distracting—but for Rastno's sake we did not wish to dishonor his best-beloved child.

Rastno was a phoenix, and he reasoned that his glass should be finest of all, since he feared no flame but his own. And true to this he filled the capital with beads and baubles and bowls and chalices, plates and amphorae and children's toys. And mirrors, mirrors of every shape. But the mirror I showed to John was his last, for when Rastno lay down in his pyre he did not rise up again—we do not know why fewer of the orange and scarlet birds return each burning season; some say the cassia crop has been bad, some say they are suicides. Rastno was one of those who went into the flame and did not come out again, but laughing before he sparked his embers, he said that the mirror he fired in his own feathers would be a wonder beyond even the churning river of stone.

When we dragged the shard of glass from the charred bones and blowing ashes of his pearl-lined nest, when we cleared from it the blackened ends of Rastno's beak and talons, and scraped the boiled eye-wet and blood from its surface, we found a sheet of silver so pure that it showed the whole world, wherever we wished to look, into any dragon-ridden corner of the planed earth.

It disturbed us all, and taught us only that our land was best, best by a length of ten giants, and we covered it—but hung it in the hall all the same, as funerary rite.

"Why did you not bury his remains, if that is what you do with your dead?" John asked, when I rolled the bronze-set glass from its resting place behind a bolt of salamander-silk. I shuddered.

"Would you love a tree whose trunk was ash, whose foliage

was burnt and blistered flesh, black with flames you cannot see, but the tree remembers? What terrible fruit it would bear! Better that he be eaten, as the dervishes do, or given to the river, like the blemmyae, than to suffer planting!"

I showed, him, yes, but he was happy in those years, and his belly was fat, and he gripped me gleefully by the hips in the late afternoons and kissed the place where my head is not, opened my legs and said his favorite mass. He hardly even insisted I speak Latin anymore, or take any saltless Eucharist he might fashion, and only cried the name of his Apostle in his sleep. How could I know?

He stood for a long time, watching a city with domes of dust and crosses of gold and chalcedony flicker by, watching its stony streets run rivulets of blood like the porches of a dozen butchers, watched horses clatter over altars and books burn like phoenix, curl black at the edges and never return. He stood with the drawn damask clutched in his white hand, and watched a sullen orange sun set on the city of dust, and his beard grew even in that moment, his scalp showed pink through his hair, and his spine became a bent scythe, until he was an old man in my sight, and he wept like a nursing mother.

X. The Moon, Benevolent Silver

"Why didn't they come?" Prester John coughed and spat; his blood was bright on the pillow, my hand. "I wrote them a letter, I sent twelve gryphon to deliver it. I wrote them, but they didn't come. I told them it was beautiful here, I told them it was full of virtuous beasts, and jewels, and every fruit imaginable. I told them about the al-Qasr and even the blemmyae, oh, Hagia, I told them you were a beauty, I told them about the mirror, I told them where I was, and that they only had to come for me and I would save Jerusalem myself. Why did no one come for me?"

"I don't know, my love," I whispered, and mopped the sweat on his brow.

"Perhaps I am being punished. I am not righteous; I have

sinned in this place. I told them I had converted the land, and you say the Ave as well as anyone, but you don't mean it, and I knew it, even in the days when I thought myself a missionary, I knew when you put out your tongue for your first communion that you had no faith in your heart, but I did not care, because my fingers could touch your tongue, the sweet tongue of your belly, and I would have given a hundred false communions for that tongue. I lied when I wrote to them, I lied, but they would not understand, they would think you were devils, and I could not bear for a friar to look on my Hagia and spit at her."

The lines around his eyes over which I had run my fingertips so many times, which I had imagined deepening into a grandfather's wrinkles, had done their promised work. I leaned over his prostrate form and let my eyelashes flutter against his cheek.

"Perhaps they never got the letter. Perhaps they did not believe it, for who would believe such a tale in a land where all men's shapes are the same? Perhaps they were too consumed with their horses and bloodletting to come so far. Perhaps they sent someone, and he crossed eight or nine rivers, an inland sea, a jungle thick with panthers and bats, only to perish in the great desert which separates us from the world. Perhaps even now there is a man—a doctor? A clerk?—lying face-down in the sand, his bones whitening under the bone-parched sky, clutching a second letter in his skeletal hand, a letter which says: *John, we hear, and we will welcome you home.* Perhaps no such man ever set out. Does it matter? I am here, your own sweet succubus—remember how long you called me succubus, after all the other names had silenced themselves on your lips?—is that not enough?"

He asked for water, and in my ears he was wretched as a baby, wrinkled and prone and motherless on a pillar, asking for water for his blistered lips. I held his cup for him, until he pushed it away.

"It is enough," he rasped, and the rasp became a rattle. "But do you think," said Prester John, "that if I could bury Jerusalem in this earth, a Jerusalem-tree would grow on the banks of the river, with little mangers for fruit, and a trunk of the True Cross?"

I pressed his clammy cheek to my breast, and our eyes fluttered together, until his were still.

XI. The Spindle of Necessity

We carried him down to the river.

There was some talk of burying him, but I knew that though his book demands burial, he would not like it. He wants the paradise that is bought with pearls, not the pearl itself, which sprouts and blossoms. I would have sat at his roots and told him how Fortunatus was trying to form a school to carry on the language of the Lonely King, but we all snickered; everyone knew that the lion-bird could never keep his declensions straight. I would have told him how the youngest dervishes barely in their first sandals jump and dance under the portico, singing: *A! Ve! Marry-A! She plays, she plays! A! Ve!* I would have sat beneath his leaves and held my tongue against his fruit, and called it Eucharist. But it is selfish of me to want to take him from the angels, who he had promised were more beautiful even than lamia.

We carried him down to the river and delivered his body to the deeps. The crush of the stones broke his body bone from sinew, and the boulders were stained red with the splash of his fluids. The current soon took him under, and we were left with the crash and grind of it echoing into the night. He had gone from us, and the procession turned under the stars, Virgo-in-Repose wheeling overhead, back to the al-Qasr which was once more the al-Qasr.

I sat cross-legged by the riverbank until the sun came rolling back around, like a whetstone strapped to a drowning man's back. Grisalba waited by me, her tail all withered and dark, her dry, splay-fingered hand warm on my shoulder.

"Salt," I said, finally. "His sweat tasted of pressed flour, pressed flour and salt water."

I took the lamia's hand and we walked from the cacophony of granite against alabaster against flint against bone.

In later years, the river would throw up a stone stained red, so bright it was as a ruby in all that dusty rock. When we see these, we throw up our arms and cry the name of Prester John, who is with the river and in the river and the river is with us, and the lapis-tree waves its branches, as if it remembers, and he is with the river and with me, his red, red stones and his high blue tree.

~

The Letter of Prester John, an anonymously composed document which appeared in Byzantium sometime in 1165, described a far-off kingdom which would be called fanciful even by today's standards of fiction. It was a truly strange intersection of literature and reality. Claiming a country full of impossible monsters and lost relics, which purported to contain mythical locales from the Fountain of Youth to the Tomb of the Apostle, the Letter fired the dreams and political ambitions of Europe for five centuries, until accurate cartography erased the possibility of its existence. This fabled kingdom was never found. Men died trying to find their way to a fictional world. This confluence of fantasy and history has always fascinated me. I wanted to treat that world as the absolute reality it always aspired to be.

Much of medieval cosmology and geography could broadly be called interstitial art, a combination of wild imagination, half-understood science, continuously reinvented religion, and deliberate lies. So too are the ingredients of this story: a painstakingly falsified version of an intentionally manipulative fiction regarding a place that never existed, but should have.

Catherynne M. Valente

Afterword: The Spaces Between

Delia Sherman and Theodora Goss

What is the Interstitial Arts Foundation?

DELIA: The IAF is a non-profit organization dedicated to examining and promoting art that doesn't fit neatly within recognized categories of genre or marketing—art that falls in the interstices, the spaces between. Most of the original founders of the IAF happened to be writers, but our Executive Board has grown to include artists and media professionals as well. As a foundation, the IAF seeks to create community among artists who feel alienated from their more mainstream peers and to encourage them to invent markets and venues for what they do. *Interfictions* is the first anthology of interstitial fiction. We intend that it be the first of many interstitial projects drawn from all branches of the arts.

Did you have a particular definition of interstitiality in mind before you began reading the stories?

DORA: I did have a general definition. But interstitiality has been defined in so many ways, at various forums where Delia and I have discussed the concept, that I wanted to forget my own definition, to say to the writers, I've asked you for an interstitial story. Now show me what you think is interstitial. And when I read a story, I considered not whether it fit my definition, but whether I responded to it in a certain way. I'll give you an example. When I read Christopher Barzak's "What We Know About the Lost Families of —— House," I thought, this is related to what I know. It is a haunted house story. But, like Shirley Jackson's *The Haunting of Hill House*, it challenges the conventions of the genre. The collective narrator, which seems to represent not only the current inhabitants of the town but also the dead ones, never tells us who is haunting the house, or why it is haunted. And what other fictional haunting involves buttons? Reading the story, I experienced both recognition and disorientation. I should have known how to read it, but I didn't really. So one response I associated with interstitiality was, "I've seen this before—but no, it looks quite different after all. I've never seen it done this way." The other response was the one elicited by Jon Singer's "Willow Pattern": "I've certainly never seen this before!" Can you think of another story that exists between two genres, one of which is science fiction, and the other of which is china patterns?

Delia: What I began with was less a definition of interstitial fiction than a short list of things I felt I knew about it. An interstitial story does not hew closely to any one set of recognizable genre conventions. An interstitial story does interesting things with narrative and style. An interstitial story takes artistic chances. These things are true, as far as they go. But the other thing I know is that every interstitial story defines itself as unlike any other. Like Dora, I had to let go of all ideas and theories. Léa Silhol's "Emblemata," for instance, looks, for the first few pages, like a realistic recreation of the journal of a nineteenth-century French traveler in the exotic Orient. But at every turn, the narrative frustrates the conventions of that form, abandoning adventure for philosophy, pausing in the external journey to pursue an internal one. Reading it, I had to suspend the expectations raised by its apparent rhetoric and just follow the story as it unfolded, trusting that it would lead me to a place that would be emotionally and intellectually satisfying. Which it did. The best interstitial work, like "Emblemata," demands that you read it on its own terms; but it also gives you the tools to do so.

Of the stories submitted, which was the first you read that you felt was interstitial?

Delia: I read several stories that were very good fantasies or mainstream stories or romances, and then I came to Mikal Trimm's "Climbing Redemption Mountain." At first, it felt like historical fiction, but I couldn't really identify the place or the time. It was utterly realistic in its details, both physical and psychological. It was clearly about redemption, but not within the theology of any historical religion. If I tried to read it as realism, I ran up against the fact that the writer had made up this world out of whole cloth. If I tried to read it as a fantasy, I ran up against the story's lack of recognizable genre markers. As far as genre is concerned, "Climbing Redemption Mountain" felt like something that was inventing itself as it unfolded.

DORA: I had a similar response to Karen Jordan Allen's "Alternate Anxieties," I think because of the way the story is told. It's fragmented because the consciousness of the narrator is fragmented. But it's also a science fiction story about alternate universes, and the story's form reflects, not just the fragmentation of an individual consciousness, but also the fragmentation of our reality, in which alternate universes are continually splitting off around us. So, what is it? Postmodern science fiction? Maybe, but it's also a story in the tradition of literary realism, about a woman coming to terms with death. The story seemed fresh, interesting, interstitial—and emotionally affecting.

Did the two of you always agree on the stories that you chose?

DORA: No! Definitely not. Delia had to convince me that "Climbing Redemption Mountain" was interstitial, for the reasons she mentioned. And I had to convince her that we should include both "When it Rains, You'd Better Get Out of Ulga" and "The Utter Proximity of God," that they weren't too similar in style and sensibility. I argued that they were influenced by different literary traditions. Adrián Ferrero's story belongs, I believe, to the tradition of Latin American magic realism, of Gabriel García Márquez and Isabel Allende, and of Angélica Gorodischer, to whom the story is dedicated—all authors I admire. Although Michael J. DeLuca says he was inspired in part by Márquez, I think his story belongs to the tradition of European surrealism, going back to Rabelais. (There I go, contradicting the author. What can you expect from someone who teaches literature for a living?) I think of it as a response to

Waiting for Godot, in which Godot, or in this case God, has arrived. But it makes no difference that God is present: the characters have to find the meanings of their own lives, even in Fecondita. And I fell in love with the styles of both stories, with their poetry. I also remember that, while we didn't disagree about Vandana Singh's "Hunger," which we both loved, we had a long discussion about whether it was interstitial. I remember arguing, finally, that although it can be read as a realistic story, it does not completely make sense, it does not allow its full meaning to appear, except to someone who is familiar with the conventions of science fiction. It's a story about living among aliens; only, of course, the aliens happen to be entirely human. So, we certainly didn't always agree during the process of choosing the stories. But by the end, we had convinced each other that these stories all belonged in the first *Interfictions*. You could say that the anthology happened somewhere in the space between us, between Boston and New York, between our individual aesthetics and ideas about genre.

These days, contemporary stories based on fairy tale are almost a genre of their own. What did you feel was interstitial about the stories you chose that have fairy tale elements?

Delia: Each of the stories we chose for the anthology plays with a multiplicity of conventions. Veronica Schanoes' "Rats" announces up front that it's a fairy tale, yet it is also, transparently, a fictionalized biography of Sid Vicious's girlfriend Nancy Spungen, which certainly does not have a fairy tale happy ending. The narrator is also a lot angrier than the dispassionate narrators of even the most violent folk tales tend to be, and a lot more present in the story. K. Tempest Bradford's "Black Feather" references a handful of fairy tales, but is equally a dream-quest out of a mystic tradition and a psychologically realistic story about unrequited love.

Dora: We could also include Colin Greenland's "Timothy" in the list of stories with fairy tale elements. Remember all the fairy tales in which men turn into animals, and animals turn into men? The most familiar example is probably "Beauty and the Beast." You could read "Timothy" as a modern "Beauty and the Beast," in which Beauty is a suburban housewife and the Beast is her household cat. I give this example to show how a story that seems so different from a fairy tale can still carrying the memory of a fairy tale within it—at least for me. And I agree with Delia that neither "Rats" nor "Black Feather" reminds me of other fairy tale retellings I have read. To the extent that fairy tale retellings have become a sort of sub-genre, these stories play with its conventions.

Why did you think it was important to include stories from writers outside the United States?

DORA: If we were going to cross borders, I thought we should certainly cross the most obvious ones—geographical borders. In a way, writing interstitial fiction outside the United States may be easier—there are national traditions of fiction that could be considered interstitial, exemplified by writers like Jorge Luis Borges, Franz Kafka, and Milan Kundera. If we have that sort of tradition in the United States, it seems to me underdeveloped and undervalued. But publishing interstitial fiction may be harder, particularly if you're writing in a language spoken by millions, not billions, of people. I was thrilled to receive submissions from Hungary, where I was born, and to include a story by a Hungarian writer, Csilla Kleinheincz. Even before I read "A Drop of Raspberry," I was intrigued by the description, in her letter, of a story "about love between a man and a lake, and the futility of keeping up long conversations with someone who freezes over in the winter." This description points to what I perceive as the story's interstitiality: the way in which it functions both as metaphor and as an absolutely realistic description of the problems you might encounter if you fell in love with a lake. I don't know if other readers will hear this, but for me, "A Drop of Raspberry," "When It Rains, You'd Better Get Out of Ulga," and "Emblemata" all have particular sounds, as though you can hear the languages they were written in through the translations. I think you can hear it in the way the sentences are structured. I've been going on about stories in translation, and I haven't mentioned stories in English but by writers from countries other than the United States. Holly Phillips is Canadian, Colin Greenland is English, Anna Tambour is Australian, and Vandana Singh is Indian, although she lives in the United States. I think that geographical diversity makes the anthology richer.

Do the stories you chose have anything in common, other than being interstitial?

Delia: Two things, really, which became clear to me only well after the fact. The first is that almost all of these stories deal in one way or another with process, journey, the space between life and death, certainty and uncertainty, the time-bound and the eternal: what Heinz Insu Fenkl calls liminality. Joseph in Rachel Pollack's "Burning Beard" is an old man on the edge of death thinking about his past and the future he has seen in visions, trying to make sense of a life lived in the shadow of prophecy. Anna Tambour's "The Shoe in SHOES' Window" focuses on a shop window, a space that brings what's inside to the attention of people outside, as a story can bring attention to the obsessions and concerns of its creator. The second is that the way these stories is told is as critical to their effect as their content. Catherynne M. Valente's "A Dirge for Prester John" and Matthew Cheney's "A Map of the Everywhere" are as much about their language as about their narrative. Even the ostensibly plain-spoken stories, like Joy Marchand's "Pallas at Noon," Holly Phillips's "Queen of the Butterfly Kingdom," and Vandana Singh's "Hunger" build powerful metaphors, sentence by sentence, that end up defining the meaning of their narratives.

Dora: One connection I see is a sort of awareness. All of these stories seem aware of their interstitial status. They are not only stories in between, they are also stories about in betweenness. For example, in Leslie What's "Post Hoc," the narrator ends up living in a post office. You could think of a post office as an ultimate liminal space—always between destinations, never the destination itself. We send mail through, not to, the post office. So, "Post Hoc" is an interstitial story about an interstitial life, about a woman who makes a home for herself and finds happiness betwixt and between.

And "A Dirge for Prester John" is about a liminal country. All of its inhabitants are somehow betwixt and between, even the narrator, whose face is on her body (like certain Magritte paintings, conflating two categories that we certainly think of as separate). It is a place of hybridities and ambiguities, but to the narrator it is home, and even Prester John eventually accepts his life there. So, strange as it may seem, since What's and Valente's stories are so different, Prester John's country is like the post office—both are liminal spaces that are nevertheless where the characters manage to create homes for themselves. I think that's what interstitial fiction is about: finding yourself at home in ambiguity, hybridity, liminality. Inhabiting the space between.

What drew you, personally, to the idea of interstitiality?

DORA: I should make clear that I love genre fiction. I read lots and lots of detective stories, and I teach a class on gothic literature, in which the conventions are so important that you see the same scenes repeated in story after story. But the space I'm most interested in, the space my own writing seems to inhabit, is the space where those conventions are—bent, broken, brought together with other literary forms. The way Angela Carter writes fairy tales, using gothic rather than fairy tale conventions. So, my interest in interstitiality is a selfish one. I wish someone else would publish an anthology of interstitial fiction, so I could submit a story!

DELIA: For me, the best genre fiction is work that pushes the edges of convention while adhering to it. I love watching a real artist claim the tropes and tame the conventions of a traditional genre. Look at Shakespeare. Many of his plays are written within the conventions of their genres: *Henry IV, Parts 1 & 2* are chronicle histories, *The Comedy of Errors* is a classical comedy, *Othello* is a tragedy. But I wrote my master's thesis on *King Lear*, about how Shakespeare used the tropes of prose romance and fairy tale to play with his audience's expectations, see-sawing our emotions back and forth between hope and despair until we are as vulnerable and disoriented as Lear himself. I think my love of genre has led me to recognize and appreciate what occurs when an artist contemplates breaking a given rule, or combining it with one drawn from somewhere else. It's certainly what I did when I started writing.

What did you learn in the process of editing the anthology?

Delia: I learned to read really fast. I learned to let a story teach me how to read it without trying to analyze it as I went along. I realized that the reason I don't enjoy a lot of short fiction is because it *isn't* interstitial: whether it's Anne Tyler's domestic realism or Isaac Asimov's hard SF, I have a low tolerance for straight up genre short fiction. But I loved reading nearly every submission for this anthology. I guess I'm just most comfortable in the spaces between.

Dora: What I learned is that interstitial stories may work differently, but they still have to work. They still have to appeal to a reader. One criticism of interstitial stories is that they are more interested in formal experimentation, in breaking genre boundaries, than in telling a story—in appealing to a reader. Although some of the stories we have chosen experiment with form (look at the formal experimentation in "Pallas at Noon," for example, in which the end of the story is really its beginning), I think they all appeal to readers emotionally. I identify with the narrator of "Queen of the Butterfly Kingdom," who has to choose between the fantasy she has created and a reality over which she has no control—a reality that is itself fantastical. That's the ambiguous reality I live in. The choices made in stories like "Alternate Anxieties," "Pallas at Noon," and "Queen of the Butterfly Kingdom" are choices I have to make. Recognition and disorientation—for me, that's the experience both of reading these stories and of living in the twenty-first century.

~

About the Editors

Delia Sherman considers herself a "recovering academic." She got her PhD in Renaissance Studies and taught at Boston University and Northeastern, during which time she wrote her first novel, *Through a Brazen Mirror*. She left the academy in 1993 to write and edit full time, co-editing anthologies of science fiction and fantasy with Terri Windling and Ellen Kushner and serving as a consulting editor at Tor Books. Her other adult novels are *The Porcelain Dove* and *The Fall of the Kings*, written with partner Ellen Kushner. In 2006, Viking published her first novel for young readers, *Changeling*. Her short fiction has appeared most recently in *The Faery Reel*, *Salon Fantastique*, *The Magazine of Fantasy & Science Fiction*, *Coyote Road*, and *Year's Best Fantasy & Horror*. She satisfies her continuing desire to teach by serving as an instructor at various writing workshops in the U.S. and Europe, including Odyssey, Wiscon, and Clarion. A founding member of the Interstitial Arts Foundation, she lives in New York City.

Theodora Goss was born in Hungary and spent her childhood in various European countries before her family moved to the United States. Although she grew up on the classics of English literature, her writing has been influenced by an Eastern European literary tradition in which the boundaries between realism and the fantastic are often ambiguous. She is completing a PhD in English literature at Boston University, where she teaches classes on fantasy and the gothic. Her short story collection, *In the Forest of Forgetting*, was published in 2006 by Prime Books. She lives in Boston with her husband Kendrick and daughter Ophelia. Visit her website at www.theodoragoss.com.

Contributors

Karen Jordan Allen spent her mostly happy childhood in rural Indiana. She now lives in Maine with her husband and daughter, a cat, and a rabbit. Her fiction has appeared in a number of magazines and anthologies, including *Century*, *A Nightmare's Dozen*, *Bruce Coville's Strange Worlds*, *Black Gate*, *First Heroes: New Tales of the Bronze Age*, and *Asimov's Science Fiction*.

Christopher Barzak spent two years in Japan, teaching English in a suburb of Tokyo, and returned home to Youngstown, Ohio last year. His first novel, *One for Sorrow*, will be published by Bantam Books in Fall of 2007.

K. Tempest Bradford is an Ohio native and alumna of the Clarion West and Online Writing Workshops. She currently lives in New York City (at the very tip-top with the ravens). She spends most of her time trying to find a place with free tea and Internet where she can write.

Matthew Cheney's work has appeared in *One Story*, *Locus*, *Web Conjunctions*, *Rain Taxi*, *Strange Horizons*, and elsewhere. His weblog, The Mumpsimus (mumpsimus.blogspot.com), was nominated for a World Fantasy Award in 2005, and he is the series editor for the annual *Best American Fantasy* anthology from Prime Books.

Michael J. DeLuca would like to tell you he lives in a cave in Western MA, pronouncing false prophecy in exchange for such essential sustenance as food, water and wireless internet. Unfortunately such caves are few and far between, and often occupied by fearsome squatters, so he advises that you not go looking for him and visit his website instead (www.michaeljdeluca.com).

Adrián Ferrero was born in La Plata (República Argentina) and attended the Universidad Nacional de La Plata, where he is currently doing his PhD. He has published academic articles in compiled editions and journals in his country, the U.S.A., France, Germany, and Spain. Fiction publications include *Verse*, a collection of short stories, and *Cantares*, a book of poetry. He is also co-editor of the digital magazine on creative writing *Diagonautas* (www.diagonautas.com.ar).

Colin Greenland is English: born in Dover, educated at Oxford, with homes in Cambridge and the Peak District. His books include *Finding Helen* and the space opera trilogy that began with the multi-award winning *Take Back Plenty*. He lives with Susanna Clarke, author of *Jonathan Strange and Mr Norrell*.

Csilla Kleinheincz is a Hungarian-Vietnamese fantasy writer living in Erkel, Hungary. Besides translating classics of fantasy, such as Peter S. Beagle's works, she works as an editor at Delta Vision, a major Hungarian fantasy publisher. Her first novel, published in 2005, and most of her short stories are part of Hungarian slipstream literature.

Joy Marchand lives in a lopsided, historic rowhouse in Salem, Massachusetts. In the last two years she's shifted her focus from short stories to longer works, and she's currently writing a series of linked urban legends for her interstitial novel-within-a-novel set in the Chihuahuan Desert of West Texas. Please visit her website at www.joymarchand.com.

Holly Phillips is the author of the award-winning story collection *In the Palace of Repose*. She lives in the mountains of western Canada.

Rachel Pollack is the author of 30 books of fiction and non-fiction, including the award-winning novels *Unquenchable Fire* and *Godmother Night*. She is also a poet and a visual artist, creator of the Shining Tribe Tarot deck. She lives online at www.rachelpollack.com, and offline in New York's Hudson Valley.

Veronica Schanoes is a writer and a scholar with a particular interest in fairy tales and genre theory. Her work has appeared in

Lady Churchill's Rosebud Wristlet, Trunk Stories, Endicott Studio, and *Jabberwocky.*

Léa Silhol was born in Africa and grew up in Europe, but considers herself a "citizen of the world." She is considered one of the leading writers in Fantasy in the French language, with four short stories collections and a novel, *La Sève et le Givre*, which won the Fantasy Merlin Award in 2003.

Jon Singer grew up in Brooklyn, NY, wanting to be a scientist. That didn't work out, but he is now semi-officially a Mad Scientist, which may even be better. You can find some of his work at www.jossresearch.org.

Vandana Singh is an Indian speculative fiction writer born and raised in New Delhi. She lives in the Boston area, where she also teaches college physics and has published a children's book: *Younguncle Comes to Town* (Viking 2006).

Anna Tambour currently lives in the Australian bush with a large family of other species, including one man. Her collection, *Monterra's Deliciosa & Other Tales &*, and her novel, *Spotted Lily*, are *Locus* Recommended Reading List selections. Her website, Anna Tambour and Others, is at www.annatambour.net, and she blogs at medlarcomfits.blogspot.com.

Mikal Trimm has sold works of speculative fiction and poetry to a number of venues in the past few years. Recent or upcoming stories may be found in *Weird Tales, Black Gate, Postscripts, Polyphony 6*, and *Shadowed Realms*. He maintains a web presence (for no apparent reason) at mtrimm1.livejournal.com.

Catherynne M. Valente is the author of the *Orphan's Tales* series, as well as *The Labyrinth, Yume no Hon: The Book of Dreams, The Grass-Cutting Sword*, and four books of poetry, *Music of a Proto-Suicide, Apocrypha, The Descent of Inanna*, and *Oracles*. She has been nominated for the Rhysling and Spectrum Awards as well as the Pushcart Prize. She was born in the Pacific Northwest and currently lives in Ohio with her two dogs. (www.catherynnemvalente.com)

Leslie What is a Nebula Award-winning author who writes short stories, essays, and novels. Visit Whatworld at: www.sff.net/people/leslie.what

Acknowledgements

For advice on anthology etiquette and procedure, the editors would like to thank Ellen Datlow, Terri Windling, Deborah Layne, and Kelly Link. For exceptional proofreading and publishing, the editors would like to thank Robert Legault, freelancer, and Jedediah Berry and Gavin J. Grant of Small Beer Press. For critical assistance with the Introduction and the Afterword, the editors would like to thank Deborah M. Snyder and Veronica Schanoes. Delia thanks Ellen Kushner for all of the above, as well as moral support and cups of tea. Dora thanks Kendrick and Ophelia Goss for their humor and infinite patience while she read manuscripts.

The Interstitial Arts Foundation is extremely grateful to the many donors who supported the creation of this volume, and particularly thanks Patricia A. McKillip and Patrick O'Connor for their generous financial assistance.